CARRERA

TRILOGY

BOOK THREE

DRAWN
BLUE
LINES

USA TODAY BESTSELLING AUTHOR

CORA KENBORN

DRAWN BLUE LINES

Loyalty is the deadliest sin

Everything has been one elaborate lie.
My name. My identity. My entire existence.
Brody Harcourt exposed me as a fraud, turning me from a
queen into a pariah.
Now there will be hell to pay.
But I'm back for more than revenge. More than blood.
My eye is on the prize.
The Carrera throne.
I'll win the kingpin's trust at any cost, even if it means crossing
enemy lines alongside Houston's political pin-up boy.
But things don't always go as planned.
Sometimes a queen has to steal her crown…
And the one man she can never have becomes the only one she
wants.

"You have to take a leap of faith in yourself. No matter what it is, take that leap of faith and know you can do whatever you want to do."

I miss you, Shanann.

PLAYLIST

Royal Blood - Krigarè
Play With Fire - Sam Tinnesz (feat. Yacht Money)
Bad Bitch - Bebe Rexha (feat. Ty Dolla $ign)
Natural - Imagine Dragons
Sorry Not Sorry - Demi Lovato
Señorita - Shawn Mendes, Camila Cabello
Come & Get It - Selena Gomez
Safari - BIA, J Balvin, Pharrell Williams, Sky
Bad Guy - Billie Eilish
A Little Wicked - Valerie Broussard
Horns - Bryce Fox
Queen - Loren Gray
Fuck Feelings - Olivia O'Brien
Heaven - Julia Michaels
Revolution - The Score
White Flag - Bishop Briggs
I Feel Like I'm Drowning - Two Feet
Born For This - Royal Deluxe
Hold On - Chord Overstreet
This Is Me (From the Greatest Showman) - Kesha

Prologue

ADRIANA

Guadalajara, Jalisco, Mexico

Two Weeks Ago

No one chooses fate. It chooses us.

I knew because I came into this world cursed, my veins poisoned with a depraved and corrupt bloodline. However, after months of running, foolish unrest drew me out of hiding and into the jaws of anarchy. War was a living, breathing thing. Nurtured and cultivated, it bloomed into an unstoppable force of nature. Left in the wild, its branches twisted into a monstrosity that eventually devoured itself.

My family's legacy had become a treacherous beast feasting on its one remaining root.

Me.

Warm blood flowed around me like an unholy baptism, soaking my hair and coating my skin. Rolling onto my side, I concentrated on breathing even though the smallest inhale shredded my lungs. The beating had been brutal, but not fatal. Not because they wanted to spare my life, but because death was more satisfying when capped off by days of torture.

I'd taught them that.

Now, here he sat in the shadows.

Watching.

The one in charge. The one whose footsteps caused all the traitors to scatter like startled cockroaches.

The muscles in his throat tightened as a dark cloud passed over his face. Out of the corner of my eye, I watched his fingers twitch against the dark denim covering his thigh. I knew nothing about the man except that he was a killer, and he wanted nothing more than to pull the blade from its holster and drive it straight through my heart.

But he wouldn't.

He could easily take my life, but it wouldn't be without consequence. Even in chaos, there was order.

I swallowed, forcing my native language from my raw throat. "Who are you?"

"A prophet without honor." He spat the words out like they were rancid, his gravelly Spanish raking over my thin nerves like fresh sandpaper.

Arrogance, a familiar yet foolish friend, filled my chest. "If you touch me, I'll kill you."

Shaking his head, he pulled a cigar from his pocket. "I don't have to touch you. I have something you need. You'll do whatever I say, when I say it." He bit off the tip and spat it at my feet, his gaze never leaving mine as he lit the end. The glowing tip sparked to life, his cheeks sinking in as he sucked a few deep puffs.

I let out a silent breath. "I am Marisol Muñoz."

The low laugh that followed nearly broke my composure. Men had underestimated me all my life. However, the one on the other side of the cold, damp room wasn't just amused by my

10

obstinance. It thrilled him. He got off on it.

My heart free fell into my stomach, and with my ear pressed against the concrete floor, I heard him get up, each step he took sounding like thunder. Bending down on his haunches, he bore stained yellow teeth in a smirk I wanted to carve off his face.

"You're no Muñoz, and you know it. I'm the one resurrecting a power you almost ruined," he snarled. "Bringing honor back to Guadalajara. Spilling enemy blood to fortify our own."

"I am Marisol Muñoz." In repeating the declaration, I couldn't help but wonder which one of us I was trying to convince. "The daughter of your former king, and the sister of your fallen leader."

He leaned down with eyes harder than stone. "You are a Carrera whore."

Before I could respond, he wrapped his hand around my blood-soaked hair and dragged me toward him. White hot pain shot through my skull, but my stumble was momentary. As soon as I found my balance, I swung.

It was just what he wanted. Easily catching my wrist in one hand, he pulled his knife with the other. Instinctively, I lunged for it, but he released my hair and shifted, causing me to slam face-first onto the floor.

I turned my cheek just before my nose made contact with the unforgiving concrete. The pain was almost unbearable, but I never screamed. This was a power struggle. Blood meant nothing to a vigilante drug runner. Fuck if I'd let it mean any more to me.

I glared as I turned, ignoring the blood dripping down my chin. "Don't call me that."

"Why not? It's your name." He resumed circling me like a lion. "Muñoz blood doesn't run through your veins. You're the enemy."

"Stop!" It was the only word I could voice.

Truth was like a splinter piercing the surface of your skin. The initial bite was painful but bearable. However, if left long enough—if accepted without a fight—it dug its way so deeply into your flesh, it became a part of you. Never-ending pain masked as masochistic pleasure.

Self-destruction was a family trait. Raised to hate and taught to avenge, obsession seeped its way into my blood from a young age, addicting me to power like the very drug our kingdom was built on.

Having it. Keeping it. Taking it.

Every spare moment I had, I ate, slept, and breathed one name. Believed one name lived to destroy us.

Carrera.

After all, that was the law of the jungle. Take or be taken. Eat or be eaten. Kill or be killed. But then three brutal words ripped away my identity and a lifetime of respect, turning survival into a goal instead of a game.

You're the enemy.

My entire existence had been a lie. I wasn't a queen. I was a pawn. I'd been robbed of the only life I'd ever known and denied the life I should've never lost.

Marisol Muñoz was dead, and it was all because of one man.

Forcing myself to focus, I met his smug gaze with one of brazen steel. Stripped of weapons, strength, dignity, and identity, psychological manipulation was all I had left. Hopefully, it'd be enough, because I'd be damned if I'd die in a decrepit warehouse in the middle of nowhere.

"Then why bother keeping me alive?" Even in the darkness, I saw the empty gaze in his eyes, and an unwelcome shiver ran down my spine.

"To determine if my instincts are correct."

A sound rumbled low in my throat—one I intended to

be apathetic but ended up as apprehensive. "I'll save you the trouble. Your instincts are shit."

It wasn't smart to antagonize the man holding your life in his hands, but showing fear was even more dangerous. I might as well have held a gun to my own head.

With a low chuckle, he leaned forward and ran the rough pad of his thumb across my bottom lip. Disgusted, I pulled away, but undeniable rage simmered beneath his thin layer of amusement, and he clamped down on the tender flesh until I cried out in pain. "Your insolence is exactly why I know my instincts are not, in fact, *shit*. You're a survivor. Most of my men would've long been dead by now."

Satisfied with my physical response to his show of dominance, he released his grip and shoved me backward. He wasn't wrong, and the backhanded compliment should've silenced me.

It didn't.

"Maybe you need better men."

"Maybe you need to hold your fucking tongue before I cut it off." He paused, waiting for another challenge. When I just glared at him, he sealed his victory with an emphatic smirk. "As I was saying, putting a bullet in your brain would be such a waste. Especially when your talents could be put to better use."

I froze, each word cramming itself down my throat until I thought I'd choke. "I'd rather die."

His distant gaze lasted only moments before understanding twisted his lips in disgust. "Don't insult me. I'd rather chop off my own dick than fuck a Carrera. I'm referring to your powers of persuasion."

"Against whom? According to you, I'm public enemy number one."

My taunt didn't faze him. Cocking his chin, he scratched his beard with the tip of his knife. "There's no truer revenge than an eye for an eye. . .is there, *Adriana*?"

"I told you not to call me that!" Consumed with blind rage, I lunged with my last burst of strength. A pathetic show he easily deflected with the back of his hand. I hit the ground with a thud, blood trickling from the corner of my mouth.

The man stood, and although instinct warned me to shut my eyes, I refused to give him the satisfaction. If he wanted to kill me, he had to look me in the face.

Instead of ramming the knife into my flesh, he tapped his heavy boot on the concrete next to my forehead. "I'm losing patience, so I'll say this once. Give me what I want, and I'll give you what you want."

"Freedom?"

"Revenge. Your poisoned bloodline already murdered one brother. You can die at my feet or use it to destroy the other." Lowering onto his haunches again, he grabbed my chin and twisted it until we were eye to eye. "Help me bring down Valentin Carrera, and I'll hand you Brody Harcourt. With what I have on that *gringo*, even you couldn't fuck this up."

I scowled. "If you think you can touch Houston's political pinup boy, you're delusional."

"You did it once before."

Memories washed over me in an unwelcome wave, but I forced a bored expression. "Tapping the same vein twice isn't my style."

"He ruined your life. It's only fair that you return the favor."

"Or I could bring you down."

"Vengeance or death," he demanded, ignoring my threat. Then I saw it. My bag. The one I never went anywhere without. He held it up like a prize, swinging it from the tip of his finger. "Let me rephrase. Vengeance, death, or more death. Lady's choice."

I had to get my hands on that bag, but negotiation was out of the question. "I'm not your fucking puppet."

"No? Then what are you?"

My swollen lip split as I smirked. "A phoenix."

He stepped back, putting more than a few inches between us. Not that I blamed him. It was a bizarre answer to give with my last few breaths resting in the palm of his hand.

The phoenix didn't wait for death to come. It took control of its own destiny and built its own funeral pyre. Igniting it with a single clap of its wings, it self-destructed in a blaze of glory only to rise from the ashes.

When one life extinguished, another one began.

The man's face twisted, deep horizontal lines slicing through the weathered skin on his forehead. "You're a crazy bitch." As soon as the words fell from his lips, his mask dropped back into place, and his tolerance faded. "You're either with me or against me. If you turn your back, I promise there are measures in place to ensure your destruction. So, do we have a deal?"

I faced him, keeping my scattered thoughts hidden. Like a prison inmate carving a deadly weapon, it was better to sharpen the mind when the guards weren't watching. Coherence held power, and power wasn't given or earned. It was stolen.

And I'd steal everything.

An eye for an eye.

I'd make a deal with the devil just to send another one to hell. The time had come to even the score, and I drew strength from the chaos.

Now, I was chaos.

I was confidence and craving and covetous power. They may have erased my past, but they had given me far more than they took away. A new day had come, and with it a rebirth. They burned Marisol Muñoz at the stake, but Adriana Carrera rose from the ashes. It was time to reclaim my birthright and take what was mine.

"No." I rasped, forcing a smirk. "A queen bows to no one."

They were my final words before succumbing to darkness.

BRODY

Chicago, Illinois
Present Day

Not everyone had a price tag. If they did, my life would be a lot easier. I sure as hell wouldn't be sitting inside a strip club, sweating through three layers of Armani and questioning my sanity.

Not that the place was a dive. The Blue Moon was one of the most elite clubs in Chicago, but at two o'clock in the afternoon, even the most elite bar looked like a shithole. Which is precisely why it was the perfect place to meet. It matched my mood— dark, dubious, and desperate. Just like my reason for being here. Even being eleven hundred miles away from prying eyes meant nothing in my world.

Someone was always watching.

But I got cocky, and arrogance blinded even the most cautious of men. Up until now, I'd managed to keep my dealings with the Irish mob quiet. The fewer questions on fewer lips, the less likely it was I'd get trapped in my own web. Not that I would've bothered explaining myself to anyone.

Despite being the head of stateside operations for the most powerful cartel in the world, I was still an outsider amongst my own men. I couldn't blame them. They were born into this life. They lived and breathed it, working their way up the ranks in hopes of one day reaching a position of power. To them, I was a *gringo*. A traitor to both sides of the law who made a deal with the devil and shit all over their sacrifices in order to secure himself a seat at the top.

They weren't wrong.

The line I walked with that devil these days was thin at best. Valentin Carrera didn't have friends; he had strategic alliances. When the kingpin gave an order, he expected it to be followed and dared anyone to defy him. Especially a man who had put half his men behind bars.

But here I sat with a noose tied around my neck, waiting to hang on my own ego. Since I wasn't looking to die today, I made sure to scan the perimeter again, rolling my phone around in my hands as I memorized faces.

"You know this place has state-of-the art cameras, right?" Slouching back into my chair, I looked up to see an explosion of blonde hair falling in a halo around two strips of sequins I assumed was supposed to be a dress. Suspicion came second nature to me, so when I narrowed my eyes, she placed her palm on the table and leaned in close. "With audio so clear, you can hear the stroke of a dick under a table."

Shaking my head, I raised my beer mug to my lips. "That's too much information."

She slid into the chair across from me with a sultry wink. "Looking for a little pleasure before business, handsome?"

"No. I never mix the two."

Especially in Chicago.

"A shame," she mused, drumming her blood red nails on the table. "You look like you could stand to loosen up."

I wondered how hard I'd have to kick her chair to send her sailing to the other side of the club. It wasn't very gentlemanly, but social etiquette and conformity weren't high on my priority list.

Plus, being kept waiting had worn my patience paper thin.

"Lady, it's been a long day, and with all due respect, I don't have time for this shit. Is your boss even here, or does he plan on dicking me around all night?"

As the dollar signs faded from her eyes, her façade dropped. Her flirty smile curled into a snarl, but before she could hurl out the insults waiting on her tongue, she glanced over my head, her eyes widening.

On instinct, I twisted around. "It's about fucking time."

However, instead of the smoky Irish brogue accent I expected to hear, a gravelly Spanish one surrounded me like rusty nails on a bullet-ridden chalkboard. "That impatient to see me, Harcourt?"

Carlos Cabello stood behind me, his gray goatee framing a smirk I wanted to punch off his face. Turning back, I shot an accusatory glare at the traitorous woman just in time to see her sequined ass disappear into the shadows.

Even rolling my eyes took too much effort.

"Fuck you." Tossing my phone across the table, I let out another slew of curses. "I'm supposed to be meeting with Ronan."

I thought I was meeting with Ronan Kelly, head of the Northside Sinners, the Irish mob in charge of every piss Chicago took. I didn't like surprises, and I sure as hell didn't like them being hand delivered by a middleman who had no direct contact with the Sinners.

"Well, now you're meeting with me."

"Oh, well, *that* explains everything." I tracked his every move as he slid into the chair opposite of me. "By all means," I said, motioning across the table. "Have a seat."

I expected a smartass retort, or at least a thinly veiled threat. Instead, Carlos offered an obligatory nod then lifted a finger and motioned to a passing cocktail waitress. I suppose the meaning was unspoken because her response was a simple nod.

Carlos let out a loud laugh. "That's what I always liked about you, Harcourt. You don't waste time with pointless small talk."

We were wasting time. This ridiculous civility dance only postponed the inevitable. "Cut the shit. What the—?"

I paused as the waitress appeared by our table, placing a shot glass filled with clear liquid in front of him. As soon as the woman came, she was gone, her presence so fleeting, if she hadn't left the drink as evidence, I'd question if she was ever really there.

"Vodka?" I asked, nodding toward the shot glass.

Carlos snorted. "Americans." Picking up the shot, he tipped it back and slammed it. "It's *aguardiente*. In English it translates to firewater." He glanced at my half-empty beer and smirked. "Want one, *gringo*?"

"I'll pass." Time was money, and this small-talk bullshit had gone on long enough. "It seems I've wasted my time. However, I'm also not driving another eleven hundred miles, so unfortunately, you'll have to do."

"Lucky me."

"My Chicago shipment never arrived."

"Tell me something I don't know." His dismissive tone grated on my nerves as he held his empty glass in the air and raised an eyebrow at the flustered waitress. Again, the woman bowed her head in swift acknowledgment. "By the way, you owe me my eight-hundred and fifty thousand dollars." When my jaw dropped, his lips twitched at the corners. "Five percent supplier fee. Did you think I was going to forget?"

I slammed my palm onto the table. "You greedy fuck. Did you have something to do with this?"

He rolled his eyes. "Think with your brain instead of your dick for once. That's *my* product coming into your port. Why would I fuck with my own blow?"

Damn. He had a point.

"Besides, if you hadn't spent the last week working your way through a bottle of scotch and paid more attention to your business, maybe you wouldn't be so fucked right now."

Because of the seventeen-million-dollar shipment that never arrived in Chicago's port. A deal I signed with my own blood.

I was in such deep shit it would take a forklift to haul my ass out of it.

"You've got Ronan Kelly and Valentin Carrera on your ass, so the way I see it, you only have two options." Holding up two thick, calloused fingers, he ticked them off. "One, pull my eight hundred and fifty K out of your ass, or two, come up with an alternative."

"What kind of alternative?"

"Find the man who stole it."

I laughed. I had no idea what the hell was in *aguardiente,* but after the crazy shit he just said, I suspected LSD. "And how do you suggest I do that?"

His eyes flashed dark with irritation. "It's pretty crystal fucking clear. Pay me my money or find the *pendejo* who intercepted your shipment, take back what he stole, and end him."

"What's in it for you?"

He shrugged. "This is a lucrative arrangement for me,

so I prefer Ronan not kill you. Plus, I don't take well to being threatened."

"Threatened?" An uncomfortable silence hung in the air. "You know who this asshole is."

It wasn't a question.

A knowing smirk crept along his face. "Possibly. And I'm feeling particularly generous, so I'll make you a deal."

"Is that right?"

"I'll replace the eight hundred kilos *and* give you a name, but I want ten percent."

"You want double?" I laughed. "Thanks, but no thanks. I can cover it." Which was a complete lie. I didn't have seventeen thousand, much less seventeen million. If I did, I wouldn't have come crawling to this dickhead instead of the main Carrera supplier.

I crossed my arms over my chest. "You don't know anything we don't know."

"You know what? I'm done fucking with you," Carlos shouted, the corners of his eyes pulled tight with annoyance. "If you'd get your head out of your ass for five seconds, I'd tell you I had a run in with the Muñoz Cartel two weeks ago."

My blood ran cold. "What did you say?"

"I thought that'd get your attention."

Muñoz was a name I hadn't heard in a very long time, and quite honestly, didn't think I'd ever hear again.

A year and a half ago, the Muñoz Cartel blackmailed me by threatening my sister. It was why I enjoyed watching a bullet tear through their leader's heart and seeing them crumble. Afterward, they were reduced to shambles while we consumed more and more power. If they'd somehow resurfaced and reorganized enough to push me out of Chicago, I needed to know everything.

However, I also wasn't stupid. I'd walked into too many

traps to watch someone bait a hook, toss their line right at me, and then just swim straight to it.

Instead of reacting, I tilted my palms up and offered a smug smile. "The name sounds familiar."

"Cut the bullshit, Harcourt. You think I don't know you were there with Valentin Carrera when his wife shot Manuel Muñoz?" he hissed, slamming a palm against the wood. "The Carreras might have crippled them for a while, but they're under a new command and stronger than ever." Downing his shot, he slammed the empty glass on the table and cut a hard stare at me.

"Who's calling the shots?"

He balanced his elbows on the table and leaned forward. "Don't know. They sent one of their lieutenants to try to strong arm me into canceling all my Carrera shipments and selling to them, but I don't take orders from anybody, much less a group of *cabrones* who don't know their dicks from their assholes."

"So, I'll ask again. Who's calling the shots?"

"Information has a price tag, *amigo*."

"Give me a name, and I'll think about it."

"Fuck your mother."

I shrugged. "Freudian shit isn't my thing. However, if that's what lifts your sails…"

"Do I look like an idiot to you, Harcourt? I'm calling the shots here, not you. I have what you need. All you have is a missing shipment and an eight-hundred and fifty-thousand-dollar debt."

"And a link to Ronan Kelly. I'm not stupid, Carlos. You're just the mediator. A man he doesn't know exists. Without me, you're just a second-rate supplier holding his dick in his hands." I sat back with a satisfied smirk. Why should I cave so easily? This was his fault. If he'd informed me of Muñoz involvement two weeks ago, we wouldn't be sitting here in the first goddamn place.

A tense breath whistled through his teeth, and another line creased his forehead before a slow smile parted his lips. "The man's name is José Rojas. I don't know how much you can find out from that, but that's all I got. We both know their reach extends far beyond border walls. They've already infiltrated Chicago. If you ask me—"

"I didn't."

The smile on his face faded, irritation flaring in his eyes. "If you ask me, whoever has the balls to rebuild is hiding in plain sight. It's the last place people ever look."

I raised an eyebrow as he stood. "What's in it for you?"

He tugged on the cuffs of his shirt. "This isn't a Colombian problem. This isn't even a Sinners problem," he continued. "What we have is a cartel rivalry that needs to settle their shit out of Chicago. I'm sure Ronan doesn't care if you bomb each other to hell and back. But, obviously, considering our recent arrangement, I have a stake in seeing the Carreras win. You get the Muñozs out of my way, and I'll replace the eight-hundred kilos they stole."

"What's the catch?" There always was one. No one did shit for free in this business.

The corner of his mouth tugged up in a half-smirk. "You find this José Rojas and make him give you the name of the *pendejo* in charge. I'll take it from there." Carlos held up a hand before I said a word. "Or I keep the kilos and you can explain to Valentin Carrera why you forged a partnership with a family he strictly forbade and then lost seventeen million dollars of his money."

I winced hearing Val's name.

"You wouldn't contact Val," I said, calling his bluff. "Then you'd have to admit to selling against his main Colombian supplier. That would be a death sentence for you."

Carlos's only response was to lean forward so that his elbows rested on the table, a patch of graying hair falling over one eye. "Let's get one thing straight, I'll do anything I want. That being said," he continued, the fire in his eyes calming, "I don't make a habit of getting involved in shit that isn't my business." Lifting his drink, he paused, holding it inches from his face as he watched me. "However, I'd bet the payout from my last job that Val has no fucking clue he's doing business with the Sinners."

And he'd walk away from that bet an even richer man.

I'd tried multiple times to force an alliance with the Chicago syndicate but always backed down when the heir to the Carrera empire swore he'd cut my balls off and shove them down my throat. He never explained his reasoning, but he didn't have to. Nobody threatened a man quite like Valentin Carrera.

I was screwed either way. If I agreed and Val found out, he'd kill me. If I refused and Val found out, he'd kill me. However, accepting Carlos's offer bought me time that refusing it didn't.

"How do I know you'll keep your end of the bargain?"

"You don't." Without another word, he stood and extended his arm across the table. "Although this has been entertaining, I have better things to do. Am I to assume we have an agreement?"

Did I really have a choice?

Allowing Carlos to dictate the dealings of the Houston leg of the Carrera Cartel was nothing less than suicide. However, calling up the head of said cartel and explaining my actions didn't fare much different of an outcome.

In our world, black and white didn't exist. Even though we lived our lives in shades of gray where lines always blurred and actions had no consequences, there was still an unspoken hierarchy. A drawn line in the sand separating the royal blue blood of Mexico's underworld and the common red blood of those who served them.

The ones trusted enough to walk the line but forbidden to cross it.

After leaving him standing in silence a few more seconds, I slowly shook his hand. "Provisional agreement."

"Meaning?"

"Meaning provisional, arranged or existing for the present, possibly to be changed later. You know how we operate, Carlos." Cocking an eyebrow, I added in a low tone, an arrogant smile tugging at my lips, "So, don't fuck me over."

I'd never seen anyone go from smug to furious so quickly. Instead of responding, he flipped his middle finger and stormed toward the door.

"Carlos?" I called out.

He hovered halfway in and halfway out, his hand gripping the doorframe so tightly his knuckles turned white. "What?"

"You didn't pay for your drinks, you cheap ass."

A slew of curses followed him out the door as it slammed behind him.

I chuckled to myself.

Being underestimated was the biggest advantage a man could have over his enemy. I'd lived long enough to know that given the right incentive, even the strongest ally could be an enemy.

Raising my glass, I conceded round one.

But it was round two, and the gloves were coming off.

I didn't go from an assistant district attorney in Houston to first lieutenant of the Carrera Cartel by waving a white flag at the first sign of a threat.

I ran that motherfucking city.

Chapter Two

BRODY

Houston, Texas

R ain pissed me off.

Not that I'd ever been a rainbows and sunshine type of guy. I preferred dark clouds and thunder. They usually brought everyone's optimism and cheerfulness down a few notches, which always improved my mood.

However, today the muggy September rain conspired against me. As soon as I got behind the wheel, the sky opened up, and now it was coming down so hard, I could barely see the car in front of me. If I had half a brain, I'd take it as an omen and turn the hell around.

No, if I had half a brain, I never would've left home in the first place.

Squeezing the steering wheel with one hand, I rubbed a damp palm across my nose and swallowed the nausea trying to claw its way up my throat.

I didn't need this shit right now. Last night, I drank my weight in cheap scotch, trying to forget my own name. Unfortunately, today, the only thing I wanted to do was crawl out of this car and throw up my spleen.

And punches. I wanted to throw punches.

It took longer than I expected for the call to come in. Forty-eight hours too long, to be exact. Someone's balls would be overnighted to their mother for the time I spent pacing my living room while waiting for Rafael to collect a thief.

I was a lieutenant in the fucking cartel.

Second in line for the bloodstained Carrera throne.

And because of it, here I was, regardless of my lack of sobriety.

Besides, as my Colombian watchdog reminded me, I didn't have much choice in the matter. It was either drive the final nail in the Muñoz coffin or climb inside my own. Since today's agenda didn't include a death wish, this seemed to be the lesser of two evils.

The more I drove, the more pissed off I became. Instead of driving on a road to nowhere, I should've been at the cantina, pretending to run it like a legitimate business instead of a one-stop-shop currency cleaner. I was the face of it, after all. Honest, trustworthy Brody Harcourt. An all-American civil servant dealt a bad hand. Righteous to his core despite being born into a band of psychos.

The pounding in my head synced with the rhythm of the rain slamming against the windshield, and my vision blurred until the whole car filled with static. I was positive I was going to have an aneurysm until the deserted service road appeared up ahead. Ignoring the railroad spikes driving through my skull, I turned right and hit the gas. Halfway down the long driveway, the car stalled. The more I slammed my foot on the gas, the more the tires spun, slinging mud across the windshield.

I couldn't help but smirk. As if being stuck would stop me. Not after how far I'd come. After all I'd done.

Killing the engine, I almost ripped the door off the hinges while stumbling out of the car, cursing as the soles of my handmade Italian dress shoes sank deep into the mud. Holding onto a thin layer of restraint, I made my way toward the building, calmly watching more expensive leather disappear into the earth.

Another piece of my identity soiled and ruined.

Just like everything else that mattered.

Lifting my chin, I glared up at the sky, a bitter blend of anger and alcohol swimming in my veins. "Is that the best you've got?"

In response, a streak of lightning lit up the sky seconds before the bottom fell out of it, turning the incessant rainstorm into a torrential downpour.

My lips twitched with a sadistic smile as I spread my arms out in acknowledgment. "Well played."

Maybe challenging God wasn't the smartest move, but recklessness had quickly become my drug of choice. It was an addiction more compulsive than gambling, producing a high twice as deadly. However, it wasn't the eventual payout that kept the cycle in perpetual motion. It was the thrill of the hunt. The crave of the kill. One hit, and it thrummed through my veins, seeking more.

Needing more.

Always *more*.

And *more* is exactly what stood a hundred yards in front of me. As I walked toward it, the rain slipped away, along with my conscience. Judgment waited inside four weathered concrete walls forgotten by time. A blood coated foundation covered in so many weeds it appeared to have grown from the earth beneath it.

Inside those walls, I unleashed the man they created.

My breathing came faster and harder, and a few steps later,

I found myself standing in front of a wooden door. The white paint peeled from every groove and edge as if mirroring the scars inflicted behind it. Unlocking it, I tucked what was left of my conscience inside a box and walked inside.

A man dangled from an overhead beam with his mouth wide open. To be fair, he didn't have much of a choice with his sock shoved in it.

Nice touch.

I slammed the door extra hard and made a show of turning the lock. Whether the move was induced by alcohol or ego didn't really matter. Once his widened eyes met mine, I committed them to memory.

Was it sadistic to savor the moment? Probably. But any benevolence I might have had disappeared when I remembered the pain the Muñoz Cartel caused the people I loved.

Rafael tilted his chair back on two legs and greeted me with a curt nod. "*Jefe.*"

That was the extent of his small talk. Not that I expected much more. My trusted soldier was a man of few words, which was fine with me. He did his job without asking questions and followed orders without expecting a pat on the back. He knew his role and respected the hierarchy.

We were associates, not friends.

And just by looking at him, I could see my associate had started the party without me. His white button-up was rolled up at the sleeves and splattered with blood, and the lines in his young face were pulled taut. A cold-hearted killer with a thirst for blood.

Quite the acquired asset.

Turning his attention back to his charge, Rafael kept one foot planted on the floor and kicked the man's shin with the other, sending him spinning in a useless circle.

"Efficient as always, Suárez." He nodded again as the chair's front two legs slammed against the concrete not far from where José Rojas still swung like a pendulum. "What's the status on the Chicago replacement?"

"Carlos came through. All eight hundred sold and distributed. After we split it up and give it a good wash through Caliente and Carrera's real estate shell, we should see a profit."

Thank God.

Step one down. Step two... Well, I suppose he was still up.

Walking past our guest, I smirked. "José, glad to see you hung around for me."

Rafael's groan quickly turned into a cough as I glared at him over my shoulder.

"Problem?"

"Nope."

Giving my associate a curt nod, I circled José, his leather jacket brushing against his ripped jeans as he spun. The man looked like hell. His breath came rough and labored, which didn't surprise me, considering the lead pipe that lay discarded at his feet. His nose was broken, his lip was split open, and blood dripped down his chin like a leaky faucet. I suspected broken ribs, maybe a punctured lung.

Rafael tended to be heavy-handed.

I couldn't decide if I appreciated the preemptive gesture or resented being denied the pleasure of inflicting the pain myself. After all, it was my business he'd screwed with.

"José," I acknowledged, clasping my hands around my back and walking a full circle around him. His swollen eyes tracked every move I made, and I had to give the guy credit; he didn't plead for mercy. Most of the assholes who'd been in his position had already pissed themselves twice by now.

Of course, he *was* still gagged.

31

The legs of the chair slammed against the concrete again. "He kept trying to give me bullshit excuses," Rafael explained with a shrug. "I didn't want to hear any more."

The attorney in me decided to let him plead his case. Years of litigation were too ingrained in me. Plus, I couldn't walk away from a trial without a closing argument. Stopping in front of him, I jerked the sock out of his mouth.

"Where's my shipment, José?"

"I don't have your fucking blow."

I should've punched out his teeth. Instead, I smiled. "Let's try this again. Where's my goddamn shipment?"

"Harcourt," he rasped, licking his lips through a labored wheeze. "I'm surprised you're still alive. I thought the *sicarios* would've taken you out by now."

I gave his cheek a tap, sending him spinning again. "José, you're acting real fucking stupid for such a smart man. I'm first lieutenant. You know I only answer to two men."

He spat at the floor by my feet, smiling with blood-stained teeth. "*Rezarás por tu vida a nuestros pies, Americano.*" *You will pray for your life at our feet, American.*

Two steps forward and we stood nose to nose. "I'm not the one hanging from the ceiling, dumbass."

José's forehead wrinkled, and I didn't bother hiding a smirk.

"Didn't expect that, huh? Well, seeing as how I run an entire stateside cartel, I thought knowing some of the language might come in handy someday." I tapped his cheek again. "What do you know? It did."

"Pinche pendejo." *Fucking asshole.*

"You know," I noted, hooking my foot under the bloodied lead pipe and kicking upward into my hand. "The disrespect seems to have gotten out of hand. Maybe Rafael needs to beat some manners into you."

José's eyes widened as Rafael rose from his chair with his arm outstretched as if we were running some sort of demented relay race. "It'd be my pleasure."

"No!" José yelled, twisting violently. "I swear I didn't do shit!"

"You really shouldn't swear unless it's under oath. But I don't blame you. I know you're just the 'yes' man, José, so tell me who's trying to reorganize your psychopathic bunch of assholes, and I might let you keep your eyeballs tucked inside your face."

He stopped twisting, and his face blanked. "Me. It's me."

Curiouser and curiouser.

"Bullshit. Okay, let's try another question. Why Chicago? Why not come straight back to Texas where the Muñozs had ties?" All I got in return was a glare of pure hatred, causing me to wave a dismissive hand. "Never mind. It really doesn't matter."

"Fuck you."

"Last chance. Who's calling the shots, José?"

"I don't know." He shook his head violently, the motion causing his body to sway even harder.

"Ah, but you've already said that." Cocking my chin over my shoulder, I caught Rafael's eye and tilted my head back toward José. "There's only one thing I hate more than a thief."

Rafael lifted an eyebrow. "An asshole?"

"A liar."

"I'm not lying! I—" I narrowed my eyes, and he stopped himself. Inhaling a labored breath, he started again, choosing his words more carefully. "Okay, fine. But you won't believe me."

"Try me."

"It's Marisol Muñoz. She's calling herself Adriana Carrera now." He smiled, his teeth coated in a thin layer of blood. "But I guess you'd know that better than anyone." When I didn't answer, his smile wavered. "Come on, Harcourt. If someone was after Val or Mateo, would you hand them over to the enemy? You'd do the same thing in my position."

He was right. I'd hold on to that shit until my dying breath.

He took my silence as an affirmation, his confidence elevating. "As long as you need a name, you needed me."

Only, I didn't. There was always another asshole left holding a smoking gun who eventually tucked his balls in his vagina and ran like a little bitch. Whether it took two more days or two months, I'd find him, too.

This wasn't the first time I had to fight my way out of a corner, and it wouldn't be the last. Stopping my circling, I stood behind him and leaned in close. "Here's the thing, José. I really don't."

With those last words, I stuffed his sock back in his mouth and pulled my gun. Aiming it at the back of his head, I pulled the trigger, watching as his broken body danced its way toward death.

"You know what to do."

Rafael dipped his chin in acknowledgment as I wiped my hands on a handkerchief from the breast pocket of my suit jacket. When not a speck of blood remained on my skin, I left them both and stepped back out into the pouring rain

I didn't waste time with small talk.

I had a queen to catch.

Chapter Three

ADRIANA

Appraising myself in the mirror, my lip twitched, curling up on one side. I looked the part. The pencil-thin black skirt fit like a glove, just as I suspected it would. The snug white blouse was a different story, but it'd have to suffice.

Sometimes assets were a liability.

No one would ever mistake the woman looking back at me for the one who stepped off that bus. Disguise had always been my specialty. Growing up in a family as notorious as mine, blending in wasn't just a learned skill, it was basic survival. There was always an enemy lurking around the corner, just waiting for me to let my guard down.

The air was thick with justice, and it was time a certain counselor choked on it.

My heels clicked against the polished tile as I made my way toward the lobby elevator.

People crammed into the tiny box like migrants sneaking

across the border. My chest tightened, but I forced myself to join them, tapping the toe of my high heel as the elevator stopped on each floor, depositing and acquiring passengers.

Fourth floor.

Tap, tap, tap, tap, tap.

Fifth floor.

Tap, tap, tap, tap, tap.

We made it to the seventh floor when a woman behind me let out an exaggerated sigh. "Do you mind?"

She looked like the woman I used to be—a revelation that made me want to sink a blade deep in her chest while watching that pretty white shirt turn dark red.

I could've stopped. I should've stopped. Adriana Carrera would've stopped. Unfortunately, there was still a tiny piece of Marisol Muñoz left inside me, and she stopped for no one.

More toe-tapping.

"I said, *excuse me.*"

I rolled my chin over my shoulder, pinning her with a hardened stare. Her wrinkled face blanched, and she swallowed so hard her throat muscles shook. "I heard you the first time."

Nobody said shit for the next three floors.

Finally arriving at the tenth floor, I stepped into the expansive lobby. It was just as I remembered—beige, bland, and boring. My heels clicked against the tile, announcing my presence as I approached the front desk. A familiar perky blonde sat behind it, trailing her freakishly large blue eyes from the top of my head down to my newly acquired heels. I stood half-amused and half-irritated while I waited to see if she deemed me friend or foe.

Women were funny creatures. We were much more powerful united, yet there was an innate instinct inside all of us to tear each other down. It was the reason men thought we were the weaker gender. If only we'd get over petty competitive bullshit, women could rule the world.

How unfortunate.

Her gaze traveled back to my face, and she broke out into a huge grin. I knew she didn't recognize me; I wasn't that sloppy. I simply didn't know whether to feel honored or insulted she'd decided so quickly I wasn't a threat.

Case in point. Women were strange.

I wanted to tell her to fuck off, but she possessed way more power here than me. Murder and annihilation were a far cry from mergers and acquisitions. Unfortunately, I had to play nice. I knew just enough about the fair city's former assistant DA to be dangerous but not enough to be deadly. From what I remembered about our mutual friend here, she'd be more than willing to fill me in on all I needed to know to tip the scales in my favor.

After all, I took the role of femme fatale quite literally.

The perky blonde leaped out of her chair. "How can I help you?"

"I'm here to see the assistant district attorney."

Her smile faded as she fiddled with her laptop. "Do you have an appointment? She's extremely busy today."

I didn't have time for this, and I sure as hell didn't need her scanning some calendar for a nonexistent appointment. "No, I don't, but I'm an old friend of his, and I'm sure if you ask…" I paused, feigning shock. "Wait, did you say, *she*?"

"Yes, Charlotte Kimbrell. I'm her secretary, Nancy Malone." She tapped her nameplate as if I cared.

"What happened to Brody Harcourt?"

Her eyebrows pulled together, little lines darting across her forehead. "Didn't you say you're a friend of Mr. Harcourt's? Surely, you know about the"—she leaned over the desk and lowered her voice—"*scandal*."

"I've been out of the country." Technically, it wasn't a lie.

"Well, I really shouldn't gossip. Mr. Harcourt was my boss for years, you know."

Of course, I knew, and I didn't give a shit. However, I dutifully nodded my head because that was what she wanted.

"It's not my place to repeat his personal tragedies."

But you will.

"But since you're his close friend and all…" Pausing, Nancy raised a perfectly penciled-in eyebrow as if waiting for approval. Of course, it probably didn't matter one way or the other. Nancy was a natural leak. The wind could blow the wrong way, and she'd take it as a sign to blab.

"Of course." I smiled. "We go way back."

That was all she needed. Nancy's mouth opened, and everything I'd missed in the last year came spewing out like a geyser. "You know he had an estranged sister, right?" Obviously, it was a rhetorical question, because she barely took a breath before answering for me. "Well, about six months ago, she came back into town. Not long after that he started missing court dates and got into some seriously deep shit… I mean hot water with the Carreras."

I gasped. "The cartel?"

"Shocking, right?" Nancy said, waving her hands around like a lunatic. "Unfortunately, one thing led to another, and she died, and then his mother got arrested."

I had to refrain from poking holes in her story. Nancy's version was like staring at a jigsaw puzzle when half the pieces were missing. "So, this is the scandal you were talking about?" I asked, shifting her back on topic. "The DA's office forced Brody out?"

Nancy shrugged and lowered herself back into her seat. "No, Mr. Harcourt resigned first. After he lost his family, something snapped up here." Tapping her finger against her temple, she sighed, the corners of her mouth turning down as her excitement faded. "Such a shame, too. He was one of the good ones."

I wanted to laugh in her face. The Brody Harcourt she knew was a façade. A skin he stepped into the minute he walked into this office and took off the minute he walked out. His palms were just as greasy as his mother's, and his loyalty was twice as thin. I wanted to take that heroic image she'd created in her mind and twist it until it was nothing but useless dust.

But I didn't.

As sickening as it was, devotion like Nancy's could be a useful tool. Besides, I still needed one more thing from her. Luckily, emotional manipulation had always been one of my finer talents.

I shot her a pleading look. "Do you have any idea where I can find him?"

"All I know is he bought that cantina from one of the Carrera wives." She glanced up at the ceiling, snapping her fingers as if it held the answer. "Crap, what's its name?"

"Caliente," I muttered, more to myself than her.

"Yes! That's it…Caliente. He bought it to make it respectable and give back to the community." She beamed with pride, and I wanted to punch her face. "Although I'm not sure he'll be there."

She might not be sure, but I was.

The only thing sure in life was that history repeated itself. This whole thing started when I walked into that damn cantina, and it'd end the same way.

"Thanks." Widening the distance between us, I turned to leave when she grabbed my arm.

"This is going to sound crazy, but do I know you? You seem so familiar."

So close.

A year and a half ago, Brody Harcourt was an overly

ambitious politician tucked into Valentin Carrera's pocket. I spent many days shadowing and interacting with him, and he never knew it. But Nosy Nancy apparently had a mind like a steel trap.

"I don't think so." Each word carried an implied message, spoken with a cold darkness that sent goose bumps scattering up Nancy's arms. Blood pulsed in my ears and every muscle in my body stiffened. Nancy's breathing quickened, those bug eyes growing impossibly wide and filling with unshed tears.

Let it go, Nancy. For your sake.

"Oh, well, maybe you just have one of those faces," she whispered, her skin growing pale.

We both knew I didn't. However, it seemed Nancy had a brain as big as her mouth. She knew she'd screwed up. She also knew she'd screw up even worse by saying a word.

Call it women's intuition. We understood each other.

Maybe there *was* hope for our gender.

I didn't offer a goodbye and neither did she. I walked out of the district attorney's office on a mission. Nancy could think whatever she wanted, but Brody Harcourt wasn't just a bar owner. Every fall from grace came with loose ends. If I tugged hard enough on one thread, the whole tapestry would unravel.

The former public servant had sold his soul and roughened up that shiny penny exterior.

He'd appointed himself my executioner…

And now, I was his.

Chapter Four

BRODY

"**A**driana Carrera," I growled into my phone, the sound of my wet shoes clapping against the dusty tiles as I pushed the door open to Caliente Cantina. "I don't know how, Carlos. But a man with a bull's-eye on his ass isn't going to throw out a name like that for no reason." Approaching the bar, I snapped my fingers at the dumb bitch behind it playing on her phone. "Yes, I'm on it." I listened to him go on and on until the last thing he said made me come to a dead stop. "Another shipment? Shit, okay. I'll handle it. I said I'd handle it!" I ended the call without waiting for a response.

Another two million dollars intercepted near Chicago.

This was getting out of control and covering my ass while pretending it wasn't on the line was getting harder. How did people do this shit day after day without staying permanently drunk? Maybe anger and guilt could coexist in some people's world, but not in mine. Spinning a wheelhouse of emotion was nothing but suicide. The only way to survive was to commit to an extreme and never look back.

Pocketing my phone, I glanced up to see the latest in a revolving door of bartender bitches lift her chin and stare at me, her red lips pressed into a thin line. I couldn't tell if it was out of intrigue, fear, or brazen pity, but I didn't give a shit. She needed to mind her own business—a point I made by meeting her curious gaze with a steeled glare and holding out my hand.

"My drink."

In response, she slid a glass of scotch toward me, eyeing my shirt while arching an eyebrow.

I glanced down and gritted my teeth. The white button-up shirt underneath my navy-blue suit was splattered with José's blood. I always kept a spare in my car for situations like this, but my mind hadn't exactly been focused lately.

I calmly stared back and waited for her to speak. She didn't, and neither did I. A successful prosecutor controlled the narrative by forcing the defendant's hand. So, we stood in silence. The longer we stood, the more unsettled she became.

Most people considered silence to be peaceful. I found it to be a necessary evil, one I masterfully manipulated to my advantage. Quite the impressive family trait. Reserve was a façade we were forced to wear like a crown.

And by the look on bar bitch's face, I was still the king.

As expected, she broke first, narrowing her heavily lined eyes. "Did you cut yourself?"

"No." My lips twitched while attempting to hold in a smirk.

Her mouth fell open, and the sound of metal crashing against tile shot through the cantina. My smirk widened. Shock value always delivered a guaranteed pick-me-up. However, as much as I enjoyed a good blindside, I also had a business to run. I couldn't have what's-her-name using this as an excuse to be late for work.

I made myself a mental note to buy her a new cell phone.

Once I remembered her name.

The thin skin underneath her eye twitched, and her whole demeanor changed. With a weak smile, she offered a courteous nod, fighting to keep her gaze impassive and failing miserably.

Not that most people would've picked up on it. Years of working in the DA's office taught me to notice the slightest involuntary human reaction. The twitch of a witness's eye told me more than their entire testimony. Hers told me she'd heard the rumors about me. She wanted to ask if they were true, but she wouldn't.

Even she knew curiosity killed the cat.

Our conversation ended as she turned her attention back to whatever the hell it was she did every day instead of her job. I wasn't offended. As long as she kept her mouth shut, I would, too, and we'd both live to see tomorrow.

Continuing down the deserted hallway, I realized being stuck at a dive bar in the middle of the day had its perks. At least I'd have a few hours of privacy before the booze brigade rolled in. Houston's town drunks were more punctual than any of its so-called professionals. They wouldn't flood the cantina until at least three o'clock.

Which gave me plenty of time to call in a favor.

Plus, we were still short-staffed, so I wouldn't have to deal with nosy waitresses who didn't know their place. That wasn't a generalized chauvinistic statement. It was a brutal fact, considering the last two employees I vouched for ended up in the obituary column.

Needless to say, women had crossed over to my shit list months ago.

Making my way to my office, I unlocked the door and collapsed in my chair. In the solitude of my own space, my lungs

43

finally began to heave much-needed air into my body, and I clicked on the desk lamp, bathing the tiny office in dim yellow light and shining a spotlight on the reason I was going to hell.

Well, one of them anyway.

Sinking into the chair, my fingers flexed around the picture frame as I dragged it toward me. Even protected by the glass, the photo was worn and faded. Destroyed by time just like each one of us.

Four smiling Harcourts. One living on borrowed time.

I closed my eyes and sighed. "None of us had to end up like this."

Sure, if my mother hadn't sold us out and my sister had trusted me with the truth then one wouldn't be in jail and the other wouldn't have been declared dead.

Unfortunately, it was too late by the time I saw through my family's carefully constructed personas. Maybe if I had, things would've ended differently. Bitter laughter rumbled in my chest.

Should've. Could've. Would've.

But didn't.

Story of my fucking life.

Of course, none of that mattered now. Things had changed, and so had I. My job wasn't to protect and serve anymore as much as manipulate and destroy. Preferably, before anyone else beat me to it.

Like the Muñoz Cartel.

Opening my suit jacket, I pulled out my cell phone and rolled it over in my palms. Carlos said he would take care of things, but I didn't like leaving my fate in someone else's hands. If there was one valuable thing I learned from my mother, it was that political officials' morality had a price tag. Luckily for me, the consulate general at the Mexican Embassy was just as corrupt as she was, only with half the intellect.

I scrubbed a hand over my face and dialed Leo Pinellas's private number. It took two rings for him to answer, his voice a satisfactory mix of fear and unease.

"Hola, *Señor* Harcourt, I didn't expect to hear from you so soon."

No surprise there, considering the last time we spoke, he put up so much resistance to my request, I had to threaten him. To be fair, he did end up betraying his own country.

"Yeah, well, I have a problem, which means you have a problem."

"*Vete a la mierda*," he grumbled. Not that I expected a warm greeting, after all this time, but telling me to fuck off was a bit over the top. "I can't be involved with you anymore. It's too risky."

"It's riskier for you to ignore me." On edge, I tossed the picture frame onto the floor. "I already made one widow today. Don't force me to make another."

Silence filled the line while I assumed he weighed his options. He really didn't have any, but I humored him and spun a full two revolutions in my chair before he came to his senses.

"Tell me what you want," Leo hissed through clenched teeth, his broken English slipping as his anger grew. "But this has to…" The rest of what I presumed to be a futile demand trailed off as a muffled voice laced with huskiness and an edge of insolence filtered through the line.

Son of a bitch.

I had enough on my plate without having to worry about some jerkoff in the Mexican Embassy hearing me spell out the details of someone's murder.

I closed my eyes and cursed. "Is someone there?"

"Just my *puta* secretary who doesn't know how to *fucking knock*," he yelled, the two words punctuated by the sound of a

45

slamming door. "As I was saying, this has to be it. The Harcourt name isn't too popular around here and unsealing Adriana Carrera's birth records for you turned too many eyes my way."

I winced at hearing her name again. It had been months since I'd thought about her, and now she was the ghost who wouldn't go away. An unwelcome pang of guilt settled deep in my stomach. The woman nearly assassinated my boss then walked out of a Houston safe house like a fucking queen. She made my life hell for months. A Muñoz creation whose mind ticked with only one emotion—hate.

Until I blew her life apart by revealing her entire existence had been a lie. Marisol Muñoz was Adriana Carrera, Val's not-so-dead sister.

After she disappeared off the face of the earth, I assumed she was buried in a shallow grave somewhere. It was inevitable. She never would've stood for her family's legacy to be dismantled, and they never would've accepted a Carrera.

I assumed wrong.

Dragging myself out of that lethal rabbit hole, I changed the subject. "Unfortunately, you don't call the shots, Leo. However, I've had a bitch of a day, so I'll make this brief. The Muñoz Cartel has restructured. I've already had a chat with a man named José Rojas. I'm sure you've heard of him." I didn't wait for a confirmation. I didn't need one. "He's given me some interesting new information on Adriana Carrera. I need you to do some recon on her last known whereabouts."

"Why don't you just blackmail it out of him?"

Smartass.

"He's missing."

"Shouldn't you be trying to locate him?"

"No."

That was all that needed to be said. Leo Pinellas was an

arrogant bastard, but he wasn't stupid. Reading between the lines wasn't a hard skill to master. Especially when his fat ass would be next.

"I'll see what I can find out."

"You have twenty-four hours."

Probably even less for me if Adriana was motivated enough.

"You'd better know what you're doing, Brody. Every time you try to fuck over a cartel boss, a woman pays the price. First, your sister, then Carrera's girl, then Carrera's sister."

My hand tore through my hair, ripping the strands at the root. "She wasn't his girl!" I let out a dry laugh. "But he sure as hell made sure she didn't have any other option."

"That's a little hypocritical, don't you think?"

The coil that had wound tighter and tighter in my chest since returning from Chicago snapped. "Twenty-four hours, Pinellas." Grinding my teeth, I jerked the phone away to disconnect the call, but at the last minute lifted it back to my ear. "Make that twenty-two just for being an asshole."

"You used to protect the law, Brody. You were a good guy." He paused, his breath uneven. "What happened to you?"

My fingers clenched around my phone, my earlier smugness brittle and hollow. "I opened my eyes." I didn't wait for a response. Ending the call, I slammed my phone onto my desk, not giving a shit if I cracked the screen.

This wasn't supposed to turn into such a clusterfuck. Of course, I shouldn't be surprised. Life had delivered one giant middle finger after another since I sank into cartel quicksand. No matter how hard I tried to claw my way out, it kept pulling me under, deeper and deeper each time. Eventually, I gave up the fight and sank to the bottom.

Now, here I sat, completely submerged, trying to fight more than one invisible enemy. How long would it be until I just stopped breathing?

"It won't be today." With fire in my chest, I spun around, ready to fire bar bitch just to make myself feel better when a glint of silver caught my eye.

Without thinking, I crouched next to the picture frame I'd tossed like a grenade and picked it up. My white-knuckled grip on it tightened. I'd be damned if I'd go down like this. Straightening my shoulders, I stood and placed the frame back on my desk.

Tugging my tie loose, I shrugged off my jacket and unbuttoned my soiled shirt, reaching for the spare I kept in the tiny closet in the corner of the office. As I rolled the sleeves of the freshly laundered shirt up to my elbows, I heard the back door slam and what sounded like a bulldozer tear through the kitchen.

I glanced at the clock and threw my head back with a groan. "For fuck's sake, Kiki, this is the third time this week. Your shift started three hours ago. Do you not own a goddamn clock?"

Tearing out of my office, I punched the wall on my way out, more than ready to hand a certain brunette waitress her ass and then toss it out the door.

It was bar bitch's lucky day.

Chapter Five

ADRIANA

How the mighty have fallen.

The phrase sat on the tip of my tongue as I rounded the building and opened the door to a pathetically empty Caliente Cantina. The symbolism wasn't lost on me, and if I had more time, I might have relished in how things had come full circle. However, I didn't come here to bask in the misfortune of others.

I came to rectify my own.

Although I did my best to blend in, my high heels clicked against the cheap floor, announcing my arrival like a grenade. Stopping mid-stride, I winced and waited for the collective gasp. Surprisingly, the handful of patrons scattered in the worn booths never bothered to look up, much less acknowledge me. Returning the favor, I ignored them, focusing all my attention toward the bar.

It didn't take long to find him. Slumped in a stool at the farthest end, Brody Harcourt scowled into his beer, gripping the glass mug as if he were squeezing out its last breath. The move might have intimidated a normal woman, but I wasn't most women.

Besides, I knew more about him in a glance than I suspected most of his "so-called" friends did in a lifetime. The simple key to reading someone was to study their body language. Yeah, he looked ready to kill someone, but his hands were his tell. The glass he held took a level of unsurmountable punishment clearly meant for someone else.

Of course, there was also the obvious alcohol he downed like water. Men tended to use liquid therapy as a crutch rather than dealing with their problems. I'd seen it all my life. Not that it was a bad temporary fix for a highly publicized fall from grace, but killing brain cells just stalled the climb back to the top.

And through all this analysis, here I stood in the middle of this god-awful, piece of shit cantina like a flashing siren. Only, like the other customers, Brody found my existence irrelevant. Not that it mattered to me. I wasn't here to have my ego stroked. There was only one thing I wanted, and I'd traveled too long and too far to hinge it on an obstinate male mood swing.

Still, observation was a useful skill, so I continued appraising him from a distance.

The way a man dressed said a lot about him, who they were; what they did; where they'd been. According to Brody's clothes, I deduced the answers were: a burden on society, two lines up the nose, and saddled up at the twenty-four-hour stripper emporium.

The wrinkled white button-up shirt he wore was half tucked in toward the front and wild and chaotic in the back. The sleeves were uncuffed and rolled up to his elbows, exposing ridiculously toned arms.

At some point, he'd undone the first button at his collar, got frustrated, then ripped the next four clean off. The evidence was scattered across the floor with one resting against the soiled toe of my high heel. I kicked it to the side, continuing to study him. With a grunt, one hand flew from his mug and yanked off the tie draped around his neck. The muscles in his forearm tensed as he balled it up and pitched it across the bar railing.

Nice throw.

This version of Brody Harcourt looked nothing like the man I remembered. Then again, I doubted he gave a damn if he lived up to dress code since his mother tried to murder his entire family.

I should know.

Bits and pieces of the last year flashed through my head. The confusion. The loneliness. The pain. Refusing to lose control, I closed my eyes and blocked the darkness from rolling in.

No emotion. Not today.

With renewed determination, I made my way to the bar, my sleek dark hair dusting over my shoulder as I slid into the chair beside him. Before I could say a word, a bleach blonde bartender in a skimpy uniform rolled her eyes as she walked toward me with a cell phone suctioned to her ear and a groan on her lips.

"I guess I'll have to call you back." Cocking a hip, she braced one hand against the bar while shoving the phone in the back pocket of her cut-off jean shorts with the other. From the way she glared at me and then Brody, I could tell her crush on him was just as big as her attitude. "So, do you know what you want or what?"

A year ago, I would've had her choking on her own tongue for that.

"*Añejo* tequila in a stem glass. Room temp, only."

I met her stare just in time to catch her raised eyebrow and quick glance to my right. When it went unacknowledged, she swallowed a few times and turned away. I sat in comfortable silence, refusing to blink. Even missing a second of this was too much.

It wasn't long before the bartender returned with my drink and a brand-new attitude. With eyes downcast, she carefully placed it in front of me and disappeared.

Maybe she wasn't so stupid after all.

"Bad day?" I pushed the tequila to the side, holding a perfect smile while nodding toward the discarded tie.

Brody didn't bother to look up, still gripping the hell out of his mug. "Something like that."

"Want to talk about it?" I urged, placing a hand across his forearm. My bold move captured his attention, snapping his eyes toward our connection.

Take the bait.

Whatever fire had lit in his eyes quickly extinguished. Turning away, he stared blankly across the bar before lifting the mug to his mouth. "Not particularly."

Okay, time to change tactics. "Well, then, can I buy you a drink?"

"I own the bar, sweetheart."

I'd learned patience. I was stellar at waiting my turn. But I'd also learned that leading a horse to water wouldn't make him drink.

Unless you shoved his face in it.

"I get it." Shifting toward him, I leaned my elbow onto the bar and dialed up the sarcasm to an eleven. "I'm just a stranger. What do I know, right? But you've got a chip on your shoulder the size of Texas. You obviously need to unload. If not me, there's got to be someone you can talk to."

Silence.

"Girlfriend?"

Silence.

I assumed that particular brand of quiet dismissal worked on bar blondie, but unfortunately for him, petulance was my specialty.

"Boyfriend?"

"The fuck? I'm not—" His widened eyes slowly narrowed as he took in the smirk plastered across my face. Rolling a heated gaze over me, he held up his palm. "Lady, if I need to unload, this does the job just fine."

Stop thinking of that hand. Focus. Stick to the plan.

"I'm told family is always there for you if you need them," I offered, clearing my throat.

The corners of Brody's mouth curled up in a cold smile. "Hard to do when they're dead."

"All of them?"

He shrugged, and I held back a smile as his fingers swiped a cocktail napkin back and forth beside his beer. He wanted to react. How could he not? The tension in the air was so thick, it could've choked us both.

"Might as well be," he bit out finally, sending the cocktail napkin skidding across the bar. "Family is just a bullshit lie anyway."

"Well, look at that, something we can agree on."

Glancing over his shoulder, Brody arched an eyebrow and gave me a slow appraisal. "You ask a lot of questions, you know that?"

"Sorry, force of habit in my line of work."

He let out a low chuckle and took another drink, a dangerous mix of intrigue and irritation flickering in his eyes. "Since you obviously can't take a hint, I'll bite. What do you do?"

A wide smile parted my lips. "I guess you could say I'm an international trade specialist."

"Sounds vague."

"Mm-hmm," I agreed, taking a small but lethal sip from my glass. Although I somewhat enjoyed our banter, I'd grown bored with small talk. Propping my elbow on the bar, I rested my chin in my hand and leaned in. "So, is this what *you* do since getting fired from the district attorney's office, Brody?"

Twisting around, he slammed his glass onto the wood, his disinterest shifting to suspicion. "I'm sorry, do I know you?"

"No, but I know you. Your Harcourt family scandal made national news, and your face is hardly forgettable, Brody."

I had no purpose in saying his name twice, other than watching the instability flicker behind his eyes. He didn't anticipate being confronted with the fall of Houston's own version of Camelot. Maybe he thought his mask was just that good, but dark-rimmed eyes and nervous twitches betrayed even the most well-crafted façade. It was obvious he'd been balancing on the edge of a breakdown for some time now.

"My last name doesn't define me."

"Well said."

"It seems you have me at a disadvantage," he accused, eyeing me cautiously. "You know my name, but I don't know yours. You plan on telling me?"

I cocked my head. "That depends."

"On what?"

"Well, my last name didn't define me either, so I got myself a brand new one. Thanks to you, of course."

That was the moment the pieces fell into place and the puzzle clicked. Beads of sweat traced the seam of his upper lip as he stopped looking at me and finally *saw* me.

"No, it can't be."

"Oh, I'm sorry, where are my manners?" Sliding off the stool, I stood barely a breath away and extended my hand. "My name's Adriana." I waited until all the color drained from his face before driving in the final nail. "Adriana Carrera."

Chapter Six

BRODY

All I could do was stare at her outstretched hand as if it had fangs just waiting to sink into an exposed vein and inject retribution and penance.

It couldn't be.

But it was.

Adriana fucking Carrera.

Speak of the devil, and she walks in your bar.

I remembered seeing the blurry college photos of her Leo managed to scrounge up when I first contacted him, but the woman in front of me looked completely different. Her hair was shorter, and the way she was dressed made it damn hard for a man to look her in the eye.

Back then, I had no idea the shitstorm I was about to unleash.

After the dust settled, Val sent men looking for her, but no one could find her. Not a damn thing. That's what made her so dangerous. It was hard to fight an invisible enemy.

But here she stood, dressed in a tight, pencil-thin black skirt, a white blouse a few sizes too small, and the highest fuck-me-heels I'd ever seen, claiming to be the missing heiress to the Carrera empire.

I didn't have to know what Marisol or Adriana or whatever the hell she wanted to be called looked like to realize my past had caught up with me. Paybacks were a bitch.

And so was the woman standing in front of me.

Curling my lip at her offered hand, I turned my back to her. "You've got a lot of fucking nerve showing your face here."

I felt Adriana's eyes boring into me as I drained the piss warm beer left in my mug. I knew she still had her arm extended, seething as she waited for me to kiss her ass, so instead, I lifted an eyebrow and waved the glass at bar bitch. Like the dutiful half-wit she was, my employee raced around the bar like her ass was on fire, sorting through chilled glasses until she found the perfect one then busied herself at the tap.

"Neat trick, Pavlov." Adriana's sultry voice trailed over my shoulder. "You might want to think about spaying her so she'll stop humping your leg."

As much shit as she'd caused, an unwelcome smile still tugged at the corners of my mouth as bar bitch shot Adriana a glare, muttering a slew of curses as my beer overflowed onto her shoes. Wiping the sides down, she slammed the mug in front of me and stomped off to the corner, huffing as she tapped away on her ever-present phone.

Lifting the new mug, I took a slow drink and shot her a look out of the corner of my eye. She glared back, with eyes identical to my boss's. A dark chocolate color with gold flecks that burned like fire when he was pissed.

Kind of like she was now.

"Something wrong?"

"How anyone didn't realize you were a damn Carrera before I blew the whistle is beyond me," I muttered around another huge drink. "You have the same condescending stare as your brother."

"I thought you two were friends."

"Respect doesn't make us friends, *princesa*."

"Yes, well, the eyes *are* the window to the soul." Tilting her chin, she held my gaze. "But the heart is the doorway to sin."

Tou-fucking-ché.

I raised my glass in a toast. "I'll drink to that."

"It appears you'll drink to anything these days."

I held her stare while taking my time drinking long and slow just to piss her off. From the way her lips pursed tighter than an asshole, I succeeded. Adriana stood there as if waiting for me to offer the seat she just vacated and invite her to join me. If she thought I still subscribed to that kind of chivalrous bullshit, she had a lot to learn. I didn't give a shit if she stood there until her fucking legs fell off.

Normally, I would've egged her on, but she'd come to me for a reason, and I was tired of dancing around the seventeen-million-dollar elephant in the room. "So, you want your revenge. Is that what stealing my shipments and this pathetic reorganization attempt is about?"

I could feel the anger rolling off her in waves, but that didn't stop her from jerking out the stool beside me and sitting down. "Not very skilled in small talk, are you?"

"I'm getting bored, Miss Carrera. You want to cut to the chase?" I lifted the mug to my mouth again, glancing out of the corner of my eye to find an angry flush rushing up that sexy, slim neck. Thankfully, my cheeks were full of beer and unable to give in to the smirk begging to break free.

She groaned, digging her palm into her forehead. "Would you stop talking and listen? I didn't steal anything, and I'm not reorganizing shit. I'm being set up."

"Right."

"You're burning the wrong person at the stake."

"And you're fucking with the wrong Carrera," I growled, leaning forward. "I'm not stupid. Shipments go missing, the Muñoz Cartel is involved, your name is given as the leader, and now here you are."

"Your point?"

"If it looks like a duck, swims like a duck, and quacks like a duck, then guess what, sweetheart? It's not a fucking chicken."

Adriana rolled her eyes. "Who wouldn't want revenge," she admitted, some of the bite leaving her voice. "You ruined my life. Why would you do that? What was so important about me that you had to do that?"

I stared at her, momentarily taken aback by her sudden and unexpected burst of vulnerability.

Nothing.

Not a damn thing was important about *her*.

It had to do with a different woman. One who'd already chosen another man, but who I still couldn't seem to let go. I did it to protect my ex-girlfriend.

Okay, that was a lie.

I wanted to prove a point. I wanted her to open her eyes and see that the man who had her heart lived in a savage world. A world where men slaughtered entire families and brainwashed children. If she'd left everything she knew to be with him, it would've been the biggest mistake of her life.

Eden would've been nothing but a pawn.

Disposable collateral.

Just like one-year-old Adriana Carrera had been.

But I said none of that. Instead, I shrugged like the asshole I'd become. "It wasn't personal. I'm a lawyer. It was my job to pick out the pieces of a puzzle that don't fit. It made no sense why your body was never found. Esteban Muñoz threw your birth mother and aunt away like trash. He would've done the same to Val if he hadn't gotten away. But you? Not a trace of your blood or DNA was found at the crime scene. It didn't add up."

"It wasn't personal?" She threw her head back and laughed so loudly the few patrons left in the bar turned a curious eye our way.

Gritting her teeth, she leaned in close enough that a sweet and spicy scent drifted past my nose, leaving a hint of licorice in its wake. A scent so complex and unique, I involuntarily tilted my head to chase it before it faded.

"Let me tell you how personal this is, Brody." Ripping the button off the cuff of her blouse, she jerked her sleeve up her arm and held it up between us, instantly breaking the spell I was under.

I blinked twice before the jagged and distorted light pink line came into focus. It ran across her wrist, marring what was otherwise perfectly flawless bronze skin. My heart seized as flashes of my sister ran through my head.

"This is where I almost bled to death from the cut of a knife," she hissed. "This?" Moving her finger from her arm, she trailed it just above the dip in her collarbone. "This is where they tried to slit my throat and missed. So, don't you sit there and tell me it wasn't personal."

"They?"

A cold smile crawled across her lips. "Muñoz *sicarios*. My soldiers. My own *familia*. It seems upon hearing that the man who I believed to be my father was actually a sadistic fuck who murdered my birth mother and raised me to hate the Carreras as some sort of demented vendetta didn't sit well with them." She gave her free arm a dismissive wave. "Something about the only

61

good Carrera blood is spilled Carrera blood."

"So, is that what you want? Blood for blood? You want to see me suffer to make your pain lessen?"

"You'd deserve it. However, for now, we have more pressing matters to discuss."

I lifted my mug again, trying hard to ignore her labored breaths and the rhythmic rise and fall of her chest. "We have nothing to discuss. You don't have a throne anymore, *princesa*."

"You're right," she admitted, rolling her sleeve back down. The cuff flapped at her wrist, and judging by her disinterest, she was either unaware that she'd destroyed the button or didn't give a shit. "But thanks to you, I do have a name, and you're going to help me claim it."

I damn near choked on my beer. "What?"

"I know the name of the man reorganizing the Muñoz Cartel."

"Right," I mocked, drawing out the word. "Because the cartel trying to kill you also gives you insider info. Nice try."

She tossed me a look somewhere between annoyance and disappointment. "Brody, you know as well as I do that true power lies in the hand that holds the truth, and effective strategy lies in knowing when to keep your trump card close and when to tip your hand."

"Then why tip to me?"

"We have a mutual enemy and tearing the Muñoz Cartel down before it rises makes more sense than wasting time doing this." She waved a hand between us. "Don't you think?"

"Give me the name, and I'll warn Val."

"No. Take me to Mexico City. I'll talk to Val myself, or I don't talk at all."

That was it. This bitch had lost her goddamn mind. Even if my damn dick didn't know the difference between a blow job and a whack job.

"Are you insane?"

She squared her chin, unbothered by my insult. "Because of you, I have nothing. Nowhere to go. No one who gives a shit if I live or die, and now another asshole is trying to take me down. You owe me this chance."

Shit.

Anyone else would throw her out on her ass. Regardless of what that birth certificate said that Leo dug up, she was raised Muñoz. She might have Carrera in her blood, but the woman had Muñoz in her soul. But as much as I tried to numb that sliver of my conscience that stubbornly refused to die, I couldn't. And right now, it stood on my shoulder yelling in my ear that she was right. I owed her. Not for revealing her true identity—whether she wanted to see it or not that was for the best. But I owed her for the torture she obviously endured.

A familiar ache seared across my chest, and I pressed my palm against my shirt, willing it to subside. Of course, it didn't. It never did. That was penance for you.

Moving my hand up, I scrubbed it over my face and sighed. "Look, Val knows about you. He's been looking for you. He wants to know you."

I didn't know what I expected. Shock? Gratitude? A blush, maybe? I sure as hell didn't anticipate the loud snort she gave me. "I highly doubt the same goes for his blushing bride. Let's not forget I was responsible for arranging the hit on her brother."

"Is that why you want me there, too? To control Eden?"

"Well, you two once had a thing, correct? You can be my buffer."

I didn't bother responding to that. It was none of her damn business.

"Why would I even consider this?" I gritted out through

63

clenched teeth. "Val is my boss. You think I want to get caught up in his shit?"

"You owe me."

Same three words, only this time my conscience flipped a middle finger and sat the fuck down. Anger took the floor, and it was like slipping into a well-worn pair of socks.

"I don't owe you shit."

"You. Owe. Me. Everything." Her voice dropped to an almost-demonic growl, her lips caressing each word as she punctuated them with dramatic pauses.

God, what the hell was it about this woman that scorched my blood and sent it rushing to parts of me that shouldn't be reacting to her? Was it my addiction to danger that made me want her? The thrill of the forbidden? Because bad blood or not, Valentin Carrera would skewer my balls if I laid a finger on his sister.

"I'm sorry, *princesa*." I winked. "I'm busy tomorrow. I have to see a man about a thing."

Silence permeated the cantina as we glared at each other. Neither of us spoke as we waited for the other to give in first. The joke was on her. Until my visit with Leo Pinellas tomorrow, I had nowhere to be and nothing to do. I could sit here and play her little pissing match all day.

I gave her intel on Val's interest in her. That's as far as I went. If she wanted more, she could walk her happy ass across the border and ask him for it herself.

I smirked.

Adriana scowled.

I leaned against the bar.

Adriana crossed her arms across her chest.

I tapped my fingers on my glass.

Adriana tapped her toe on the tile.

I scanned my eyes down her legs, and the color of her face turned to lava. Just as she opened her mouth, a crash and the sound of shattering glass turned both our heads toward the bar.

Bar bitch stood on her toes with her palms held high in the air, her mouth rounded in a tight "O". She stared down at the floor, and when I lifted myself over the bar, I saw why. Two bottles of Val's most prized tequila lay shattered on the floor, the contents now rolling under the anti-slip mat.

"Well don't just stand there!" I yelled. "Get a mop, for Christ's sake!"

"I-I'm sorry," she stammered, bending down and picking up random pieces of glass, slicing her hands to hell and back.

With a mop in one hand and a towel in the other, I managed to stop the bleeding and prevent this from turning into a major worker's comp catastrophe. As I put pressure on her wounds, bar bitch looked up at me with hearts in her eyes, and it was all I could do not to fire her on the spot.

By the time I returned to my seat at the bar, Adriana was gone.

Lifting my abandoned glass, I raised it in the air and toasted to small victories. "Better luck next time, *princesa*." I drank slowly, savoring my victory. This wasn't the last I'd seen of Adriana Carrera. She'd be back.

Just as the glass hit my lips, I saw it. A cocktail napkin covered in blood. Slamming the glass back onto the bar, I slid off the seat and snatched it from the puddle of water soaking the edge.

Only, it wasn't blood. It was red lipstick.

Your *thing* isn't that impressive.

And your man is for sale.

Never dip your dick in the same pool twice.

Regency Court – Room 233

"Fuck!" I balled it up and threw it across the bar.

She knew about Leo Pinellas. Worse than that, now I had no choice.

Her trump card ended up being my Achilles heel.

Chapter Seven

ADRIANA

The scotch smelled like Band-Aids soaked in disinfectant. I had no idea how he drank this shit.

Picking up the clear plastic cup, I popped the pills in my hand into my mouth and tossed back what was left, shuddering at the vile taste.

It tasted just as bad.

Crushing the flimsy cup in my hand, I crossed the tiny motel room and dropped it in the trash can. Then again, I was drinking cheap booze out of a plastic cup I found on the bathroom counter. I wasn't exactly the epitome of class. I might as well have sipped Cristal from a salad bowl.

My father would roll over in his grave if he saw how low I'd sunk.

My father.

The words hit my chest, knocking the breath out of me. My lungs seized as if I'd run full speed into a brick wall. I groped the scalloped neckline of my dress, desperate for something to ground me to this room. Far away from the lies whispered to a little girl or the truth beaten into a defiant woman.

But this was reality, and the truth was, my father wouldn't care what I'd become. He wouldn't care because he wasn't my father. He never had been.

The same numbness started to surface, and I closed my eyes and squeezed my fists by my hips, fighting it with every fiber of my being. I refused to drift in between worlds, hovering in that fragment of space where no light could penetrate.

A void.

An abyss.

I squeezed my fists tighter, my nails digging hard into my palms. "No," I whispered. "I won't give you power. Not here. Not now." Opening my eyes, I blinked a few times as the room came back into focus.

I was still here in this crap-ass motel room.

Slowly, I unclenched my fists and glanced down at my phone.

And he was late.

Running a hand down the front of my dress, I straightened the tight lacy material, and a small smile tugged at one corner of my mouth. The royal blue lace overlay hardly masked the body-hugging nude lining. It had better do the trick because I was running out of options.

Grabbing my phone off the stained red and lime green bedspread, I tossed it between my hands a few times and then checked the time.

9:36 p.m.

I had to give Brody points for self-control. After leaving Caliente a little after two o'clock, I would've bet money he'd have beaten my door down by at least four. Although, to be fair, the note I left wasn't exactly inviting. I'd wanted to antagonize him. Maybe push his buttons a little.

I eyed the offensive scotch bottle sitting on the small table as the clock on my phone changed to 9:41 p.m. If he dragged out this pissing contest much longer, I might be tempted to drink more than a sip just to block out the image of the dark ring around the bathtub and the stains on the bed.

God, I missed having money.

I had just grabbed the last plastic cup from the bathroom and filled it with the vile liquid when the sound of repeated fists pounding on my door diverted my attention.

"Adriana! Adriana open this damn door right now, or I swear to God, I'll break it down."

For reasons I couldn't explain, I smiled and swayed my hips, sashaying across the room until I was pressed against the cheap metal. Holding the bandage flavored disinfectant in one hand, I pressed the other against the door. "Who is it?"

"You know damn well who it is. Now open the door."

I trailed a nail across the metal, and it scratched like nails on a chalkboard. "I'm sorry, I don't answer the door for strangers. A lady can never be too careful, you know."

"Adriana," he warned, the low growl in his voice drawing me closer to the door until I pressed flush against it. "You're staying in a motel that's in the heart of a Carrera-run neighborhood. If you don't open this fucking door by the count of three, I'm going to open fire on this lock, and no one will give a shit. Do you understand me?"

My smile faded.

I did understand him, and I wanted to slam my head against the door for being so stupid. Yeah, I didn't have the extra cash to go to a fancy hotel, but I should've remembered the Carreras had a lockdown on this part of town.

He was right. He could empty the gun in the door and me, and no one would bat an eye.

Moving quickly, I opened the door with a scowl. "You're a real *aguafiestas*, you know that?"

Brody stood at the threshold with his palms braced against the molding. "Thanks. And you're one hell of a *perra tramposa*."

"I call you a buzzkill, and you have to take it over the line with sneaky bitch?"

"Be grateful," he gritted through clenched teeth. "That was me censoring myself."

My scowl deepened, but it didn't stop me from taking him in. He was still dressed in the same half-destroyed button-up shirt and slacks as earlier but whereas before they just looked disheveled, now they appeared to have survived a three-day bender. One wrinkled sleeve was rolled up past his elbow while the other flapped loosely around his wrist. Only four, maybe five, buttons held the whole damn thing together, the others scattered on a breadcrumb trail from here to Caliente.

But his clothes weren't what tightened my chest and sent my pulse skyrocketing.

It was his face.

Brody clenched his jaw so hard, the muscles in his neck twitched, and a vein running down the center of his forehead throbbed with barely-restrained rage. He was more than pissed off. He was a man whose hands itched to feel the life drain from my body. Chills scattered over my skin, and for a moment, I considered backing off.

Then he opened his mouth.

"Drinking alone?" His lips curled in a smirk, and he nodded his head at the forgotten cup in my hand.

"Well, when in Rome…" I motioned to where he still stood in the doorway.

"What's that supposed to mean?"

"I assumed all the women who spend time in your company erase the memory with booze." His face flushed a heated shade of crimson as I swung my hips back toward the table. Lifting the bottle of scotch in the air, I licked my lips and winked. "It's your favorite, rock bottom scotch. I'm out of cups, but feel free to wrap your lips around the tip and suck."

Okay, admittedly, maybe I took it too far. Way too far, because Brody stormed through the motel room like a charging bull and caged me against the table. His palms slammed against the wood on either side of my ass, and I fought hard not to breathe in the intoxicating scent of scotch and sage. But not the kind in my hand. I recognized indulgence when I smelled it. Single malt scotch, expensive as hell, and hard to come by. Paired with the rugged earthy sage scent of his cologne, the combined effect knocked me off track for a moment.

"Did you hear me?"

I blinked him back into focus. "Huh?"

He rolled his eyes. "I said, what the fuck did you do with Leo Pinellas?"

"Who?"

Brody shifted forward, the hard planes of his chest crushing my lace bodice. "Don't play innocent, Adriana. It doesn't suit you. After I read your little love note, I had one of my men go to the Mexican Embassy to check on him. He never returned from his lunch break, so I told them to check his apartment. I'm sure it comes as no surprise to you he wasn't there either."

I set my drink down with a shrug. "Why are you asking me? Isn't he your stool pigeon?"

Brody's eyes turned black, and an inhuman sound rumbled in his throat. Before I could process what was happening, one hand from the table buried in my hair. Tightening his grip, he jerked my head back and forced me to look up at him.

"You don't understand what's at stake here." His fingers twisted tighter around the strands. "I need him. Tell me where he is!"

Dios mío. Why the hell was I turned on? In one show of dominance, my heart raced, and an unbearable ache hit hard between my legs. What was wrong with me? The man was seconds away from putting a bullet in my head, not his dick in my vagina.

I had to get it together.

Curling my fingers around the edge of the table, I gripped the wood tightly. "Oh, I understand a lot more than you think I do, *counselor*."

"What's that supposed to mean?"

"Instead of swinging your dick around, you should be thanking me."

He let out a dry laugh. "For killing my informant?"

"For saving your ass!" I yelled, the truth barreling into me like a hurricane. *Me.* Adriana Carrera did something unselfish. Something that didn't directly benefit me. Maybe I *did* take too many punches to the head in that warehouse. "Leo Pinellas was playing both sides—a game I believe you know quite well, if I remember correctly." I smiled as he shot me a look that said he wanted to tie me to a concrete block and toss me into a river. "It blows my mind you couldn't see what was right in front of your face."

A rogue piece of blond hair fell across his eyebrow as he leaned over me. "Bullshit."

"Pinellas was reporting to the men trying to frame me, you idiot! How you ended up in charge of US operations, I will never know. *Dios mío,* you're gullible. Do you still believe in Santa Claus, too?"

"How do I know *you're* not lying? You were once leader of the Muñoz Cartel yourself. Why would you suddenly turn against them?"

That was just it. He didn't know I wasn't lying, and it was the reason he was wound tighter than a nun's asshole. The biggest sacrifice anyone could make in life was trusting a proven enemy. It was the ultimate gamble. You either walked away with everything, or you didn't walk away at all.

Checkmate.

"Shipment for seventeen million, right? Disappeared near the Chicago port?" He didn't answer, but he didn't have to. "Brody, open your eyes. Every contact you have is being turned. You can't trust anyone. Not your friends, not your contacts, and certainly not your informants."

That damn condescending smirk returned. "Not even *you*?"

"Especially not me," I shot back, letting go of the table and shoving my hands hard against his chest. The sudden move knocked him off balance enough that he released my hair, and I slipped around him. "I wouldn't, if I were you."

I spun around and faced him, ready to do battle. Instead, I met with sculptured lips that twitched with obvious unwelcome amusement.

Or it could've been anger.

Or lust.

Or hate.

The gamut of emotions we ran through in the span of ten minutes exhausted me. Or maybe it was the scotch. Both were extremely bad for me.

"So, why bother? I exposed your real identity, Adriana. I turned your life into a nightmare. Your words, remember?" he accused, pointing a finger at me. "I should be the last person you'd want to help. You should want to strike a match, watch me

73

burn, then dance in the ashes. So, again, why? There has to be something in it for you, other than clearing your name and taking down the Muñozs, or you wouldn't be here."

"There is," I admitted, hating the slight wobble in my voice. "I want you to convince Val to accept me into the Carrera family."

"And I'd like to have my dick sucked by a Victoria's Secret model every day of the week. We don't always get what we want, *princesa*."

Of course. I let down my guard for one minute and got slapped in the face.

I sighed. "Can you take something seriously for five minutes, please?"

He crossed his arms over his chest and leaned against the table. "Yes, if I really thought you wanted to be his sister, but I'm not a moron. I see what you're doing."

"And what am I doing, exactly?"

"You lost control of the Muñoz Cartel, and now they're restructuring. You don't give a shit about Val. You want what comes with the Carrera name, and you're using this situation to get it. I took your crown, so you want to take his."

"Are you done?"

"For now."

The rational side of my brain pleaded with me to not even dignify that with an answer. However, the batshit crazy side screamed at me to shove his words down his throat and make him choke on them.

Guess who won.

"Let's get something straight, counselor," I hissed, my hands fisted by my side. "I don't give a shit about wearing a crown or sitting on some goddamn blood throne. I was tortured by the same men who used to bow at my feet. If you don't think I know how easily loyalty can fade, then you can go to hell. You have no idea what I've been through. Loyalty is only a word, Brody. Anyone can say it, but only actions prove its worth."

Were those fucking tears in my eyes?

Adriana Carrera did not cry. I didn't cry when my own men sank a blade into my flesh, and I wouldn't cry over a few stupid words. Especially in front of *him*.

"I didn't know," he said softly.

I blinked until my eyes cleared. "Well, now you do. Things at first glance are rarely what they seem. Dig deeper, and you'll find the truth lies more in what you don't see than what you do. Arrogance is the eye's worst enemy, Brody. Men always make the mistake of looking at what's in front of them instead of watching out for what's behind them."

Thankfully, Brody let the subject die, redirecting his focus back to the subject at hand. "Still, even if I thought about humoring you, which I'm not, approaching Val is something that has to be eased into. Just flying to Mexico City and playing house like you didn't try to kill him a year ago isn't going to happen."

Ouch.

"I don't want to play house, and I'm not looking for instant absolution. I'm looking for a chance to prove myself by warning him."

He raised an eyebrow. "Ah, yes. About this infamous man of mystery."

Here it was. Time to show my hand.

"When I was being held captive, there was a man who seemed to be in charge. I barely saw him for the first day or so, but then he came to taunt me. He never told me his name, but he knew things about me. Things no one should know. He offered me a place in the new Muñoz Cartel if I'd turn Val over to him."

"Wait, *this* is your argument for me to take you to Val?" I glared at him, and he rolled his eyes. "Fine, continue. Let me guess, you told him no."

"What? Hell, no. I couldn't agree fast enough." Brody's lips thinned, and his eyebrows drew together. "Oh, don't look so constipated. It was my only way out of there. Do you think if I had refused they would've said, '*Oh, bummer, well, look us up sometime… We'll do lunch.*' They would've slit my throat right then and there. I did what I had to do to secure my freedom."

"Then you came here to…do what?" He asked, throwing his arms out wide. "Warn Val about the impending threat?"

"Exactly."

He dropped his arms by his side with a slap. "Well, mission accomplished, sweetheart. You've told me, and I can relay the message. No need for you to go anywhere."

"There is if you want to know his name."

Like I said, checkmate.

"Sweetheart, you don't know his name." His burst of arrogance caught me off guard, but before I could come back at him, he reached forward and pinched my lips shut. "That's what the hell I mean. Like most women, you don't know when to stop talking."

With his fingers holding my face in a vice grip, I channeled the words trapped in my mouth into a glare that could plow through plaster. In response, a slow, purposeful smile crept across his lips as he brushed them against the shell of my ear.

"You just said yourself he never told you his name."

It took everything I had in me not to knee his nuts halfway up his throat.

Jerking away from him, I forced this deplorable union of hate and desire into a mask of control. "I said *he* wouldn't tell me his name. I never said I didn't overhear it from another *sicario*."

He stepped forward, his eyes blazing. Something primal lurked in them. An innate need to dominate and control. "Tell me."

"No," I repeated, standing my ground. "I tell Val, or I tell no one."

"I don't take well to threats, *princesa*."

"Well, maybe it's time you start, considering I know all about your dirty little Chicago deal."

There was nothing but silence. Brody's body went completely still. He didn't move. He didn't blink. I almost wondered if he was even breathing. But unlike before, this time, his silence didn't mean acquiescence.

It was just the calm before the storm.

"Son of a bitch!" Coming out of his catatonic state, Brody whirled around and grabbed the scotch bottle from the table by the neck. Hitching his arm back, he pitched it across the room, his chest heaving as he watched it slam against the wall and shatter into pieces.

"Well, that was a little—"

He cut me off with another low growl, his disheveled hair brushing over his face, hiding all but one wild eye. "Fuck your ultimatums. I'm not going to be blackmailed into doing shit. I'll tell Val about the impending threat, and he can handle it on his own. If there's someone to be found, he'll find him—without your help." He stalked forward, his hands opening and closing by his side as if seeking more destruction. His moves were quick and efficient, and my heart slammed against my ribcage as he brushed past me in search of the doorknob.

I did everything I could to avoid this.

Despite what people thought of me, I wasn't completely heartless. I'd attempted to exhaust every path before leading my enemy to slaughter. Damn it, I'd even cracked a little for him. But Brody Harcourt was so damn stubborn, he wouldn't recognize an olive branch if it was shoved up his ass.

I had to get to the Carrera Compound, and unfortunately for Brody, I still had an ace up my sleeve.

"Brody," I called out, biting my tongue so hard I tasted blood.

Spinning halfway around, he glared over his shoulder, rage etched all over his face. "What?"

"You need to call Val tonight. We'll want to fly out first thing tomorrow."

His mouth dropped open. "Did you not just hear a damn word I—?"

Before he could finish his rant, I moved toward him until we stood chest to chest. "Oh, I heard you, but none of it matters. I was hoping it wouldn't come to this, but you've certainly become a pompous blowhard since we last did business. The thing is that you don't have a choice." Lifting onto the toes of my high heels, I placed a hand on his shoulder, and mimicking his arrogant power play, I brushed my lips against the shell of his ear and whispered, "Because if I don't get what I want, I'll make sure Val knows the real reason you ruined my life."

Chapter Eight

BRODY

I felt all the blood drain from my face. "What did you just say?"

"You heard me." Her dark, sensual voice sounded like a hushed prayer, whispered against my ear in a promise of desecration.

I closed my eyes, forcing the sound out of my head. "Look, I don't know what you think you know, but—"

She shifted, her breathy chuckle skating across my neck. "Oh, *qué chingados*. You're such a bad liar, Harcourt. Did you ever win a case when you worked for the DA's office?"

I should've been insulted. Hell, I should've been on my sharpest game. She just threw down the gauntlet—the woman who eighteen months ago used my sister to blackmail me into betraying Val Carrera, the man who was already blackmailing me. If that wasn't some fucked-up shit, I didn't know what was.

Back then, she had an army behind her, but now, she was alone.

Knowledge might be power, but both ended up being worthless without the credibility to sustain them. One of us was bluffing their influence, and it sure as hell wasn't me.

I jerked the door open. "I'm leaving."

Her toned arm snaked around my left side, and her palm connected with the door, slamming it closed. "Are you sure you want to do that? The way I see it, you're out of options, counselor."

I dropped my chin and let out a low laugh. Not because I was entertained by the situation. Far from it. I laughed because if I didn't, the rage boiling inside me would take over, and I'd turn around and swing. I'd never hit a woman in my life, and I didn't plan on starting just because I let Adriana Carrera get under my skin.

"I'm sorry, did I say something to amuse you?"

Instead of punching her, I punched the door and plastered on a fake smile before facing her. "There's always an option, *princesa*. I haven't survived this long without having a backup plan. So, you go right ahead and think you have me cornered with your Hail Mary bullshit."

Adriana's dark eyes searched mine in the dimly lit room, and her full lips twisted into a cocky smirk. "Lie to yourself all you want, Brody. Pretend your heart isn't riddled with sin. Ignore the voices you hear with your own ears. Slam the door on what you know is the truth. Tell yourself whatever makes you sleep better at night, but know, when you wake up, nothing will have changed. I know what you've done, and I'd bet my life on the fact that Val doesn't."

Pretend my heart isn't riddled with sin?

What the hell was that supposed to mean, and why did it sound so familiar?

As her accusing glare entwined with mine, time tumbled

backward. To a surprise meeting. To a heated exchange. To haunting words that came barreling back in a rush of unfortunate foreshadowing and impending ruin.

"Yes, well, the eyes may be the window to the soul, but the heart is the doorway to sin."

The meaning of her words finally sank in, and I realized how screwed I was.

Ignore the voices you hear with your own ears.

"Is someone there?"

Slam the door on what you know to be the truth.

"Just my puta secretary who doesn't know how to fucking knock."

My pulse pounded in my ears, and all the air rushed out of my chest in one breath. The minute I picked up that phone, Leo Pinellas was a man living on borrowed time, and when Adriana walked into my cantina, it was as judge, jury, and executioner.

Since becoming entangled in cartel life, I'd memorized Marisol Muñoz's playbook. Although merciless and at times, brutal, her methods were formulaic. Once she needled through her enemy's defenses, she openly exploited their weaknesses until they caved to her demands. But Adriana Carrera's innate Machiavellian nature rewrote the rules of the game.

Not only had I met my match, but I might also have met my undoing.

"That was your voice I heard in Leo's office. The door slamming...he let you in. That's how you knew."

I didn't have to elaborate. The truth stared me in the face and shrugged.

"As I've already told you, the man has been on the take for a while now. He'd sell out his own mother if the price was right."

"Where is he?"

"If the whereabouts of a traitor is your main concern, we

have bigger problems, counselor."

She was right. I shouldn't give a fuck about Leo. He sold me out, and now she had me backed against the wall.

But if I was going down, I was going down swinging.

"You wouldn't risk the fallout."

Of course, she would.

"Admittedly, I'd prefer to avoid a scene." She shrugged, and for the first time, I saw indecision on her face as worried lines darted across her forehead. "Ratting out his trusted lieutenant isn't exactly the way to endear myself to my brother." As soon as the brief moment of weakness broke through her shell, it disappeared. "But if you force my hand, Brody, I won't hesitate to go to Mexico City myself and serve your head on a platter. Don't think I forgot you were about to serve mine up for your Chicago bullshit."

"Then why come for me in the first place?"

"Didn't you just hear me? You're his *trusted* lieutenant. If you bring me there and convince him I'm worthy of that same trust, things will go a lot faster." She turned her back to me, walking away as she bit out her confession. "If I have to do it on my own, the walls I'll have to tear down will take a lifetime."

"And blackmailing me is just an added perk, I suppose."

"Don't flatter yourself," she tossed out over her shoulder. "You're just an insurance policy. I had a feeling you'd be resistant to my attempts at a reconciliation, so, as someone I know once said, 'I haven't survived this long without having a backup plan.'"

"Throwing my own words back in my face, huh?"

"Listening is a useful skill." She winked. "You should try it sometime."

She had me by the balls. She didn't have to say the words to confirm it. I didn't want to hear them anyway. Especially from her. There was no point in denying it now. The only thing left to do was figure out a way to turn this around and beat her at her own game.

Besides, if I was good at one thing, it was causing women to self-destruct.

I scrubbed my hands down my face. "They weren't together, you know."

Adriana glanced down at the shattered scotch bottle in front of her feet and sighed. "Does it matter? It was a selfish, risky gamble with low odds, Brody. One that an attorney such as yourself should know better than to attempt." The shitty blue carpet squished under her high heels as she kicked a large piece of glass.

"Well, obviously, my *gamble,* as you call it, didn't pay out, so why turn Val's life upside down over a bad roll of the dice? You wouldn't be his savior. You'd be his destroyer. Would selling me out be worth the wrath that might come with that title?"

Crossing her arms over her chest, she whirled around and glared at me. "A bad roll of the dice?"

"That's what you got out of all that?" I pressed, trying to ignore the way her crossed arms exaggerated her already displayed breasts. "Were you even listening?"

"To every word." The cords in her neck tightened, venom dripping from the forced pause between every word.

"And?"

Adriana took a calculated step, her stare hardening as broken glass crunched under the toe of her high heel. "And why not? I seem to have acquired a nasty little habit of reinventing myself these days."

One more step. *Crunch.* Two more steps. *Crunch.*

Darting her tongue out, she licked her bottom lip while curling a finger around my tie. "Plus, no risk, no reward—and whatever wrath comes our way, I'll just chalk up to a *bad roll of the dice*." She gave my tie a hard tug. "At least this time, it'll be on my terms."

"You're insane."

"And you've been drinking since I left. What are you up to now, Brody? Half a bottle a day? More? I mean, you're a bountiful mixed bag of sin. What are you trying to forget?"

"The fact that you're here."

"Maybe it's the fact that you love the power of pulling that trigger a little too much. Quite possibly, it's that your little rebellious phase caused you to go against a direct order and align with the Northside Sinners anyway."

"Don't push me, Adriana. I'm warning you."

"There could even be a tiny part of you hidden away in whatever's left of your conscience that's haunted by what the roll of your dice did to me. But what you're really trying to numb is buried deep within the dark and twisted layers of that 'don't give a fuck' exterior. That's where the real fear lives."

"Shut up!"

"The fear that the all-powerful Valentin Carrera will one day find out the truth. That when you rolled the dice, you bet everything on the fact that her hatred for me would outweigh any love she had left for him."

"That's quite a story."

"Yes, and quite cliched, if I'm honest. Even if you lost in the end, as long as Val lost, too, that's all that mattered, right?"

Son of a bitch.

This game of wits had turned into a battle to the death and sensing impending defeat, I flipped my middle finger in the air and headed for the door. "I'm out of here."

"Stop!"

And like an idiot, I paused mid-stride, my hands clenched

by my side with one foot in front of the other.

The room went silent.

"You're running because I'm right. Because to look me in the eye would force you to see yourself. Not the man you pretend to be every morning, but the one you drown every night."

I closed my eyes, my jaw clenching so hard my teeth cracked. "You don't know anything about me."

"Don't I?" she said, the jagged rawness in her voice tearing at my skin. "You don't think I know what it's like to crave escape from your own darkness? To want something to stop the voice in your head that whispers it all would end if you turned that gun around?"

I snapped. Suppressed rage erupted, hotter than lava and twice as destructive. Twisting around, I reached underneath my shirt, drew my gun from its holster, and pulled back the slide.

"Shut up!" In three wide steps, I had her shoved against the wall, my hand wrapped around her throat and glass crunching under our feet. Before she could say a word, I pressed the Glock against her temple. "You know so much, huh? Did you know I came here to get rid of you, Adriana? Did you know if I pulled this trigger right now, Val wouldn't know any different?"

I waited for her to plead for her life. I wanted her to beg. I needed her to beg. I wanted to hear the words come from those tempting lips. All night I'd listened to them hurl insults and threats like it was her goddamn given right.

Taunting me.

Teasing me.

Making me want things I had no business wanting.

And that dress didn't help.

That tight, lacy, scrap of a dress that hugged her voluptuous body in all the right places. A dress that turned a man into a type of crazy that should never be left alone in a motel room with his boss's sister.

"Then what are you waiting for?" she rasped as my grip tightened around her throat. "Do it."

My gaze shifted to where my hand gripped her slim neck, and I lifted my thumb, trailing it along the side of her jaw. The move was simple but undeniably erotic. A strange buzz swayed me off balance, forcing our bodies together until there wasn't an inch of space between us.

"You'd like that, wouldn't you?"

She laughed, the force of her hard exhale pushing her breasts against my chest. "Am I supposed to be intimidated?"

"Most women would be."

"Sorry, counselor. You're not the first man to pull his gun on me." The tip of her tongue rested at the center of her top lip as her eyes lowered between us, then trailed back to mine with a wicked glint. "You won't be the last."

The hell I wouldn't.

As if drawn by a magnetic force, my head lowered, my lips hovering so close to her I felt her sweet breath against my skin. Adriana inhaled sharply, swallowing hard as I pressed my erection against her. Her inhales turned to pants, the battle raging inside her playing out across her face as she tipped her chin down, her eyes squeezing closed.

We stood there, immoral and reckless, toying with manipulative and dangerous. Two pinnacles of destruction that, if joined, would rip each other to shreds just to watch the other bleed.

As the implications of what I was about to do hit me, I came out of my haze of lust and turned my face, slamming my gun against the wall. "Fuck!"

Adriana flinched, but I didn't stop. I slammed it over and over until the Sheetrock gave way under my repeated abuse. It wasn't until I noticed blood running down my wrist that I spun around and stalked toward the door.

"Where are you going?" she called after me.

I swung the door open and stepped out onto the rickety balcony. "If you make good on your threat? To hell." I stiffened as I heard her move behind me, refusing to look at her as I delivered my promise. "But don't worry. No good deed goes unpunished. I'll save you a seat."

Chapter Nine

BRODY

The scotch bottle was empty.

So were the other two.

Frustrated, I swept my arm across the desk and watched as all three clattered to the floor. Grimacing, I rubbed my eyes and ran my tongue across the roof of my mouth. *Ugh.* It was as dry as the Sahara and tasted like a camel shit in it.

This was what she'd reduced me to.

After leaving Adriana's motel room last night, the last place I wanted to be was alone in an apartment filled with ghosts. So, I did the only thing I could think of—I drove to a bar filled with even more ghosts and spent the night having myself a one-man party. A deeper descent into an alcohol-induced stupor in an effort to maintain control. A Band-Aid for the inevitable.

A decision that didn't seem as intelligent in the light of day.

Plus, it solved nothing. My problems were still there, only now they were compounded by a raging hangover. The upside was, as long as that jackhammer continued pounding in my head, I didn't have to think about missing consulate generals or Colombian drug lords or pissed off Irish mob bosses or lost shipments or disgraced cartel princesses who fucked with my head more than I cared to admit.

Who said alcohol didn't solve anything?

Pressing the heel of my palms against my eyes, I forced thoughts of her out of my mind and typed out a quick text to Carlos I put off last night. Yet another forbidden thing I flipped a middle finger at and did anyway. Val hated texts. He claimed anything written came back to haunt you.

Bullshit. Everything came back to haunt you sooner or later.

Cancel the manhunt. Adriana Carrera showed up at Caliente yesterday. She's not the one in charge of reorganization. She has a name. Will update soon.

I barely put the phone down when it chimed with a reply.

Fuck you. Fuck this. And fuck your mother. Delete this shit and get a new phone.

What was with the sudden fascination with fucking my mother?

The phone chimed again.

Now deal with it.

I rolled my eyes. Carlos's subtly was on par with an atomic bomb.

I let out a breath, trying to redirect my energy and failing miserably. This was ridiculous. I put an end to her bullshit last night. She was probably on a bus back to wherever the hell she came from.

Swiping a folder from my desk, I attempted to do something productive, but the fight with Adriana kept replaying in my head. The crazy thing was I didn't know if I was more pissed about her threats or the fact that I wanted to rip that dress off her and bury my cock between her legs.

She was trying to blackmail me with the one thing that could destroy me. I hated her, but I was also man enough to admit I'd never wanted a woman more than when I had her shoved against that wall. Just thinking about it crossed all kinds of wires in my head again, and I threw my pen across the office.

The ache was unbearable, and I adjusted my hardening erection, trying to find some relief and failing miserably.

Fuck it. This was my office.

Popping the button on my slacks, I pulled my zipper down and freed my cock. It sprang up, hard as steel, the tip weeping in gratitude.

I closed my eyes and leaned back, wrapping my hand around the base and giving it a few rough pumps. It jerked in response, and with thoughts of her still fresh in my mind, I knew it wouldn't take much.

My face twisted as the image of Adriana in that tight lace dress filled my head. I pumped harder, taking my frustration out on the traitorous appendage that couldn't seem to grasp the fact that she was trying to get both of us killed.

Thoughts of her flashed through my mind. I imagined her walking in and finding me like this, that wicked grin creeping along that plush mouth of hers as she stalked toward me.

I could hear her sultry voice begging me to forgive her, the conversation playing out in my head as I stroked.

"I came here to apologize."

"Say that again; I think I'm hearing things."

"Don't be an ass. After you left last night, I realized how wrong it was to hold something so personal over your head. That was low, even for me."

"What's the catch?"

"No catch. I want to make it up to you."

"Is that right?"

"We may be enemies, but our bodies don't care. I saw the look in your eyes when you pushed me against the wall."

"So, what are you waiting for? Apologize."

Without another word, Adriana crossed the room and dropped to her knees in front of me. Holding my stare, she swirled a red nail around my wet tip, then slowly dragged the rest of them down the length of my shaft. My body responded like a ball being shot out of a cannon. My back arched, and my ass levitated off the chair.

"Christ!" I growled, sucking air between my teeth. Grabbing her long, dark hair, I twisted it in my hand. "You want my forgiveness?"

She nodded. "More than anything."

"Then fucking earn it." Tightening my fist, I shoved her head down. "And don't disappoint me." She opened her mouth, taking me in until my cock hit the back of her throat.

I threw my head back, my hips already thrusting. "Oh fuuuuck!"

"Oh fuuuuck," I groaned out loud, the fantasy egging me on. I squeezed my eyes tighter and pumped harder, pretending my hand was her wet mouth. The line between fantasy and reality blurred so fast I didn't hear the door open or the sharp gasp that followed.

"Holy shit! I mean, that Rafael guy told me it was okay to come in. I, uh, he said you were just playing with your balls… I mean paying your bills."

My eyes popped open, and for a moment, I thought I was still trapped in my fantasy, but the horrified look on Adriana's face told me otherwise. She widened her eyes and clamped her lips together in a bizarre expression somewhere between mortified shame and hysterical laughter.

I wasn't sure which one was worse.

"Jesus!" I scrambled to tuck my dick back in my pants before I did something to make the situation worse. "Don't you know how to knock?"

Adriana's lips pulled back in a dazzling grin. "Yes, but to be fair, most bar owners aren't jerking off in their offices at nine-thirty in the morning."

Smartass.

I cupped my balls and smirked, nodding to the floor between my legs. "Maybe if you'd gotten here at nine-twenty-five, I wouldn't have had to jerk off."

"Interesting… And what would we have done with the other four minutes and forty-five seconds?"

Damn.

It was physically impossible to one-up this woman. Not like there was a good comeback for being called a one-pump chump. And for that matter, why couldn't she have walked in here looking like the rest of my men's sisters?

I didn't want to fuck them. Hose them down, maybe, but definitely not fuck them.

But Adriana was a woman who knew her value and had no problem using it to her advantage. From yesterday's tantalizing corporate secretary look to the sex-kitten dress she tried to distract me with last night, clothes were just the window dressing to her inner chameleon. I wasn't sure what today's outfit was supposed to portray, but at the moment, I really didn't care.

The tight black skirt she wore was short enough to drive a man to his knees but modest enough to allow her to bend over in mixed company. Long bronze legs extended from the edge, leading down to the same black heels. However, had my dick not already been hard enough to chop wood, her shirt would've given it a standing ovation.

Her shoulders were bare, that thick dark hair pulled back in a high ponytail. My gaze trailed down to where two full sleeves covered the length of her arms, which was good because combined, they probably contained more material than the rest of the shirt. Two white bands of spandex crisscrossed over each breast, attaching to the upper part of each sleeve, exposing miles of cleavage.

I swallowed hard. Somewhere in the past twenty-four hours, she stopped being Val's sister and started being a woman. That was a dangerous park to play in, so I needed to calm down before I did something stupid.

"What do you want, Adriana? I'm busy."

Her dark eyes crinkled at the corners. "Yes, I see that."

Like I said, impossible.

She should've been shocked and embarrassed, or at the very least, profusely apologetic for barging in unannounced to a private area. Instead, she leaned against the doorway of my office with her hip cocked and arms crossed, wearing the unmistakable look of triumph.

"We need to talk."

"I'm pretty sure we said all there was to say to each other last night."

"No, you said all *you* had to say, and then you ran out like a little bitch." Her lips quirked, trailing a pointed gaze down to where my erection still tried to break free from the confines of my pants. "I'm here to finish what we started last night."

My dick leaped at her words, beating against my zipper like a provoked gorilla. Instinct riddled my mind with images of bending her over my desk, jerking up that tiny black skirt and pounding into her from behind until we both collapsed from exhaustion.

What the hell was wrong with me?

Pulling the folder from my desk, I dragged it onto my lap and opened it, studying the stack of invoices to try and force my body into submission. "Maybe some other time. I'm swamped today, Miss Carrera."

Undeterred, Adriana pushed off the doorframe, sauntering over until she hovered directly above me and placed a hand on each arm of my chair. My brows dove together as I forced myself to focus on the blurry numbers in my lap while swimming in the intoxicating sweet and spicy aroma of licorice.

"Brody…" she purred.

Lust.

Pure, unadulterated lust.

That's all this was. It had been way too long since I'd gotten laid. I should take bar bitch up on one of her many offers. Maybe if I had empty balls, I could handle this damn woman with a clear head and get myself back on track.

Then I reminded myself she was a master of deceit.

Don't be an idiot.

"Like I said," I repeated, clearing my throat, "I'm busy with these invoices, so make sure not to let the door hit you in your ass on the way out."

She cocked her head, her heart-shaped mouth puckering into a luscious pout that did nothing for my waning self-control. "Yes, I can see how stressful that might be. Allow me." Without waiting for a confirmation, she grabbed the end of the folder and flipped it around in a complete one-eighty. "There. That should speed things along."

It was only then I realized I'd been staring at the damn thing upside down. I fought the urge to smirk. I already struggled with wanting to fuck my enemy, but here I was dangerously close to actually liking the woman.

Hell, no.

Slamming the folder closed, I threw it across my desk. "Get out."

The smirk faded from Adriana's face, quickly replaced by something far more deadly. Something I knew too well. A fusion of a silent predator and a raging storm. A dichotomy born by blood and cultivated by power. It surfaced on impulse and flipped on a dime.

It was something I'd witnessed firsthand from her brother the two times I chose to disregard the proper chain of command. The first time Val was too concerned with rescuing the woman we both loved to bother with me. The second time would've guaranteed my death had he not owed me for finding her.

She leaned in closer. "I indulged your tantrum last night because let's be honest, I beat you at your own game. I figured you needed some time to cool off and lick your wounds." She paused, the flecks in her midnight eyes flashing like streaks of gold-plated lightning. "I came here this morning to offer you a chance to apologize and reconsider my offer."

The heat boiling inside me turned to stone. "You want me to apologize for getting pissed at being insulted and threatened with blackmail? Are you kidding me?"

"You put a hole through my wall."

"You're lucky I didn't put a hole through your head."

"I'll chalk that one up to the hangover. Regardless, my offer has an expiration date. I'm not a patient woman, Brody, and contrary to the lenience I've given you, I don't tolerate being jerked around."

"And this offer would be?"

Smiling, she toyed with the loose threads on my shirt where the buttons used to be and trailed that damn red painted fingernail down my chest. I held in a groan, the fantasy of where the nail swirled earlier dancing around in my head and causing beads of sweat to break out across my upper lip.

My brain sent flares up, screaming for my cock to stand down.

It's a trap. It's a trap. It's a trap.

"Either you call Val and tell him we're coming, or I call him and tell him the only reason he's married is because your plan backfired."

My cock sighed as my brain took a bow.

Told ya so.

God, I needed space. I needed to think. Wrapping my fingers around her upper arms, I gave enough of a push that she released her grip on my chair and stumbled backward. Breathing in gulps of air instead of just her, blood finally rerouted to my brain.

"You don't have any proof."

"I don't need proof." She punctuated each word with a dramatic pause.

"I don't think you have the balls."

Adriana let out a husky laugh. "Oh, counselor, I have them, and they're way more than you could ever handle." Perching her ass right on my desk, she grabbed my cell phone.

I lunged. "Give me that!"

Bad move.

My close proximity gave her perfect positioning. She quickly turned my phone around, holding it just long enough for the facial recognition to unlock the damn thing before jumping off the table. "I'll put it on speaker just so you can hear it for yourself."

"I swear, Adriana, if you—"

"Brody, is everything okay?"

I froze as I heard the familiar voice. The one that still made my stomach flip.

"Good morning," Adriana said, in a sing-song voice, her

accent heavier than usual. "I'd like to speak to Valentin Carrera."

"Who is this? Why do you have Brody's phone?"

"I'm a friend of Brody's."

There was a long pause, and my heart slammed against my chest so hard, it might have broken a couple ribs. A door closed in the background, and the voice on the line hardened. "I'm a friend of Brody's, too. I'm also Valentin Carrera's wife. Anything you have to say you can say to me."

"Eden Lachey." A catlike smile spread across Adriana's lips. "I don't think so."

"Eden *Carrera*."

"How traditional of you."

"Look, lady, I don't know who you think you are—"

Adriana held my stare. *"Trust me, he'll take my call when you tell him who's on the line."*

"And who is it?"

"Adr—"

I knocked the phone out of her hand, lunging for it before she could drive the final nail in my coffin. Luckily, my reflexes weren't as sluggish as my brain, and I grabbed it seconds before she did, ending the call with a glare. "What the hell is wrong with you?"

She shrugged. "You forced my hand."

"I thought you wanted my death to be slow and drawn out, not over in the next five minutes!"

Adriana cocked her head. "You still love her."

"Eden is married to Val, and Val is the head of the cartel I've sworn a life oath to. For fuck's sake, they have a baby."

"Thanks for the biography. However, you didn't deny it which tells me I'm right."

The headache that had been pounding behind my eyes suddenly became a full-blown explosion. Pinching the bridge of my nose, I closed my eyes as a heated conversation from over a year ago broke through the incessant hammering in my head.

I shed my suit jacket and raced to catch up with him. "You need me, Carrera. I know where she is, and I need you. I can't go in there alone. I'll never make it out."

"You've got that right."

"Look," I said, placing a hand on his shoulder and stopping our movement. "She doesn't want me, man. I don't know what you've got going on with Eden, but it's obvious you care about her. I may not like you, but that's enough for me. I just want her safe."

"She's mine."

"Fine, she's yours. Can we go get her now?"

His eyes narrowed in suspicion. "If you have no interest in her, why are you so dead set on walking into a massacre? You do understand this isn't the movies, right? These men are real. They have real guns with real bullets, and a lot of people will die. I can't guarantee you won't be one of them. My only concern will be Eden."

I didn't flinch despite his warning. "Let's just say, I'm hoping if I do this, you'll owe me one."

I was right. I may have lost Eden to Val, but I gained something almost as valuable.

An owed favor.

A favor that I cashed in trying to protect my sister. Now my safety net was gone. I didn't have anything to shield me from Val's wrath should Adriana follow through with her threat. Our relationship was already shaky due to my history with his wife. If Adriana told him I exposed her identity just to sever his hold on Eden, he'd happily gut me himself.

I might be reckless, but I wasn't suicidal.

I squeezed my phone so hard, I was surprised it didn't crack.

"Fine."

Adriana cupped a hand behind her ear. "What was that?"

I ground out the words as if I were chewing sand. "I said, fine."

"Well?"

"Well what?"

She pointed at the phone in my hand. "Aren't you going to call him?"

"With you here? I don't think so."

"You're seriously taking all the fun out of this for me," she huffed, crossing her arms.

"I thought this was about family and saving the Carrera siblings from impending doom?"

"It is. Watching you squirm is just a fringe benefit."

I lowered my head into my hands, rubbing my forehead. "I can't believe I'm even considering this. He's not going to be happy I'm leaving Houston unmanned."

She nodded toward the bar area where Rafael was probably fending off bar bitch. "Your boy seems more than capable of handling things. Arrange a flight for this afternoon. I'm sure there are washed funds tucked away somewhere in this office."

I swore, the woman lived to make my life hell. "Get out of here before I change my mind."

She dropped her arms by her side, her sulky attitude fading. "Fine. I have to pack, anyway. Pick me up in an hour?"

Rolling my chair against my desk, I stared at spreadsheets I didn't give a shit about. "Meet me here in two."

One hour. Two hours. Who cared? Timing meant nothing. Not letting her get her way meant everything.

"So bossy," she chided, swaying her hips as she made her way toward the door. I almost let out a breath when she glanced back over her shoulder. "Oh, and Brody?

Turning my head, I glared at her between two fingers.

"Don't ever fuck me over again. Sometimes I forgive, but I never forget."

Chapter Ten

ADRIANA

After throwing what little I owned into the tattered bag I carted across the border, I walked in the door of Caliente exactly fifty-nine minutes after walking out of it. Brody demanded I wait two hours, but I'd lived long enough to know anything could be a trap.

Sometimes the element of surprise was the sole difference between survival and ambush.

Setting my bag on a nearby table, I surveyed the scene. It was too quiet. Granted, it was still only eleven o'clock in the morning. The lunch crowd probably wouldn't swarm in for another half hour, but I didn't like the unnatural silence.

"You're early."

I yelped and spun around with my hand shoved in my bag, in position to knee somebody in the balls then blow them off. Luckily, I recognized that steel cut jaw from earlier and punched him in the shoulder instead.

It was like punching a brick wall.

"Jesus!" I hissed, glaring at Brody's lapdog as I shook my injured hand by my side. "Don't you know you're never supposed to sneak up on someone who could blow your dick off?" I glanced down to find my knuckles red as hellfire. "*Dios mío*, do you have concrete under that T-shirt?"

He cocked an eyebrow. "Brody told you not to be here for another hour."

"Aw, that's cute. Do you wipe his ass for him, too?"

"Look, lady, I don't know who you think you are, but when Brody Harcourt gives an order around here, you listen."

He was like an obedient little Rottweiler.

If Rottweilers were ten seconds away from stabbing you in the face.

I rolled my eyes. "Don't get your panties in a twist, puppy. I had to check out of the motel by eleven, or I would've had to pay for an extra night. Let's be real here. If he had to choose between having me show up a little early or having $65.60 charged on his credit card, I think we both know what he'd prefer."

"I don't know if…" His voice trailed off, and those dark eyes gave me a few slow blinks. "Wait, how do you have his credit card number?"

Because I stole his wallet last night.

"Is that really important? I think we have bigger issues to worry about, such as the fact that it's way too quiet in here." Tucking my hand back inside my purse, I turned my attention back toward the open cantina.

"You'd prefer a bar brawl?"

"I don't like quiet." I narrowed my eyes and glared at him over my shoulder. "If you were any good at your job, you wouldn't either."

Technically, I was right. A second in command should be

patrolling the area with an eagle eye, watching for anything out of the ordinary. An unfamiliar face. An anxious stare. Eyes fixated on a watch. Especially with my former men edging dangerously close to Carrera territory.

"That's Frankie." He moved beside me and nodded at an older man sitting at the bar, shoveling chips and salsa in his mouth so fast I half expected him to choke. "He's been a regular for years. Comes here every day for lunch, then drags his ass back in at night to drink himself into oblivion."

"Why?"

He shrugged. "Why not? Maybe his job sucks. Maybe he's in debt up to his eyeballs. Maybe he found out his wife's fucking his best friend. Who knows? It's not my business to ask."

Before I could argue that everything happening on Carrera property was his business, he continued assaulting me with everyone's life story.

His gaze shifted across the bar to a lone booth. "That's Antonella Reyes. Her husband died about six months ago."

"Emilio Reyes's widow?" The words were out of my mouth before I could stop them.

Puppy nodded, and I made a noise somewhere between a grunt and a growl. Emilio Reyes was once one of Valentin Carrera's most trusted men. Not only did he own Caliente, but he also ran all stateside operations before becoming one of the worst traitors the cartel had ever seen.

"That's exactly what I'm talking about," I fumed, staring crater-sized holes in the woman. "Why would you let her in the door, much less serve her?"

He bumped my shoulder. "Put your claws away. She wants no part of the family. She proved that by selling this place to Brody for a dollar."

"So why would she come back here? Is she masochistic?"

I didn't like the pity in his eyes as he tilted his chin and studied me. "Emilio chose the wrong path, but that doesn't erase the twenty years she spent loving the man who didn't."

And just because Esteban murdered my family, it doesn't erase the twenty-four years I spent loving the man who spared me.

Yeah, yeah, I get it. You know all about me.

Good for you.

"Hey, you okay?"

I vaguely heard his voice echoing over the sound of my heart pounding in my ears. When I didn't respond, he called my name louder and louder until the fog finally dissipated.

"Adriana?"

"What? Oh, yeah." Shaking my head, I cleared my throat and pulled myself together. "I'm fine. Long trip and too little sleep. You know how it goes."

I diverted my attention back to the bar area then felt a strong hand on my shoulder. "Look, I know it's none of my business—"

"You're right. It is none of your business." Picking up two of his fingers, I slid his hand off my shoulder. "Well, this has been fun, but I think I'll go freshen up. Point me toward the ladies' room?"

He offered a lackluster motion toward the left of the bar. "Down the hallway to the right."

Stepping behind him, I dragged my suitcase off the table and gave him a tight smile. "Thanks, puppy."

"It's Rafael."

"Huh?"

"You keep calling me puppy. My name is Rafael."

"Oh, I know who you are, *papi*." Smiling, I tossed him a wink before making my way down the hallway.

For once, luck seemed to be on my side.

I stood in the bathroom with my head poked outside the door, listening for the slightest sign that Rafael Suárez had changed his mind and decided to get rid of his boss's burgeoning problem before it could wreak any more havoc.

The problem, of course, being me, and the havoc being the fact we both knew I had as much intention of freshening up as he did.

But as the minutes ticked by, other than the expected clatter of pans and dishes from the kitchen, the hallway remained silent. Either Brody's enforcer didn't believe I had a gun in my bag, or he had this insane notion I wouldn't open fire in the middle of the bar.

He was wrong on both counts.

The muscles in my neck twitched, my shoulder aching under the weight of my overstuffed bag. So even though it had only been a little over five minutes, I pushed the door open and stepped out into the hallway.

The darkened hallway.

I paused, surveying my surroundings and absorbing the unusual dimness. I had to admit it was a little bizarre. The rest of the cantina had plenty of windows scattered along the perimeter, and the sun was probably almost directly overhead by now. Not that the lack of light bothered me. I felt more at home in the dark. At least in the shadows, I knew what to expect.

Pain. Shame. Hate. Betrayal.

Emotions as familiar as my own skin.

It was the uncertainty of the light that terrified me. Fear of being stripped of my armor and revealed to be what I'd always fought to never become.

Weak.

The air in the narrow hallway seemed to thicken, and with every breath, I felt my lungs fill with water. Dropping the bag on the floor by my feet, I forced myself to calm down. This wasn't a shitty warehouse in the middle of nowhere. Within these walls, I was no longer just a girl dealt a shitty hand in life. I was Adriana Carrera. An heiress. Sister to one of the most powerful men in the world...

And that made the light my bitch.

So instead of drowning in the past, I floated in the present, and swam toward the future. Only one person stood in my way and maneuvering around him wouldn't be easy.

Brody and I had a river of bad blood between us. We'd toyed with each other's lives not for the love or hate of each other, but for the love and hate of other people. I forced him to set up a man I was groomed to hate, and he unsealed records for a woman he loved enough to let go. The nobility of each act depended on who you asked. Was a motive driven by revenge any more honorable than one driven by hope?

You tell me.

Brody let everyone believe he gave Saint Eden my birth records so she'd get off her self-righteous throne and follow Val to Mexico. He was praised for swallowing his pride and urging her to wave stolen papers in Val's face, so he'd fall at her feet in gratitude, and they'd live happily ever after.

Please.

Anyone who bought his act was a fool. Humans weren't wired for self-sacrifice, and I doubted my dear brother believed in his pure intentions any more than I did. Brody may have spent years studying the art of persuasion and even longer practicing it in a court of law, but Val and I grew up in the court of the cartel. Listening to what was said around us gave us power while finding out the things that weren't kept us alive.

However, I had to remind myself that trust wasn't given freely in either world. It was earned, and so far, I hadn't given Brody much to work with. To get what I wanted, I needed him amiable and compliant. In the last forty-eight hours, I'd killed his ally, threatened him, blackmailed him, and then topped it all off by stealing his wallet and his phone.

Not exactly winning any popularity contests here.

I suppose making a few concessions wouldn't kill me. Technically, I was early. Maybe I could knock on his office door and offer an apology for walking in earlier while he was, um... busy relaxing from all the stress and tension from the...

Oh, for fuck's sake.

Fine, I'd apologize for barging in while he was beating his dick like it stole something.

Although it went against my every instinct, I bit the bullet and stepped forward just as Brody's heated voice carried into the hallway from a small opening where his office door was ajar.

"Don't you think I know that? I've tried everything I can think of, Val! Reasoning with that woman is like trying to herd cats."

As soon as I hear Val's name, I knew "that woman" was me, and I didn't know whether to be flattered or offended. I didn't come here to be his bestie, so I had no idea why the insult bothered me so much. To be honest, he wasn't wrong. I *was* unreasonable.

But then I realized he'd delayed his conversation with Val, which was why he wanted me to stay away an extra hour. And exactly why I didn't.

I strained to hear more, but as the lunch crowd began to arrive, their incessantly boisterous chatter caused Brody's voice to become muffled.

Glaring at them over my shoulder, I willed them to burst into flames. "Inbred assholes."

I'd just have to move closer.

Just as I took another step forward, the toe of my high heel caught under something huge and heavy. My arms windmilled in a valiant effort to delay the inevitable, but it was useless. With my feet anchored to the ground, gravity took over, and my knees slammed against the top of the box right before my body propelled into the wall.

"Ooooof."

"Hold on a minute, Val."

I froze, my hands planted against the stucco wall and glass rattling under my knees as the sound of his footsteps moved toward me. *Shit*. Adding eavesdropping on top of all my other infringements wouldn't bode well in winning over a king.

Thankfully, at that same moment, all hell broke loose in the kitchen. Glass shattered, men shouted, and multiple mothers were insulted. I held my breath as Brody stood right outside the door. One more step and I'd be up close and personal with a part of him I'd already seen way too much of. Thankfully, he grumbled and kicked the door shut.

Exhaling hard, I dislodged my foot and tip-toed toward his door until I could press against it. With the war going on in the kitchen, it made it almost impossible to hear, but I didn't give up so easily.

As gently as possible, I gripped the doorknob and gave it a slight twist. With minimal effort, the door pushed open no more than a fourth of an inch.

Just enough to hear the end of an important conversation.

"I know it's not a good time, but let's be honest, is there ever a good time to meet one's dead sister?"

Balling my fist, I gritted my teeth.

"Of course, you're right. Look, I know Eden's worried, and you both have a lot going on, but I wouldn't bring her if I didn't think this threat was real. It's not the first I've heard of Muñoz reconstruction and infiltration." I caught a quick glimpse of him as he paced across the office. "No, I'm not hiding anything from you, Val. I'm not a damn moron. I just didn't want to come to you until I had full recon and intel. Adriana has the name of the man leading the charge. It's foolish not to hear her out."

For a moment, I almost believed the shit he was shoveling. Then I remembered he was so desperate to hide his Chicago dealings and indiscretions, he'd sell his sick grandmother beachfront property in Colorado if it meant saving his own ass.

Hypothetically speaking, provided he had any family left.

Which he did not.

"Yet again, she won't tell me." I cocked an eyebrow at his tone. It bordered on mocking, a dangerous line to walk for a man in his position. I suppose he knew it, too because he returned to his chair and slumped down. "I ripped the floor out from underneath her, Val. She wouldn't trust me with her drink order, much less valuable information."

That's true.

"No, she won't be here for at least another forty-five minutes."

I laughed to myself. That's what he thought.

After a long stretch of silence, Brody let out a relieved sigh. "Perfect. I'll have the pilot on standby."

Pilot?

Clamping a hand over my mouth, I crept over to where I'd dropped my bag. Collecting my belongings, I quickly slipped inside the ladies' room before being discovered. Once inside, I leaned against the tiled wall, the bag falling from my shoulder again. This time, I didn't care. All I could do was stare at my reflection in the blurry mirror, the reality of what I'd heard finally sinking in.

This was it. There was no turning back now.

We're going to Mexico.

Chapter Eleven
BRODY

My patience was running low.

Bouncing my knees up and down, I watched. Tapping my fingers against my chin, I waited. Finally, seconds after the plane leveled out, the pilot's voice crackled over the onboard PA system.

"We've reached our cruising altitude, Mr. Harcourt. You're free to move about the cabin."

Thank God.

I didn't waste another minute. Unbuckling my seat belt, I pressed a hidden button on the inside of the arm rest, causing the back to recline and a footrest to pop out. The groan that followed bordered on obscene. Whether out of embarrassment or courtesy, I tilted my chin to the left and offered an unenthusiastic apology.

"Don't worry. Everything's still tucked in and zipped."

Silence.

"Adriana?"

Silence.

I popped an eye open to find the bane of my existence sitting across from me with her head bowed, waves of long onyx hair covering her face like a curtain. Her entire body was rigid, and all hunched over so that she looked like one of those weeping angel statues. In fact, with the soft sounds coming from the other side of the plane, she could even be…

No way.

I glanced at her again. "Are you praying?"

Adriana slowly lifted her head, her thick hair falling back to reveal a clenched jaw, thinned lips, and a glare so sharp it could cut glass. "What? Like I can't pray?"

"I didn't say that."

"You think I'm going to burst into flames or something?"

"Damn, forget I asked." I rolled back over, perfectly content to doze off and dream of a world where Adriana Carrera skipped her ass back to wherever the fuck she came from.

The hell of the last few days had just started melting away when disturbing noises assaulted my ears. Gagging would be too tame of a word. It was more like an overweight cat coughing up another cat. I opened my eyes to find Adriana, crouched forward with one hand clamped over her mouth while the other frantically patted down every inch of the recliner.

She wore the look of a woman about to defile a multi-million-dollar jet.

"You're not gonna puke, are you?"

Giving up on her quest, she scowled before closing her eyes and sinking back into the chair. "No. I'll be fine once this death box levels out."

"Well, then you might have a problem since that happened five minutes ago."

Her eyes popped open, and she gripped the arms of the chair

with such force, I wouldn't be surprised if a few of those red nails slashed through the leather. "Tell me you're joking."

"Sorry, *princesa*. Maybe you missed the announcement from the cockpit while you were wheeling and dealing with the man upstairs." I jabbed my finger in the air a few times for emphasis.

She opened her mouth and took a deep breath. But instead of insulting me, she rubbed her temples, releasing her breath with a slight frown. "I hate flying."

"I'm shocked. You hide it so well."

She rolled her chin toward me, eyes blazing. I had her riled up, and it was about time. The woman was a pain in my ass who blackmailed her way onto a kingpin's private jet, but at least she was a distraction.

The brief moment of peace ended as the curtain at the front of the jet parted. Immediately, Adriana's walls shot back up, and she glared at the flight attendant as she made her way toward me.

"Mr. Harcourt…" Turning, she smiled brilliantly at Adriana, who scanned the woman's navy-blue pantsuit like it was loaded with contraband. "Miss Carrera, would you like anything to drink?"

I bit the inside of my cheek to keep from laughing. "I'll have a scotch on the rocks, thanks, Tia." I motioned toward Adriana. "She'll have water and a barf bag."

Giving a small tight smile, she nodded, disappearing as quietly as she'd appeared.

"You drink too much," Adriana grumbled.

"You talk too much." It was on the tip of my tongue to ask if Tia had anything to dislodge the stick from someone's ass when the plane dropped, leaving my stomach hovering about two feet above the rest of me.

I grasped the chair just as Adriana let out a high-pitched

scream.

"It's just a little turbulence," I assured her. "We hit an air pocket. It's fine."

"Couldn't you have just rented a car?"

I rolled my eyes. "Because a nineteen-hour road trip with you would have been so enjoyable."

That was when I noticed she had her arms wrapped around her body, and she was shaking. The woman who led an entire cartel actually had a horrific fear of flying. Everything about me was designed to seek out weakness and exploit it. Adriana's shield was up most of the time, but no one could run from demons at forty-one thousand feet.

This was my chance. I should go in for the kill.

"Look, if it makes you feel any better, you're two-thousand times more likely to be in a car crash than a plane crash."

Or I could toss out random statistics to help the enemy. *Whatever.*

"Yes, but if I'm in a car crash, I have a chance of surviving. If this abomination of gravity goes down, they'll have to piece us back together like a damn puzzle." As if the mental image wasn't enough, she put her fists together then opened her palms and threw her arms out wide in a physical reenactment of our deaths.

I dismissed her dramatics with a wave of my hand. "Don't be ridiculous. If that happened, the engine would explode, and we'd fry to a crisp before even hitting the ground."

Just a little dig to remind her who called the shots once we hit Mexican soil.

Crossing her arms, she turned her back to me. "Don't talk to me until we're on solid ground."

Well, shit. If I knew describing our hypothetical deaths in graphic detail would shut her up, I would've done it a long time ago.

"With pleasure." After Tia returned with our drinks, I took a much-needed sip and placed it in the chair's drink holder. Folding my arms behind my head, I stretched out and enjoyed the first moment of peace I'd had all week.

As if pulled by some unknown force, my gaze wandered back to Adriana. She still sat as rigid as before, except the cup of water in her hand shook so hard, droplets spilled over the edge and scattered across the leather. I assumed air sickness had struck again. I had no idea how to comfort an ally, much less an enemy. Normal emotion wasn't something I felt anymore.

The only thing that felt natural was sarcasm, but just as I opened my mouth to insult her, I noticed her face. It was no longer green but pale. So pale, if she wasn't almost panting, I'd wonder if she was breathing at all.

"Adriana…"

She cut a sharp stare at me, immediately setting down her cup and clasping her hands together. "So, what kind of shit show am I walking into?"

I motioned toward her tight grip. "Are you sure you're—?"

"I assume when you convinced Val to let you bring me to Mexico City, you conveniently left out the reason you'd suddenly joined Team Adriana." Her face tightened, either in pain or in anger. Whatever the cause, the message written across it clearly said back off.

So, I did.

I rattled the ice in my glass. "As far as Val knows, my concern for the cartel outweighs any risk you might pose."

"And?"

"And I told him I believed you were sincere."

"And he believes it?"

"Mmmhmm," I mumbled, around a mouthful of scotch.

Adriana's pale lips twisted in suspicion. She had every right

117

to doubt me. The conversation wasn't quite that cut and dry. I left out the part where Val more or less threatened to castrate me.

"This is not a time for a family reunion, Harcourt. In case you forgot, Adriana had my wife's brother tortured and killed. I put you in charge of Houston for a damn reason. If you can't handle the job, then maybe I should—"

"I can handle it. Look, I know there's bad blood with Eden, but I wouldn't bring her if I didn't think this threat was real. It's not the first I've heard of Muñoz reconstruction and infiltration."

"And you're just now informing me? ¡Hijo de tu puta madre!" Son of a bitch.

"Val, I'm not a moron. I didn't want to come to you until I had full recon and intel. Adriana has the name of the man leading the charge. It's foolish not to hear her out."

"Force the name out of her. When did you become such a pussy?"

"Yet again, she won't tell me. And nobody has the balls to employ torture techniques on the boss's sister."

"You're a resourceful man. Figure something out."

"I ripped the floor out from underneath her, Val. She wouldn't trust me with her drink order, much less valuable information."

"Dios mío. Fine. I'll have Walker prep the jet. But, Brody?"

"Yeah?"

"She's your responsibility."

As usual, with Val the real threat lay more in what he didn't say rather than what he did. He agreed to open his home to us, pull back the veil and bare a vulnerability few ever witnessed. However, reward never came without risk. I swore on my life his family would be safe. I personally guaranteed Adriana would prove both her loyalty to him and herself worthy of the Carrera name.

She had to…

If she failed, we'd both die, and I wasn't so sure Val would be the Carrera to pull the trigger.

Chapter Twelve

BRODY

Mexico City, Mexico

I whistled as we approached the opulent excess of the Carrera mansion. "So, this is how the other half lives."

Adriana paused on the first step, her bag sliding down her arm. "What are you talking about? You grew up in a mansion."

Shoving my hands in my pockets, I swiveled around on my heels to face her. "Well, if it isn't the pot calling the kettle black. For your information, I grew up in a modest three-bedroom house until my dad died. It wasn't until my mom remarried that we shot up into an obscene tax bracket."

"But you've been to Val's estate before, right?"

"Meetings in Mexico, yes. House, no." I fought a smirk as Adriana's brow furrowed. As fun as it was to toy with her, I had no desire to encourage more of her questions. "Look, you grew up in this life. You know better than anyone that the people in a man's business inner circle aren't necessarily the ones in his personal one. Val has a wife and a son to protect. I get that."

"But you're his second in command," she argued. "Besides, regardless of what happened between you and Eden in the past, you said it yourself. She's his wife, and you saved her life."

I shrugged. "Sometimes a person's mistakes will always haunt them and overshadow any good they'll ever do."

"That's depressing," she huffed, turning to climb toward the front steps.

Chuckling, I followed behind her. "That's life, kid."

As we both stood outside the enormous archway that framed the front door, our limo driver held out his hand, preventing us from moving any closer.

"What?" I asked, almost barreling into him. "Is there a password?"

He grunted and turned his palm up. "Guns."

Adriana's eyes narrowed, and before she could make this worse, I clarified things for the idiot. "I'm Brody Harcourt."

"I don't give a fuck if you're *Santa Muerte*. No guns."

Crossing her arms over her chest, Adriana nodded toward the estate. "And what about their guns? I suppose if we use the wrong fork, they're allowed to shoot us in the face?"

Jesus Christ.

"Adriana!"

"What?"

"Shut up and give him your gun."

She shot me a wry look. "I don't have a gun."

As much as I understood her reluctance, I also knew this guy had orders, and they stated the line stopped here. We didn't cross unless we caved.

"Adriana…" The word was her name, but the warning was clear.

This is what you wanted.

"Oh, fine, here." Reaching under her skirt, she unclipped a

thigh holster and slammed a small revolver into the man's hand, glaring at me the whole time. "Happy?"

Handing over my own gun to the man's waiting hand, I smirked. "Ecstatic."

As soon as we crossed the threshold into the house, I whistled again, ignoring Adriana's glare. The Carrera estate made the elaborate display of wealth I spent my high school years living in look like a run-down backwoods shack. Intricate framework, brushed gold, museum quality artwork, and enough square footage to house a small neighborhood closed in on me, tightening the already snug tie around my neck.

Pulling on my collar, I leaned close to Adriana. "Maybe this is a bad time. We should go."

"But you just got here." The commanding and authoritative voice slithered down my back, and as if we'd been struck by lightning, Adriana and I spun around to find the source.

Like a panther watching its prey from a higher vantage point, Valentin Carrera nodded, acknowledging our presence from halfway up the winding staircase, then slowly and meticulously descended, his predatory eyes watching me the entire time. He exuded confidence. It poured out of him, coating the very floor the man stood on. He was danger wrapped in a designer suit, and intimidation masked as an ordinary thirty-one-year-old man.

But there was nothing ordinary about Val Carrera. From his slicked back black hair to his heavier-than-normal beard, the kingpin of the Carrera Cartel wielded power most men could never fathom. With a simple nod, he decided who lived, who died, and who suffered until madness took whatever remained.

And if that weren't enough, trailing behind him was the second most feared man in Mexico. Val's most trusted confidante. The prince who'd become king should Val's enemies ever succeed in taking him out.

Mateo Cortes.

A man who'd both killed for Val and nearly died for him. His family was the cartel. His loyalty knew no bounds. He was younger and more impulsive, but just as deadly.

He was also my brother-in-law.

"Val." I nodded in return, watching him just as carefully. Then I turned my head. "Mateo."

Mateo dipped his chin. "Brody."

Adriana stood motionless beside me as Val made his way toward us. I followed his gaze, identical eyes meeting for the first time in over a year.

"Marisol." He spoke the name slowly, as if tasting the word on his tongue.

"Adriana," she corrected, not an ounce of fear in her tone. I didn't particularly like the woman, but I had to admit, hearing her talk back to Val Carrera did something to me.

Something that, if I didn't get under control, would embarrass all of us real soon.

Instead of launching into his usual tirade about respect and authority, the corners of Val's mouth curled in the barest hint of a smile. "Of course. Adriana. My mistake."

"Where's Eden?"

Fuck.

Yeah, I thought it, but I sure as hell didn't mean to say it. The words just slipped out, and as soon as they did, I wanted to stuff them back down my throat.

Mateo raised a questioning eyebrow, and if looks could kill, Val's narrowed stare would've incinerated me to dust.

"My wife is out."

I heard the meaning behind the words loud and clear.

Stay away from her, asshole.

"Besides, I thought it would be best if Eden wasn't here

when she arrived," he added, nodding toward Adriana.

Adriana opened her mouth to object, but I stomped on the toe of her high heel, causing her to swallow a muffled groan instead.

"Of course," I answered for her.

While Adriana shot me death glares, Val headed into a sitting area to our right and straight for the fully stocked bar nestled in the corner of the room. Filling a stem glass full of what I knew to be *Añejo* tequila, he placed one hand on the marble and drank leisurely before saying a word.

"So, Adriana, I suppose I should welcome you home."

I glanced at Mateo who simply shrugged.

This whole situation was a grenade waiting to explode, and at any moment, either Carrera sibling could pull the pin. To prevent a disaster, I did the only thing I knew she couldn't resist. I stared hard into her gold-flecked eyes and dared her to play his game.

Adriana Carrera never backed down from a challenge...

And judging by her defiant stare, it was game on.

She turned a brittle smile Val's way. "Thank you for having us."

We stood in silence for a moment, each of us staring at the other, unsure of what to do or what to say. Finally, Val offered her a curt nod and motioned for us all to sit, breaking the tension.

"I'm sure we'll have plenty of time to catch up later, but Brody tells me that we have pressing business to discuss. My men have heard rumblings of a new leader attempting to reassemble the Muñoz Cartel, but no one has managed to gather useful intel on him. I believe you have some information for me."

Her hands tightened by her side. "Yes. I have the name of the man in charge of restructuring them."

"I'm all ears."

He wasn't the only one. Since returning from Chicago, I'd waited to hear the name of the man who stole my shipment and set this whole thing in motion. The man who'd made enemies of two powerful crime syndicates then opened the door for the woman who stood beside me to hold my life in the palm of her hand.

"His name is Ignacio."

Taking a slow drink of tequila, Val studied her while running a thumb over his beard. "Ignacio…*what*?"

"That's all I know."

Val cocked his chin toward me, a smug smile twisting his lips. "That's all she knows."

I whipped my head around, clenching my fists just to keep from wrapping them around her neck. "You lied to me?"

"Brody, I—"

"You told me you had inside information Val had to know in person. I put my reputation, not to mention my life on the line for you!"

Her cheeks flushed. "If you would just listen to me for a damn—"

A low chuckle from across the room caused us both to turn just as Val set his empty glass on the bar. "Well, this has been enlightening, but if you two will excuse us, Mateo and I have real intel to find before shit gets out of control."

"Val," I called after him.

He paused at the entrance to the sitting room. Tipping his chin over his shoulder, he leveled a hard stare at Adriana. "Brody will make sure you get back to Houston safely."

"You need me."

"Adriana!" I was going to fucking kill her.

Provided she didn't get me killed first.

Val held up his hand. "No, let her speak, Brody. I'm

intrigued." Taking a few steps back into the room, he locked his hands behind his back. "And why would I need you?"

I'd seen grown men fall to their knees under the predatory hunt of Val Carrera. He stalked, they retreated. However, Adriana didn't back down. She lifted her chin and met him eye to eye.

Carrera to Carrera.

"I'm the only one who knows the inner workings of the Muñoz Cartel and how they operate. To find Ignacio—to figure out who he is and stop him—you need me. If you send me back to Houston this little scavenger hunt of yours will take three times as long."

Little scavenger hunt.

Mateo and I locked eyes across the room, and this time it was my turn to shrug. I had no idea what she thought she was doing. I wasn't a pussy. I'd walked into massacres unarmed. I'd taken more lives than I could remember. I'd outsmarted some of the world's most sophisticated criminals. But not once had I mocked a cartel boss to his face.

And even though I knew allowing the repercussions for her actions to play out would solve most of my problems, I found myself standing in front of her.

I made myself a goddamn human shield.

For Adriana fucking Carrera.

"She doesn't mean that."

Adriana shoved her way around me. "Don't answer for me like I don't have a brain. I meant every word of it. He needs me, and he knows it. The three of you can stand around here congratulating yourselves on how big your dicks are, or you can go on the offensive and strike first. It's your choice."

If and when we made it back to Houston, I'd kill her myself. Slowly.

"Val," I started, raising a hand. "Call your driver. I'll take care of this myself and make sure she never—"

"She's right."

"What?" I whipped my head around sure I'd heard him wrong.

"She's right," he repeated. "By the time I tracked this *pinche cabrón* down, the damage he might inflict on us could cripple our distribution channels and our infrastructure. We need to end him, and we need to do it now."

Mateo raked a hand over his long hair and let out a harsh breath. "So, what do we do?"

Val never took his eyes off Adriana. "We strike first."

Unbelievable.

Adriana managed to do something very few ever accomplished. She forced her way into the inner circle of two cartels and dragged me along with her. If she succeeded in drawing out the Muñoz organizer, my position within the cartel would be solidified.

If she failed...

Well, I didn't care to think about that.

Adriana fought a smirk as she dipped her chin. "I'll do whatever I can to help."

A glint flashed in Val's eyes. "Do you mean that?"

I didn't like the way this conversation was going. Something felt off. Like a sizzle running along an invisible current. Adriana was too confident, and Val was too agreeable. A combination as natural as oil and water.

"I wouldn't be here if I didn't."

"*Muy bien.* Then I want you to go to Guadalajara."

"What?"

Val smiled. "This is where you heard this Ignacio name in the first place, yes?"

"Well, yes, but you can't expect me to—"

"Good," he said, cutting her off. "Then it's settled. You'll leave first thing in the morning. You grew up there. You know the area better than anyone. Find out what you can and report back."

"What will walking into enemy territory prove? That I'm suicidal?"

"No, that you have no lingering Muñoz loyalty, and you're completely invested in keeping the Carreras in power."

I couldn't blame him. It was a dick maneuver, but a shrewd one. Besides, at least with Adriana gone, I didn't have the black cloud of her threat hanging over my head.

"Fine." The word crawled out of her throat like a beast trying to claw free from her chest. Pushing past me, she stomped toward the front door. "Whatever it takes, *brother*."

"Adriana…" Hearing Val call her by her given name, she froze, her hands fisting by her sides. "I'm not a stupid man. While I'm willing to give you a chance due to the blood we share, I'd be foolish to trust you because of the same reason. Our mother gave love unconditionally, while our father used it as a weapon. Where your genetics fall remains to be seen, and until then, I can't put anything past you, especially betrayal."

"So, what are you going to do?" she taunted, popping a hand on her hip. "Send a group of spies to report back to you?"

"Close. I'm sending Brody."

Chapter Thirteen

ADRIANA

I spun around so fast the room blurred. "I'm not going anywhere with him." To make my point clearer, I flung an arm in Brody's general direction.

"Over my dead"—a low grunt broke his protest as the back of my hand slammed against his chest—"body."

The stealth of his movement and the sudden impact caught me off guard. Without thinking, I turned away from Val and stared blankly where my hand still pressed against his chest. Even through the layers of his pretentious suit, the hard muscle molded against my hand, and my head filled with flashes of being pressed against a wall.

The sound of a throat clearing broke the moment, and all eyes turned toward Val. He stood with one arm crossed over his chest, stroking his chin with the other, his eyes bouncing between us.

He said nothing. In fact, the entire room had gone silent.

Jerking my hand away from Brody, I ignored the heat burning my cheeks and scowled at both of them. "No."

Well, *that* sounded convincing.

Val quirked an eyebrow. "No?"

"No." Why did my voice sound all breathy? Squaring my shoulders, I tried again with more conviction. "I work alone."

"And I sure as hell don't want to babysit her."

I inhaled slowly, forcing myself not to turn around and punch him in the face.

"Val, come on," Brody protested, stepping in front of me like a damn caveman. "That's not feasible. I can't drop everything and spend God knows how long in Guadalajara. I have an entire stateside operation to run, in case you've forgotten."

I stared at the back of his head like it had grown horns.

Insubordination. I would've shot him on sight.

Apparently, Mateo had the same thought. In the blink of an eye, he crossed the room and stood beside Val, his hand disappearing under his black leather jacket. However, Val held up his hand and Mateo's relaxed, dropping to his side.

"I'm sure you've left it in capable hands with Rafael," he said, his tone slow and calculated. "Besides, you owe me for the mess you made in San Marcos, don't you think?"

Brody's face blanched. "Val—"

"I'm the head of this cartel. It's time you remember you take orders, not give them, lieutenant."

A tense silence filtered around the room, and for once in my life, I didn't know what to say. All eyes were on Brody, and all ears waited on his response. I had no idea what happened in San Marcos, but his entire body language changed at its mention. The fight drained out of him, his shoulders dropping, as if those two words carried the weight of a mountain.

I'd found another chink in his armor, and I tucked it away

for later.

Lifting my eyes, I met Brody's tortured gaze, but it wasn't focused on my face. It was locked below my chin with a resigned intensity so strong it commanded my body without my permission. As he stared, my fingers brushed over the scarred skin at the base of my neck. I swallowed hard, the moment uncomfortably intimate.

Too intimate.

It was like he saw through my scars and forced his way into forbidden territory. My fingertips danced along my chilled skin, and as my hand shook, he caught my eye.

A simple glance.

No smirk. No wink. No words.

Just silent acknowledgment of an unintended show of weakness.

Pulling his eyes away from me, Brody stepped forward and settled them on Val. "Message received, boss. However, there's no way Adriana can get inside Muñoz walls after they—"

"After they found out I was a Carrera," I interrupted, commanding Val's attention. "It's all about protecting the bloodline…right, *brother*?"

Brody glanced back at me with a question in his eyes I ignored.

My words hung in the air, and Val's grip on his glass tightened. Lines sank deep into his chiseled face, and the corners of his eyes pulled downward. "Adriana, I want to believe you. For almost a year, I've tried to find you. I…" His voice trailed off, and he lifted his glass, draining half of it. When he spoke again, his voice was clipped, all emotion on his face erased by the hardened mask of a ruthless leader. "My men will ensure you have all you need. I'll expect regular updates."

Without another word, he finished what was left in his glass, slammed it onto the marble bar, and stormed out of the room.

Mateo started after him, then paused, turning back toward us. As usual, his expression held both the unreadable secrets of an exclusive brotherhood and the transparent loyalty that said he wouldn't hesitate to take us both down to protect them. "Try not to kill each other. I'll be back to show you to your rooms."

Brody and I stared after him, speechless for what seemed like forever. Scrubbing my hands over my face, I slumped against the wall, slowly sliding down until my ass hit the floor.

Well, that went well.

A shadow crossed in front of me. "Why wouldn't you let me tell Val they hurt you?"

Every muscle in my body coiled as I peered up at him through a small space between my index and middle fingers. "Even though he doesn't trust me, he wouldn't have let me go if he knew." Dropping my hands, I rolled my head against the wall and gazed up at him with a half-hearted smirk. "Come on, even a former Muñoz knows Val's strict code against violence toward women. I told you I want to prove myself, and I meant it. If this is the way I have to do it, then so be it."

"Are you willing to die for your cause?"

At that moment, the sarcastic shield Brody Harcourt wielded as a weapon failed him. Gone were the dozens of masks he hid behind, leaving only the raw power of a man on the verge of anarchy. A man caught between fighting for a life he never wanted and against his natural instinct to throw me to the wolves.

And in that same moment, I stared down the quiet hallway where the only family I had left disappeared, and the carefully constructed walls I built around myself bent.

"I already have," I whispered. "Dying isn't the hard part, Brody. Living, now that's the real torture."

An hour later, I settled into a quiet room on the third floor of the Carrera estate. A place that, despite being the hub of everything I was raised to hate, felt oddly familiar. Almost as if the walls themselves whispered my name.

Dropping my bag on the oversized bed, I found myself drawn to an antique dresser that sat tucked against the opposite wall. Muted and worn, it seemed almost out of place, considering the over-the-top grandeur of the rest of the estate. Closing my eyes, I fought a wave of emotion as I trailed my fingers along the dark wood, every divot and crevice painting a picture of a life I couldn't remember. A life as real as the wood under my skin, but as ruined as the scratches that marred it.

A life just like this antique dresser. Preserved, yet somehow still lost in time.

Ghosts lived in this room. I heard their whispers, and they tore at my soul. I heard the lullabies coated in the soft, soothing voice I used to hear in my sleep. One I convinced myself over the years was nothing but a hallucination. Only it wasn't because if I listened hard enough, I could hear it now. I felt her in the air. I felt her in the wood under my fingertips, and I knew it was no accident I'd been put in this room.

I'd been here before.

I'd lived here before.

I'd died here before.

My back slammed against the wall, my eyes squeezing shut to block out the memories assailing me like snapshots from a photo album I'd never seen but knew all the same. The father who never once held me or allowed my name to pass his lips. The small brother who sat outside my bedroom window, watching and protecting as if he somehow felt the end nearing.

And the mother who, in the midst of a massacre, gently sang *Duérmete Niño*, keeping our family together until the last note took both of us away.

The words echoed within the confines of the four walls.

Duérmete niño, duérmete ya.

Sleep, baby, sleep now.

As pain tore through my chest, I pressed my hands against both ears, but it did nothing to block it out.

Que mientras tanto te canta Mamá.

While Mommy is singing to you.

Louder and louder, the lyrics seeped into my soul. Taunting me. Filling the hollow spaces with a dark warning as the edges of my vision blackened to a dull haze.

"Stop!" The word tore from my chest in a violent scream so loud I slapped a hand over my mouth in horror that someone heard.

I had to get out of here.

As if pulled by instinct, I stumbled down the hallway, past closed doors without giving them a second glance. The entire floor seemed deserted, yet I still moved, drawn toward a destination I knew nothing about. It wasn't until I turned left and neared the end of another hallway that I heard a familiar voice.

"...doing well. Barely remembers anything that happened or anyone involved."

Mateo.

"That... That's for the best."

And that voice was unmistakably Brody's. I'd recognize the deep timbre and rough edge anywhere, a fact I didn't care to analyze.

Pressing my back against the wall, I lifted onto my toes and slid quietly along the floor, willing the backs of my high heels not to fall off. Just as I pressed the side of my face against the frame of the open door, the voices stopped. My heart climbed into my throat, and for a moment I thought they'd heard me until Mateo's thick accent broke the silence.

"Aren't you going to ask?"

"No."

"She remembers you. She asks about you."

My grip on the doorframe tightened. Who was *she*?

"Mateo, I can't…" Brody confessed, the pain in his voice palpable. Almost as if the fight in him had died and he was one blow away from breaking.

"Don't do this, man. She's just a little girl."

Wait, what?

"I can't hurt them again."

At that moment, my high heel slipped off the back of my foot and slammed against the marble floor. I tipped my head back and winced, but at the same moment, the wall behind me vibrated with what I could only assume was one hell of a punch.

"You don't think refusing to see them isn't hurting them?" Mateo roared. "*Dios mío*, do you think I'd let you anywhere near them if I thought you were a threat to their safety? You're *familia*, Brody, but I'd put you in the ground before I'd put them in danger."

"I know."

The quiet response intrigued me more than the testosterone show Mateo put on. I'd spent no more than forty-eight hours with Brody, but even I knew his two-word compliance was completely out of character. The man lived to argue, and contrary to my insults, he'd made quite a successful career out of it. Whatever they discussed was serious enough to disarm a man who used words as a weapon.

"So stop feeling sorry for yourself and man the fuck up,"

Mateo growled, and I couldn't tell if he meant it as a suggestion or a warning. "You're the only family they have left. You made some bad decisions, but you didn't hurt them on purpose. The only person punishing you for your sins is you."

"I'll think about it."

Mateo barked out a sardonic laugh. "Don't hurt yourself on your sister's account."

Hold on a damn minute.

Sister?

My mind spun a hundred miles an hour as bits and pieces of an earlier conversation clicked into place.

"You know he had an estranged sister, right? Well, about six months ago, she came back into town. Not long after that, he started missing court dates and got into some seriously deep shit... I mean, hot water with the Carreras."

"The cartel?"

"Shocking, right? Unfortunately, one thing led to another, and she died, and then his mother got arrested."

Oh, hell no.

My days of being left in the dark were over. With fire shooting through my veins, I hobbled around the corner. "I thought your sister was dead?"

Chapter Fourteen

ADRIANA

Both men turned at the sound of my voice. Mateo faced the wall where I'd just been eavesdropping, his palm braced next to an impressive dent. Brody leaned against the opposite wall, his arms crossed tightly over his chest, the vibrant green in his hazel eyes all but swallowed by a lifeless brown. However, once they landed on me, a rough smile tugged at the corner of his mouth.

Mateo, not so much.

"Don't you know how to knock?" he growled.

I glared at him. "Don't you know how to close a door?"

"Calm down, Mateo. It's fine."

"It's fine?" Mateo pushed off the wall, his hands fisting by his side. "I'm sorry, have you forgotten she blackmailed you into betraying Val by having Leighton stalked?"

Brody shot him a pointed look. "No, I haven't forgotten." Both men stared at each other, their restraint razor thin. However, instead of volleying another insult back to Mateo, Brody shifted his attention back to me. "As far as the US government knows, my sister and niece are missing and presumed dead. Before I left the DA's office, I faked passports for both of them so Mateo could get them out of the country."

"Why?"

"With the mess my mother's arrest made, it was the only way to ensure their safety and privacy."

"You haven't seen them since they left?"

"No," he admitted. Pushing his shoulders back, he tossed a heated look Mateo's way. "And contrary to popular opinion, it should stay that way."

My brows knitted together. "Huh."

"What does 'huh' mean?"

"Nothing. Just that the US has this huge intelligence cooperative, and all this time the two people they've been looking for have been—"

Mateo came off the wall like he'd been shot out of a cannon. "Stay away from my wife and daughter. You got that?"

To be honest, I forgot he was even in the room.

"Wow, the nice guy routine doesn't last long, does it?"

Antagonizing my new brother's foot soldier probably wasn't the smartest move, but the guy acted like I planned to toss his family into a bonfire and watch them burn.

He shoved his finger in my face. "Look, you bit—"

One minute, the Carrera underboss stood inches away from wrapping a hand around my throat, and the next he sailed across the room like a frisbee, creating a second dent into the wall not far from the first.

"That's enough!" Brody growled. "Do I need to remind you that Adriana is a *Carrera*? She's Val's sister, which means you'll treat her with the same respect you would any member of this family."

Being thrown like a human lawn dart by his inferior didn't seem to faze Mateo. Instead of coming barreling back, he tugged a hand through his long hair and gritted his teeth so hard I heard his teeth clack together. "She hasn't earned it."

"It's not your call to make, is it?"

I'd witnessed brutal murders that didn't fill a room with as much tension as the stares those two men passed back and forth. I almost felt guilty for stirring the pot of whatever friction boiled between them.

Almost.

Without another word, Mateo turned away, slamming his hand into the wall on the way out.

Three dents.

What fascination did Carrera men have with destroying drywall?

Flopping down on the bed, I leaned back on my hands. "That guy needs to lighten up or he's going to have a stroke before he's thirty."

I glanced at Brody discreetly out of the corner of my eye as he fumbled around in his suitcase. Finally, his head popped up, and with his toothbrush in one hand and a bottle of shampoo in the other, he disappeared into the adjoining bathroom. I wasn't sure whether it was to unpack or get away from me, and the fact I even cared irritated me.

"Back off, Adriana," he called out over the sound of running water.

I sat up. Surely, he wasn't taking a shower *now*. I twisted my fingers around the bedspread, battling the urge to go in and see for myself. A battle I almost lost until he poked his blond head around the corner.

"Just because I defended you doesn't mean I don't agree

with him. Stay away from my sister and my niece, and this will go a lot smoother."

I winced. For reasons I didn't care to explore, Brody standing up for me felt good. Maybe because for a second, I actually let myself believe what he said was true.

I quickly turned my back to him. "Does this have anything to do with San Marcos?"

"I'm not discussing this with you."

I sighed. I'd let it go for now. "Okay, then tell me why you defended me. You don't even like me."

"You're right, I don't. But I also don't like exclusion. I know what it's like to be the outsider. The top layer of the Carrera empire is like a tightly-woven shield—tied together and almost impossible to get through. I may not trust you, but I hate seeing someone bounced off it without being given a chance."

"If you don't trust me, why did you tell me about your sister?"

"I don't know. I have no basis for it, considering what you've threatened me with so far. But something tells me you draw the line at hurting children."

A sharp pain tore through my chest, and it wasn't until I glanced down that I realized it came from my own nails.

"Adriana?"

I slowly turned around, expecting to see his messy blond hair still peeking out from behind the bathroom door. But it wasn't. It was right in front of me, connected to a bare chest leading to trousers popped open at the button. And leading right to that button was a trail of blond hair that disappeared where his zipper started. A zipper playing referee between two prominent slopes that formed a perfect V cutting sharply down to his groin.

I was staring, but I couldn't help it. I grew up cartel. Every male I'd ever known looked the part—rough and lethal with slivers of bronze skin peeking through a litany of colorful tattoos. Tattoos that meant they'd met certain standards in a life of power, murder, and crime.

But Brody Harcourt was nothing like them.

He was a privileged *gringo* whose sun-kissed white skin stretched over every taut muscle in his chest. Deep lines defined his pecs and abs, the toned peaks and valleys rolling over a deceptive blank slate. Unstained by ink. A fresh canvas for the sin that dwelled within him.

The perfect contradiction of deceptive boy next door and soulless viper.

"Adriana?"

Blinking, I realized he'd called my name again. "I'm sorry, what?"

The bed dipped as he knelt in front of me and gently pulled my hand away from my chest. "You looked like you were trying to claw your heart out of your chest."

I was.

His fingers traced the red marks I'd left on my skin, and I flinched. "Hey, what's going on? Talk to me."

"Why?"

"Because when I mentioned you'd draw the line at hurting children, you went somewhere else."

I couldn't think while he was touching me, so I scooted backward until his hand fell away. "I may have done a lot of things. But I never have, nor will I ever, hurt a child. They're the only innocent thing in this world. Nothing that happens to them is their fault. Sometimes…" I sucked in a sharp breath. "Sometimes even the people they grow up to be isn't their fault."

Brody was silent for a minute, and I thought I'd said too much until he shifted closer. I didn't move. I didn't even blink until he lifted his hand and reached for me. All the breath left my lungs in one hard exhale, but instead of returning to my chest, his fingertips brushed the scar on my neck.

"No one has ever really seen you, have they, Adriana?"

I shook my head because speaking the words would've been too intimate. This was the man who uprooted my life and destroyed my future, then tried to stain the only name I had left with false accusations. I hated him, and once I was accepted into this family, I planned to return the favor.

So why did I want his lips on me more than I wanted my next breath?

"I see you."

"Don't…" I shook my head, trying to pull away, but his long fingers curled around the back of my neck, holding me in place.

"You fight dirty, Carrera. You want everyone to think you're this heartless bitch who'll eviscerate anyone to get what she wants, but that's a role you play just to get noticed."

"Stop."

"You dominate and exploit your enemy's weakness because that's the only way you know how to feel wanted."

The air felt heavy, clogged with tension so thick I could taste it. As much as I wanted to throw every vile and hateful word I knew at him, the self-assured stare in his darkened eyes held me hostage, crashing through my barriers and holding me immobile.

He was right. He did see me. He saw right through me to the core of something I couldn't rationalize, and it both infuriated and calmed me.

Why him?

Why did the man who ruined me, understand me?

My chest rose and fell in arduous waves as his hand slid up my neck. It was pure torture, a disturbing sensuality that resonated within the darkest depths of my soul.

Up my throat. Across my chin. Brushing my cheek.

I shivered the moment his hand dove into my hair, his fingers tightening to the perfect amount of pain.

"There are better ways to feel wanted, *princesa.*" The deep timbre of his voice was rough. Low and controlled, yet still hinging on the brink of destruction.

It was me he'd destroy, and God help me, I wanted it.

"Adriana," he whispered my name again, and it sounded like a wicked prayer. He was breathing so hard my hair fanned across my face. This was wrong. So wrong. But I craved more, hating myself for it, but unable to stop.

Until the door slammed and the perfectly fucked-up bubble we crawled into burst.

"Well, I sure as hell didn't expect this."

Chapter Fifteen

ADRIANA

I had no idea who moved first. All I knew was that Brody and I sprang apart like two ends of a snapped rubber band. The fire that moments ago had my blood boiling extinguished, leaving nothing but withering smoke.

I knew who was there without turning around.

Brody's eyes widened as he stared over my shoulder. All the color drained from his face, a sudden discord etched across it. Like he'd suddenly found himself trapped between two worlds without any means of escape.

Maybe it stemmed from coming face-to-face with the living embodiment of torture. Either way, the sadistic craving that almost seduced me into trading vindication for gratification faded leaving only a bruised ego and a renewed will.

"Eden…" Brody murmured her name with such reverence I twisted my fingers together to stop myself from putting a fourth dent in the wall. "We, uh… I didn't know you were back."

Oh, for fuck's sake.

"Obviously," she quipped.

I barely refrained from rolling my eyes.

Brody raked a hand through his hair. "It's not what it looks like. I mean, this isn't... We aren't..."

"Fucking," I finished for him. Spinning around, I flashed her a wicked smile. "Well, not anymore, thanks to you. You'll cockblock him until the day he dies, huh, Lachey?"

"Adriana!"

Yeah, that might have taken it a bit too far, but damn, it felt good, and even *he* had to admit she had it coming.

Twisting around, I met his narrowed eyes. "What?"

"Be nice!"

"Give me one good reason."

"Because we're guests in Eden's house, that's why." Lowering his voice, he hissed a warning through a forced smile. "*And because Val values her opinion.*" Turning his attention back to Eden, his whole demeanor changed. "Seriously, we were just talking."

I was pissed. Partly because of his slingshot attitude, but more so because I hated that he was right. I was caught between wanting to see Saint Eden suffer for her sins and needing her approval in order to win Val's.

It was like teetering on the edge of a cliff with my only options being to jump off or face a hungry pack of wolves. Either choice ended in sacrifice. Whether it would be a sacrifice of pride, blood, or my life remained to be seen.

I had no doubt the wolf at the door right now wanted all three.

Cocking her hip, Eden leaned against the doorframe, flipping her unnatural cherry-red hair over her shoulder. "You know Adriana, you'd think you could scrape together a little gratitude I opened my house to you, considering you ordered a hit on my brother."

"And you put a bullet in mine. I'd say we're even."

"Even?" She threw her head back and let out a laugh so ridiculously loud it echoed down the hallway. "Your brother held a gun to my head then shot Val. What I did was self-defense. What you did was premeditated and heartless. My brother was an innocent pawn in your sick game."

"So were you yet here you are."

A flush crawled up her neck, painting her face the color of her fake-ass hair. "You bitch…"

I yawned, patting my mouth for a dramatic flair. "Try again. I've already heard that one today."

I caught a blur of movement out of the corner of my eye moments before Brody stepped in between us, arms stretched wide like some kind of bitch war referee. "All right, that's enough."

The insult was right there on Eden's lips. I saw it. I waited on it, but her eyes darted toward Brody, and much to my dismay, it died. Sighing, she gave him a weak smile which quickly faded as her eyes trailed back to me. "I'm watching you, Marisol."

Resting my chin in the palm of my hand, I tapped my index finger against my bottom lip. "Adriana."

"We'll see. You may've been born a Carrera, but you haven't earned the right to call yourself one. My husband wants to give you a chance, so for him, I've allowed you in my home."

Leaning back on one hand, I flipped my hair over my shoulder. "Don't break your back rolling out the welcome mat."

"Ladies!" Brody groaned. "Can we take this down a few notches? You're not going to be best friends; we get it. Will you at least agree to be civil and try not to kill each other for the next twelve hours?"

Obviously, I had no intention of falling on my sword first, so I settled a hard stare toward the doorway and waited. The silence was deafening, and the longer it went on the more agitated Brody became. We were clearly taking too long to answer, evidenced by his clenched fists and the gaze that bounced angrily between us. Just as he opened his mouth again, Eden cut him off.

"Fine."

Twisting around, he cocked an expectant eyebrow at me.

I shrugged. "Maybe."

"Adriana…"

God, I hated it when he drew out my name like that. It made me feel like a petulant child. "Oh, all right. I'll pretend to be nice to the bitch."

Brody threw his head back, exhaling hard as he stared at the ceiling.

"Starting now," I grumbled.

I expected more arguing, but to my surprise, Eden let it drop. It was just as well. I'd only been here a little over an hour and I'd already provoked everyone in the house. Not exactly the best first impression. I had to find a way to keep my resentment compartmentalized if I hoped to have a chance of becoming a permanent fixture in the Carrera family.

"It's good to see you again, Brody." She took six steps inside the room and stood in front of him, placing a hand against his chest. I knew. I counted them. "You know you're welcome here any time."

Brody flinched at the contact. "I wish that were true."

I wanted to grab her hand and twist it until it snapped.

I tensed at the bizarre surge of jealousy. Angry at my unwelcome reaction, I tore my eyes away, only to glance down and see my hand once again fisting the bedspread.

Get a grip.

Disgusted with myself, I released the material and swung my legs around until I faced the wall. Being alone in the room I knew belonged to my mother was the last thing I wanted to do, but it beat the hell out of watching whatever this was. However, just as I was about to make my exit, a faint but shrill cry filled the room.

Eden smiled. "That's my cue. We'll talk soon, okay?"

"Yeah, sure."

Giving him one last pat on his chest, she took a few steps backward. "Well, then, I'll see you both at dinner."

"She means *la comida*," I interrupted, irritated at the way she bastardized my culture. Two sets of eyes turned my way, and I snorted. "It's like your version of dinner only we have it in late afternoon. Americans are the only gluttons who stuff themselves like pigs right before bed."

Brody glanced at Eden for confirmation, and my blood boiled. As if the whitest woman in Mexico would know anything about tradition. For once, she didn't argue, offering a slight dip of her chin as confirmation, and then slipped out the door as quietly as she'd slipped in.

Oh, good. My first dysfunctional family meal.

In the wake of Eden's departure, an awkward silence filtered through the room. Brody and I argued with each other. We insulted each other. We threatened each other. We occasionally defended each other. And, in a surprising new twist, we inexplicably wanted each other. However, the one thing we never did was ignore each other.

It unsettled me.

I climbed off the bed, wracking my brain for something to say when out of the corner of my eye, I saw steam billowing out of the open door of the adjoined bathroom.

Which of course reminded me he was standing in front of

me half naked.

"There's probably no hot water left," I mumbled, motioning behind him.

Brody's forehead wrinkled, and he blinked a few times before glancing over his shoulder. "Oh, yeah. Forgot about that. Guess I'll be taking a cold shower."

That makes two of us.

"Well, I'll leave you to it."

Still, he didn't move. "I guess I'll see you in an hour for lunch."

"*La comida.*"

"Right," he said, a smirk teasing across his lips. "I'll see you in an hour for *la comida.*"

Nodding once, I turned just as he called my name.

"Adriana?"

Just let me go. Please.

However, my body gravitated toward his voice, and I twisted back around, my gaze falling to where his hands were shoved in his pockets, the weight drawing his open pants farther down his hips.

"You're wrong," he said, and the force of the two words snapped my eyes back to his, but it was too late. He sighed heavily. "You accused me of still being in love with Eden. I'm not. There's no justification in holding on to something that was never yours. In the end, not only will you lose, but you'll also answer for it for the rest of your life."

The room popped with the electricity of his confession. Or was it a warning? I didn't know, and I had no desire to find out. My heart thundered harder in my chest until I was halfway down the hallway, far away from his probing eyes, seductive scent, and duplicitous words.

Collapsing against the wall, I braced the heels of my hands

against my temples, forcing myself to remember what Brody Harcourt had done. We didn't have a connection. What happened in that room was two dominants engaging in sexual warfare.

But I wasn't about to win the battle just to lose the war.

At the end of the day, Brody and I would never trust each other. Our paths had tangled in such destructive ways that anything other than a shared goal between us was implausible. But even I wasn't stupid enough to deny the obvious physical attraction between us. The chemistry we shared wasn't just palpable—it was combustible. One touch was like flicking a lit match into a puddle of gasoline.

Brody fought it because he didn't understand it, but I'd lived a life built on hypocrisy. It made perfect sense to me, which was why I knew eventually the storm would consume us.

Everyone equated passion with love, but hatred was a much stronger and more volatile emotion. It drew out our most primal response, the human instinct to control and punish. Desire and hatred were separated by only a fraction of a degree, and that was why neither of us would be satisfied until we'd torn each other to pieces.

We desired because we hated, and we hated because we resented.

I resented him for what he stole from me, and he resented me for forcing him out of the dark hole he'd buried himself in. Come tomorrow morning, there would be no estate to separate this chaotic storm brewing between us. Nothing but a road leading me back to a place I once called home...

And a choice to give up the man who claimed it, or give in to the man who destroyed it.

Chapter Sixteen

BRODY

No one died during dinner.

It sounded ridiculous, but when you sat at the table of a man whose wife you used to fuck and sister you resurrected from the dead, a closer inspection of the *pozole* he served seemed warranted. Not to mention his most trusted confidante had done the exact opposite of what I'd asked and showed up for dessert with my sister and niece in tow.

So here we sat, three hours later, all gathered in what looked to be a botanical garden disguised as a backyard, still alive for the time being. That is, assuming Adriana kept her mouth shut about my port deal with the Sinners and…other things.

Speaking of which…

Swirling the scotch in my hand, I sat back in the ornate hammock and took a long drink. "Are you serious about being a part of this family?"

Adriana tensed beside me. "What kind of question is that?"

"A valid one. You have to know that this hostility between you and Eden can't continue. Val won't stand for it."

"I was perfectly civil during *la comida,* just like you requested."

I shot her a cynical stare and snorted. Either she didn't catch the blatant sarcasm, or she chose to ignore it.

"Come on," she groaned. "I even asked her to pass the salt nicely."

"You said, 'please pass the salt, whore.'"

"What? I said, please." She met my eye roll with a smirk and pushed her foot hard into the grass, all the muscles in her leg contracting.

I tried not to look. Well, I tried not to let her see me look. After all, she was the woman who was threatening to ruin me, and I was the man trying to figure out a way to even the playing field. But I *was* still a man, and I dared any guy with blood still flowing to his dick to turn away from those long legs and curvy thighs that spilled out of tiny white shorts barely containing her ass.

"You all right there, counselor?"

I cleared my throat, shifting my eyes to her face. "Yeah. Just wondering what you plan on doing."

"This…" Leaving us suspended for a moment, she watched for a reaction. When I offered her nothing, she kicked out her foot, smiling as we free fell into a hard arc.

Neither of us spoke as we watched everyone scattering around the grounds, enjoying what was left of the sunlight. My gaze bounced from my sister and niece to a few of Val's top lieutenants to the first family of Mexico's underground. However, Adriana's eyes never left her brother. If persuasion could be attained by sheer willpower, she would've had him in her pocket five minutes ago.

"If you make him choose, Adriana, it won't be you."

She shook her head, strands of her dark hair sticking to her red lipstick. "We share the same blood. I'm his sister."

"And she's his wife," I reminded her. "Not to mention the mother of his child. Besides their baby, there's no one more important in his life. For Christ's sake, he took a bullet for her."

"Why am I always the villain? Blowing my brother doesn't absolve her of sin, you know. Have you forgotten that she strung you along for months until something better came along?"

"That's not true! She—"

"And of course, there's the fact that after Val took a bullet for her, as you were so kind to point out, she left him lying alone in a hospital bed because she"—rolling her eyes toward the darkening sky, she curled her fingers into air quotes—"was too good to live the life of a cartel queen."

"Adriana…"

"Oh, and let's not forget that you risked your reputation and ruined my life just to remind her how the horrors of our world would clip her saintly wings, and she threw it in your face. Know why, Brody? Because underneath that sanctimonious exterior lies a soul just as ruthless as the rest of us. I just don't get why I'm the only one who sees it."

She wasn't. But giving credit to her already rabid contempt would only make things worse. I knew exactly who Eden had become since getting tangled up with Val. She'd always been headstrong, but there was a void nothing ever filled. Almost as if something inside her locked her away against her will. Becoming part of the most feared family in Mexico set it free, unleashing a ruthless side of her that consumed the girl I fought so hard to save.

Who never wanted to be saved in the first place.

However, the stone walls around the cartel queen's heart

cracked for her family, especially her two-month-old son, Santiago.

Across the immaculately manicured garden, Eden bounced the small bundle in her arms, a smile on her face as she talked with my sister. The visual was kind of comical. Santiago's dark fuzzy hair stood out like a beacon next to the stark contrast of his mother's long cherry-red locks. The little prince peered over her shoulder, alternating chewing on his fist and her neck.

I know nothing about babies, but I swore the kid saw me staring at his mother and scowled.

"Santi!" Eden laughed, wedging a finger in between his slobbering lips to pry the suction hold his mouth had on her neck. "You're going to give me a hickey."

I smirked at him.

Yeah, have fun explaining that one to your dad, you mute little bastard.

"What's that smirk about?"

There's no use in denying it. Judging by her reclined position in the hammock, Adriana watched the entire thing play out across my face. Maybe I could use it to my advantage and use her own words against her.

I shrugged, tipping my chin to where Eden cuddled Santi in her arms. "Think about what you're doing, Adriana. If not for anyone else, at least for that innocent baby. You said it yourself, children are the only innocent things in this world."

As expected, she tensed, drawing her leg away from me and locking it against her chest with a tight grip. Adriana's temper was like a powder keg, and I'd already lit a match and waved it over the barrel.

I'd burn some fucking sense into her or ignite a hell storm.

"Val's not rational when it comes to Eden, and if you reveal what I did to keep her from him, there's no telling what he might do. You know better than anyone that truth can destroy lives. Is that what you want for Santiago?"

Adriana's feet flew out from under her, slamming onto the grass as she spun around. "Don't you dare use what you did to me as a crutch," she warned. Dragging in a deep breath, she geared up to toss out what I anticipated to be some insult/threat hybrid when she stopped and narrowed her eyes, those plump lips curving into a wicked smile. "Oh, well played, counselor."

Christ, what now?

She was supposed to knock the match out of my hand, not blow it out. "What the hell are you talking about?"

"I'm not stupid, Brody. This isn't about the potential fallout if I continue fighting with Eden. This is about the potential fallout if I decide to rat you out to Val. You're protecting yourself."

I pushed off the hammock. "Look, I brought you here on a mutual agreement. You give Val a name, and I convince him to give you a chance not to fuck it up. Well we both lived up to our word, and that was supposed to be it, but here we are." I threw my hands out wide, barely missing clipping her chin. "So forgive me for being a little pissed that this mutual thing isn't so damn mutual anymore. You have me by the balls, and because of it, I'm stuck with your crazy ass until we can find this Ignacio and shut this reorganization bullshit down."

She stared at me, blinking as if waiting for more. "That's your idea of a motivational speech? You were a prosecutor. I thought you persuaded people for a living."

"Fuck off, Adriana."

"See, this is why you don't have a girlfriend."

"And this is why you don't have an argument. As much as it pains you to admit, *princesa*, you need me. We have a common enemy and taking him out is more important than tearing me down."

She turned her eyes away and brushed her hair over her shoulder. "There are always casualties of war, counselor."

There wasn't much to say to that, so I didn't. Instead, I followed her gaze to where my sister and Mateo chased my niece around as she shrieked with delight. Joy and peace radiated from them. This was what I wanted. I gave up the last piece of my soul and pushed them away, so they'd have a chance at a normal life. I should've been ecstatic.

So why did seeing them happy make me so goddamn miserable?

"You ever think about having one?"

"One what?"

She laughed, and if I hadn't heard it with my own ears, I wouldn't have believed it. It sounded light and airy, a pleasant change of pace from her usual demonic growls. "Kids, you idiot. You know, a wife, house, white picket fence, dog…the whole plastic package."

Now it was my turn to laugh, but it was neither light nor airy. It was an obstinate bark weighted in irony. "Hell, no. A kid is the last thing I need. I'm lucky to keep myself alive." I raised my glass in a silent toast.

"Speaking of which," she noted, taking it out of my hand. "How about slowing down, *por favor*."

"I've only had two."

"You've had six."

I reached for my drink just as she tipped it upside down, pouring what was left of my scotch in the grass. Leaping forward, I grabbed it out of her hands mid-stream, trying to salvage what was left, but it was too late.

I glared at her while rolling the glass in my hand. "I don't need another mother, Adriana."

"Not trying to be one. I just don't want to have to carry your

160

drunk ass upstairs. I'd hate to have to blow your dick off for chipping a nail."

I didn't want to smile. I wanted to grab the bottom of the hammock and flip her ass upside down, but my brain and my face miscommunicated somewhere, and I grinned.

I fucking grinned.

"You really should back off the booze. Excessive drinking can kill you, you know."

"All the more reason."

She let out a sigh. I knew that sigh. I'd heard it so many times in the past year, it'd become an old friend. A lonely, old, asshole of a friend who showed up when others stopped trying to figure me out. I couldn't blame them.

Hell, I couldn't even figure me out.

"You should have a few. Maybe it would knock that chip off your shoulder."

She eyed the glass still rolling in my hand. "No, I can't have... I don't drink."

I could've called bullshit. Not twenty-four hours ago, she stood in a run-down motel room, taunting me with a bottle of cheap scotch. But something in her voice stopped me. A sliver of weakness that any other time I'd wedge my foot into and pry open. But now wasn't the time.

"No, I meant, do you think about having kids?"

"I'm kind of tired," she announced abruptly. Standing, she grabbed the glass out of my hand and tapped her nails against the side. "I'll take this inside for you."

She was gone before I could point out that it was barely seven o'clock. Whatever. It was a moot point. Her excuse, while transparent, peeled back another layer of raw truth. I'd leave her alone to lick her wounds tonight.

But the real Adriana was showing, and eventually there

would be nowhere for her to run.

Chapter Seventeen

ADRIANA

"**A**driana, stop."

I had no idea what compelled me to obey. I was a grown-ass woman not an errant child, but Val's voice stopped me mid stride, preventing my escape from his mandatory fun.

My grip tightened on the staircase banister. "Is something wrong?"

"I was hoping we could talk for a few minutes. Alone."

Here it comes.

Clearing my throat, I peered over my shoulder, trying to look sorry. "Look, I didn't mean to call her a whore. It just slipped out."

Val squinted, his eyebrows drawing together. "What?"

"What?" I repeated. Because everyone knew when you were about to make an ass out of yourself, the best defense was a confusing offense. The trick was to bite your bottom lip and glance to the side. It activated some repressed Neanderthal instinct in men to pat us on the head and send us back to the cave while they congratulated themselves on being rulers of the universe.

He palmed the back of his neck, and I could see the wheels turning in his head. "What did you say?"

Nice try, Carrera, but I can dance around in circles with you all night.

"I said what because *you* said what." *Cue the lip bite.* "You know, never mind." Facing him, I waved a dismissive hand in the air. "What did you want to talk about?"

He blinked a few times before tilting his chin sideways. "Let's sit down."

The minute he turned his back, I smiled.

Works every time.

"Nothing good ever follows those words," I muttered, following him into the same room we were ushered into when we arrived. Val motioned for me to sit, and I didn't argue. Setting Brody's empty glass on the coffee table, I sank onto the plush couch, running my hand over the expensive leather.

Val watched me from the wet bar, quirking an eyebrow as he poured a drink. "Are you always this suspicious?"

"Yes. Aren't you?"

"Point taken." Neither of us spoke as he poured tequila into a shot glass until it almost overflowed. Picking up a second glass, he paused before pointing the mouth straight at me. "If you tell me that you drink this shit over ice, I'm disowning you."

"First of all, you can't disown me. You're my brother, not my father."

"Oh, Adriana…" My jaw tightened at the snide way he said my name. "I can do whatever I want."

If he weren't completely serious, I would've laughed. "Have you always had a god complex, or did it materialize with

164

all of this?" Holding his stare, I gestured at all the pretentious excess surrounding us.

"So, what's the second part?"

Biting my lip, I glanced to the side, adding in a hair twirl for good measure. "What?"

Val smirked and wagged a finger. "Adriana, never pull the same con twice. It makes you predictable."

"Meaning?"

"Meaning, I indulged your 'confuse and deflect' act once. Don't insult my intelligence or test my generosity. I do have limits."

Limits I couldn't afford to test right now.

"Secondly," I continued, glancing down at the twisted fingers in my lap. "My father... I mean, Esteban drank a lot. It turned me off to the stuff. So, thank you, but I'll pass."

Val remained quiet, and I wondered if I'd crossed another one of his imaginary lines. Finally, he picked the tequila bottle up, the muscles in his neck straining as he held the neck in a tight grip. *"Gran Patrón Burdeos Añejo.* Our father's favorite." His gaze flicked from the bottle to me. "I grew up on this stuff. Had my first drink when I was nine years old. Most fathers teach their sons how to ride a bike or catch a fish at that age." Letting out a dry laugh, he shook his head. "Mine taught me the difference between fine tequila and piss water by making me drink shots until I blacked out."

"Sounds like he was a real winner. Hate I missed out on that."

His eyes narrowed. "Don't act like the man you grew up with was Father of the Year, Adriana. He stole you from your mother's arms." He lifted the glass to his mouth, and just before taking a generous drink added, "Right after he put a bullet in her brain."

I winced, his callous summary hitting a nerve. "Don't you think I know that?" I hissed. "That's become my legacy. Stolen from one sadistic fuck only to be raised by another. Esteban Muñoz lied to me my entire life, and for what? To get his kicks watching me grow up to hate my own family?" I slammed my palms on either side of me against the leather, the sound echoing all the way up to the vaulted ceiling. "Do you know how confusing it is to be me, Val? Six months ago, we wouldn't be having this conversation. I would've shot you in the back while you walked in here. Conditioning like that doesn't just disappear."

"Yet here we sit, and I'm very much alive. Why is that, sister?"

Patronizing fuck.

"I don't know." I tried to glare at him, but rippled waves masked my view. It wasn't until I scrubbed a hand over my face that I felt the dampness.

Oh no.

Oblivious, Val continued berating me. "Is it because your loyalties are shifting, or because I'm still of use to you?"

My shoulders hunched, and I pressed the heels of my hands against my eyes as if reining in a tirade. "I'm already risking my life by walking in front of a firing squad tomorrow. If that doesn't answer your question, then you can go fuck yourself. Find somebody else to insult. I'm going to bed." In a flurry of movement, I stood, wiping my hands on my shorts.

Val's voice was sharp and loud. "Sit down."

"I prefer to stand, thanks."

Was that a glint of approval in his eyes? I couldn't be sure because as quickly as it appeared it, it was gone. "Suit yourself." Refilling his glass, he strode toward me, one step at a time, until he stood in front of me, staring at me as I stared back.

That was when I saw it.

The last time we met in a stash house in Houston, I'd won. I looked Valentin Carrera in the eye and recounted all the ways I'd trapped him in my web. I was too busy gloating to realize I'd been staring into a mirror.

The war raging inside my head radiated to my fists, and I clenched them by my side. Whether he took it as a sign of insolence or not, it was Val who finally broke the silence.

"I took a chance in allowing you to come here, against my better judgment. Against multiple better judgments. And it wasn't only to draw information out of you."

I needed air. Slumping my ass against the back of his overpriced couch, I spread my arms wide, forming a tight grip on the leather. It was probably bad etiquette. Like I gave a shit.

"I'm listening."

He let out a tired sigh, his iron mask slipping. "Adriana, you're my sister. When Eden brought me the proof Brody found out about you, I didn't know if you'd ever accept who you were. Even if you did, I had my doubts we could repair what has been broken for twenty-four years."

Why did everything always circle back to Eden? I glanced at Val, the words sitting on the tip of my tongue. But as much as I longed to say them, I swallowed them.

Today I suffered alone.

Tomorrow, I made no promises.

Instead, I offered an alternate truth. "You have no idea what it's like to suddenly find yourself alone in the world without a damn person to care if you live or die."

"Actually, I do."

"What?"

He shifted his weight, his eyes not quite meeting mine. "I came to Houston to get away from our father, Adriana. As far as I was concerned, he was dead long before he took his last breath.

But the damage had been done. He succeeded in turning me into the same heartless bastard he'd been. So, I lived in isolation."

"To protect yourself?"

His laugh made my skin crawl. "No, to protect everyone else. Alejandro Carrera created a beast, and it feasted on the pain of others. It controlled me. It smelled fear and hungered to hear their screams." Palming the back of his neck, Val turned away, pacing the room as he spoke. "I'm not a good man, Adriana. I know a seat in hell awaits me, for the things I've done. But that beast?" He shook his head, his hand slipping from his neck to the collar of his black button up shirt. "It wasn't just criminal," he said, unbuttoning the first two buttons. "It was demonic. It craved the blood of the innocent."

"What did you do?" I had to know because the beast he spoke of was an entity grown and cultivated by the very culture of a life centered around death.

I knew because I fought the same one.

He dragged his hand across his mouth. "I did the only thing I could do. I starved it. I built a fortress of solitude around myself, and I still felt it clawing at my chest."

"But how did you beat it?"

"Beat it?" His lips twisted in a sardonic smile, and he huffed out a breath. "It's still with me. You can't slay a dragon when you're the one breathing its fire."

"But how—?"

"Eden." The moment the word is out of his mouth, his whole demeanor changed. "She crashed into my life and refused to let me shut her out. She was the first person to look the beast in the eye and tell it to go fuck itself."

"You really love her, don't you?" It was the same question I asked Brody.

"Love her?" Val dipped his chin, a piece of midnight black

168

hair escaping his slicked back style. "I refuse to live without her." Raking his hands through his hair, he forced the errant chunk back in line. "You'll find someone who won't run from your beast, too, Adriana."

Not in this lifetime. That took trust, and trust took time, and that was something I didn't have to offer.

"Is that all?"

Val stiffened, the brother fading as the ruthless king reared his head. "No. I want to discuss what's expected of you on your trip to Guadalajara."

"Ah, yes, where I prove my worth." I rocked back on my heels and shoved my hands in my pockets. "Well, let's hear it."

"I don't have to tell you what the Muñoz Cartel has done to our family in the past. Another cartel war not only weakens our hold on our ports and distribution channels, but it also causes unnecessary bloodshed I don't need. Whoever is restructuring your former soldiers is good, I'll give him that. I've had my best men and associates pulling intel and they've come up with nothing."

"And they won't."

"How can you be so sure?"

I considered a straightforward answer, but having the upper hand felt too good. Plus, I wanted to push his buttons a little just to see how he'd react.

"Because I know how these men think. Muñoz soldiers care nothing about order and protocol. Your wife murdered their leader, and your lieutenant exposed their queen as a fraud. They're blind ants in a constant state of anarchy who'd follow the great and powerful Oz if he promised to avenge what they lost." Emboldened, I poked a finger against his chest. "Let me be clear. His name is Ignacio, but it could be Francois for all they care."

Val's face darkened. "You need to back up and remember who you're talking to."

"There he is." I smirked. "The real Valentin Carrera. The one who hates me. Nice to finally meet you, *sir*."

"*Dios mío*, would you stop being so fucking dramatic," he growled, batting my hand off his chest. "I don't understand some of the things you've done, but you're my sister, Adriana. I don't hate you."

"Your wife hates me."

"Eden is protective, that's all." He stared at me as if those five words wiped the slate clean.

They didn't.

"We had quite the chat earlier. Did she tell you that? The one where she barged into Brody's room to accuse me of murdering her family."

"Didn't you?" It wasn't a question.

"Sure, take her side."

Val chuckled on his way back to the bar. "You two are more alike than either of you will admit. Both of you were deceived by the one person who was supposed to always protect you. You both lost your brothers to a war that should've never escalated to the point it did. You're both headstrong, stubborn women with too much pride and not enough tolerance. But mostly, you're both survivors."

"I'm assuming there will be a point made eventually in this rousing speech?"

He poured his drink, and I held my breath as he sauntered toward me. Taking my chin between his thumb and forefinger, he tilted it up, forcing me to look up at him. "Tell yourself you're here to prove your worth and stake your claim in this family. Make up whatever excuse you need to in order to justify why you're really here."

"And why am I here?"

"To face your fear of isolation."

I jerked my chin out of his hold, my fingers curling around the back of the couch. "That's bullshit."

"It goes against everything you know to hand over control to me, Adriana, yet here you are. You and I, we live in a world of lies. *Narcos* don't trust easily, but when we give it, it's unwavering. To be honest, the real power begins the moment you and my wife stand on the same side of the battle line." Raising his drink, he winked before downing the whole thing. Without another word, he turned, and I stared openmouthed at his back as it rounded the corner and disappeared.

"Don't hold your breath."

Chapter Eighteen

ADRIANA

I'd never sat on a throne before.

It wasn't comfortable, but then again, we were criminals. Comfort led to complacency which opened the door to weakness. But this one suited me, and the moment I leaned against the black velvet, I felt at home here.

Wherever here was.

The room held nothing but silence. Stagnant, metallic-scented smoke clouded around me, close enough to lick my skin while maintaining a thin level of restraint. I should've feared it. I was always taught where there was smoke, there was fire, but this was my throne.

I was invincible.

Besides, if there were a fire, I would've already been consumed by flames.

"You craved the blood of the innocent."

My heart slammed against my chest, and I gripped the chair

until my arms shook. I knew that voice, but I couldn't remember why. All I knew was that the soft melodic cadence didn't belong in my circle of hell.

"Who's there?"

In response, the temperature plummeted, and the short, ragged breaths torn from my lungs materialized in front of me as a labored mist. The smoke didn't part, and she didn't walk through it, but a dark-haired woman in a white flowing dress emerged, almost as if they were two combined entities. When she lifted her head, I stared into familiar warm chocolate eyes dotted with gold.

Mother.

It was an illusion. The human eye was nothing but a passive slave to the brain's whims. The mind was a sadistic bastard, easily tricking it into seeing whatever it wanted.

"Was it worth it?" Raising a hand, she pointed toward my chest. My eyes followed her finger, trailing down to the source of that pungent metallic smell. Every part of me was covered in blood. But it wasn't mine.

"They were all guilty," I said, offering an emotionless stare to the death lying at my feet. "They hurt me. They deserved this."

"Not all of them." Her haunted eyes lowered directly in front of the base of the throne. I really didn't have time to play games with her, but I leaned forward to humor her.

Then I screamed.

Two tiny hands. Two tiny feet. Two dark and empty eyes begging me why.

My stomach roiled, and the world spun as their burned and bloodied bodies lay tattered before me, their innocent faces frozen in fear.

"No!" I screamed again. "I would never hurt a child! I only took revenge on those who hurt me so I could kill the beast!"

"Cariño, you can't slay a dragon when you're the one breathing its fire."

My eyes popped open at the familiar words, only to look into the cold eyes of my brother. "Val?" His name broke as the bravado I'd held onto came crashing down around me.

"Pity that it was all for nothing," he taunted, baring his teeth in a chilling smile while nodding at my bloody clothes. "It appears the dragon doesn't need you anymore."

"What?" I looked down to find a gaping hole in my stomach. "No!" I cried as I pressed both hands over the wound in a pathetic attempt to stop the bleeding, but it pumped out faster than I could stop it.

I slumped against my throne, a damned queen living her inevitable truth. As more blood spilled, I grew weaker. With my last breath, I turned to face my brother, but he was gone. In his place the glowing tip of a cigar sparked to life and a man's cheeks sank in as he sucked a few deep puffs.

Leaning down, his weathered face split into a stained smile. "You're a Carrera whore."

I sat up and screamed his name until I was hoarse, thrashing against a cocoon of sheets and blankets. Caught between two worlds, I desperately clawed my way out of hell, the image of his smile shoving me to near hysteria.

"Adriana!"

I wouldn't go down without a fight.

There was a groan, and fire ignited behind my eyes. "Jesus Christ, Adriana! Wake up!"

Brody?

Brightness burned my eyes the minute they cracked open, and my body felt like it had gone twelve rounds in an octagon. Fighting the urge to lash out, I shielded a hand over my eyes, squinting as they adjusted to the invasion. When the spots finally cleared, I scanned the room only to find it empty.

"Over here, genius."

Suddenly wide awake, I turned toward the sound of his voice with both barrels loaded only to stare openmouthed at what stood in the doorway.

Brody had both hands over his head, palms splayed and braced against the side molding. His sleepy face was framed by what could only be described as wild and chaotic sex hair. Yet again, he was shirtless, his arm position accentuating every toned muscle. Loose fitting sleep pants hung low on his waist— untied, of course, because, *why not*. But tied or untied, loose fit or suctioned with a vacuum seal, none of it mattered. Nothing on Earth would hide the imprint resting on his right thigh.

"See something you like?"

My head snapped up so fast, I about gave myself whiplash. "What the hell are you doing in my room?"

"You were screaming my name."

"I was not."

Releasing his hold on the doorframe, he took a few wide steps into my room, stopping at the edge of my bed and leaning one hand against the bedpost. "Right, because I'd wander down the hall half-naked at three o'clock in the morning because you screamed out Mateo's name."

I wanted to smack the smirk off his face. "Well, if I called your name, it's because I was having a nightmare. You tend to provoke those."

"Yeah?" He paused, hooking his thumb in the waistband of his pants. "Well call someone else's next time. I thought someone was killing you."

He laughed at his own joke, but his words brought my dream back in vivid color, and with it, his face. The man who gave me the choice of accepting death or delivering it was now the hunted.

In an ironic twist, Ignacio sent me to destroy Val, and now Val was sending me to destroy Ignacio. Two powerful leaders sending a woman to do their dirty work. If only men realized how predictable they were. I guided them. I moved them around like pieces on a chess board.

However, for all my bravado, here I sat unable to stop seeing *his* face. I felt his breath on my skin. I smelled his breath on my cheek. I heard the warnings in my ear, and I couldn't help but wonder if the destruction I'd so masterfully crafted would be my own.

I barely registered movement before the bed dipped with added weight. "Shit, you're shaking." There was a brief hesitation, and then two arms wrapped around me from the back.

I glanced down to see my upper arms completely engulfed in Brody's huge hands. They felt warm and safe, and I hated that I liked it, so I jerked away. "Don't touch me!"

Brody's hands flew in the air like I'd pulled a gun. "Okay, fine. I'll leave." Muttering under his breath, he got to his feet and stomped toward the door.

"Where are you going?"

He planted his feet with his back to me. Placing his hands on his hips, he tossed his head back and let out a labored breath. "Not gonna lie, Adriana, you're making it real hard to be nice to you right now."

Seconds ticked by when finally, he turned to face me. Still, I said nothing, and neither did he. The longer the silence rolled on, the more awkward it got until he caved first, dropping his chin to his chest in frustration.

A whoosh of air blew past my lips. *Thank God.* At least frustration prevented us from making eye contact. The last thing I needed was for him to see me gawking at him *again*.

"What is it you would like me to do, *princesa*?"

That was a loaded question.

I stared at the empty space next to me. The king-sized bed was ridiculously big for one person, and as much as I hated showing weakness, I hated the idea of being alone more. Clenching my teeth and my fists, I looked up at him. "Can you just sit here until I fall asleep?" Upon watching the cocky smirk peel across his face, I added, "And not make a big deal out of it?"

"Right. So, I'll just sit here and stay wide awake while you sleep."

Rolling my eyes, I flopped back down and rolled over. "Just go."

The bed dipped again, an unexpected flush spreading across my chest as he rolled against me, his unrestrained cock pressing against my ass. "No, it's fine," he said, his warm breath fanning across my bare shoulder. "At least I can keep an eye on you this way."

He shifted, and I swallowed a groan. "If I hear you jerking off, I'll dick punch you."

"You're never going to let me live that down, are you?"

"Nope."

Brody's deep throaty laugh was the last thing I remembered before drifting off into a peaceful sleep.

I woke to an empty bed.

I didn't know whether to be grateful or pissed off that Brody ditched me like a drunken one-night stand and the fact that I even wasted time caring annoyed me more than anything.

After throwing on a pair of cut off jean shorts and a black scoop-necked top, I swept my hair in a loose messy bun, grabbed my newly-packed suitcase, and headed downstairs.

I heard their whispers as soon as I reached the bottom of the staircase. Indistinguishable words, but three voices I knew weren't four for a reason. My blood heated with irritation, so lifting my heels off the marble, I shuffled on my toes toward the sitting room to find Mateo, Val, and Brody standing in a huddle. I couldn't hear what they were saying, but apparently it was serious.

Which meant I was just in time.

I placed my suitcase on the floor and flounced into the room with flair. "*Hola*, boys," I announced. "I didn't see a No Girls Allowed sign hanging outside the clubhouse, so I assume someone will fill me in on what all the secret whispering is about."

Three pairs of eyes turned my way, but when Brody's dropped from my face to my feet, then slowly slid back up again, my smirk faded.

"That's a lot more stuff than you came here with," he said, nodding at the suitcase at my feet.

I shrugged. "Your sister brought me some things this morning." Turning, I winked at Mateo. "She's a chipper one in the morning, huh?"

As usual, Mateo just raised an eyebrow.

"*Dios mío*, will you all shut the fuck up?" Val motioned for us all to sit as he made his way to the bar tucked at the front of the room.

I cocked a hip. "Don't you think it's a little early for that?"

The suction from the tequila top released with a pop.

"No."

"Well aren't you going to sit down?"

He lifted the glass of tequila to his lips with a smirk. "No."

"Can you say anything else besides, no?"

179

"No."

"Oh, for fuck's sake." It was all I could do not to roll my eyes as I sank into the same damn leather couch from last night. Mateo sat across from me, his finger rubbing back and forth across his goatee as he watched Brody's eyes bounce between the empty seat beside him and the one next to me.

This was ridiculous. Tired and irritated, I motioned to the seat next to Mateo when a slow smile broke across his face, and he lifted a long jean-clad leg, stretching it across the length of the couch.

"What are you doing?" Brody asked.

Mateo's grin widened. "Getting comfortable. There's a seat over there. Have at it."

They stared each other down, Brody scowling as Mateo smirked. Finally, Brody flipped his middle finger up and collapsed next to me muttering to himself. "Jackass."

"Well," Val said, moving in between the two pieces of furniture, a deep vertical line sinking between his eyes. "If we're done acting like *pinche idiotas*, I suggest we devise a cohesive strategy before you two go off and get yourselves killed."

Brody leaned forward with his elbows on his thighs and his hands clasped in front of him. "What did you have in mind?"

"Not fucking up."

"I'm serious, Val."

"So am I. This may be Adriana's chance to prove her loyalty to the Carreras but consider it your chance, too."

Brody's forehead wrinkled. "To do what?"

"To prove to me I shouldn't put you in the ground right next to your predecessor."

Mateo's hand dropped from his chin. "Val!"

Val didn't acknowledge him. Shoving one hand in his pocket, he lifted his glass again, his eyes locked on Brody.

"Fuck you." Brody's quiet response wasn't out of fear. It was forced control. Like when a child turned the crank on a Jack-In-The-Box as fast as they could only to suddenly stop because they knew that one last turn would cause a puppet to explode in their face.

"Brody!" This time, Mateo's shock was aimed at the man sitting beside me.

His game of chastise ping-pong grated on my nerves. "Seriously?" I growled. "Pick a side, *güey*."

Val swung his drink in Mateo's direction. "No, it's fine. I'd be angry, too, if I were about to track down the man who stole seventeen million dollars of my *jefe's* money."

I stiffened. "You know?"

Val cocked his head. "And so do you, apparently."

There was a distinct warning in his voice that self-preservation should've heeded, but defiance took over, snapping my head toward Brody. To my surprise, I found him stone-faced except for the steady tick of his jaw.

His gaze flicked up to meet Val's. "How did you find out?"

Val smiled, his lips stretching so tightly over his teeth they seemed to disappear. "I have eyes all over the world, Harcourt. You couldn't take a shit in Somalia without me knowing. However, in this case, your friend Leo Pinellas thought a breach in my highest ranks would go a long way in funding his nose candy habit."

Brody closed his eyes and tilted his head back, his steel composure cracking. "Motherfucker."

He didn't have to elaborate. I knew the words he bit back because they were the same ones sitting on my tongue. If Leo told Val about the missing shipment and the Chicago deal, what other information did he try to sell?

I wet my lips. "What else did he say?"

Val lifted a dark eyebrow. "Oh, you mean the part where you showed up at his office demanding information on one of my lieutenants?"

Shit.

I flinched, and the knee jerk reaction sparked Brody back to life, his voice as dark as his penetrating glare. "Yet you never said a word when I spent half an hour convincing you to let me bring her here."

"And neither of you questioned why I was sending you to Guadalajara together. Interesting. I expect such careless bullshit out of you, but Adriana"—Val raised his glass in my direction before turning toward the bar—"you were raised to question everyone's motives."

"Great. You knew this whole time he opened up Chicago and lost your money, and that I used it to get here." Holding Val's gaze, I gave him an intentionally loud slow clap. "Do you want a cookie?"

"Adriana!"

Twisting around, I pointed a finger at Mateo. "Okay, just so you know, that's getting really fucking annoying." Ignoring his snarl, I shifted my attention back to Val. "So, what does this mean? This whole thing was bullshit, and you're sending us to slaughter?"

Val's lips twitched, and if I didn't know any better, I'd swear he was getting a kick out of watching this play out. "Quite the opposite, actually. You see, in an interesting turn of events, I now have leverage over both of you, and your success is even more vital to your position in this cartel," he said, locking eyes with Brody. Then he turned toward me adding, "And in this family."

I watched Brody with curious eyes as he flung himself off the couch and threw his arms out wide. "Then let's do what we came here to do."

I shuddered. Not because of Val's accusation, or that we were moments away from walking into what was most likely a trap. But because for the first time since he held me against the wall of my motel room at gunpoint, I saw that flicker of darkness and an overwrought need to break and control. The perfect combination of grace and civility packaged in a man whose veins coursed with poison.

God, we were both fucked up.

"You're both to look for intel," he said. "Adriana, I need you to sniff around your old contacts and see what you can find out about this Ignacio person." I nodded, which seemed to appease him, or he lost interest because he turned his focus back to Brody. "Should you find someone of interest, your job is to secure him and call for backup." Rocking back on his heels, he shrugged. "Or if needed, eliminate the problem. Be discreet and don't raise any flags."

Right.

Because the former queen of the Muñoz clan and a blond snowflake would blend in with no problem.

Brody and I exchanged curious glances as Val walked back to the bar and opened the lower cabinet. After retrieving what he wanted, he slammed it closed and crossed the room until he stood in front of us holding four metal objects.

"Two burner phones, and two revolvers," he announced, handing one of each to both of us. Ignoring the phone, I went straight for the gun and opened the chamber.

"It's not loaded. You'll get your ammo and more weapons when you're escorted off the estate."

I slammed the chamber closed and scowled.

Brody tucked his phone and gun away. "Where are we supposed to stay?"

Still pissed off, I held the useless gun in my hand, tuning

them out as Val rattled off directions and addresses. "They should be empty. If not, make them empty. When you get to Guadalajara, you're on your own." Pausing, he reached into his pocket and pulled out a wad of cash and a set of keys, handing them to Brody. "You understand for security reasons, once you're in Muñoz territory, the Carrera name doesn't pass your lips."

Brody pocketed the cash and twirled the key ring around his finger without answering. No one said another word until he glanced down at me. "You plan on getting up, or do you expect to be carried out of here?"

Rising to my feet, I found myself face-to-face with my brother. I started this, but he'd commanded control of it. Now, I had no choice but to trust him, but there was an air of uncertainty around him that I couldn't put my finger on…

And feeling like I'd disappointed him really pissed me off.

"Val, I—"

He held up a hand. "Adriana, I told you last night I brought you here against my better judgment."

"I know."

"I also told you to never pull the same con twice. It makes you predictable, and I don't give second chances. Are we clear?"

"Very." Picking up my suitcase, I pushed all the unfamiliar emotions out of my head. I had a job to do, and nothing would stop me from seeing it through.

"Adriana?" Pausing, I glanced back over my shoulder. Val opened his mouth to say something, only to close it and shake his head. "Don't die."

Chapter Nineteen

BRODY

Morelia, Michoacán, Mexico

Adriana propped her legs up on the dashboard and groaned. "How many times are you going to mess with that thing?"

I ground my teeth, turning away from her smirk while pressing the tuner button on the radio for the tenth time. "As many times as it takes."

"Okay, suit yourself. But, look around you, counselor." She waved a hand beside me, gesturing toward barren fields. "We're in the middle of nowhere. If you think you're getting anything but static on this piece of shit," reaching over, she gave the decrepit dashboard a firm pat, "you're dreaming."

I turned the damn thing off and squeezed the steering wheel so hard my knuckles turned white. "Fine, but I'm not driving three and a half hours to Morelia in silence. It'll drive me batshit."

"So, what do you suggest?"

I shrugged, doing my best not to stare at her bare legs. "We could play *I Spy*."

She rolled her eyes. "What are we, six?" Drumming her fingernails against the console, she chewed on her lip for a moment before slamming her palm against it. "Oh, I know. Let's play truth or dare."

"In a car?"

She turned to me, a glint in her eyes. "Are you scared?"

"I'm driving in a piece of shit Toyota into Muñoz-infested territory with a woman who I'm fairly certain is the antichrist. What do you think?"

She pursed her lips. "A simple no would've sufficed." She was quiet for a moment, and I thought she let it die until a slow grin pulled at her lips. "When we get to where we're going the loser has to do whatever the winner says, no questions asked."

I wasn't stupid. I knew a con when I heard it.

"Your rules are flawed."

"How so?"

"What's to stop either of us from lying?"

"One," she said, holding up her index finger, "I don't have to lie, counselor. I've led a very full life. And two"—dropping the first finger, she lifted her middle and smirked—"I'll know if you're lying."

I decided to ignore the fact that she was still flipping me off. "How?"

"You have a tell."

"What is it?"

Folding down her middle finger, she waved her hand. "Telling you would ruin all my fun. Now stop stalling. I'll even let you go first."

"No, I insist, ladies first." I cocked my chin. "However, since there doesn't seem to be one around, you can start."

Her cocky smile faded into a scowl. "Fine. Truth or dare?"

"Truth."

"Boring." She stared out the windshield in deep thought. After five minutes of silence, she twisted in her seat, her eyes flashing. "Have you ever had sex with a *sicario*?"

"That's not fair. All my *sicarios* are men."

"Hey, it's not my fault you discriminate."

The smug grin on her face was almost enough to make me slam on the brakes just to watch the seat belt slingshot her back into the seat.

"Truth or dare?" I growled.

"Truth."

"Well, look who jumped on the boring express." I rolled my eyes as I racked my brain trying to think of something to knock her down a couple notches. Then I remembered when she barged into my office, and I smirked. "Have you ever gotten yourself off to the thought of someone in this car."

I was staring out the windshield, so I couldn't see her reaction, but I felt her body shift, and from the sudden silence, I knew I had her.

"Funny, you never stop talking, but you're suddenly really quiet, Adriana."

"Shut up."

"You have, haven't you?" I couldn't resist anymore. Turning my head, I saw that her cheeks were the color of fire, and the moment we made eye contact, she turned away.

Shit, this was better than any radio station, and I wasn't about to let it go.

Keeping one hand on the wheel, I grabbed her chin with the other and forced her eyes on me. "Oh, no, *princesa*, this game was your idea, remember? Tell the truth. Have you touched yourself while thinking about me?"

She jerked her chin out of my hold. "Maybe. It's not a big deal."

"Oh, I think it is. When did this happen?"

It took her a few moments to find her voice. "After you left my motel room, all right?"

"You mean after I had you pinned against the wall, completely at my mercy?"

Her lips thinned, but she didn't respond.

Stubborn-ass woman.

"I walked away because two more seconds and I would've kissed you while ripping that little lace dress off," I admitted, pushing her defenses a little harder.

That earned me a sharp glare. "I don't kiss."

My tongue burned with a dozen questions but asked none of them. Instead, I kept myself in check and forced her hand.

She sighed. "You kiss someone you love. I fuck, Brody. I don't kiss."

I was stunned but focused on proving my point. "Fair enough, no kiss. Want to know what I would've done after that?"

"I'm on pins and needles."

"I would've run my hands down those curves you keep throwing in my face. You wouldn't have had to get yourself off, Adriana, because right up against that wall, I would've made you come so hard, you would've collapsed."

She curled her lips and stared at the roof of the car. "*Uh-huh*, right."

"Don't believe me?"

"Oh, I'm sure the socialites you've been with have no complaints, but we're talking apples and oranges here." She tossed out one open palm and then the other to demonstrate as if I were a complete moron. "I'm not saying your vanilla way is bad, but we'd never be sexually compatible."

I was fucking with her before, but now I was pissed.

"How would you know?"

"Let's just say my sexual appetite is like a car's engine, and yours is more like a bicycle pedal." Again, she demonstrated holding on to invisible handlebars as if I were a chimpanzee who'd just learned to eat with utensils. "You strike me as more of a candlelight-and-roses-by-a-four-poster-bed type of guy. That's not me, counselor. I'm more of a dirty-fucking-on-the-hood of a car type of girl."

I should've let it die. My brain knew nothing good could come of taking this any further. Unfortunately, it wasn't my brain that was in control.

"Who are you trying to convince, *princesa*? Me or yourself?"

"What's that supposed to mean?"

"I think for once in your life, you want to hand over your coveted control and know what it feels like to submit. Only nobody has ever had the balls to make you do it."

There. I said it, and every word was true whether she wanted to admit it or not. I saw how she responded when I had a gun to her head and my hand around her throat. I understood her better than she thought. Maybe I was the only one who'd ever come close.

Our lives paralleled, forming an extremely warped yin and yang. Adriana grew up in darkness, fighting for respect, blood and death her closest childhood friends. I, on the other hand, grew up in what I thought was the light, freely given respect and adoration, ignorance and justice my most trusted confidants. Somewhere along the way, our worlds imploded and reversed. I fell into darkness while Adriana, whether she saw it or not, desperately sought out the light.

Black and white.

Dark and light.

Yes and no.

Control and submit.

She'd spent her life fighting. I'd spent my whole life giving.

For once, she wanted to surrender. For once, I wanted to take.

Yin and yang.

The sun kept me from seeing her face, but the tension in the car was palpable.

"You're wrong."

I'd had enough of this back-and-forth bullshit. Jerking the wheel to the right, I pulled the car over to the side of the road and threw it in park. Unbuckling my seat belt, I pressed one hand against her headrest and the other against the dashboard.

"Am I? Then tell me you wouldn't have loved it if I'd pressed your hands against the wall and made you watch while I took out my cock and stroked myself. Tell me you wouldn't have wanted me to grab you by the back of the legs and slam you into the wall so hard it would've knocked the breath out of you."

"Brody…"

Taking a chance, I leaned over the console until there were only inches between us, her breath heavy as I took her face in my hands. "I would've stood there making you both fear and want what I would've done next, and when you were about to break, I would've driven into you so hard, you would've screamed mine and God's name until you cried. It would've been rough and brutal until we both came harder than we'd ever come in our lives."

Her eyes fluttered closed, and her tongue darted out to lick her bottom lip. Mesmerized, I brushed my thumb against it. She rewarded me with a whimper, wrapping her hands around my forearms.

"Adriana…" I groaned, my voice rough.

"Yes?"

Grazing my lips across her cheek, I traced them against the

190

shell of her ear before whispering, "I win."

I pulled back just as her eyes popped open and her jaw dropped. Letting out an almost inhuman growl, she flung herself back into her seat as I put the car back in gear and pulled onto the road wearing a satisfied smirk.

Yin and yang.

SHE DIDN'T TALK TO ME THE REST OF THE WAY, AND BY THE TIME WE got to the stash house, it was dark, which was a good thing since it was exactly what I expected it to be—a piece of shit. A run-down barnyard red box house. Not the most subtle of colors, but that was probably why Val picked it. No one in their right mind would think the most feared man in Mexico would paint a bright red bull's eye on himself.

Which is exactly why he did.

Human instinct was trained to dismiss the obvious.

Adriana's face puckered as soon as we walked in the door. Granted, the sheets slung over the windows and the stained mattress on the floor didn't scream hygiene, but unless she wanted to sleep in the back seat of the Toyota, we didn't have many options.

Of course, saying the words out loud probably wasn't the best idea. After growling at me, she stomped into the shoebox of a bedroom and slammed the door.

An hour later, she still hadn't opened it.

Not that I'd tried to see what she was doing. I had enough on my mind without wasting time trying to decode her hot and cold routine. Grabbing a bottle of scotch from my backpack, I kicked one of the splintered chairs away from the rickety kitchen table and sat down, not even giving a shit when the bottom rung snapped in half.

Fuck it. If I fell, I fell.

Unscrewing the cap, I tipped the bottle back, draining a good four shot's worth before taking a breath. My throat ignited, and my eyes watered, but I welcomed the burn. I knew from experience it was only temporary. A few more like that, and I'd feel nothing. Numb and sedated. Just the way I liked it.

Besides, drunk me was a hell of a lot more rational than sober me.

With eighty-proof logic coursing through my veins, I could devise a plan on what to do about the shitshow my life had become without all the useless guilt getting in the way.

Men like Val and Mateo were born in this life possessing the ability to compartmentalize their conscience. I wasn't wired that way. I felt like Jekyll and Hyde molded together and stuffed into the same suit. The constant conflict between fighting to hold on to the honorable man I was and fighting the monster clawing inside my chest was wearing me down. I wasn't sure how much more I could take before Hyde turned on everyone.

Of course, that was provided I lived long enough for it to be an issue.

Letting out a huff, I turned the bottle up again. Val knew I went against a direct order and contacted Ronan Kelly personally to set up the Chicago port. If that weren't damning enough, when the Muñozs hijacked my shipment, not only did I not come clean, I let myself get backed into four different corners by Leo Pinellas *and* Adriana Carrera. Luckily, Val hadn't said shit about going through another Colombian supplier yet. Dragging Carlos into the mix might send him over the edge.

Dropping the bottle between my legs, I scrubbed a hand over my face, unfamiliar stubble raking across my palm. "What a fucking mess."

"You're just now realizing that?"

I rolled my eyes to the side, ready to tell her to go back into whatever hole she crawled out of when my mouth went dry and every drop of blood in my brain free fell straight to my groin.

Adriana leaned against the kitchen counter with her arms crossed, wearing Leighton's Texas State University T-shirt.

Wearing *only* her Texas State University T-shirt.

It hit her mid-thigh, leaving the rest of her long shapely legs to spill out of the bottom. My eyes went all unfocused, and all I wanted in life at that moment was for her to bend over.

My hand fell from my chin, almost knocking the bottle off my chair.

Cocking a hip, Adriana traced the pad of her index finger around her bottom lip. "Everything okay? You look a little flustered there, counselor."

That's the understatement of the year.

I didn't have to look down to know my cock was about to punch its way through my pants, so I dragged the bottle tight against my crotch. "Did you need something, or did the rats get tired of your bullshit, too?"

"Funny." Pushing off the wall, she pulled out the chair beside me and flopped down, legs splayed.

Fuck me.

Her T-shirt rode up her thighs, and my dick leaped with a battle cry, fighting against the constraints of the bottle. I looked everywhere but directly at her, and when she leaned forward with her hand extended, I wondered if it was possible for a human penis to shatter glass.

I pushed my chair back. "Whoa, what are you doing?"

Whatever it is, do it fast.

And hard.

With both hands.

Jesus, where did that come from?

She paused, her hand hovering over the bottle. "I'm shoving this bottle up your ass if you don't let go." When I didn't move, she sighed and wrapped her hand around the neck. "Brody, it's been a shitty day, and I want a drink. Are you going to make me beg, or not be a giant dick for once?"

"You said you didn't drink."

"Forget it." Shoving the bottle against my chest, she stood to leave when I grabbed her arm. It went against everything common sense told me to do, but I didn't want to be alone. "Fine, sit down. I'm the last one who should be casting stones here."

Her eyes narrowed, but she didn't argue, slowly sinking back into the rickety chair. "Hand it over," she demanded, holding her hand out for the bottle, but I shook my head and dug around in my backpack until I found what I was looking for. She lifted an eyebrow as I slid a crystal shot glass adorned with a golden crowned skull clutching a rose in its teeth. "You stole one of Val's personal shot glasses?"

"Correction," I said, pulling out an identical glass. "I stole two of Val's personal shot glasses."

I filled them to the top and threw my shot back immediately while Adriana wrapped her fingers around her glass, the corners of her mouth turned down as she stared into the liquid. I recognized the look on her face. I saw the same one etched across it last night.

"Do you want to tell me about your dream now?"

"It was nothing."

"It didn't seem like nothing. I've never seen you that shaken up."

Adriana glanced up, her mouth twisting into a snide smirk. "You've known me for all of four days."

"I was an attorney, Adriana." Ignoring her little pretend

yawn and eye roll, I poured myself another shot. "My job was to read people the minute they stepped up on the witness stand. I was damn good at what I did."

I prepared myself for one of her smartass comebacks but looked up to find her staring down at her glass again in silence. Finally, she gave it a spin, scotch spilling over the rim and soaking into the wood. "Do you ever have a feeling that no matter what you do things are going to end badly?"

"Yeah," I admitted, lifting another shot to my lips. "Every day of my life."

"Come on, your life can't be that bad."

Slamming the glass on the table, I sat back with a bitter smile. "The only girl I ever loved dumped me for the man who kidnapped her, and now I've sworn an oath to kiss his ass for the rest of my life. How's that?"

"You really love throwing pity parties for yourself, don't you?"

"Excuse me?"

"Oh, boo-hoo," she whined. "My unrequited love married someone else, and I can't get over it, so even though the man she married defied tradition and made me, a white man, second-in-command of an entire cartel, I'm just going to be a little bitch and whine about it."

"Jesus, what the hell is wrong with you?"

She jumped to her feet, her hands clenched into fists by her side. "Why don't you try watching the cartel you grew up believing was your destiny implode in front of your face? I ran for my life because I found out what you'd done. Instead of taking what I'd rightfully earned, I was shunned."

"Adriana…" Not sure what else to do, I stood and held out a hand, unprepared for her to slap it out of her face.

"That was my time to shine, Brody." Balling her fist, she

beat it against her chest. "That was my chance to show everyone that Marisol Muñoz was smart and brave and capable. That was my time, and you cheated me out of it!"

This time, I didn't back down. If we were doing this, we were going to do it. I was tired of dancing around it. What better place to have a shitty showdown than in a shitty shack in a shitty part of Mexico. Closing the distance between us, I wrapped my hands around her shoulders and pulled her toward me only to have her twist out of my hold.

"Don't touch me," she hissed. Swiping the back of her hand across her eyes, she picked up the still full shot glass off the table and stomped into the kitchen. Even from across the room, I could hear her labored breathing as she fought for control. Dumping the contents of the glass down the drain, she tossed it in the sink and braced her hands against the counter. "*Hijo de su puta madre.*" *Son of a bitch.* "Everybody causes cracks in me, Brody. Maybe you'll be the one who finally breaks me."

I watched her.

I listened.

And then I finally learned.

Adriana Carrera was a damn liar. She claimed she didn't want me to touch her, but nothing could be further from the truth. She pushed me away because she used control not only as a weapon but as a shield. But it was breaking her piece by piece until eventually there wouldn't be anything left but a shell.

Despite our differences. Despite our past. Despite our dislike for each other, there was a magnetic force drawing us together. Energy that left alone was destined for self-destruction, but combined, it ignited a power capable of deadly strength.

Her vulnerability awakened the monster in me...

And he was ready to feast.

Chapter Twenty

BRODY

Pouring one more shot, I tossed it back and followed her into the kitchen. I didn't ask permission. I just placed both hands on her back, feeling her body go rigid and still. Without saying a word, I dragged them down her spine to the small of her back and rounding over the ass that had played a starring role in every single dream since she stormed into my bar. Her broken groan was music to my ears, but I didn't allow myself to linger. Stepping forward, I grabbed the indentations in her hips.

"I said, don't touch me," she rasped, her breath stuttering.

She didn't mean it. We both knew it, so I pushed her into the counter, grinding against her ass. "Quiet," I commanded, dipping my nose into her hair. The minute I got a whiff of her sweet licorice scent, my cock swelled. "The rules from the game stand. You have to do what I say, no questions asked."

Adriana opened her mouth to argue, so I dug my fingers into her hips. As expected, she shut it. Such a small power play spoke volumes.

"Look at me." The minute she tilted her cheek toward me, I traced my lips across her jaw, slowly making my way to her ear. I was treading on dangerous ground, but the high was too addictive not to chase.

"I—" she whispered, trying to turn away, but I cut her off by sliding one hand from her hip up to her throat. I stroked my thumb over her pulse, feeling it dance under my command.

"No questions."

I watched the conflict play out on her face. Her every instinct told her to fight me, but she didn't. Rolling her lips over her teeth and pressing them together was her single act of defiance. I wasn't pissed. In fact, it made me smile. I knew her rules against kissing, and I had no intention of breaking them. Besides, I didn't want her mouth.

Reaching under her T-shirt, I ran my hand along her stomach, feeling her sharp inhale as I toyed with the lace at the top of her panties. Her fingers curled around the counter and the steady *thump thump thump* of her pulse under my thumb detonated as I slipped my hand inside. I closed my eyes at her tortured groan and sank my finger deep inside her.

Fucking hell, she was wet, and I couldn't get enough. I pumped faster, adding a second finger. The more I pumped, the tighter her walls gripped me, and I almost came undone imagining what they'd do to my cock.

Adriana's head flopped back against my chest. "Oh, fuck."

Keeping up my brutal pace, I shifted my hand, pressing down on her clit as I thrusted. We weren't looking at each other, but neither of us cared to. This was primal need in its most basic form. Adriana's clenched hands shook against the counter as she whimpered, a sound magnified by the feel of her ass grinding against my cock.

Jesus, if she didn't stop, I was going to come in my fucking pants.

"Give me what I want, Adriana," I growled in her ear. Curling my fingers, I sought out the one spot I knew would bring her to her knees.

"Shit!" she screamed, shaking violently. "*Ay Dios mío, por favor no pares. No pares.*"

No worries, princesa. I have no intentions on stopping.

"Scream my name, Adriana, or I swear I'll throw you on this counter and eat your pussy until you pass out."

I hit the fleshy button inside her again, and she erupted like a volcano, convulsing and clawing my arm as her ear-piercing scream rattled the thin windows. "Brody! Brody! Brody!"

I released my hold on her throat, and she collapsed against the sink, the demon that haunted her gone, at least for now. She was spent but calm. Almost as if by stripping away her control, I actually restored it.

It was a heady feeling. And then the reality of what we'd just done crashed down around her. Adriana's spine stiffened, and she pulled away. I could see her frantically rebuilding the wall I'd just knocked down, and if she thought I'd allow it, she was crazy.

Laying a hand on her shoulder, I spun her around, making her watch as I sucked the taste of her off one finger at a time. When the last one was licked clean, I straightened her T-shirt and ran the pad of my thumb over her bottom lip. "Get some sleep, *princesa*. We have a long day tomorrow."

She blinked. "There's only one mattress."

"I'll take the couch."

"Are you sure?"

I smirked at the subtle question in her voice. I'd have to jerk off all night just to be able to function tomorrow, but tonight's experiment was over.

"Adriana, if I lie next to you, I'm fucking you."

All the color drained from her face, and she took a step back.

I walked away with a wink. "That's what I thought."

I CHECKED MY WATCH AGAIN, CURSING UNDER MY BREATH AS I POUNDED my fist on the door for the third time. "Adriana, this isn't a damn vacation. Get your ass up and get dressed. We still have a three-hour drive to Guadalajara."

Silence.

Propping my free hand against the doorframe, I pressed my thumb against my temple, trying to ward off the headache brewing behind my eyes. Most of it stemmed from irritation from Adriana's stubbornness. However, spending the night wide awake while jerking my dick raw didn't help my mood.

I pounded again. "Adriana, open the door, or I'm leaving your ass here."

Lie.

There was no way in hell I'd walk my ass into Muñoz territory without her by my side. I had a reckless streak, not a death wish. Still, I had the keys and a drug house in the middle of Mexico was the last place I assumed she'd want to be stranded.

Threats had a fifty-fifty payout, but I was getting antsy.

Silence.

"Fuck this." Planting one foot on the floor, I grasped the doorframe and pushed my heel out. I let out a grunt as my foot thrust against the flimsy wood. Once, it rattled. Twice, the center bulged. On the third kick, the hinges tore away from the wall, sending the whole damn thing crashing inward. As I stepped inside the tiny room, it took me a minute to realize what I saw.

And then I got pissed.

Adriana lay curled into a little ball on the dirty mattress, her knees tucked into her chest and her arms crossed low around her waist. Her long hair hung like a blanket over her face, but I had no doubt she was still asleep.

My entire life was on the line, and she slept like a baby.

I sank the toe of my shoe in her ass cheek. "Adriana, if you don't get up in the next five seconds, I'm dragging you off that mattress by your feet."

She didn't move. In fact, as still as she was, it didn't look like she was even breathing.

Fuck.

Blind instinct brought me to my knees next to her, my hand pressed against her back. I held my own breath until I felt the shallow rise of hers, rattled, but steady. My head dropped back in relief, and I sank onto the mattress next to her. "Jesus, Carrera."

My unguarded relief confused me. It wasn't like I wanted her dead, but the fear that shot through me in those few seconds unnerved me. The conflict sparked a wave of anger in me I never saw coming, and my fingers dug in between her ribs.

"Brody?"

I had no idea if it was the confused, fragile look in her dark eyes that did it, or if it was the gray tint of her skin, but the need to lash out diffused. It was only when her eyes creased in pain, that I realized how hard I still gripped her. Snapping my arm back, I ran my hand through my hair, tugging hard at the strands.

"You wouldn't wake up." Clearing my throat, I scratched the back of my head and stared through the destroyed doorway. "I called you four times."

"I'm tired."

"Yeah, well take a number, *princesa*. We all are," I huffed, wincing as the words left my mouth. I knew I was being a dick.

Adriana groaned behind me. "I just don't feel so good. Must be the scotch."

"You didn't drink any," I muttered. When she didn't answer, I risked a glance over my shoulder, noticing she now sat hugging her knees against her chest. "You poured your shot down the sink remember?"

Her gray skin flushed a bright pink. "Right."

"Yeah, right," I echoed.

I didn't have to elaborate. I could tell by the way her breath hitched that she was thinking about what happened after that. I had no doubt we'd send each other straight to hell, but if last night was any indication of what was to come, the ride would be worth the fall.

I climbed to my feet before I started the descent right here. "Get dressed. We have to get on the road if we want to be in Guadalajara by noon."

Offering me a quick nod, she tightened her arms around her middle and grimaced. "I'll take a quick shower. I'll be ten minutes."

I raised an eyebrow. She sure looked hungover. "Are you sure you're all right?"

Forcing a smile, she tossed out a weak excuse. "I'm just hungry. Once we stop for breakfast, I'll be fine."

I didn't buy the smile or the excuse, but I didn't push it. I turned to leave when my eye landed on her dingy army green bag lying on the floor. I didn't even remember her bringing the damn thing. Jesus, like one packed suitcase wasn't enough? We were cartel runners on an intel mission, not rock stars on a world tour.

Fucking women.

Grumbling, I grabbed it off the floor. "I'll take this to the car."

"No!" I didn't even have time to react before Adriana

launched herself off the mattress and ripped the bag out of my hands. Stepping back, I eyed her suspiciously, and she offered me another fake grin. "I mean, I need that. Girl stuff." Climbing to her feet, she ran into the bathroom and slammed the door behind her, leaving me with a whole lot of questions and no answers.

Like the line of bullshit she just tried to sell me.

That woman rode my hand like she was on the final straightaway at the Kentucky Derby, came like a tsunami, then watched me lick it off my fingers like it was goddamn candy.

Girl stuff, my ass.

She was lying, and I'd find out why.

I didn't have the highest conviction rate in Texas for nothing.

Chapter Twenty-One

ADRIANA

Guadalajara, Jalisco, Mexico

Besides the crackling static from useless radio stations, Brody and I spent the first hour and a half of the drive to Guadalajara in complete silence. Since the last twenty-four hours spun on a continuous loop in my head, I couldn't decide if I was grateful for it or unnerved by it.

I was grateful he didn't care to analyze and dissect what happened between us. And what happened was that everything had turned upside down. Layers of skin were shedding, and I felt more exposed sitting in this car than when I hung half-naked from the rafters of a warehouse.

I came to Houston with a plan. Everything so far had fallen into place. Box after box checked off as if I'd bound everyone to marionette strings. I made them move. I made them dance. Then I somehow twisted the strings.

However, I was unsettled because last night should never have happened. As confident as I was playing the seductress, I'd never found myself so entangled in a web that I couldn't walk away. But the minute Brody touched me, not only was I entangled in his web, I wanted to be his prey. Breathlessly waiting to be devoured inch by inch.

In one weak moment, the tables turned, and I found my wrists bound by wires and dancing to his command. My body was his to manipulate and his to control. My lips called out his name both pleading for mercy until I shattered into irreparable pieces.

And the worst part of it all?

I wanted more.

If he hadn't walked away, I would've handed over something he hadn't earned, and would never deserve.

The more I thought about it, the more claustrophobic I got. Passing cars became a swirl of blurred colors, and my vision darkened. I gripped the edge of my seat, a thin layer of sweat beading across my top lip.

I had to get out of this car.

"I have to get out of this car," I blurted out, shocked to hear the words in my head come out of my mouth.

Glancing briefly away from the road, Brody nodded toward the passenger door. "Be my guest."

"I'm serious."

"Me, too."

"Brody, I'm not jumping out of a moving car."

Taking one hand off the wheel, he fumbled with the radio tuner. "Then I suggest you sit back and ignore me for another hour and a half."

I stared at him, waiting for the punchline, only there wasn't one. He just kept punching buttons, catching seconds of a song before it was swallowed by static. Letting out a growl, I knocked his hand out of the way and turned the damn thing off.

"Hey, I was listening to that!"

"Yes, unfortunately, I was, too. A hundred and eighty minutes of choppy static, and it's driving me fucking *loca*!" I screamed the last word, wishing I could've punched him without risking an accident.

I wasn't surprised he was acting like such an asshole. He was pissed about my overreaction about my bag, but if he was waiting for an explanation before dropping the attitude, the next few days would be very quiet.

I let him pout for a few minutes before trying again. "Are you hungry?"

"I could eat."

"Good. In about twenty minutes take a right. I'm about to introduce you to food cart dining."

Brody's eyebrows shot up, worried lines creasing across his forehead. "I'm sorry, did you say food cart? As in food made in a cart?"

"You're not just a pretty face, are you?" Laughing at his pissed off glare, I sat back in my seat and smirked. "Don't worry, counselor. If you get sick, there's a hospital van just down the road."

WIPING A STREAM OF *CREMA* FROM HIS CHIN, BRODY GAVE ME A reluctant stare and mumbled around a mouthful of food, "Okay, I admit, you were right."

Leaning back, I popped the last piece of bread in my mouth and grinned. "I'm sorry, could you say that again a little louder?"

He flipped his middle finger and swallowed. "Don't push it." Attacking the last bite of his sandwich with gusto, he crumpled up the paper, tossing it on the hood of the car before leaning back on his palms. "What was that again?"

"*Pambazo*. It's fried bread dipped in red *guajillo* pepper sauce filled with *papas con chorizo.*" At his lifted eyebrow, I added, "Potatoes and spicy sausage. My *mamá…*" I paused and stared at my lap. "I mean, Josefina used to make them for Manuel and me all the time."

"It's okay to remember the good times with her, Adriana. She wasn't a part of what happened to you."

Tilting my chin toward him, I squinted into the sunlight. "Wasn't she? Can you honestly tell me that hours after Alejandro Carrera's wife, sister-in-law, and one-year-old daughter were murdered, her husband showed up with a one-year-old baby, and she didn't know exactly what happened?"

Brody thought for a moment. The lawyer in him wanted to argue for the opposition but he couldn't. There wasn't one. "No," he said, letting out a breath. "I can't."

"Just because there's no blood on the hand, it doesn't mean the stain isn't there. Guilt is guilt. The only difference is the perception of severity. So, you tell me, which is worse, committing a sin or hiding it?"

Brody didn't say anything, and I didn't expect him to. If I hadn't figured it out in six months, how could I expect him to do it in six seconds? There was no quick and easy answer.

"Come on," I said, gathering our trash and sliding off the hood of the car. "We have places to be and people to see."

Following after me, he leaned forward, pressing his palms against the hood. "Do you have a lead?"

It was a loaded question, but one I expected. I considered my answer as I chucked our food wrappers in a nearby trash can. Dusting my hands off, I turned around and winked. "I just might."

"I don't like when you get that look on your face."

"What look?"

"That one," he said, jabbing his finger across the hood. Just to rile him up, I turned my smirk into a pout, and he responded with crossed arms and a stony stare. "Don't be cute. When your eyes get all shiny, I end up blackmailed into doing shit that could get me killed."

He made it too easy sometimes.

Trailing a finger along the front of the car, I put an extra sway in my hips and sauntered toward him. "Aw, you noticed my eyes?"

A groan rumbled in his throat. "You're such a pain in my ass."

I had to admit, as much as watching Brody go from polished to prickled entertained me, we had more important things to do. "Relax. I've got a connection."

"What kind of connection?"

"I know a guy who owns a club. There's a good chance he might have some information."

I glanced at him out of the corner of my eye, because I knew what he was thinking, and I was right. His face said it all. Eyes narrowed. Lips pressed tightly together. Arms locked over his chest. "Don't look at me like that, you'll be fine." His nod wasn't exactly a ringing endorsement, but I'd take it. However, when he dropped his arms, my eyes locked on the light blue tie hanging around his neck. "Well, maybe."

He rolled his eyes. "What now?"

"Your clothes."

"What's wrong with them?" His confusion would've been almost comical if he weren't dead serious. "This is an Armani suit."

"You look like an investment banker. Did you bring anything else?"

"I brought black slacks and a polo."

I pressed my hands over my eyes. If I made it back to Mexico City alive, I'd kill Val for this. I had to think fast. Waiting until we made it to Guadalajara wasn't an option. I was good, but I wasn't sure I could pull a miracle out of my ass.

Opening my eyes, I held out my hand. "*¡Hijo de tu puta madre!* Give me the keys. I'm taking you shopping."

"The hell you are."

"I don't remember asking for your opinion." Dirt kicked up around my heels as I stomped around him and snatched the keys out of his hand. "Now get in the damn car. As impossible of a task as it is, you have to try to blend in. If you walk into this place looking like a Wall Street Ken doll, you're going to get us both killed."

"Jesus, who owns this bar?"

I flung the driver's side door open and paused, questioning my own sanity. "My ex."

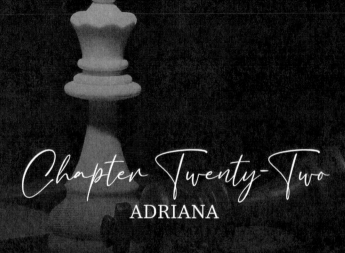

Chapter Twenty-Two

ADRIANA

If there were a rating system for stash houses, this one would be a two star. A step above last night's which would've received about fifty health code violations and a tetanus shot.

At least I didn't hear the sound of rodents running through the walls, and there were real beds instead of roadside mattresses. Plus, the shower had hot water and a tub that didn't look like the remnants of a crime scene.

My standards had seriously taken a nosedive.

However, there were so many cracks in the bathroom mirror, it was like trying to get dressed in a funhouse. I had no idea if my smoky eye makeup made me look like a sultry vixen or a rabid raccoon. Sighing, I tucked a stray piece of hair inside my wig and gave myself one last check.

"I'm not wearing this," Brody called from the bedroom.

"Yes, you are."

Our shopping excursion was an exercise in patience and

restraint. Both of which were required not to kill him and dump his body on the side of the road. He argued with everything I said, refused to try clothes on, and sulked the rest of the way to Guadalajara.

"Stop being so dramatic. I'm sure you look good." Giving my lips one last swipe of red lipstick, I swung the door open and froze. My mouth went dry, and I couldn't speak. All I could do was stare.

Black boots replaced his pretentious designer dress shoes, and the tailored suit pants I had to pry out of his hands were gone. In their place were black jeans that hugged him in all the right places. Wall Street Ken left his starched white shirt, power tie, and jacket behind and got dirty with a fitted black button up, and I couldn't help but wonder if I was a mad genius or a witch with a death wish.

His eyes were still lowered as he held out his arms, the sleeves rolled up. "I look like I'm about to tie a woman to some train tracks."

I wasn't listening to a word he said. I was too busy following the sculptured muscles up his thick forearms until they disappeared under the dark fabric of his shirt. Before I could stop myself, I moved from the doorway and stood in front of him, my hands on his collar.

Brody's head snapped up, his jaw going slack as he took in my dress. "Jesus."

Folding down the upturned side of his collar, I smoothed it over the tight cords in his neck. The air between us crackled with unleashed tension, and the way he looked down at me had me struggling for words.

Clearing my throat, I lowered my hand and stepped back. "There. It's fixed."

"That dress is…" He swallowed and shook his head.

"Damn."

I felt my cheeks flush and lowered my gaze at the skintight red dress while trailing a hand over my stomach. "Do you like it? It's your sister's."

He glanced down at the prominent bulge pushing against his zipper. "I'm going to defer to visual cues to answer your question and pretend like I didn't hear that last part."

I laughed. "Fair enough. Are you ready to do this?"

His response was quick and simple. "Not in the least." Pushing his fingers into the small of my back, he maneuvered me toward the front door. Just as I was about to open it, he tightened his hold on my waist. "By the way, what's with the wig?"

I was waiting for that.

Did I pick the color on purpose? Maybe. Maybe I wanted to see how he'd react. Maybe I wanted to prove a point. Maybe I wanted to give him a subtle reminder of what was at stake. Or maybe a part of me had an innate need to correct the imbalance of power he'd created.

Glancing over my shoulder, I ran a piece of the bright red, bob-cut wig between my fingers. "Camouflage. I can't risk being recognized. It only takes one Muñoz asshole to spread the word I'm looking for Ignacio, and this will be over before it even starts."

"So, this ex, how close are you two?"

"Not very." My answer seemed to appease him. He ushered me out the door, the deep line between his eyes relaxing, only to reappear when I added, "I mean, how close can you be after breaking off an engagement?"

EL PALACIO WAS ON FIRE TONIGHT.

Flashing strobe lights flickered around the darkened nightclub, painting everything in shades of magenta and purple as the rhythmic beat of reggaeton vibrated the walls. Brody stood behind me scowling as I paid our cover fee, and I would've slapped him if it wouldn't have drawn even more attention to us. He already stuck out like bright yellow caution tape. Causing a scene wouldn't help the situation.

"If it wouldn't be too much of an inconvenience, could you take that stick out of your ass?" I hissed, tucking a wad of pesos back into my purse. "People are staring."

"We waited in line for over an hour."

"Your point?"

His nostrils flared, shifting closer as more people filtered in. "I would've thought the owner's fiancée would have expedited entry."

I groaned. "Ex-fiancée, and are we still talking about this?"

"You tell me." Clenching his fists, he crowded against me. "Up until an hour ago, I was under the impression we were going into this thing blind. As crazy as it sounds, I thought maybe we were on the same side, but you keep doing shit to prove my instincts were right about you."

"And what instincts would that be?"

Crowd. Step. Crowd. Step.

To the casual onlooker, our habitual catch and release ballet seemed like a mating dance. In reality, it was a never-ending chase between stalker and prey. Only the roles weren't defined and always reversed in the middle of the hunt.

"That you're hiding something." He tilted his head, and the scent of scotch and sage hit me so hard I stumbled. Without hesitation, he slipped an arm around my waist, pulling me close to his chest and further toward the edge.

I felt myself weakening. Every time my head put an iron

214

wall between us, my body reminded me it wasn't the only one in control.

With one hand digging into my hip, Brody wrapped the other around the back of my neck, stroking his thumb up the length of my throat until it came to rest under my chin. "Maybe you're being set up, but there's something else going on." He tilted my head back, forcing me to look up at him. "You can spin all the bullshit lies you want, Adriana. I'm going to find out what it is, and when I do, you'd better hope it doesn't involve Val or his family or—"

"Or, what?" I challenged. "You'll kill me?"

A small smile tugged at the corner of his mouth. "Don't push me, Carrera. You won't like what happens."

"Don't threaten me, Harcourt. You already know what happens."

His face boiled with rage, and at that moment I had no idea if I wanted to watch him burn and dance in his ashes or stoke the fire and get licked by the flames. Twisting out of his hold, I glared at him before heading toward the bar, his mocking voice echoing in my ears.

"So, do you actually have a plan, or are you winging this whole thing?"

"Watch and learn, counselor."

I assumed he followed behind me, but I didn't particularly care. By the time I pushed my way through the throngs of people, my walls were firmly in place, and it was showtime.

No fewer than four bartenders raced around filling drink orders, sweat pouring down their temples. Leaning over the bar, I put my assets on display while watching everyone's movements. When I caught the one in the middle sneaking repeated glances at my chest as he wiped down the bar, I smiled.

Folding my arms over the chrome railing, I painted on a

seductive smile and crooked a finger, beckoning him over. Ignoring the protests and raised hands, he made his way toward me.

"Busy night?" I purred in Spanish.

The bartender's lips twisted. "Are you going to point out the obvious or order a drink?"

"That depends"—narrowing my eyes, I peered at his nametag—"Tomás. What's the most expensive scotch you have?"

Dropping the rag, he glanced behind him at the rows of liquor bottles spanning the length of the bar. "I think we have some Johnnie Walker Blue. You sure you can afford it, *mami*? It's twelve hundred pesos a shot."

I had no intention of paying for it, but he didn't have to know that.

"Make it two."

I didn't have to wait long before he set two shot glasses and a bill in front of me. "Twenty-four hundred pesos." I raised an eyebrow, and he shrugged. "I have rules against running tabs for Johnnie."

I let out a heavy sigh. I'd hoped to coax the information out of him, but it was obvious he'd played this game before. He was good, but I was better.

"I'm the exception to your rule."

He snorted, turning away to take another drink order. "Says who?"

"Cristiano." The name rolled off my tongue with ease. "Care to ask him, or would you like me to?"

Tomás froze, the woman waving money in his face forgotten. My pulse raced as he turned his narrowed eyes back to me. "Who *are* you?"

"I'm someone who's going to have your ass fired if you

don't tell me where to find Cristiano in the next five seconds."

"I don't know where he is."

"Four."

Bending down, he dug a beer bottle out of the cooler and popped the cap. "I said, I don't know."

"Three."

"You've got *cojones*, you know that?" he growled, handing the bottle to the annoying bitch with the fistful of pesos.

"Two."

He was in my face before I could hit one. "I haven't seen him tonight, but I can take you to his office." He held up a hand as I indulged in a victorious smile. "You're on your own after that." After stopping to have a few heated words with one of the other bartenders, he rounded the corner and glared at me.

I slid off the bar stool and turned halfway around when I remembered the scotch. Grabbing a shot in each hand, I spun around and slammed into a wall of hard muscle.

"What the hell was that?"

"Why? Are you jealous, *papi*?"

"No," Brody bit out through clenched teeth. "I'm tired of standing over here with my dick in my hand while you run a solo operation."

Glancing down, I cocked an eyebrow. "You really shouldn't have your dick out in here. It isn't that type of club."

A low growl rumbled in his throat. "You know what I mean, Adriana. What the hell were you trying to sell over there?"

"Nothing. I was buying." I held up the glasses. "Two shots of Johnnie Walker Blue." Noticing they were half empty and the front of his shirt was soaked, a wicked smile curved my lips. "Well, now I guess it's technically only one shot of Johnnie Walker Blue." Shoving a glass in his hand, I pinched his drenched shirt between my index finger and thumb and winked. "But if you want the other one, you'll have to suck yourself."

The cords in Brody's neck strained so hard, I was afraid they'd snap. As entertaining as this was, I caught Tomás's impatient stare out of the corner of my eye. Clinking our glasses together, I poured what was left from mine into his and tucked the empty one into his shirt pocket. "Try not to get yourself killed while I'm gone."

I took one step before he grabbed my arm and snapped me back. "Where do you think you're going?"

"To get information. You really should keep up."

"Not without me."

I laughed, and then his eyes darkened. Holy shit, he was serious. "I don't think so."

"Is that him?" he asked, nodding toward Tomás. "Is that your *fiancé*?" He growled the word with such contempt, I found myself torn between being wanting to laugh in his face and wanting to kick his ass.

I settled for jerking out of his hold and crossing my arms over my chest. "Ex-fiancé, and no. That's a random bartender. However, he's taking me to Cristiano's office."

"Then I'm definitely going."

"Okay, pump your brakes, caveman. I can handle this myself. Besides, if you think a Muñoz associate is going to say shit with you in the room, you've lost your damn mind."

I realized that was probably the wrong thing to say the minute his face turned blood red and a vein in the middle of his forehead started pulsing. "He's a fucking Muñoz?" he roared. "Are you crazy?"

"Would you keep your voice down?" I hissed. "Yes, but he's not a part of this."

"You can't be that stupid."

This fucker wants to die tonight.

"Look, *gringo*," I warned, jabbing a sharp nail into his chest. "Cris would never hurt me or betray me. I'm safe with him."

"So now he's Cris, huh?"

I threw my hands in the air. "*Dios mío*, I can't win with you."

"*¿Vas a venir hoy?*" *Are you coming today?*

I glanced over my shoulder to where Tomás impatiently tapped his toe. *Shit.* I'd forgotten all about him. Scrubbing a hand over my face, I steadied my voice, leaving no room for argument. "Look, this might be our only chance to find out where Ignacio is hiding. Don't screw this up for me, Brody. You're not the only one who has a score to settle."

He stared at me before finally exhaling a hard breath through his nose. "If you're not back in ten minutes, I'm coming after you."

I didn't say anything. What was the use? He'd only argue and waste more time. Besides, I knew his threat was empty. Cristiano had guards stationed at every possible entrance to the second level. He'd never make it past the dance floor.

Without another word, I walked away, following Tomás through a secured doorway, down three darkened hallways, and into a familiar elevator that let us out in front of an ominous black door.

He stopped so suddenly I almost barreled into the back of him. "I need a name."

I blinked up at him, debating what to say. The one on my tongue burned and to speak it out loud felt like serving myself up on an altar of the damned. But, to cross that threshold, I knew there was only one answer. "Marisol."

"Stay here," he instructed as he knocked an intricate code on the door and waited. Eventually, the door clicked, and he disappeared inside.

I hated the way my stomach seesawed back and forth while I waited for him to return. A few moments later, the door opened, and Tomás nodded. "Go on in."

Blowing out a nervous breath, I pushed my shoulders back and moved past him, the words I assured Brody now singing in my ear like a taunting child.

"Cris would never hurt me or betray me. I'm safe with him."

However, the moment I stepped into his office, my past circled around me.

It watched.

It waited.

And then it swallowed me whole.

"Marisol Muñoz. I've been waiting for you."

Chapter Twenty-Three

ADRIANA

Cristiano Vergara sat behind a sleek black desk, his elbows propped on the arms of his chair and his fingers steepled together under his chin. He looked older. Colder. Iniquitous with a razor edge that sent a chill down my spine. His eyes, the same ones that hypnotized me as an impetuous young girl, now held me immobile in the open doorway as a grown woman. Blue as the ocean with a depth that hid just as many secrets, they ripped back the layers of time as if they never existed.

Forcing my body to relax, I cocked my hip against the doorframe and shrugged the opposite shoulder. "I like to make an entrance." My confidence sounded weak, but there was no turning back now.

Cristiano raised a dark eyebrow. "You always did. But a man has his limits, Mari. My patience isn't infinite."

I swallowed hard, trying not to cringe at that name. "Well, you know what they say, good things come to those who wait."

"Do you also know what they say happens when a woman keeps a man waiting?"

I flashed him a wicked grin. "She holds all the cards?"

"He reflects on her shortcomings." His familiar eyes flashed, sending an unspoken message.

Our past granted me certain privileges, but my silence set limitations. At the end of the day, a Carrera was still a Carrera.

My name was a ticking time bomb, and that was why I pushed past his blatant intimidation and walked into his office with conviction, closing the door behind me. Standing in front of his desk, I glanced down at the wingback chair beside me with disdain. It was just a chair but lowering myself in front of him created uneven ground. So instead, I braced my palms on the edge of his desk and slid on top of it, crossing my legs with a wink.

The permanent scowl he wore in response to my defiance was remorseless and calculating. He looked decades older than his twenty-four years, and that was what made him so dangerous. Tall, muscular, with skin dark enough to earn a rank but light enough to raise an eyebrow. Men let their guard down around him because he didn't look the part. He looked more like an underwear model than a ruthless killer. Underestimating him was always their downfall.

"It appears good news travels fast."

He didn't waste any time getting to the point. "They're looking for you," he said, lowering his hands. "It took balls to come here."

"Yet, you knew I would."

That earned me a ghost of a smile. "A tiger doesn't change her stripes. It doesn't matter what ambush she belongs to."

Underestimating Cristiano was both a mistake and an asset. No one on Earth knew me like he did, which gave him the unique ability to anticipate my moves before I made them. Five minutes ago, I would've sworn on my life he'd never use that power against me, but now, I wasn't so sure.

My hands clenched the edge of the desk, and I looked away. "Am I that predictable?"

"No, you're that proud. And a fighter. I knew you'd come to clear your name eventually."

It was time to address the elephant in the room. Twisting around, I braced a hand behind me and held his stare. "Speaking of which, I go by Adriana now, not Marisol." I held my breath, bracing for the storm to roll across his face, only to find an indecent smile.

"So I've heard." Leaning forward, his smile widened. "Kind of scandalous to know I slept with the enemy for so many years."

"Nothing about this is funny, Cris."

"I know." His voice lowered, his smile fading. "I told you, I've *heard*." A sudden rustling drew my glance down to a stack of papers mangled in his clenched fist. "If I ever get my hands on the man who touched you—"

I laid my hand over his fist. "You won't do a damn thing. This is my fight, not yours."

Cristiano's eyes went unfocused, and his face pinched together. For a moment, I thought I'd gone too far. But as soon as they opened, the icy blue flooded with warmth, and the lines in his face turned downward.

Moving his hand out from under mine, he pushed out of his chair and paced. I couldn't help but smile as he dove a hand in his hair, tugging at the brown strands until they pointed in every direction except the ones they were meant to. The ritual was so familiar that it was almost comforting.

This was the Cristiano I knew.

This was the one who would help me.

I watched and waited until his frantic pacing came to a stop right in front of me. Pulling back, he studied me. "How are you?"

I snorted. "Oh, just great. Escaping certain death by my own men kicked off one hell of a summer but kissing a man's ass who I was groomed my whole life to hate really enhanced the excitement."

"Mari…"

"But the biggest thrill has come from fighting an invisible man who's decided to stir up a pot of shit soup and slap my name on it." I clapped my hands together for dramatic effect.

He engulfed my wrists between two strong inked hands and gave me a pointed look. "I'm not talking about that, and you know it. How *are* you?"

"I'm fine."

"Bullshit."

I dropped my head back. "If you don't believe me, then why ask?"

"Stay with me."

I laughed out loud. "Yeah, okay." Sliding off the desk, I tried to pull away from him when his grip tightened, his serious expression taking me off guard.

"I have connections, people who can get you to the top of—"

"No!" I yelled, jerking away from him, his eyes narrowing at the force of my outburst. Shit. He'd taken this conversation to a place I refused to go. I needed to redirect it back on track before he forced me to sever what little connection we had left. Palming my forehead, I let out a frustrated breath. "Look, Cris, I know you're trying to help, but I don't have a lot of time."

"I know."

"Then stop arguing with me and help me stop this *pendejo*."

He crossed his arms, his stare evasive. "Even if I know

something, what makes you think I'll tell you? After all, *El Palacio* is still a Muñoz front."

"Because a lion doesn't stop protecting his mate just because she left the pride," I said, throwing his own metaphor in his face.

I waited. For what, I wasn't sure. For an argument? For vindication? For the door to be slammed in my face? What I got was a genuine smile as he shook his head in concession. "This is new," he said, running a lock of my red wig through his fingers.

I grinned. "Do you like it?"

"No, but it definitely matches your temper." Tapping me on the nose, he leaned against the edge of his desk. "So, what do you know so far?"

Now it was my turn to pace. "His name is Ignacio. I know he has hijacked at least three Carrera shipments worth over thirty million. I know the Carreras captured one of the men who pulled the Chicago job." Stopping to take a breath, I turned on my heels and launched into more word vomit. "His name was José Rojas, and yes, that's in the past tense because he's dead. He was the asshole with my name in his mouth who set this whole thing in motion. I also know this Ignacio fucker scared the shit out of Leo Pinellas enough to put a gun in his own mouth right in front of me."

"You *have* been busy," he noted, stroking his chin.

I groaned, my nerves almost shot. "Cris…"

Closing the distance between us, he settled a heavy hand on my shoulder. "I don't know who he is or his last name." He tipped my chin up, and I met with eyes so serious I had to remind myself to breathe. "But I can tell you to stop chasing ghosts and start opening up closets. They're full of skeletons that have been locked up for a long time."

"What does that even mean?"

"This isn't about an outsider coming in to take over. This is a vendetta. You want to find the truth? You need to look in your own backyard."

"How would you know something like that?" I swallowed hard, not sure what I was more afraid of—his silence or his answer.

He didn't answer, and we stared at each other in silence, the words he said breaking apart and piecing back together in my head

"I don't..." Still in a daze, my voice trailed off as distant shouting drew my attention toward the closed door. Maybe subconsciously, I knew, and that was why I waited, listening as they grew closer and louder until finally capped off by the sound of bone hitting bone and a muffled grunt.

I should've reacted faster.

I should've held my ground with Cristiano.

I should've done a lot of things.

But I didn't.

Instead, I stood there like a statue as the door flew open, slamming into the wall behind it and then bouncing back into an open palm.

An open palm attached to an arm wearing a black button up soaked with Johnnie Walker Blue.

"Your ten minutes are up."

Chapter Twenty-Four

BRODY

The command may have been directed at Adriana, but my eyes never left the asshole with his hands all over her.

Rage tore through me, my hands fisting by my side itching to take another swing. Coming here was risky, if not suicidal. I had a feeling not too many Muñoz men would dare bulldoze their way into this guy's office, let alone a Carrera.

The man's gaze shifted from me to Adriana. "Friend of yours?"

Adriana shifted under the weight of his hands, pulling away and crossing her arms over her chest. "Not even close."

Not even close? Was she serious? Every fiber in my body wanted to yell, *"Last night I had my hand buried in your pussy. How's that for close?"*

I scowled, and a clamor in the hallway broke the tension. All three of us turned as one of his men pushed past me, a stream of red blood pouring from his nose, his expression a cross between fury and fear.

"I'm sorry, *jefe*," he whined, pointing back at me. "I had him, but he pulled a gun on me, and—"

"It was a finger gun, you pathetic sack of shit!" Pointing my index finger, I cocked my thumb while tucking the other three fingers into my palm, and the guard's hands flew in the air. I blinked at him a few times before swinging around to face his boss. "Where the hell do you recruit these guys? Walmart?"

His boss crooked a finger over his lips, attempting to hide a smirk. "Let him in."

The guard reluctantly stepped aside, and I stormed past him, only stopping long enough to kick my heel back and send the door slamming into his face.

"Was that necessary?" Adriana hissed.

The condescension in her voice kicked my temper into overdrive. In three wide steps I stood in front of her, rage vibrating off me in waves. "I said ten minutes. I don't make idle threats. You should know that by now."

"Brody…"

The smirking man perked up at the mention of my name, appearing by her side out of nowhere. "Brody Harcourt," he said, and I wanted to punch that smug look off his face. "I've heard a lot about you."

"Funny, I've never heard a damn word about you."

It took everything I had in me to remain in control. My body felt like a stripped electrical cord, and the more agitated I got, the more it seemed to amuse him.

"Cristiano Vergara," he said, sticking out his hand.

The infamous Cristiano.

I hated him.

I stared at his offered hand, ignoring it to turn toward Adriana. She'd been gone so long, I'd convinced myself she was being held against her will, enduring all kinds of horrific torture. So, the first thing I did was search her skin for signs of bruising.

The tension in my body uncoiled as my hand grazed her flawless cheek. "Are you all right?"

She swallowed hard and nodded, the anger on her face fading. The movement inadvertently caused my thumb to caress her skin. I didn't want to admit what that small touch did to me. I only wanted to do it again. So, I did, this time brushing the pad of my thumb over her cheekbone.

"Why wouldn't she be?"

The moment shattered, and my eyes snapped toward Cristiano. "Oh, I don't know. Maybe because the cartel you're with tried to kill her? It tends to make people jumpy."

"It's not *my* cartel," he growled, "and I'd never hurt her."

I let out a sardonic laugh, my hand falling from her face. "Right. All Adriana has ever been is a cartel play toy. Why should I believe that?"

Adriana charged toward me, holding up a finger. "Back the fuck up! I—"

Cristiano cut her off, pushing her away as he squared his shoulders and bowed up to me. "First of all, you should believe it because you're in my office and don't have a choice. Secondly, not that it's any of your business, but I was protecting her. Something you obviously can't handle."

I pushed forward until we were nose to nose. "Step outside. I'll show you what I can handle."

Adriana let out a scream, turning both our heads for half a second, but it was all the time she needed. Forcing her way in between us, she pressed a hand against our chests and shoved us apart.

"*Dios mío*, are you two going to whip out your dicks and have a pissing match soon? I'm not a carnival prize, you know."

"Stay out of this," I warned, cracking my knuckles.

Cristiano bared his teeth in response. "This doesn't concern you."

"Doesn't concern me?" She repeated each word with a hard punch to his chest. "I'm so deep in this you couldn't dig me out with a shovel, motherfucker."

Both of us backed off at the same time, staring at her like she'd sprouted horns and a tail. Apparently, a well-timed outburst from a deranged, ex-communicated cartel queen got shit done.

Who knew?

Cristiano sucked a breath in through his teeth, not moving despite the fact she'd just used him as a punching bag. "I've given Marisol all the information I can." Glancing at her out of the corner of his eye, he gently removed her hand from his chest and took a guarded step toward me. "I'd lay down my life for her, and if this Ignacio asshole were here, I'd rip his throat out and shove it up his ass. No man puts his hands on Marisol and lives."

"Adriana," I mumbled, and when he furrowed his eyebrows, I scowled. "Her name is Adriana, and trust me, you'd have to get in line. Between me, Val, and Carlos, you'd have a long wait."

He hitched an eyebrow. "Carlos?"

I waved my hand. "Freelance Colombian supplier. This Ignacio has made a habit out of intercepting my Chicago shipments. Carlos gets a little cagey when his product disappears."

Before he could respond, the wall behind us opened up, and a different man with arms the size of tree trunks appeared out of nowhere. Adriana and I exchanged glances as he whispered into Cristiano's ear. Whatever he said wasn't good because his eyes darkened, revealing the ruthless killer I suspected him to be.

He cleared his throat and tugged on an impeccably straight jacket. "I'm going to have to cut this meeting short. It seems there's a problem that needs my attention. Drinks are on the house, of course. Please, enjoy yourselves." Adriana stiffened as he approached her, and my fists shook from the force of holding them back when he touched her. "Mari…" He paused, offering a smile that didn't quite reach his eyes. "Forgive me. Old habits die hard. Adriana, don't make me wait so long next time, or I might have to come find you instead."

The hell he would.

Giving her one last squeeze, he turned toward me, but I wasn't feeling as benevolent. I'd had enough, and the minute I stepped in front of him, my silent stare said more than any threat ever could.

Cristiano nodded. "Harcourt."

"Vergara."

Shoving his hands in his pockets, he leaned in making sure he was out of Adriana's earshot. "I know who you are and what you did to her. Keep her safe."

I smirked and tossed his threat back in his face. "Or what? You'll come find me, too?"

His lips pulled into a slow, sadistic smile. "I wouldn't have to. I've always known where you were." Brushing past my shoulder, he dropped his final bomb before turning around. "I would've never let her stay in that piece of shit barn house in Morelia."

Fuck.

My mind spun in fifty different directions. I didn't give a shit what Val had to say. I just added a second name to our intel mission. Every man had a story, and every story had a villain. Cristiano's role in Adriana's seemed to be a mystery, but one thing was for sure—I planned to find out.

He made his way over to Adriana and crooked a finger under her chin. "*Hasta la próxima, mi amor.*" *Until next time, my love.*

Before she could answer, he joined the man waiting at the

opening in the back wall. Within seconds, two doors slid in from the side, and the minute they sealed, they were gone, leaving no trace of them ever being there in the first place.

My gaze shifted to Adriana. She stood in a daze, her fingers pressed against the place on her chin where Cristiano touched her before running inside his wall like a fucking rat.

"Screw this," I muttered, turning around and stomping out of the office.

"Brody!" she yelled, her high heels clacking against the floor as she ran to catch up with me. "Brody! Jesus, would you slow down?"

I didn't slow down, and she didn't catch up until we reached the elevator. Dropping her head, she pressed her hand against the wall, her breath coming hard and fast. "I said to let me handle this."

"And I said you had ten minutes," I snapped, punching my fist against the call button. "Seems like neither of us listened."

She tilted her chin toward me and glared. "You know this whole sit-there-and-look-pretty-while-the-men-talk-bullshit is getting old, Harcourt."

"That man is dangerous, Carrera."

Adriana rolled her eyes just as a loud ding announced the elevator's arrival. "Here we go again," she muttered, stepping inside the opened doors.

Her ignorance fueled an already lit fire raging out of control. My knuckles were white from clenching my fists too hard, and I gritted my teeth in a futile attempt to remain silent. But I followed behind her, caging my anger until the doors closed.

Once I knew we were alone, I snapped, grabbing her around the waist and pushing her against the wall. "He knew the exact stash house we stayed at in Morelia. If you don't think he's balls deep in this, you're kidding yourself."

Her face paled. "You're wrong about him."

"Jesus Christ, Adriana! How can you be so ruthless and so blind at the same time? He's giving you just enough information for you to hang yourself."

The tension inside the tiny metal box was so thick I could barely breathe. She didn't answer me, and I didn't give a shit. I was mad, but not for the reason I should be.

She'd given me nothing but trouble. She'd threatened me and blackmailed me into lying to the one man I should never lie to. She'd made my life a living hell and would probably get me killed. She insulted me, berated me, and disobeyed every order I gave her. But what pissed me off the most was that despite all of it, I wanted her. I wanted every goddamn inch of her. I wanted to wrap her legs around my waist and drive into her so hard, she'd forget how to speak.

The most pathetic thing was I wanted her to want me, too. I wanted her to willingly give herself to me. And yes, fuck it, I wanted her to kiss me.

But I didn't want her to do it with that damn wig on.

The thought barely formed in my head before I had my hand on it. "I hate this damn thing. Take it off."

"Are you insane? I need it to—"

"Take it off, or I'll take it off for you." I had no idea where the command came from, but I wasn't backing down. When she hesitated, I gave it a sharp tug, and she yelped.

"Fine, Jesus. It's pinned. Give me a damn minute." Pins flew at my head like small torpedoes, but I got my way. The bright red atrocity landed at my feet, and I looked up to find her glaring at me, fists clenched and mad as hell.

With long dark hair falling over her shoulders.

The elevator stopped, and whatever force held us together snapped. Adriana shoved both hands against my chest, running a hand through her hair as she stomped into the darkened hallway leading toward the club.

In a complete reversal, now I chased her as the muffled beat from the club vibrated the walls around us. "Adriana! Would you slow down? Christ, how do you run so fast in those things?"

She was already halfway across the club when I caught her arm. Spinning around, she jerked out of my hold, eyes blazing. "*Dios mío*, are you always this suffocating? Because if so…" Her tirade trailed off as her eyes drifted over my left shoulder then widened in panic. "Oh shit."

"What?" I turned to see what she was looking at when she jerked my arm and tugged me back.

"Why don't you send up some flares while you're at it?" Glancing over my shoulder again, she groaned. "Fuck, they're blocking the exit."

"Who's blocking the exit?"

She grabbed my hand. "Come on."

I didn't have a chance to argue before she dragged me toward the dance floor, refusing to stop until she had us sandwiched in the middle of what could only be described as a human petri dish. Bodies writhed around us in a hedonistic orgy as people grinded, touched, rubbed, and stroked to Latin-infused rap music set to a techno salsa beat.

I'd never seen anything like it.

Adriana turned around and pressed her ass so hard against me I groaned. "We're being watched," she whispered, wrapping her arms around my neck. "Act like you want me."

"Tell me what the hell is—"

Lifting her chin, Adriana plastered a fake smile on her face, and that's when I saw the fear hiding behind her eyes. The rare show of vulnerability struck a familiar chord inside me.

I stepped back, but Adriana held tight, sliding a hand to my cheek and running her fingers through the stubble. "Play along, counselor. Your life may depend on it."

Whatever little control I had left splintered. Grasping her hips, I hauled her against me, pressing every inch of her body against mine. We fit together like a puzzle. Soft curves molded into hard muscle, and wrapping my hands around her waist, I rolled my hips to the sinful beat. I smiled at her sharp inhale and trailed a hand up her stomach, my fingers barely grazing the edge of her breast before sinking deep into her hair.

"Brody?" The breathy way she said my name was so damn sexy I almost forgot why we were doing this. Good thing I was one hell of a multitasker.

Tightening my hand in her hair, I pulled just hard enough for her ear to land by my mouth. "We're going to play a game, *princesa*. It's called I ask a question, and you answer." Just to drive my point home, I ground my erection against her ass.

She pressed her lips together, trying to hold in a lusty whimper. "Fine."

"Who's here?" Sweat rolled down my temple as we dipped and swayed to the evocative rhythm. When she didn't answer, I ran my hand down her thigh and slipped my fingers under her dress.

"Men," she groaned, digging her nails into the back of my neck. "Muñoz men. They…*fuck*…" Her knees buckled as I toyed with the edge of her panties. "They know me."

"See? This isn't so hard." I chuckled and nipped at her ear. "Or maybe it is. You tell me." Bending my knees, I gave a sharp upward thrust under her dress. Taking advantage of the position, I moved my hips, my jean-clad cock rubbing against the outside of her drenched panties.

"*Ay, Dios mío.*"

"Let's try another one. Is this what your fiancé left to

arrange?"

"Ex-fiancé." Her breath hitched as I hooked my finger in the scrap of lace, pulling it to the side while continuing to roll and thrust my hips. "And no, he has nothing to do with this."

I stilled all movement. "I don't share, Adriana."

She looked up, raw want in her eyes. "There's nothing between us."

I didn't answer. Partly because I wasn't sure if I believed her, and partly because I was suspicious as to what she was doing. Was she giving into whatever was building between us, or was I simply getting played? She was supposed to fight me, flip me off, and tell me to go to hell. Instead, she wiggled, forcing the friction I denied her, and I let out a low curse.

I stood still, my conscience at war with my cock. The choice was mine. Did I take what I knew we both wanted, or did I draw a line in the sand? Maybe on neutral ground, it would've been a fair fight, but standing in the middle of a hedonistic hurricane, my conscience never stood a chance.

Throbbing with need, I resumed my slow grind, enticing a broken moan from Adriana's lips. I glanced around at the sweaty bodies surrounding us. The dance floor was crowded, and nobody cared what anyone else was doing. The whole place looked like one big orgy anyway. We already looked like we were fucking. The only thing stopping it from happening was a scrap of denim and a thin layer of restraint. All I had to do was free both, and I'd sink right into her.

Fuck it.

Releasing her hair, I reached for my zipper when I heard the first gunshot.

Chapter Twenty-Five

ADRIANA

Brody's hand hit the back of my legs, and I closed my eyes. I could've stopped him. I should've stopped him. I knew what he was doing. I knew the complications it would cause and the consequences.

I just didn't care.

I couldn't lie to myself anymore. Brody Harcourt and I stood on opposite sides of the battle line, but hating the lieutenant didn't stop me from wanting the man. And I wanted him with a desperation that clawed at my soul. He'd become a drug, poisoning my body with a fatal addiction I craved. Touching him was like flirting with death. I found myself risking everything for the high. But with risk came consequence, and tempting the devil never promised another breath.

I felt him fumble for his zipper, and I bit my lip. Muñoz *sicarios* weaved through the crowd like mice, and I had no doubt Cristiano watched everything from one of the hundreds of hidden cameras, but the danger only added to the intrigue. This was the highest level of insanity, but I wanted it more than my next breath.

I tightened my hold around his neck in preparation when a loud pop jolted me back into reality. I recognized the sound immediately. Growing up cartel, it was the nature of the beast. By age two, I knew the sound of a gunshot better than my mother's voice.

Brody's hands fell from my body, our close embrace disintegrating as his head jerked up. A handful of people stopped to cast a curious glance around, but the majority of them ignored the prelude to chaos, continuing to dance in indulgent ignorance.

A heavy hand landed on my shoulder, and I looked back to see Brody's eyes wide and wild. "Adriana, get—"

Then all hell broke loose.

Shot after shot ripped through the club, confused partygoers standing stock still until people collapsed to the floor, blood splattering across their faces. Then screams drowned out the still thumping music and mass panic ensued. People were shoved, pushed, trampled, and used as human shields.

Trying to stay on my feet while being shoved around like a pinball, I shoved my hand under my dress and unsnapped my thigh holster. Within seconds, I pulled my Colt 380 from the inside of my left thigh and scanned the chaos for a familiar face.

Just not the one that showed up.

"Son of a bitch!" Cristiano came barreling past me in a blur of rage and shoved Brody into a screaming wall of people. "Get her out of here!"

All I could do was watch as Brody came back with a vengeance. Grabbing a handful of Cristiano's shirt, he wrenched him forward and growled through clenched teeth, "You're the one with invisible doors. *You* get her out of here!"

Before Cristiano could react, Brody shoved him backward with so much force he tripped and slammed into the mirrored wall behind him. I stood there with my mouth open and a loaded gun in my hand in shock. I'd never seen anyone manhandle Cristiano Vergara like that. I'd never seen anyone dare try. I was surprised Brody was still breathing, and from the look on Cristiano's face, so was he.

I jumped as a new round of shots rang out. Steadying my trigger finger, I turned to shout orders when Brody's muscular arm hooked around my upper back.

"What the—?" That was all I got out before the room spun in a frenzied swirl of light and sound as I crashed into Cristiano's hard chest.

"*Dios mío,*" he wheezed.

It was dark, but that didn't hide the glint of steel I saw in Brody's hand. My stomach dropped. What the hell was he planning to do? Take them all out by himself? We were supposed to be in this together. I was a trained killer, not some damsel in distress.

Stupid motherfucker.

I scrambled to my feet, only to be spun back around into the arms of the abnormally large dickhead from upstairs. Cristiano took my gun out of my hand and nodded to him, something unspoken passing between them. "Take her to the rattle room," he instructed, pulling his own gun from inside his jacket. "Keep her quiet by any means necessary."

"Give me back my gun!" I yelled. "And what the hell is a rattle room?" He didn't answer. His back was already turned as he walked away, swallowed into the thinning but still hysterical crowd. When the guard started toward a door near the corner of the room, I did the only thing I could think of. I went limp and became one hundred and twenty-seven pounds of dead weight.

He dragged me two feet before turning to glare at me. "You think I won't throw your ass over my shoulder, *puta*?" I pinched my lips together and glared right back at him. Sighing, he bent down, scooping me up like I weighed nothing and tossed me over his shoulder. "Now shut up, or I'll gag you. *Jefe's* orders."

I lifted my head, a cold numbness spreading through me as I took in the destruction and carnage. The room that moments ago was alive with the scent of desire now smelled metallic, a stench fueled by blood and revenge. Death never bothered me before, but as I watched Brody and Cristiano grow smaller and smaller with every step, my heart lodged in my throat

I couldn't leave them.

I struggled, beating my fists against his back, but the harder I hit, the tighter his grip became. "Let me go!"

"Don't make me hurt you."

"Don't make me hurt *you*."

He laughed. "Yeah, right."

I sighed. "Have it your way."

I had long legs. They came in handy during strenuous physical activities like running, rock climbing, or kicking a man in the balls while hanging upside down.

Plus, they looked great in heels.

Bracing my hands on his back and my knee against his stomach, I swung my foot as hard as I could and prayed. His muffled grunt was my only warning before we both hit the floor. Luckily, my hands took the brunt of my fall, and I quickly got to my feet, leaving him groaning on his knees.

Brody and Cristiano stood back-to-back, guns firing when I ran toward them. Cristiano saw me a fraction of a moment too late. I pulled my fist back and swung, his head snapping back with the force of my momentum.

Damn, that hurt.

He grabbed his chin. "What the fuck?"

"Give me my gun." I half expected him to argue, but to my surprise he dug inside his jacket and dropped it my waiting hand. "If you ever pull that shit again, I'll shoot your dick off and shove it up your ass."

He glanced at Brody. "Is she like this all the time?"

"Yep." Brody shrugged, and his face contorted in pain. That was when I noticed the sheen of sweat coating his forehead and the rip in the arm of his shirt.

"What's wrong with you?" I didn't wait for an answer. My hands were on him despite multiple attempts to push me away. I prodded at the hole, my fingers coating in warm, sticky wetness. "*Dios mío*, you're bleeding!"

He'd been shot, and I wasn't here to prevent it.

Brody gently held my wrist. "Adriana, stop. A bullet grazed my arm. It's nothing."

"It's not nothing!" I yelled, a foreign panic tearing through me. "You could've been killed! Do you think about anybody but yourself?" Gasping for air, I braced my hands on my thighs and looked up to see both men staring at me like they'd encountered an untamed animal in the wild.

Shit.

Avoiding their eyes, I stood and cleared my throat. "Status."

Cristiano nodded. "They were definitely Muñoz. Five of them. Two at the entrance, one at the bar, and two at the east and west side of the dance floor. Three confirmed dead, one ran like a little bitch. I've got men on him now."

"And the fifth?"

The two men exchanged glances. "That's why we're still shooting."

"But you're an associate. Why would they turn on you like this?"

He steadied his eyes on the entrance, then, drawing in a deep breath, he exhaled hard and leveled a stare at me. "I've told you, Mari. Information comes with a price."

Deep down, I already knew it, but it still cut deep to hear the words. "They came for me and sacrificed you." For the first time, I really saw what I caused by coming here. The blood, the death, the bodies. The dozens of lives lost because of a last name that was never even mine to start with. "All these people…" I swallowed, glancing up at Brody, guilt washing over me in a sickening red wave. "We have to go."

"Adriana," he said, his tone cautious. "If they found us here, they can find us anywhere. We can't go back to the stash house. That'll be the first place they look."

"I have a place you can go to." We both turned toward Cristiano, still rubbing his now swollen jaw. "No one knows about it, not even my own men." He shot me a pointed look. "You know the code."

Brody stiffened beside me, and I blew out a breath. I knew the place Cristiano referred to, and he was right. I did know the code. I knew it because I chose it, and the thought of being there with Brody sent my heart free falling into my stomach.

Then reality arrived with a sharp reminder. "I don't think…" I winced, blowing out a painful breath. "I mean, I have to go…"

Cristiano held up a hand. "It's okay. I have you covered. There's still plenty—"

"Perfect!" Taking Brody's hand, I rushed toward the entrance before he said anything else. "We'll go now." Glancing back, I nodded toward his gun. "Got my back?"

I blinked, confused at the hint of sadness that flashed in his eyes.

"Always."

Chapala, Jalisco, Mexico

AFTER I CONVINCED BRODY TO WAIT UNTIL TOMORROW TO CALL VAL with an update, we drove in silence for an hour in the rain before reaching Cristiano's Lake Chapala house. As soon as the stone staircase came into view, I tensed.

I spent sixty minutes steeling myself for Brody's reaction, but still cringed when I heard the low, *what the fuck* muttered under his breath.

I could've prepared him, but what was the use? It was going to be a fight regardless, one which I preferred not to have at sixty miles per hour.

And one we still hadn't had half an hour later.

At least, not about that.

"I told you it's fine," he growled.

"And I told you even flesh wounds can cause gangrene if they're not cleaned. Now shut up and let me look at it."

It was a little extreme, but he was being unreasonable. We were too close to uncovering the truth for him to die from septic shock and a petulant male ego. Plus, I could tell by his parted lips and labored breath he was in more pain than he let on.

Groaning, he slumped onto the three thin steps dividing the kitchen from the living room, slamming his feet onto the bottom step, and hooking his elbow onto his knee. It wasn't exactly an open invitation, but knowing Brody, it was the closest I'd get.

I rummaged through the kitchen in search of a first-aid kit, flinging open cabinets and cursing Cristiano's name and still coming up empty. Frustrated, I collapsed against the counter and scrubbed my hands down my face.

Could one damn thing go right tonight?

I'd already gotten a few dozen people killed. All I wanted was a bandage and some fucking antiseptic. Was that too much to ask? Tipping my head back, I pressed my palm against my forehead and twisted a handful of my hair between my fingers.

God, I needed a drink.

My head snapped up so fast the room blurred. Holy shit, that was exactly what I needed.

I searched the kitchen again, this time focused and methodical. By the time I plopped down next to Brody, he was half-asleep, his forehead pressed against his opposite knee.

"Rise and shine, counselor. It's time to play doctor."

He popped one eye open. "Is this a joke?"

"Nope. Take off your shirt." Rolling my eyes at his smirk, I held up a pair of scissors. "You wish. I need to make a bandage."

He narrowed his eyes, clearly not trusting a word out of my mouth. Not that I blamed him. But he didn't have much of a choice, and he knew it. I waited as he opened one agonizing button at a time, and the minute the fabric slipped off his shoulders, all the air sucked out of the room. He paused, raising an eyebrow at my choked gasp, our eyes tangling with ferocity.

"Are you all right?"

I forced my eyes away from his chest and settled them on the blood coating his arm. His beautiful unmarred skin was now stained a deep scarlet. Luckily, most of the bleeding had slowed down, only a trickle of red still snaking down in a jagged trail toward his wrist.

He was right. It was a flesh wound, but a few inches to the right and we wouldn't have been having this conversation. Pushing it out of my head, I busied myself cutting his shirt into strips, trying to ignore the heat of his stare. Setting them out in front of me, I forced everything out of my mind but the task at hand.

"Face forward and put your elbow on your knee."

He did as I asked without arguing. Wadding up a few strips of his shirt in one hand, I picked up the bottle with the other and unscrewed the cap with my teeth. I'd barely tipped the neck when he flinched, and his elbow knocked against the side of the glass, dousing my legs instead of his arm.

"Hold still and stop being such a baby."

He gritted his teeth and scowled. "It fucking burns."

"It's eighty proof vodka," I snapped. "It's supposed to fucking burn." Done coddling him, I trapped his injured arm between my forearm and his knee and turned the damn bottle upside down, watching most of what was left splash on his skin.

He sucked in a harsh breath, muttering a slew of intelligible curses, but didn't pull away. I didn't know whether it was out of trust or necessity, and I didn't care to dig deep enough to find out. Keeping my head down, I cleaned, dried, and wrapped the remaining strips around his arm until there was nothing left to do. No reason left to touch him.

Rubbing my thumb across the secure knot I made in the bandage, I gave his shoulder a soft pat. "There, I think you'll live." Gathering the scissors and empty vodka bottle, I started to stand when he grabbed my arm.

"It was supposed to be yours, wasn't it?"

"What?"

Lifting his uninjured arm, he motioned around us. "This place. You knew the code because he bought it for you."

Chapter Twenty-Six

ADRIANA

I swallowed hard while taking in his tightened jaw and pinched expression. "Brody, come on, don't do this."

"What happened between you and him?"

"Does it matter?"

He released my wrist, a flicker of emotion crossing his face before a vicious laugh wiped it away. "Considering it rained a fuck ton of bullets in the middle of his nightclub tonight, I'd say, yeah, it matters a lot."

Sighing, I set the supplies down and rubbed my palms up and down my still damp legs. I didn't want to have this conversation now. I didn't want to have this conversation ever. But it was naïve to expect Brody to stay in another man's house without demanding answers. But how did I give him answers to a question I still didn't understand myself?

I considered lying, but what was the use? We were too deep into this for such barrier tactics to work, and I had too little time to reap the benefits even if they did.

Stepping off the final two steps into the living room, I crossed my arms over my chest. "I met Cristiano when I was nineteen," I said, staring out the sliding glass doors at the falling rain. "He was a low-level runner trying to work his way up the ranks by doing all the wrong things. He had a chip on his shoulder and a problem with authority. Esteban and Manuel hated him, but in less than a year, he was our highest earner, so there wasn't much they could say. Cris was one of the few who didn't think the path to the top detoured through my pants." I laughed. "In fact, he hated me."

"You do have a pattern."

I glanced over my shoulder and shrugged. "You know how it goes. Tell a kid they can't have a piece of candy, and they want it twice as much. When I wasn't attending *universidad*, I hung around him and—"

"Let me guess; you wore him down until he fell in love."

"Actually, I pissed him off so much he ratted me out to Esteban."

"You're a glutton for punishment."

"What can I say? I love candy." Flashing him a lethal smile, I cocked a hip against the back of the couch. "Esteban was so impressed he had the balls to do that, he took the time to get to know him and ended up making him a top *sicario*. I guess that was what finally pushed us together. Two years later, we were engaged, and he was about to make him a lieutenant."

"But he didn't."

I shook my head. "No. Esteban died two days before it was supposed to happen. By default, Manuel took control of the cartel, and Cris's chance was gone. Manuel was already threatened by him, so he took immense pleasure in denying his rank. That was the beginning of the end."

"So, how did he end up with *El Palacio*?"

I narrowed a suspicious gaze at him, wondering what angle he was pushing. However, he lost the snide tone and seemed genuinely interested in the answer, so I opened up and spilled my most private secrets to the one man who'd proven he couldn't be trusted with them.

"I didn't have the power to make Cris a lieutenant, but no one could stop me from giving him one of our clubs. *El Palacio* is one of the cartel's biggest money laundering fronts. Every Muñoz deal eventually runs through him. Manuel may have pushed him out of the inner circle, but I got the last laugh." My eyes drifted toward the ceiling. "In the end, Cris had more inside information and power than any lieutenant ever could."

"So why the split? Did you get cold feet?"

"No, he did." The shocked look on his face made me chuckle. "It was for the best. I'm not cut out to be someone's wife. You said it yourself; I'm selfish. Marriage is about compromise, and I'm not sure I know the meaning of the word. He's better off without me."

Brody turned away, his voice rough. "I'm not so sure. I saw the way he looked at you."

My breath hitched, but it had nothing to do with what he said and everything to do with what he didn't. I had no idea how Cristiano felt about me, and I didn't care. He was part of my past, a part of my life I'd long since buried along with Marisol Muñoz. My reaction came from the possessive shift in his tone. The subtle growl in his voice. The corded muscles in his neck that snapped to attention along with his clenched jaw.

The more I stared, the murkier the line between lust and retribution became. His heated gaze met mine, a similar battle for control brewing in his eyes. Whatever this was, it was dangerous, and if I let myself burn in the fire behind his eyes, we'd both go up in flames.

"What about you?" Walking toward the ledge behind the staircase landing, I trailed my hand along the wood. "Ever come close to tying the knot?" Lifting my hand, I blew the dust off my fingers.

"Hell, no. I was too focused on law school. Even after I started at the DA's office, that didn't change. I've fucked lots of women but never considered caring for them." His eyes turned hollow. "Emotions complicate things, and I've been down that road before."

He didn't have to say the words. He was talking about Eden. Before tonight, I wouldn't have hesitated to rub salt in his wound, but my confession left me too raw.

The corner of Brody's mouth quirked up. "What, no cheap shot about Eden dumping me for Val? Come on, I left the door wide open. You love to make fun of me."

"It's not so funny anymore."

The smirk fell from his lips, his hazel eyes darkening. Adrenaline rushed through my veins, and my mouth went dry. Not thinking, I darted my tongue out to wet my lips, which was the wrong thing to do. A low growl rumbled in his chest, and once I saw him move, I did, too.

I was too late.

He was already across the room, both hands caging me against the landing before I could get away. "What changed?"

"Let me go."

"Not until you tell me what changed."

"Nothing's changed."

He slapped his palm against the stone. "That's a lie, and you know it. We can't go on like this, Adriana. This thing between you and me is a ticking time bomb. Something has to give, or someone's going to get hurt."

He was right, but I'd be damned if I'd admit it. "What do you suggest we do?"

He slid his hand around to the back of my head. "Fuck each other out of our systems."

"You can't be serious."

Electricity sizzled in the air as Brody pressed closer, his hard arousal letting me know he was very serious. The green and brown in his hazel eyes was completely gone, swallowed by a dark, conflicted desire. It was like looking in a mirror. Both of us pretended to be something we weren't, but underneath it all, I was broken, and he was lost. We were one empty soul drawn to another.

I told him once that the eyes were the window to the soul, but the heart was the doorway to sin. To survive, I had to close both.

"Go fuck yourself." Pushing him away, I threw the sliding glass door open and ran. I barely got outside when a solid sheet of rain hit me, drenching me from head to toe. Clenching my fists, I threw my head back and yelled toward the sky, "You can go fuck yourself, too!"

It wasn't like I was getting my ticket punched at the pearly gates.

I stumbled along the uneven walkway muttering to myself when my one of my heels sank in between two stones, snapping it off and sending me sprawling onto my ass.

This fucking day.

Letting out a scream, I kicked off the bastard shoe and stomped the rest of the way to the car, still holding the other one like a weapon. I had no idea what I was going to do when I got there. It wasn't like I brought the damn keys. Frustrated, I slammed the perfectly intact heel onto the hood, jumping as a low chuckle rumbled behind me.

"You know that's Val's car, right?" Brody leaned against one of the columns, looking infuriatingly calm while I beat the hell out of the car with a shoe.

"What do you want?"

"I wasn't finished talking to you."

"That's too bad. I was." Turning back around, I resumed attacking the hood. I didn't know what it was about him that sparked such a volatile side in me, but it made me want to put my fist through every window of this car. Unfortunately, this place lacked adequate medical supplies, and *someone* had been a giant man-child and wasted all the Stolichnaya.

"Huh. Well, then, maybe I should take a page out of Vergara's playbook."

I paused my destruction to glare at him over my shoulder. "What's that supposed to mean?"

Pushing off the column, Brody walked the few feet separating us until he stood beside me, his jaw ticking. "If I call Val and tell him you're being a cock tease, will you open your legs for me, too?"

I didn't think. I dropped the shoe and swung. A loud crack broke the sudden silence as my hand smacked across his cheek with such force his chin snapped back.

He didn't say anything. He just stared at me as the rain pelted his smug face.

Letting out a frustrated scream, I did it again, this time harder and higher, connecting right below his eye. He still didn't back down, turning back toward me with rage in his eyes.

I should've stopped. I should've backed off and begged him to leave me alone, but the anger and lust inside me ignited into a fire that burned out of control. Needing to lash out, I drew my arm back to slap him for a third time, but this time, he grabbed my wrist and held it tight while slamming me against the side of the car.

Brody's chest rose and fell with labored breaths as I held mine. His hooded gaze settled on my mouth, and I stiffened as his other hand cupped my jaw. Panic tore through my body, but it wasn't at being chased down or held immobile.

Don't kiss me.

The words screamed over and over in my head until my mouth spoke them out loud.

Brody turned my chin to the side and whispered in my ear, "Don't worry, *princesa*. It's not your mouth I want tonight."

I didn't know who moved first, but in a blur of rain and frantic need, I found myself spun around and bent over the hood of the car. On instinct, my hands flew out in front of me and grasped onto the metal. Behind me, Brody jerked the hem of my dress over my hips, a groan tearing from his throat.

"Fucking beautiful."

Anything could've happened. He was in complete control, and as much as I should've loathed being at his mercy, I'd never wanted a man more.

Brody slipped two fingers under the string at my hip, and with a hard tug, ripped my panties off. I pressed my forehead against the metal, a broken moan battling with the rain as he sank two fingers inside me. The harder he pumped, the louder I became, not giving a damn who heard me.

"No running this time, Adriana. I'm giving us what we both want tonight."

"*Sí.*" It was the only word I could manage.

"Say it."

I opened my mouth to oblige him, then clamped it shut. He wanted me to beg him to fuck me. It wasn't an outlandish request. A little overbearing, maybe, but not unreasonable. I did want him to fuck me, and I had no problem asking for it, but as the rain pelted my back, my own words came back to haunt me.

"Everyone causes cracks in me, Brody. Maybe you'll be the one who finally breaks me."

"Don't fuck with me, *princesa*. I've had a shitty day. Say the words, or I'll stand here and jerk off on this gorgeous ass of yours."

"Break me," I whispered.

Brody stilled. "I don't want to break you."

I didn't believe him. However, it didn't matter if he wanted to break me or not. This had nothing to do with him. Clinging to a life that was no longer mine kept me in a glass box filled with resentment and rage. Maybe I'd never learn to forgive or make peace with the wrongs done against me, but I didn't want to close my eyes still trapped inside a prison of my own fears.

"You have to. It's the only way to fix me."

"Adriana…"

"Fuck me, Brody."

Those three words were the key that unlocked the savage inside the suit. As if waking from a restless sleep, Brody roared, grabbing my hips and dragging me toward him. Pressing one hand on my back, he tore open his jeans and shoved them down his thighs. As if in response to his hunger, the rain came down harder, forming a secret wall between us.

It was because of that wall that I wasn't prepared when he buried his cock deep inside me with one punishing thrust. The ferociousness of his possession buckled my knees, and I dug my nails into the car's paint while crying out his name. Every time I tried to breathe, my body clenched around him, drawing a groan from his chest.

"Jesus Christ."

Those two words were the calm before the storm. Or maybe they were a prayer for forgiveness for what was to come. It didn't matter because only seconds later, he did exactly as I asked him to.

He broke me.

Vicious drives forced me up onto my toes, his hips slamming harder and harder into mine with each thrust. I cried. I begged. Tears streamed down my face, mixing with the rain as he grabbed a handful of my hair while digging his fingers into my hip.

"Is this what you wanted? For me to make you cry?"

"Yes!"

"Goddamn, you drive me crazy!" His thrusts became faster, harder, more brutal, and I felt his cock jerk inside me. He was about to come, and knowing that flung me over the edge first.

"¡Valió la pena morir por esto!" I screamed until my voice shattered, my body convulsing violently around him.

"Fuck!" My release triggered his, and he gave one final thrust before roaring out my name, his body jerking as he came inside me. Exhausted and spent, he slumped on top of me, his chest molding against my back as his hand braced on the hood.

Neither of us spoke a word, and the rain continued to pelt us as if trying to wash away what we'd just done. But that was impossible.

He did exactly as I asked. He broke me, but it didn't fix me. Instead of turning me into a blank slate, all he created were jagged shards of glass.

Brody exhaled hard, his breath fanning against my neck as he pulled away. Pushing up on his palm, he stared down at me as I stood to fix my dress. "I should apologize."

"I told you to do it."

He shook his head, his blond hair now wet and stuck to his forehead. "Not for that. I sure as hell won't apologize for what happened. I meant for not thinking clearly enough to… Adriana, I—"

"You didn't use a condom. I know."

His eyes narrowed. "And you're not mad?"

"Look, I'm clean, and you're still not over Saint Eden, so I know you are, too. It's not a big deal. Don't worry."

"That's not all that can happen." He said the words slowly as if I were a child. I knew exactly what he was implying, and I was tired of the inquisition.

"I said, don't worry." Picking up my shoes, I headed toward the door, the earth squishing under my bare feet. I heard his footsteps close behind me, so I picked up my pace. Barely two feet from the door, he swung me around to face him.

"Why did you say this was worth dying for?"

"What?"

"You yelled it in Spanish. Why did you say it?"

Damn. I forgot he knew basic Spanish.

"No reason." I jerked away from him, only to have him pull me back.

"Are you seriously shutting me out now? Now? After what we just did?" He flung his uninjured arm back toward the car as if it were a shrine.

This was what I was afraid of. This is why I knew it was a bad idea.

I tried to remember how it felt to hate him. How much I wanted to destroy everything good in his life when he destroyed me. But the driving hatred that brought me to Houston was gone.

He broke that, too.

So instead, I fueled myself with hatred for wanting something I could never have.

I curled my lips into a cold sneer. "What we just did was fuck, Brody. Nothing more. I gave you my body. It doesn't give you access to anything else. Stay in your lane or go back to Val. I have no problem handling this on my own."

I'd just grabbed the glass door when his accusation hit my ears.

"Or with Vergara."

I whipped back around, eyes blazing. "Are you deaf? I said by myself! I don't want either of you."

"Does it matter what I want?" he asked, his voice dangerously calm.

He didn't move, his gaze steady as he watched me. I asked him to break me. My words. My request. None of this was his fault, yet I kept my eyes averted as I returned the favor.

"No. Just chalk it up to a bad roll of the dice," I hissed, leaving him in the pouring rain as I stepped inside the house. "You're good at that."

I didn't wait for a reply before slamming the door.

Chapter Twenty-Seven

ADRIANA

Typing out a quick text, I hit send and tossed my phone next to the sink with a groan. It was too early for this shit, and the coffee was taking forever to brew.

The half-hour of sleep I managed to get was anything but restful. Not when the man sleeping like a damn baby in the room down the hall invaded every minute of it with his sinful words and commanding touch.

I hated him for it.

But it did give me the excuse to get a head start on preparations for what I anticipated to be the turning point of this whole trip. Brody wasn't going to like it, but since the sun had barely broken over the horizon, I still had time to figure out how to tell him without causing him to have a stroke.

Propping my elbow on the counter, I slumped forward and tucked my chin into the palm of my hand as I counted the rhythmic drips one by one. Big mistake. By the time I hit twenty, my eyes were closed, and my head fell heavy into my palm.

"Adriana!" Brody shouted from the living room, and I jumped. Disoriented, I blinked the haze out of my eyes and twisted around in a circle until my eyes landed on the full coffeepot.

Shit, how long had I been asleep?

"Adriana, get your ass in here!"

Grabbing a mug from the cabinet, I filled it to the top with the now lukewarm liquid and downed half of it before sauntering into the living room and leaning a hip against the wall. "Yes?"

Brody stood in the middle of the room, in nothing but a pair of black boxers, his hands fisted by his sides as he glared at the scattered artillery. Thankfully, I still had the mug shoved between my lips because it stopped me from licking them while I devoured his body.

"What the fuck is this?"

His irritated growl dragged me back to reality, and I swung an exaggerated glance around the room, then shrugged, swirling the liquid in my mug before taking another sip. "They appear to be guns."

"I see that," he seethed, baring his teeth. "Where did they come from?"

I pushed off the wall, trying not to wobble down the steps into the living room. Ignoring his heated stare, I bent down in front of him and picked up a shiny new Glock from the coffee table. Holding it up, I tilted it to the side and cocked my head. "Smyrna, Georgia," I announced with a smirk.

Brody's nostrils flared. "You know what the hell I mean."

Of course, I knew what he meant, but I also knew he wasn't going to like the answer. "Cristiano had them delivered early this morning."

As predicted, Brody's sharp jawline twitched, his hand

squeezing the gun as if he couldn't decide whether to shoot me or throw it out the window. "Any particular reason?"

"Probably because I called him and asked him to have them delivered early this morning."

He stared at me, and I stared right back. The standoff lasted until he let out a harsh breath, slamming the gun back onto the table. "It's too goddamn early for this."

"Coffee?" I smiled, pushing my half-empty mug of coffee in his face.

His eyebrows pinched together, and for a moment, I thought he was going to take it, but then he turned around and sank onto the couch, his hand dragging through his hair. "Okay, let's start over. Why did you call Vergara and request"—pausing, he shifted his gaze toward the coffee table while counting—"eight guns?" Cocking an eyebrow, he shook his head and sat down, draping an arm across the back of the couch.

This was going to get a little ugly.

"Oh, I'm glad you asked. Because I thought I'd pay a visit to my childhood home today."

"I'm sorry, *what*?"

Okay, maybe a lot ugly.

"Cristiano gave me some solid leads last night when I was in his office. He said my family had secrets that would give us answers." As soon as Brody's mouth opened, I held up a hand. "I would've told you last night, but if you remember, we got a little sidetracked."

I remained quiet. Not because I had nothing else to say, but because leaving the ball in Brody's court was a strategic move. It was time for him to put up or shut up. Either he proved he was all in, and I could believe him when he said he didn't want to break me, or he proved me right when I said if given a chance, he'd drive a knife in my back.

Which was exactly what I thought he was about to do when he pushed off the couch. "No fucking way," he growled, pressing into me.

His fiery stare sent a chill across my skin, reminding me how little clothing I wore. Not to mention *what* I wore. All I could find after storming into the house last night was one of Cristiano's old T-shirts, which was another argument I didn't wish to have with him.

I had to stand my ground or get bulldozed.

"I don't remember asking for your permission."

"Adriana, you can't go to Esteban's estate."

"What's the worst that could happen?"

"You'll be shot on sight!" he yelled, throwing his arms out wide.

"A possibility, I'll give you that."

His eyes bore into me as if trying to pick apart the warped patchwork of my brain. "You're really insane, aren't you?"

"Aw, and they say chivalry is dead." Winking, I gave him a patronizing pat on the chest before walking toward the kitchen.

"I can't believe this," he fumed, tearing across the room. "You're risking your life on a few cryptic words from Vergara?"

Dumping the coffee down the drain, I whirled around. "Do you have a better idea? You have to check in with Val tomorrow. What do you plan to tell him? That we have a few irons in the fire?" Rolling my eyes, I curled my fingers into air quotes. "We've been at this for three days now, and I'm not sure if you've noticed, but we've got nothing."

"Val wouldn't want you to risk your life for him."

I blinked. "You don't get it, do you? This isn't about him." His eyebrows drew up, and I palmed my forehead. "Okay, maybe it started out as a way to clear my name while working my way into the Carreras, but don't you see what has happened? I've tried so hard to outrun Marisol Muñoz that I couldn't see that she was the problem."

"How so?"

"Cristiano told me to stop chasing ghosts and start opening up closets. He said they were full of skeletons that have been locked up for a long time."

"What does that even mean?"

"I asked the same thing, and he just said this wasn't about an outsider coming in to take over. That it was a vendetta, and if I wanted to find the truth I needed to look toward my own family. This whole time we've been looking for this enigma who'd come in and taken over what was left of the Muñoz Cartel. We've been racking our brains to figure out who it could be. Is it a former lieutenant? Disgruntled *sicario*? An outsider who saw an opportunity?" I pushed away from the sink and moved toward him until we stood only inches apart. "What we failed to do was see what was right in front of our faces. How could someone command control of a cartel unless they had the name to back it up?"

Brody looked me up and down, his eyes clouded with doubt. "But that makes no sense. Esteban and Manuel are gone. People can't come back from the dead, Adriana."

Maybe I baited that out of him. It was possible I dug that hole just waiting for him to fall into it. Unresolved issues didn't go away just because bigger ones pushed them under the rug. Eventually, they crawled out and showed themselves.

A slow smile tipped the corners of my mouth. "Are you sure about that? I did."

His Adam's apple bobbed hard in his throat, and he chewed on his words before responding. "Are you insinuating one of them is alive?"

And they're back under the rug.

I sighed, fatigue catching up with me. "No, I'm insinuating that just because something isn't visible doesn't mean it's not there."

"Stop chasing ghosts," he grumbled, stalking toward the coffee pot, his eyes wild. Grabbing a mug out of the cabinet, he slammed it shut and poured.

"It's cold."

"Don't care." Brushing past me, he stomped up the stairs without another word.

I didn't go after him. He was furious, and I got that, but I also didn't have the time for bruised male egos. I'd give him until ten o'clock tonight, and then I was going with or without him.

Guadalajara, Jalisco, Mexico

I FOLDED MY ARMS ACROSS THE TOP OF THE HOOD AND GRINNED. "Ready to open up some closets, counselor?"

Brody climbed out after me, the look on his face not as pleasant. He was lucky I let him come with me at all after he made me waste two hours driving to Guadalajara and back just so he could get his own clothes. I suspected it had to do with me suggesting he wear one of Cristiano's T-shirts since I'd turned his into a sleeveless crop top.

Crossing his arms, he moved toward the front of the car. "No, but I'm not letting this asshole take a shot at Val."

My grin faded. "Right."

"Or you," he added, glancing over his shoulder. "You said being together was worth dying for. Maybe so, but it won't be today." I met his stare, expecting to see his eyes swimming in lies, but I found stormy defiance. I didn't know what to say, so I said nothing. As if expecting my silence, Brody nodded at the backpack slung over my shoulder. "Are you ready to face Marisol again?"

Using that name wasn't a slip of the tongue. It was a dart aimed at my heart intended to dissuade me from continuing and proved his blindness.

However, darts couldn't pierce what didn't exist, so ignoring him, I drew my gun and walked toward my past.

As a precaution, we parked far enough away from the estate so as not to cause suspicion. However, it was an unnecessary tactic because the closer we got to the iron gate Brody's stride slowed. A few more steps and my jaw dropped.

"Well," he said, lowering his gun. "I didn't expect this."

That was an understatement. The estate where I grew up was a palace. A house built for opulence and excess. It was a labyrinth of mazes Manuel and I would purposely get lost in until someone sent a servant to retrieve us.

Esteban Muñoz wanted the people of Mexico to revere him, and the world to bow to his power. It was why everything had to be bigger and better than the Carreras. A bigger and more lavish mansion. A deadlier and more heavily armed army. Smarter and more ruthless children.

More, more, more.

The more he pushed, the weaker everything became. The inside of our house turned chaotic. Our army turned on itself. And his children became self-destructive machines.

However, it didn't matter what lay behind the curtain as long as people believed what they saw in front of it. I wondered if he'd stand by that creed if he saw what had become of his precious legacy.

The gate swung on bent and torn hinges, opening and closing as if daring us to enter, and once we did, my mouth dropped open. Large chunks of the three-level stone staircase leading up to the front were strewn about the lawn, and jagged, sharp holes existed where windows once stood. But it was the white exterior, barely visible behind a rainbow of spray-painted gang signs that had me stumbling backward into Brody's chest.

"You're not going in there. There's no way, Adriana."

Spinning around, I waved my gun like a crazy woman. "Why? It's not like we have to fight our way in. Obviously, nobody gives a shit."

"Then let me go."

I let out an incredulous laugh. "You have no idea what you're looking for."

"Neither do you!"

I pursed my lips and glanced up at my childhood home, a distant memory humming low in my throat. "I wouldn't be so sure about that."

"Then I'm coming with you."

"Look, I appreciate the offer, but you would be more helpful watching my back out here and letting me know if anyone is coming." I started toward the door when he pulled me back.

"What am I supposed to do, strike up a conversation and keep the nice vandals busy while you sift through garbage?"

"I'm sure you'll think of something." Patting his shoulder, I stepped through the open door before he could drag me back.

"Adriana!" he called after me, but I was already headed toward the only place I could think of to go. Cristiano said to stop chasing ghosts and open up my family's closets. If there were skeletons hidden in any room in this house, it would be the one I was always forbidden to enter.

Keeping my head down, I stepped over trash and cracked marble as I made my way through the deserted hallways. After swallowing the lump in my throat, I stopped outside the door to Esteban's office, closing my eyes and taking a breath before pushing it open. Stumbling through the darkness, I felt my way to the enormous oak desk situated near the back of the office activating the flashlight on my phone so I didn't break my neck.

Once I was seated, it only took a moment for the smell to hit me. Even in the destruction it lingered. *Cohiba Siglo* VI Cuban cigars. Rain-soaked earth. A dank, sweet leather scent that hurled me through a black hole of time. The smell surrounded me. It covered my skin, seeped into my pores, and killed everything inside.

Just like he did.

I gripped the edge of the desk until my arms shook. Spilling blood created this mess, and doing it again was the only way to end it. "Okay, Esteban, twenty-four years of silence for five minutes of my time. The clock starts now."

I wasn't surprised when I found the drawer under the desk missing.

Fucking thieves.

Undeterred, I searched for the other four only to find the same situation. Flopping back into the chair, I curled my fists and dug my nails into my palms.

Well, that was pointless.

Time was ticking, so I scanned the room, frantic to find something—*anything*—I could get my hands on, but there was nothing. There wasn't a damn thing that wasn't destroyed, and to make matters worse, my eyes started to sting.

I will not cry.

I refused to let fear control me anymore.

"I'm coming for you, Ignacio," I announced, pushing back my chair. "And I'm pulling back the curtain." With renewed determination, I stood and slammed my hand against the desk, knocking off something metal, heavy, and extremely loud. "Shit!" Scrambling around the desk, I bent down, and my fingers brushed against cold steel. I knew what it was without looking. That stupid pendulum. The one that echoed outside his office day and night. The one I still heard in my sleep.

Click-clack.

Click-clack.

Click-clack.

The rhythm pounded in my head, causing my brain to swim. I wasn't surprised the vandals didn't want it. It was a useless piece of shit belonging to a selfish monster who valued power and revenge over a child's innocence.

I was a *thing* to him. A possession.

Gripping the pendulum tightly, I turned to slam it back on the desk when the light from my phone passed over a glint of gold. It sat in front of my shoe, inviting me to come closer. Daring me to listen to its secrets. Beads of sweat scattered across my forehead and my heart felt like it had clawed its way outside my chest only to be left swinging like his stupid pendulum.

Click-clack.

Click-clack.

Click-clack.

I picked it up with a shaking hand, curious and afraid of what I might find. And then I laughed. Low at first, and then uncontrollably with my head thrown back. I laughed until I couldn't breathe.

It was a motherfucking key.

I turned it over to find three engraved numbers on it.

384

No location. No nothing. Just a numbered key to an unknown lock, which I had no doubt hid all of Esteban's skeletons. Who better than me to open it and watch them all tumble out?

"Nice try, old man. You're good, but I'm better."

It was a pretty safe bet that somewhere in Guadalajara, there was a safe deposit box housing a ticking time bomb, and here I was with a key in one hand, a pendulum in the other, and a lot of questions for Cristiano Vergara.

The weight of the pendulum caused it to shift in my hand, and I felt the small slit underneath the base. Without hesitation this time, I flipped it over and held it next to my phone.

"I'll be damned."

The light shined on a perfectly cut rectangular opening, no more than an eighth of an inch wide and just long enough to fit a key. I'd bet my life that lying somewhere around here was a piece of wood that once sealed all this illogical secrecy.

My grip tightened on the pendulum as footsteps shuffled outside the hallway.

"Adriana! Where are you?"

Shit.

Why couldn't that man listen for once? Standing, I dropped the pendulum back on the desk and pocketed the key. "I'm coming," I yelled.

I'd gotten a lot of things wrong in life. I'd made wrong calls and trusted the wrong people. Maybe I didn't know how I planned to stop myself from ending up the final Muñoz casualty, but I did know two things: one, my father was a psychopathic narcissist who kept a detailed log of everyone's dirty little secrets, and two, I was about to reveal them all.

Chapter Twenty-Eight
BRODY

"You're going to do what?"

I held the phone out and let Val yell while opening a can of what I hoped was soup. When he brought it down to a low roar, I held it up to my ear. "I said we're going to check banks and see what we can find. It's like playing slots. Sooner or later, one has to pay out."

"I'm going to kill you."

"Promises, promises."

"You get yourself and my sister involved in a shooting at a club belonging to her ex and you don't call me. Then you trespass on rival property, and you still don't call me." He let out a low laugh, but it wasn't out of humor. "My charitable side is wearing thin, Harcourt."

"As soon as I have more information, I'll call back."

"Brody," Val said, hesitation in his voice. "Adriana's back is against the wall. She has nothing to lose and everything to gain.

While I'm willing to give her the benefit of the doubt, I won't trust without verifying. You should do the same."

"Right."

"By the way, I've got some news on your friend Leo Pinellas."

Ten minutes later, I ended the call, my chest tightened, but it had nothing to do with Leo.

Everything he said about Adriana was true. I knew better than anyone lies were told by the sweetest of lips. I had to remind myself she was a dangerous killer, just like the one I'd become.

Unfortunately, I didn't know if that deterred me or excited me.

I GLANCED UP AT THE BIG ROUND CLOCK ON THE WALL.

4:47 p.m.

If the bitch in front of us counting out coins like she was about to play slots until her next birthday didn't move, the bank would close before we had our turn. Clearing my throat and tapping my toe did nothing but feed my irritation. Finally, she swept them into her huge old lady bag and waddled past us, returning my glare as she walked by.

Last night, we determined the key Adriana found was to a bank safe deposit box, so after we got up this morning, we set out to find the bank it belonged to. Only now, it was eight hours later, and after driving from bank to bank, my patience ran on fumes.

"¡Próximo!" Next!

Adriana and I stepped up to the teller window, and I ground my teeth as Adriana held up the key she stole from her father's house, reciting the same ridiculous speech in Spanish I'd heard six times already. If there was a seventh speech, I couldn't promise that damn key wouldn't end up shoved up someone's ass.

Because to tell the truth, I was fucking tired of not knowing what they were saying. *"¿Alguien de aquí habla inglés?"* Does *anyone here speak English?*

Adriana glared at me, but thankfully, the bank teller flashed an overly white smile. "Yes, of course. I speak very good English."

"Good. Use it," I growled, her overly perky attitude grating on my last nerve.

Her lips wavered a little at my tone, but she was still smiling when she turned back to Adriana. "Yes, Miss Muñoz, box 384 does belong to Esteban Muñoz. According to our records, it has been untouched for three years." A line formed between her eyebrows as she stared at her computer screen. "Very strange."

"What's strange?" Adriana asked.

"Usually, our customers pay yearly, but when Mr. Muñoz rented the box, he prepaid ninety-seven thousand pesos. It's highly unusual. I've never seen anyone do that before."

"He knew he wouldn't be around to make the payments," I muttered.

The teller tilted her head. "What was that?"

"Nothing. Look, we're on a tight schedule. Can we just see the box?"

"I'm sorry, that's not going to be possible."

Adriana's head shot up. "Why the hell not?"

The teller gave her a thin smile. "Mr. Esteban Muñoz is the only name listed on the safe deposit box. Just because you have the key and claim to be his daughter, that doesn't give me authorization to allow you access, Miss Muñoz." She tapped a pink painted nail against her computer screen as if we could see it. "Your name has to be on the account itself. I'm sorry."

She was sorry?

Somewhere in that vault was a truth bomb ticking away the seconds of the Carrera Cartel's destruction. Unless I could convince some half-wit to stop wasting my time and unlock the gate, it would detonate, and Adriana and I would both be as good as dead.

And she was fucking sorry?

With a quick look around, I noted there were only two tellers and one office manager in the entire place and made a snap decision.

Pulling my gun, I glanced at her nameplate while aiming it at her face. "Here's what's going to happen, Maya. You're going to let Miss Muñoz back there to get her father's shit right now. If not, I'll put a bullet in your head, and"—I swung the gun toward a younger woman two windows down from her—"I'm sure Selena over there would be happy to do it for you."

Maya nodded like a bobblehead and let out a high-pitched wail while she blubbered, snot flying everywhere as she begged for her life.

"What the fuck are you doing?" Adriana hissed beside me.

"Shut up and take this." Keeping my gun level, I reached for my ankle holster and handed her another one.

Her eyes widened. "Where the hell did you get that?"

From Guns R Us… Where the hell did she think I got it?

"Oh, I don't know, maybe from the haul you requested from your fiancé. Now stop asking me stupid questions and go!"

Taking the gun, she pointed it at Maya and motioned her toward the back. Once they disappeared, I turned my attention toward Selena, the catatonic teller.

"What's your boss's name?"

"Vicente Hernandez." Selena spat the name as if it was the vilest thing she'd ever tasted.

I was starting to like this girl.

I let out a loud whistle. "Hey, Vic, I'm going to need you to come out here, and I suggest you do it now because I promise you don't want me to come get you."

The fucker had been hiding out in his office the whole time.

Coward.

Slowly, the office door opened and a middle-aged man wearing a cheap suit and a bad comb-over walked out with his knees shaking and his hands up. "*Por favor* don't hurt me. I'll do anything you want."

"Anything?"

"*¡Sí!*"

I turned toward Selena and pointed the gun at her head. "Tell you what, Vic, I'll make you a deal. Only one of you is walking out of here today, so since you're the man in charge, you tell me who it's going to be. Do I shoot Selena or you?"

I was only half-serious. That was the lawyer-half. However, the lieutenant-half was still waiting on his answer.

He didn't hesitate. "Her. Shoot her."

Piece of shit.

"Unfortunately, that's the wrong answer, Vic." Swinging the gun around, I fired once, and Vicente Hernandez hit the ground. Shaking my head, I noted Selena's shocked face. "I can't stand a weak man," I explained. "At least die with dignity."

"Are you going to kill me?" They were the first words she'd spoken since giving me a dead man's name.

Never leave a witness.

It was the cartel's number one rule, but something in her eyes that told me she understood the value of silence.

Call it instinct.

"Selena, I want you to listen very carefully," I said, lowering the gun. "I will know where you sleep, where you eat, and the names of your family. If you open your mouth to say anything other than, '*I don't remember,*' I will find you and kill you slowly until you beg for death. *¿Me entiendes?" Do you understand me?*

Instead of breaking down, Selena dipped her chin. *"Te entiendo." I understand you.*

"Now, just so things don't look suspicious, I have to do this." Lifting my arm, I pulled the trigger and sank a bullet in her shoulder. She screamed and crumbled to the floor. "Don't worry, it's not fatal. Been shot there myself."

I heard shouting and another high-pitched wail just before another shot rang out.

"Let's go!" I yelled toward the vault.

Before I could say another word, Adriana ran out from the back holding a brown envelope in her hands. She didn't give the bodies on the ground a second glance as she tore out the door.

Once we were a safe distance away, I called Rafael and instructed him to use his more useful talents to hack into the bank's surveillance system and erase the feeds from the last half hour.

We drove in twenty minutes of silence before Adriana turned to me. "You shouldn't have left a witness."

"Don't start with me."

"Wow, someone's in a bad mood."

I gritted my teeth. "I'm fine."

I caught her bored stare out of the corner of my eye and hated the sudden rush of blood through my veins as she raked that sultry gaze down my body.

"You don't look fine. You look like you're about to rip that steering wheel off and beat somebody with it." I forced myself to look away as she settled her attention back on the road.

"Pretty and perceptive. Tell me again why some lucky guy

hasn't snatched you up yet?" Before she could respond, I answered with a smirk of my own. "Oh, that's right, it must be because you learned your social skills from a bunch of psychopaths."

"Wow, that was a good one," she exclaimed, giving me a slow clap. "It must be nerve-racking throwing all those stones inside that glass house of yours."

My smirk faded. As much as I enjoyed this push and pull between us, I couldn't forget what Val said.

Adriana's back was against the wall. She had nothing to lose and everything to gain. While he was willing to give her the benefit of the doubt, he wouldn't trust without verifying. He was right, and I needed to find out what he'd uncovered and give him an update on whatever was in that envelope. Especially since there were now two more bodies to contend with. He wouldn't be happy we left them there, but without the surveillance tape, nothing could be traced back to us.

I had no doubt this Ignacio posed a real threat against Val. The man I reported to was a walking bull's-eye. However, Adriana was hiding something else. Originally, I convinced myself it involved an intricate plot to take me down simply for screwing her over, but now I had a feeling what lay behind that secret smile was much worse.

"I said I'm fine. I'm just ready to get this shit with you over with and get back to Houston."

Adriana's eyes snapped back to mine. "I'm sorry, what was that?"

"You heard me."

Silent for a moment, she squinted and studied me. "You're punishing me for turning you down the other night."

"That's funny, I don't remember you turning me down. What I remember is fucking you over the hood of this car."

Her cheeks flushed. "That's not what I meant. I'm talking

about afterward when you insinuated that you wanted more."

A confession said in the heat of an argument I wished I could take back. I swore to never let my guard down, but despite every effort, she managed to slip behind my defenses. A mistake I didn't intend to repeat.

Glancing at her out of the corner of my eye, I snorted. "Don't lean too far forward, or you're going to fall off that pedestal you've put yourself on, *princesa*."

Adriana reared back as if I'd slapped her. A few tense moments passed as we stared at each other. Eventually, the shock on her face faded into suspicion. "Why do you do this?"

"Do what?"

"Live this life. Cartel life. Val and I were born into it, but you chose it. It's going to be a hard existence for you. Our world is too blood tied for you to ever truly belong to our *familia*." Shifting, she waved a hand from my shoulders to my waist. "I mean, *Dios mío*, look at you with your Armani suit and your manicured hands, and…"

"My white skin?"

Adriana's lips parted. "I didn't say that."

She didn't have to.

"You don't think I have to work three times as hard as anyone else just to prove myself?" I didn't bother hiding the steel in my voice. "I have more eyes on me than I care to count. Hell, half the time I don't know if someone wants to shake my hand, cuff it behind my back, or cut it off at the wrist."

"So, why do it?"

Baring my teeth in a cold smile, I cupped her cheek. "Newsflash, sweetheart, other than a six-by-eight jail cell or a three-by-six grave, this is all I have left. Until I'm forcefully shoved in one or the other, I *am* your fucking *familia*."

Her eyes darkened as she slapped my hand away. "How

dare—"

"So," I continued, cutting her off. "You'll have to excuse me if I'm still figuring out the proper protocol for entertaining my boss's recently resurrected petulant sister while she holds my balls in her hands."

"I'm not petulant," she growled, folding her arms across her chest.

For the next thirty minutes, we gave each other the silent treatment, the conflict inside me driving me insane. I'd never had such a violent urge to simultaneously sink a blade and my dick in a woman before. I hoped for both our sakes she kept her mouth shut, but by the time we made it back to Chapala, my anger gave way to curiosity.

Tilting my chin, I nodded to the envelope resting in her lap. "Are you going to look inside that thing or what?"

"Later."

"Adriana…"

"Don't push me," she warned, placing a protective hand over it. "You may have been the boss in Houston, but you're in Muñoz territory. That means I call the shots here, not you."

"Fine," I growled, flinging my door open. "But if you think I'm calling you *jefe*, you can shove that crown up your ass, *princesa*."

Chapter Twenty-Nine
ADRIANA

Chapala, Jalisco, Mexico

"You can't put it off forever you know." Brody's eyes shifted to the unopened letter, still sitting in my lap.

We sat on the stairs in between the kitchen and the living room, just like when I tended to his injury. Only this time, he wasn't the one who was bleeding. At least, not in the literal sense.

My wound went much deeper than the simple graze of a bullet, and there wasn't enough vodka in the world to cleanse it. Its gnawing presence never left me. It kept me on edge, pulling me forward while pushing others away. Hiding its dark secrets while slowly destroying me.

The sins of the father are to be laid upon the children.

Sometimes I wondered if a part of me always knew things would end this way. That sins of the past would come full circle, and the one who was spared would be the one who ended the reign.

"Adriana?" Brody lightly bumped my shoulder, and I

blinked away the burn behind my eyes. "Did you hear me?"

I picked up the envelope and ran my fingers along the edge. "Yeah, I heard you. Listen, before I open this, I need to say something, but I need you to not make it weird."

"I'll do my best."

"When I came to Houston, I wasn't lying. Adriana Carrera was the only name I had left, and I wasn't going to sit by while some *pinche cabrón* ruined it. I never hid that I knew bargaining information would force Val to align with me."

Brody's eyebrows hit his hairline. "Bargaining? Is that what we're calling it now?"

"Would you shut up and let me finish?" I growled, slapping the envelope across his injured arm.

"Ow! Jesus, okay!"

"I'm trying to apologize for what I said in the car. You've had every opportunity to turn on me, and if I'm being honest, every right to. I threatened to ruin your life, yet when shots were fired at *El Palacio*, your first instinct was to protect me." I turned to him, the envelope crinkling in my hand. "Why?"

He stared with a widened curiosity. "No one has ever risked anything for you, have they?"

Flinching, I immediately started to argue, then remembered my own words to him. How I told him in detail how Cristiano left me once a rank was no longer on the table. I lowered my eyes and rubbed my chest, trying to relieve the suffocation slowly building behind it.

"Adriana, you fight me because you fear me."

I snapped my head up, eyes blazing. "I don't fear anyone."

"See, that right there." He blew out a heavy breath, his thumb leaving a trail of fire as it traced the corner of my mouth. "That's your go-to response for everything. You talk a big game, and it's pretty damn convincing to anyone who doesn't know you."

"And you think you know me?"

"I don't think it. I know it. You keep people close enough to watch them, but far enough away that they don't realize all this…" He waved a hand down the length of my body. "…is just an act. The real Adriana fears everyone."

"You're wrong."

I'd perfected evasion into an art form. Hid behind it. Worn it as a suit of armor. There was no way he could've seen through it.

"You think if you let someone close enough to get to know the real you, they'll reject you, and that's worse than having the world hate you. That's why I didn't think twice to protect you at that club, Adriana. Because despite all that you've done, and as hard as you try to hide from me, I see you. And maybe for the first time in my life, I don't feel like a placeholder."

Stop it.

The words echoed in my head, taking root and refusing to let go. He was digging too deep. It felt too personal. My world was black and white, but the things he was saying dragged it into a muddled gray area.

"I think you see me, too."

I should've pulled away. As soon as his thumb slid across my bottom lip, drawing it open, I knew what he wanted. My breath hitched as he leaned forward, his hooded gaze on my mouth. I'd already given him my body, but I couldn't deny how much I wanted to let him have the one thing I'd never allowed any man.

I craved it.

I feared it.

I turned my cheek just before he kissed me. "Don't."

He pressed his forehead against my temple, a ghost of a smile on his face. "You have rules." Sitting back, he scrubbed his hands down his face, discreetly adjusting his pants. Letting out a long, drawn-out sigh, he nodded to the letter still clutched in my hand. "Open it. Time's wasting."

Slipping my finger underneath the seam of the envelope, I tore it open and pulled out the multiple pieces of paper tucked inside. Brody sat quietly, giving me space as I unfolded them, scanning the handwritten pages.

"It looks like pages ripped out of a diary."

Brody cocked an eyebrow. "Does it say whose?"

It didn't have to. "It's my grandmother's." Then realizing what I said, I shook my head. "I mean, Esteban's mother. It's dated fifty-five years ago."

Scanning the pages, I read aloud, my hand shaking.

"'Today I followed Pablo to where he keeps his whore. He thinks I don't know. Men with his power aren't expected to be faithful, but he hasn't been discreet with this one. I hid in an abandoned house across the street until he left then confronted the woman sleeping with my husband. I threatened her just like all the others. We both may lay with the same man, but we are not the same. Rosita can spread her legs for my husband, but I can break them. I gave her a choice—walk away from Pablo or never walk again. That was when she told me why she'd summoned him. Pablo's infidelity has shamed our family, and the sins of the father are to be laid upon the children. Poison has infected our bloodline, and it will eat away at our souls for generations to come.'"

The sins of the father are to be laid upon the children.

Brody's eyes flicked toward me. "He got her pregnant."

I nodded a weak affirmation, and as I flipped the page, every bone in my body snapped to attention. Swallowing uneven breaths, I felt an inescapable coldness settle into my soul.

"Jesus, you're shaking." Brody's concerned voice sounded

far away as I stared at the paper in my hand. "What is it?"

"It's a birth certificate," I whispered.

"For whom?"

"Ignacio Vergara."

HOLDING UP MY PHONE, I POINTED TO THE DUSTY ROAD TO MY RIGHT. "The GPS says this is it. Turn here."

Giving the wheel a sharp turn, Brody grumbled, "I don't see why we're bothering an old woman who may or may not have given birth to this asshole. We should be going back to Guadalajara and tracking down—"

"My ex," I finished for him, rubbing my temples in frustration. "I know, you've said it six times already." It was the same argument we'd had for the last hour, but apparently, one he wasn't about to let die.

"You'd think maybe after the first couple of times, some common sense would've gotten through to you."

I didn't have time for this. We already went to *El Palacio* and searched for Cristiano. We threatened, I begged. No one was letting us into that club in the middle of the day. He wasn't answering his phone, and I couldn't waste any more time. When you had a smoking gun in your hand, you didn't tuck it away to search for the missing bullet. You went straight to the hand that fired it.

Besides, Brody called Val before we left the club, and he had already deployed a swarm of Carrera soldiers before they ended the call.

"Would you stop with that? I'm not accusing him of anything until I have proof. You're a damn lawyer. Aren't people innocent until proven guilty?"

Brody squeezed the steering wheel. "If it looks like a duck, swims like a duck, and quacks like a duck, it's—"

I glared at him. "It's not a fucking chicken. I know. I've heard this one already. Get new jokes." He didn't answer, and I didn't elaborate. "We're here," I announced as a tiny house came into view.

With the papers in hand, we walked in silence along an overgrown walkway toward the front door. I knocked twice, drawing the ferocious barks of what sounded like extremely large dogs. *"¿Señora Vergara, estás en tu casa?"* Miss Vergara, are you home?

The dogs kept barking, but no one answered.

Brody sighed, the lines around his eyes deepening. "See? She's not here, can we go now?" Just as he turned around, a frail voice filtered out from behind the door.

"¿Quién está ahí?" Who is there?

Grabbing his arm, I pulled him back and continued in Spanish. "Miss Vergara, my name is Adriana, and this is my friend, Brody. We have a few questions we'd like to ask you. It won't take much of your time."

"Go away!"

I pounded on the door again. "Miss Vergara, please. This is important. It's about your son, Ignacio."

There was a moment of tense silence before a makeshift curtain rustled against a window beside the door. I held my breath as a weathered face appeared. "I know no Ignacio."

That was a lie. I saw it in her eyes when she said his name. I didn't wish this woman harm, but I wasn't leaving without the answers I came for.

Pulling out the birth certificate, I turned it around and slammed it against the window. "I think you do."

She raised a shaking hand, tracing the handwritten words.

"Where did you get that?"

"In a safe deposit box belonging to Esteban Muñoz. I know you know who he is, just like you knew Pablo and Carmen Muñoz. Now you can let us in, or I have no problem standing out here all day."

The old woman's hand dropped, her dark eyes lit with renewed fire. "I'll call the police."

It was the response I anticipated. "You do that," I challenged, pulling the certificate away from the window. "I'd love to tell them how your son hunted me then chained me up like a dog. Or how he's the one rebuilding the Muñoz Cartel." She jumped as I slapped my palm against the glass. "How many people do you think you'll have at your door then, Rosita?"

The curtain fell, and she disappeared. I couldn't breathe. My lungs felt too small, and the air too thick.

Brody placed his hand on my shoulder and gave it a firm squeeze. "Adriana, it's okay."

"No, it's not okay! She can't just—"

There was a soft click, and we both turned as the wrinkled face from the window appeared in the doorway. "Come, I'll put the dogs away."

Ten minutes later, Brody and I sat on a stained floral couch in a pathetically bare house. A few pictures hung on what was probably once vibrant orange walls, and a small square table sat tucked in the corner covered in a serape.

That was it.

A door opened near the kitchen area, and she made her way toward us, the battered cane she gripped in her gnarled hand scraping along the dusty floor. Lowering herself into a rickety chair, she settled a hesitant eye on me and waited.

However, Brody waited for no one. "Is Ignacio Vergara your son?"

I glared at him, but he kept his eyes on Rosita, who shifted her attention toward him, transitioning into broken English. "Yes. But I haven't seen him in many years. Not since…" She looked away, a sudden cloud shadowing her face.

"Not since what?" he pushed.

"Not since…" Her frail voice trailed off, and tilting her head, she narrowed an accusing gaze at me. "How do you know Esteban?"

I froze, the words stuck in my throat. Panicking, I looked at Brody, who gave an encouraging nod. "I'm his daughter," I said.

She studied me. "His daughter is Marisol. You said your name was Adriana." My name barely left her mouth before recognition sparked. Her eyes widened, and both hands wrapped around her cane as she flung herself out of the chair and snatched the crucifix off the wall. Holding it close to her chest, she dropped to her knees and closed her eyes, chanting a prayer in frantic Spanish.

Ave Maria. Hail Mary.

She knew who I was.

There was a harsh edge to Brody's face, and his eyebrows pinched together in confusion. But I knew exactly what was going on, and if I was going to get answers out of her, it had to be woman to woman.

Victim to victim.

I fell to my knees beside her and wrapped my hand over hers. Raising my voice, I overpowered her chanting with rapid fire Spanish.

"You know who I am. You know Esteban murdered my mother and stole me from her arms. Now you tell me what Pablo Muñoz's bastard son has to do with it!"

Without warning, her incessant chanting stopped, and her eyes flicked toward mine. "Esteban wasn't the one who killed your mother, child. It was my son."

I released her hand, falling backward as if I'd touched fire. "What? Why?"

"Adriana, what the hell is going on?" Brody shot off the couch, but I didn't move. I never averted my eyes as the harsh truth spilled from Rosita's parched lips.

"It was a test," she said, her eyes locked on mine. "To prove his loyalty. All my boy wanted was to be accepted by his brother, and Esteban used him as a pawn." She spat the words like poison. "Pablo refused to acknowledge Ignacio, so no one knew my son existed. Esteban used our shame to his advantage. He sent Ignacio away for months to make a trade alliance with promises to make him lieutenant of the new syndicate."

"Let me guess; Esteban lied."

She didn't answer, pressing her lips in a thin, tight line. "He gave him one last task to complete. 'All or nothing,' he said. If he succeeded, the new territory was his, but if he failed..." She trailed off, her eyes brimming with unshed tears. "The task was a revenge mission in Mexico City. I told him it was too dangerous, and Esteban couldn't be trusted, but he wouldn't listen. He was willing to risk everything to return to what he'd built. But I was right. Alejandro Carrera demanded justice, and that lying *pendejo* handed Ignacio over like a sacrificial lamb."

"Obviously, he didn't kill him."

"No, Ignacio overheard the conversation and ran for his life."

"You act like he was innocent!" I yelled. "This wasn't a cartel hit, Rosita! Your son went after women and children. He killed my mother and my aunt. Had my brother not escaped, he would've been slaughtered, too."

I vaguely heard Brody's voice, and when his firm hand landed on my shoulder, I knocked it off. I only hoped he didn't try dragging me out by force. I couldn't promise I wouldn't turn on him.

Rosita's cold eyes softened. "You still don't know, do you?

"Know what?"

"Why you were taken. It wasn't to punish Alejandro Carrera. It was to punish his wife."

All the air whooshed out of my lungs. "What?"

"Alejandro didn't want another child, so after you were born, he rarely came home. Liliana was a lonely woman, and Esteban was a very handsome and powerful man who saw an opportunity. They became lovers, and Esteban found himself so enamored with his rival's wife, he would've left his own for her. However, she feared Alejandro's wrath too much to risk the same." She looked upon me with pity. "Jealousy has more power than love. Your mother ripped out his heart, so Esteban—"

"Took hers," I whispered. "He ripped me out of her arms…"

"She rejected him," she finished for me. "She wasn't supposed to die, but she fought for you."

As the words sank in, so did the surge of hatred. Climbing onto my knees, I clenched my fists, the accusation boiling on my tongue. "Your son has my mother's blood on his hands."

"He had no choice."

"Don't!" I growled, squeezing my fists so tightly, my bones cracked under the pressure. "Everyone has a choice. Ruining my life once wasn't good enough for your *boy*. Now he's trying to do it again. You've kept your mouth shut for twenty-four years, and you'll have to answer for that, but you make this right, old woman. You tell me where he is."

I waited as she did nothing but stare at me.

"I know he's in Guadalajara because he held me here against my will. Are you still proud of your son, Rosita?"

A tear rolled down her cheek, and while part of me knew

berating guilt into an old woman was wrong, I refused to stop.

"If you don't tell me where he is, you might as well put that crucifix down. When he kills again, it will be your hands stained with the blood."

That was the straw that broke her. Rosita let out a wail, her aged hands cupping her face. "There's a warehouse near *Tlajomulco de Zuñiga*. It's about half an hour from here." Rattling off the address, she pressed her palms together under her chin. "He's all I have left. Please show mercy."

"I'll show him exactly what he showed me." Climbing to my feet, I left her sobbing on the floor and flung open the front door. My chest burned as bile crawled up my throat. I didn't know where I was going. All I knew was that I had to get out of here.

I made it halfway to the car before Brody grabbed me by the shoulders and spun me around, his face barely containing his rage. "You're not going anywhere until you tell me exactly what the fuck just happened in there."

"I can't…" The words stuck in my throat like cotton. "Get me out of here. Please."

He stared at me, and I knew his internal debate was between losing his shit in public or private. Either way, he wouldn't back down. Not this time. Closing his eyes, his nostrils flared, as he inhaled a deep breath before blowing it out hard and fast. "Get in the damn car."

Chapter Thirty

BRODY

Adriana had gone rogue, so whether I liked it or not, I needed back up.

I contemplated calling Val again, but it was too soon. I couldn't call the head of the Carrera Cartel with half a story and an excuse of, *"My Spanish is shitty, so I missed half the conversation. However, I'll call you back with more of an update as soon as I fuck it out of your sister."*

Obviously, calling Leo was out of the question. Not after what Val told me.

That left only one person, and I had no doubt his help would cost me almost as much as the debt that got me into this mess in the first place.

Karma was a hateful bitch.

I dialed his number, watching Adriana through the glass doors as she paced a continual line outside, her thumb in her mouth, chewing on her nail like it was her last meal. All of this could've been avoided if she'd just been straight with me and stopped trying to do shit on her own.

"Harcourt. *¿Cómo estás?"*

He didn't care how I was doing any more than I cared about him. So, I got straight to the point. "I need you to find everything you can on Rosita Vergara and Ignacio Vergara from Guadalajara."

"That's interesting. Last time I checked, I wasn't your bitch."

"I don't have time to fuck with you, Carlos," I growled, now starting to fall in line with Adriana's pacing. "Just do it. And get back to me as fast as possible."

A low laugh rumbled in my ear. "Information has a price—"

"Yeah, yeah, I know. Information has a price tag, *amigo*. I remember. I'll get you your money. Just do it."

"These Vergaras," he said, his voice becoming deadly serious. "Are they the ones responsible for fucking with my kilos?"

"I think so. But it goes a lot deeper than that." I stared through the glass at Adriana's hunched shoulders, her body a coiled spring ready to snap. "They're both tangled in the Muñoz family tree, and I want every root dug up."

"*Muy bien.* I'll be in touch."

"Oh, and Carlos? Find a location on Cristiano Vergara as well as any background information." Disconnecting the call, I dropped my phone on the coffee table. I'd given Adriana enough time to pace. It was time to talk.

She jumped at the click of the sliding glass door but didn't turn around. "Are you going to tell me what you tattled to my brother about?"

"Depends," I said, shoving my hands in my pockets. "Are you going to tell me what the hell happened back there?"

She snorted, wrapping her arms tighter around her chest. "You've learned fast. Good for you."

"Meaning?"

"It's the cartel way. Answer a question with a question. Never give without getting. Keep your friends close and your enemies closer." Adriana brushed her chin over her shoulder, a distant smirk pulling at her lips. "Well played."

I wanted to grab her and kiss that damn smirk off her face. Spending twenty-four hours a day with someone for almost a week stripped away all their plastic bullshit. I knew her well enough to recognize a stone wall when I saw one. Whatever happened with Rosita Vergara tore her apart, and now she'd built a shield around herself to keep me out.

"Well, I did get a crash course this week."

She whipped around, her cheeks flushing blood red. The violent reaction confirmed my suspicions, and I almost pushed her just to see if I could get her to crack, but that was what she wanted. Provoking me gave her justification and a clear conscience for shutting me out.

But I was done playing that game.

"They found Leo Pinellas."

"Oh?"

"Official cause of death was a self-inflicted gunshot wound." She stiffened and turned away. Sighing, I pushed off the glass and stood beside her while staring out at the water. "It took so long to find him because he was listed as a John Doe in the morgue at Houston Methodist." I faced her. "*You* dropped him off at the hospital?"

She shrugged. "Not personally. Leo had a full wallet. You'd be surprised what a few street thugs will do for a couple hundred."

"Why not just get rid of him?"

"Did you know my mother…?" She sighed. "I mean

Josefina. Did you know she shot herself?" When I shook my head, she glanced down at her feet, her voice losing its edge. "Right in front of me. Esteban was so shamed by it, he didn't give her a funeral. He just cremated her and tossed her away like garbage. I couldn't do that to him."

Her confession was like a punch in the gut, and I couldn't stop myself from curving my palm around her jaw. "Adriana…"

But the floodgates had opened, and words came spilling out in an avalanche of truth. "Do you know why I was in Leo's office that day?"

"I have an idea."

"No, you don't," she countered, pulling away. "There was a price on my head for something I didn't do, so I came to Leo for information. When I heard him on the phone with you, I knew I could get him to tell me anything I wanted to know, and he did." She let out a dry laugh, a rare breeze blowing her hair across her face. "Sang like the piece of shit canary he'd always been. When he told me you ruined my life just for Eden, that was when I knew I had you. I'd won."

The weight of her words sank in. "You were going to tell Val regardless of whether I helped you or not." It wasn't a question. "You were going to ruin me, and you didn't even know me."

"You didn't know me either. That didn't stop you."

"Why are you telling me this?"

"To let you off the hook. I still think what you did was shitty, but you can stop pretending to like me. No matter what happens, your secret dies with me."

I let out a harsh laugh. "Is this where I'm supposed to thank you? To be grateful that you're so selfless to deny me what I want?"

Chuckling, she brushed past me while walking into the house. "You don't want me, Brody. What you want is redemption."

I stopped her and turned her around. "Redemption for what?"

I saw the wall coming down moments before it slammed into place. "You think you failed Eden," she hissed. "You're convinced you failed Leighton and your niece because you couldn't protect them from your batshit crazy mother. You have a damaged hero complex, and you think saving me will absolve you of your sins." Anger tore through her as she shoved both hands against my chest. "News flash, counselor, I can't be saved."

"Jesus Christ, I'm not trying to save you, Adriana! I'm beating my head against the wall trying to help you, but you keep fighting me for no damn reason!"

"I'm fighting you because you won't admit I'm exploiting your insatiable need to punish yourself, and you're using me to make yourself feel better about it!"

Her words burrowed deep into a decayed part of my mind and detonated, severing the last thread of my self-control. My smile was not a gentle one as I stalked toward her. "Well, if you're going to convict me without a fair trial, I might as well make good on what I'm being accused of."

Adriana parted her lips, stumbling as she backed up. "What do you mean?"

"I mean, if that's all you think I'm doing, then I should use you to make myself feel better. Right here. Right now. Because I'll feel good, Adriana. I'll feel so fucking good."

"Go fuck yourself!" she yelled, stepping back until there was nowhere left to go. She was trapped, her back pressed against a bookcase as tall as the ceiling. Her gaze lowered, and I wasn't sure if she knew whether it was out of fear or anticipation.

"Look at me."

She pushed her hand out in a weak attempt at stopping me. "Don't."

"I said, look at me." She did, those damn gold flecks in her eyes as electric as the sun. "No one decides what I want for me, Adriana. If I want these," I pulled down the top of her shirt along with her bra and exposed her breasts, cupping them in my hands. "I'll have them." I ran my thumbs over her puckered nipples. She was so damn tempting. Leaning down, I took one in between my teeth, biting down gently as I sucked.

"Ah, shit!" Adriana went off like a firework, grabbing handfuls of my hair as she moaned.

But I wasn't done. Dislodging her hold, I shifted her wrists into one hand and held them over her head. "If I want this," I said, daring her to look away as I released the button on her shorts and dove a hand inside, "I'll have it."

As soon as my finger slipped in between her wet folds, her mouth dropped open in a wordless whimper. I allowed a cruel smile just before sinking it deep inside her.

Jesus fuck, I was getting off just on the sounds she was making. She was up on her toes, grasping for purchase onto books and then tossing them off the shelf as her moans became more frantic. She begged for mercy, but I wasn't letting up for shit.

Her pleasure was mine, and I was taking it.

The minute she cried out my name, it was like a symphony in my ear. Tired of not seeing all of her, I pulled my hand out and tugged both her shorts and panties down her legs in one hard jerk. Her eyes went a little unfocused, and I watched curiously as she lifted a shaking hand toward my pants. My cock was hard enough to cut steel, but I was trying to prove a point, and coming in her hand didn't support it.

I grabbed her wrist and held it between us. She blinked in surprise, but I didn't waver. "Both hands on the shelf and don't let go." Once she reached behind her and held on, I soaked in the control I'd commanded, taking my time unzipping my pants. Her eyes followed my every move, so once I had them pushed over my hips along with my boxers, I stroked myself, letting her get a good look at what had already claimed her.

"If I want this inside you," I growled, stroking harder, "I'll fucking have it."

She groaned and licked her lips.

"So don't tell me what I do or don't want. I don't take orders." She expected me to take her against the bookshelf, but this was my show, and I was the goddamn ringmaster. Turning around slowly, I walked to the oversized chair in the corner and sat down. "I also don't feel like chasing you tonight. So, if you want me, you're going to have to come over here and work for it."

I fully expected her to flip me off and walk away. To my surprise, she released the shelf and stumbled toward me, blinking as if not sure what to do next. The power fucked with my head, and I was half tempted to tell her to get on her knees and wrap those smartass lips around my dick, but that wasn't what I really wanted.

I wanted her to own this fucked up thing between us.

"Tick tock, Adriana. Are you going to show me you know how to fuck a man, or do I do as you asked, and go fuck myself?"

A fire ignited in her eyes so intense I almost lost control. Adriana braced a hand on the arms of the chair and knelt on either side of my thighs. She didn't say anything. She just held my gaze and reached between us, wrapping her hands around my cock and circling the head around her entrance until I thought my eyes were going to roll back into my head. I gritted my teeth, forcing myself not to grab her by the hips and impale her.

Sweat beaded across my forehead as she teased me by sliding down a few inches before lifting back up. I bit my lip so hard I drew blood, five seconds away from throwing her on the floor when she sank down slowly, and I slipped fully into her wet heat.

All the air sucked out of my lungs in one breath.

Holy fucking hell.

She shifted her hands, gripping the back of the chair behind my head as she lifted her body up and down so agonizingly slow, I swore I was losing my mind. We were nose-to-nose. My eyes dimmed. My hearing muddled. My insides twisted.

But damn, could I feel.

Adriana's pace picked up, her body rising and falling with frantic speed. It wasn't enough. Giving up, I dug my fingers into her hips and lifting her up, I pulled her down rough and hard on my cock. Over and over, we worked in tandem, her riding me on top as I pumped my hips from the bottom.

Faster.

Harder.

Deeper.

My balls tightened, and the pressure built to the point that I knew if we didn't stop now, I'd come inside her again. I opened my mouth to tell her to slow down when she came.

Hard.

Her hands dove into my hair, her eyes squeezed shut, and her mouth dropped open as her body spasmed, wave after wave claiming her and dragging her under. The violent contraction gripped my dick like a vice, and I came with a roar, my hands holding her hips down until I had nothing left.

We sat there, stunned as we gasped for air. Adriana was still holding the back of my head when we opened our eyes. Her long eyelashes fluttered as we sat pressed together from our foreheads to our noses to our mouths.

Our open mouths.

Stealing breath and flirting with danger.

It would've been so easy to kiss her. I didn't think she would've stopped me. But she had rules, and rules weren't made to be broken.

They were meant to be changed.

So, without breaking our connection, I picked her up and carried her into the bedroom.

I WOKE UP THE NEXT MORNING, STILL EXHAUSTED.

Rolling over, I peered at the clock on the nightstand and groaned. Three hours of sleep wasn't nearly enough, but I'd trade sleep for sex any day. I smiled, remembering how I took her three more times once we made it into bed, and how she'd fallen asleep curled up next to me.

I couldn't remember the last time I'd slept with a woman in my arms.

Whatever this was between us, I'd be damned if I'd let her shut me out again. We were going to talk about what happened at Rosita Vergara's house and stop all this secretive shit.

"Adriana, baby, we have to get up." Still half asleep, I flung my arm across the bed, only for it to fall on top of a cold sheet.

I ignored the rock settling in the pit of my stomach as I grabbed my discarded boxers off the floor before stumbling into the attached bathroom. "Adriana?"

It was silent.

A combination of dread and rage fueled me as I tore through the house, searching every empty room, the call of her name becoming angry shouts.

Then I looked out the window toward an empty driveway.

"Fuck!" I slammed my palm against the glass, trying hard to

resist putting my fist through it.

If she wanted to have conversations behind my back, so could I. All Carrera vehicles were equipped with specialized GPS. One call to Val and he'd track her down in five minutes.

Turning around, I stalked toward the living room and reached for the coffee table where I left my phone only to find it missing, too.

"Son of a bitch!" Hurling a nearby lamp across the room, I cursed as it shattered against the wall into hundreds of irreparable pieces.

Chapter Thirty-One

ADRIANA

The longer I drove, the hollower the ache in my chest became. Why did selflessness hurt so damn bad? Having a taste of happiness last night made leaving him this morning the hardest thing I'd ever done.

Whereas most people hungered for light, I found solace in shadows. But last night, Brody stripped my defenses, and I let myself need someone. Want someone.

I almost kissed him.

His lips were right there. I wanted to kiss him—something I'd never done. I'd fucked many men. I'd pleasured them with my mouth. But I'd never kissed one. However, last night, I was about to give the one thing I held the most sacred to the man who ripped my life apart.

And then he pulled away.

I had my rules, and maybe he had his, too. I needed the words to justify the kiss, and he needed the kiss to justify saying the words. But maybe kisses and words weren't important when actions spoke louder.

Was what I felt love? Was it lust? I didn't know. I'd never truly been in love before. But if it meant shielding me from gunfire in a crowded nightclub or doing whatever it took to unlock the secrets to my past or lying to a man who could end his life just to give me more time to figure out mine—then I guess that was exactly what it was.

But love didn't invite danger. It met it head-on.

And that's why I left him sleeping.

Love also knew when to walk away.

He never would've let me leave, or even worse, he would've tried to come with me. This was dangerous cartel territory. To these men, oaths meant nothing. Pledges meant nothing. Affiliations meant nothing. I would've never forgiven myself if something happened to him.

It took a little over an hour to get to the *Tlajomulco de Zuñiga* address Rosita gave me. The warehouse was hidden three miles down a secluded road. It was everything and nothing I expected it to be. Run-down, gray, plain, and boxy. It blended in as nothing special which was just what he wanted.

As soon as I stepped out of the car, a thick foreboding hung heavy in the air, and the quiet hum of destiny whispered in my ear. That's when I felt it. That's when I knew.

He'd been waiting for me.

I didn't bother to knock. There was no use. I pushed the latch down and opened the door, knowing it wouldn't be locked. A dank, musty smell hit me as soon as I walked in, a metallic rust that only lingered with the stain of blood. As much as it turned my stomach, I ignored it, keeping a blank face as the heavy door slammed behind me.

My eyes fought to adjust to the dim overhead lighting,

scanning for hidden Muñoz soldiers, but there were none. Only a folding table with a metal chair and the bright glowing end of a lit cigar.

"Ignacio Vergara." The words slithered past my lips.

He removed the cigar from his mouth, his voice echoing off the bare walls. "Marisol Muñoz."

"It's Adriana Carrera." I squared my shoulders. "You're a hard man to track down."

His lips parted in a sadistic smile. "Invisibility is a learned skill. I'm good at it."

"Well, I found you, so obviously, not that good." Clasping my hands behind my back, I walked a strategic line parallel to the table. "Plus, I know who you are now, so I suppose the only question I have left is to ask what the hell you think you're doing."

"I told you before. I'm taking what's owed to me."

I paused and lifted an eyebrow. "Am I supposed to know what that means?"

I knew exactly what he meant, so I was shocked when my abrasive belligerence came out of nowhere. I didn't fear his aggression. I wanted it.

We locked eyes. "The Muñoz name," he growled.

"See, that's where you're wrong." Turning toward the middle of the table, I placed both palms down and leaned forward. "The Muñoz name died with Manuel. You're not a Muñoz, Ignacio. You're just Pablo's bastard son, and Esteban's little bitch."

I barely saw him lift the back of his hand before my head snapped over my shoulder. "I would be careful what I said if I were you."

I should've walked away. I should've run out that door, got in the car, and never looked back. But I was done running, and I refused to spend the time I had left looking over my shoulder. So

I braved the consequences and faced him.

"Was being accepted by a brother who hated you worth killing two innocent women? Destroying a family? Ruining a child?"

"You know nothing."

"I know he lied to you. Esteban used you to satisfy his vindictive jealousy then sold you out. He never had any intention of giving you a rank. That would've forced him to acknowledge his family's dirty little secret."

Ignacio raised his hand again, and damn it, I flinched. A sick smile broke across his face as he traced my face with the back of his hand. "Little Marisol. Never fear the knife to your throat as much as the one in your back."

I knocked his arm away. "I didn't escape before. You let me go."

He laughed. "Why chase a rat when you can set the kitten free and wait for her to drop it at your feet?" Pulling the cigar back to his mouth, he took a long puff, blowing out the smoke in a cloudy haze. "You think this is about you? *Puta*, you're nothing but my puppet. I barely did any work. I just stole a few Carrera shipments and put your name out there. You and your new boyfriend, Brody, did the rest." The orange end of his cigar zigzagged as he pointed it at me. "Gotta admit, that one took me by surprise."

"You set me up."

Tucking one hand in the pocket of his dirty black pants, he rounded the desk with a confident swagger. "I simply put cheese on a plate. You're the one who gobbled it up and got your fucking neck snapped. You did exactly what I thought you'd do, which was to try to save your ass by selling mine out." We stood face-to-face, the low laugh he let out slithering down my spine. "You thought you were so smart, getting revenge on Brody Harcourt and shutting me down, all while using that new name to work your way into the Carrera family. You didn't count on that being exactly what I wanted you to do."

"You think you can take him down from the inside?"

"No, but you can."

"Fuck you!" I exploded, but my outburst only seemed to amuse him.

"How do you think Valentin Carrera and Brody Harcourt would react if they knew that you were behind all this from the beginning?

I clenched my arms by my side so as not to take a swing at him. "They wouldn't believe you."

"No, *puta*, they wouldn't believe *you*," he sneered. "Not when they find out you were engaged to *my* son." His words sank low and hard in my stomach. "Not when they find out you gave him *El Palacio* to launder all Muñoz money. Not when they find out you lured Harcourt to his club and tried to get him killed."

Brody was right, and betrayal hit hard with a vengeful hand.

"Cristiano." I stared at him, silently watching as my misguided thirst for vengeance stole every trace of the fragile humanity I'd reclaimed.

I was trapped, a pawn in my own game, with death at both ends of the board. Ignacio Vergara's blind ignorance might have changed my fate, but in a cruel twist of irony, it was my own that sealed it.

"What do you want?" I whispered.

"I want Alejandro Carrera's son to kneel before me. I want him to beg for my mercy, just as his *pinche cabrón* father expected me to do."

"Val kneels for no one."

The glowing tip of his cigar magnified the hatred in his eyes. "He would for *his* son."

My body stiffened, blood roaring in my ears as I made the connection between his cat and mouse game and his end game. "No."

No. The ironclad will that moments ago looked my mother's killer in the eye shriveled behind that one word. He told the truth. This was never about me or claiming either of our birthrights. This was retaliation twenty-four years in the making.

He warned me. I heard him say the words. I just refused to listen.

"Putting a bullet in your brain would be such a waste. Especially when your powers of persuasion could be put to much better use."

"Against whom? According to you, I'm public enemy number one."

"There's no truer revenge than an eye for an eye... Is there, Adriana?"

"No. No, no, no, no, no." The same word fell from my lips over and over, my voice breaking with finality.

Ignacio grabbed my chin, his calloused fingers digging into my bruised skin. "This sanctimonious act is getting old. Don't lie to yourself, *puta*. Santiago Carrera is the heir to the throne. You're nothing but an afterthought. A useless inconvenience. Without him, Valentin and Eden Carrera implode. It's what you wanted, remember? Reclaim who you really are and stop pretending to be this pathetic shell of a queen. Besides," he added, his knowing smirk sickening me as he loosened his grip to trace the traitorous dark circles shining under my eye. "I'll put you back on top and make sure you live to see it."

"You can't want me to—"

"I want Valentin Carrera to remember my name," he hissed, his grip tightening as he stalked forward, forcing me backward toward the door. "So you go back to Mexico City, Adriana

Carrera, because I have a task for you. Don't fuck it up, or I'll kill you. But first, I'll make you watch everyone you love suffer, including Brody Harcourt. I'll enjoy the look on his face when he sees how blind he's really been."

I HAD TO STOP FOUR TIMES ON THE WAY BACK TO CHAPALA TO THROW up. The rest of the drive was a never-ending blur of cars, trees, houses, and static. By the time I pulled into the driveway and around to the back of the house, my head felt as empty as my body.

That's how I felt as I stumbled toward the house.

Empty.

"Adriana!" Brody stormed toward me, his green and brown eyes blazing with deadly fire and the strong smell of alcohol on his breath.

"You've been drinking again."

"You're damn right I have. Where have you been? No, don't answer that. I already know you confronted Ignacio alone. You don't…" His hand flew to my chin and turned it to the side. "Is that a bruise? Did that motherfucker hit you?"

I didn't know what to say. The truth would send him into a drunken rage, but lying was pointless, so I said nothing.

"He's a dead man." He spoke the words with such cold malice, I shivered. Diving both hands in his hair, he pulled at the roots as he paced. "Who the fuck do you think you are, Adriana? I'm not one of your soldiers. I don't answer to you, and you sure as hell don't get away with stealing from me! I'm a goddamn Carrera!" His voice boomed, rage pouring out of him as he hauled me against him. "Do you hear me?"

All I could do was nod.

"That's it? A nod? After what you did, that's all I get?" Brody threw his head back and let out a harsh laugh. "Fuck this. I'm done." Shoving both hands into my jeans pockets, he pulled out the keys to the car and his phone. "You won't be needing these." He tucked them away, and seizing ahold of my arm, dragged me inside the house. I didn't resist. Truthfully, I was thankful for the help.

Once we were inside, he threw me onto the couch, where I collapsed, my body giving into fatigue and strain. My head lolled back, and I stared up at the man looming over me, his muscular body taut with unleashed rage.

"You need to lay off the booze. I'll never understand why people willingly destroy their bodies. It's disrespectful to those who never got to make that choice."

"Thanks for the PSA. Now, explain yourself."

"I swear, I—"

"Don't!" he yelled, his fists balling. "No swears. No promises. Just truth."

I winced at the disgust in his voice, but I couldn't fault him for it. Truth was a two-faced beast dancing on my shoulders. Each whispered words of evil in my ear that would damn me if spoken out loud.

So, I gave him the only truth I could.

"Yes, I went to see Ignacio, but it's not for the reasons you think."

He stood still as a statue while I gave him a very abridged version of Rosita's story. I told him about Esteban's rank promises to Ignacio. About his ultimatum. About the affair and how Alejandro knew about it. I also told him how Esteban handed Ignacio over to the Carreras without a second thought.

I did not tell him about Cristiano, and I hated myself for it.

"So, why reorganize after twenty-four years?" he asked.

"Why implicate you? The shit doesn't add up."

He was right. It didn't. But only because I left out pertinent information that incriminated me.

"Ignacio was a hunted man, so he had to bide his time. After Esteban and Alejandro died, he only needed Manuel out of the way. Once that happened, there was nothing preventing him from reclaiming what he believed to be his birthright." I shrugged. "He was the only one left alive who knew it wasn't mine."

"So, now what?" A distant black calm deadened his voice. "That's it? You just exchanged contact info, and now you'll send each other Christmas cards once a year?"

"What did you want me to do, Brody? Challenge him to a duel? You're lucky I came back in one piece."

I glanced up to see the tight lines in his face fading, his anger slowly dissipating.

He bought it.

A fact that should've relieved me. Instead, I'd never been more miserable.

He let out a heavy sigh. "You can't keep doing this shit."

"I didn't want you to get hurt, and that would've happened if you'd gone with me."

He reared back, a stricken look crossing his face. "So, what if you'd gotten hurt, or God forbid, killed? What would I have done then?"

I lowered my eyes. "Lived your life."

"What life?" he roared, casting his arms out wide. "Christ, Adriana, do you understand I've felt more alive in the last five days than I have in the last five months?" He balled his fist, beating it against his chest with each word. "Do you know what it's like to feel nothing?"

"Yes, I do."

Rough, ragged breathing echoed in my ears moments

before strong hands landed on the back of the couch, caging me in. "Adriana, you're the only light I see. If you die, so does any hope of me living again."

He couldn't say those words. Not now.

"You've been drinking," I repeated.

"Yes, but I'm very aware of what I'm saying."

I tried to force him to hear words I wasn't saying. "I'm not light, Brody. There's nothing but darkness in me. Darkness you couldn't possibly understand."

"I don't believe that. But you do. So, if the only way for you to accept you're worth love is for me to accept you'll never give it, then I don't care to ever see the sun again."

I shattered. A million pieces, broken and jagged.

There was no thought. No reservations. No hesitation. My hands cupped his face, the now thick growth on his once clean-shaven face brushing against my palms as I pulled him toward me.

My breath hitched.

And then I kissed him.

Reckless and without rules.

It was everything I never imagined it would be.

I covered his mouth with mine, sweeping my tongue against his as if I owned it. As if I knew what the hell I was doing. Brody stilled, his eyes open wide with shock.

This was a mistake.

Just as I was about to pull back, he let out a low curse and cupped the back of my head, pulling me back against his lips. I started the kiss, but Brody owned it. His hands maneuvered my face, twisting it to his advantage so he could dive deeper, taste more, take as much as I'd allow. His primal groans awoke a dormant fire inside me, and I chanted his name in between kisses.

A low growl rumbled in Brody's throat, and I found myself

in his arms as we made our way toward the bedroom, hungry kisses now frantic and fevered.

Once we fell onto the mattress, he leaned back, and the sound of his belt buckle hitting the floor drew my eyes up. He crawled over me and took his time undressing me, revealing each piece of skin as if he were unwrapping a present.

"You're so beautiful, Adriana," he murmured, kissing his way down to my belly button and across to my hip. "So fucking beautiful." His lips moved inward, his breath hot against my thigh.

I knew what he wanted, and any other time, I would've welcomed it. But not tonight. Tonight, I wanted his tongue inside the one place that only belonged to him.

"Brody…"

Hooded eyes gazed up at me, and then he smiled. He knew what I needed, and he waited to give it to me until I understood that asking for it didn't make me weak. It empowered me.

His mouth found mine, his cock pressing at my entrance, hesitating as if asking for permission. I nodded, but he just stared at me, the want in his eyes relentless.

Say the words.

A surge of courage swelled in my chest, and despite the ruin that awaited us on the other side of that door, I gave him what he needed to hear.

"Make love to me," I whispered, brushing a hand through his thick hair.

He closed his eyes as if soaking them in and then slowly pushed his hips forward, sinking inside me so torturously slow, every inch felt like a mile. When we were fully joined, he stilled, dropping his mouth and taking my lips in a deep kiss that took my breath away.

Then he loved me.

The muscles in his back bunched under my fingers as he moved. There was no frantic rush. No punishing thrusts. Just raw connection. We never stopped kissing, our tongues moving in sync with our bodies.

This was how I wanted it to end.

I was so lost. Our mouths remained connected, sharing the same breath as the tension peaked.

"Tell me," he growled in between pants. "Tell me in Spanish, I don't care, but tell me."

"Te amo. Me hiciste amarte, y ahora estoy perdida."

He fell over the edge, dragging me along with him. Our combined groans were only masked by the sound of each other's names. In the silence, Brody dropped his head in the crook of my neck, his damp hair sticking to my skin as I traced my fingers down the claw marks on his back.

Tomorrow we'd return to Mexico City, and everything would change.

Which was why I hoped Brody could only translate the first part of my confession. Even if he asked me to explain the part he didn't understand, I'd refuse.

It'd be a blessing when I turned the only ones he did to ash.

Chapter Thirty-Two

ADRIANA

Mexico City, Mexico

We were three hours into the seven-hour drive back to Mexico City the next day when Brody turned to me, a deep line sinking between his eyebrows. "You're quiet."

I drummed my nails against my armrest. "Just thinking."

"About what?"

"What I'm going to tell Val."

He reached across the console, gently tilting my chin toward him. "You mean what *we're* going to tell Val."

I shook my head and faced my window. "This isn't your problem, Brody. I'm the one who chased a ghost. I'm the one who dragged you to a club and put you in the middle of a massacre. I'm the one who convinced you to hold up a bank. I'm the one who harassed an eighty-year-old woman. And I'm the one who went off to see Ignacio alone. I'm not letting you take the fall for my mistakes, past, present, or future."

Dios mío, just saying it all out loud turned my stomach.

Was this the person I'd been all my life—selfish without a shred of compassion for anyone but herself? There was no wonder everyone believed me to be the root of all evil.

That was all I'd ever been.

Brody sighed, running a hand through his unruly blond hair, the front of it flopping defiantly over one eye. "Adriana, you're Val's sister. He's not going to kill you for acting like a Carrera."

Amidst all the lies, my watery smile was genuine.

Because the irony was too poetic.

He wouldn't kill me for acting like a Carrera. He was going to kill me for acting like a Muñoz.

"Besides," he said, pulling the car over as he spotted the food cart he'd been looking for. "This isn't over. Val's soldiers are searching for Cristiano. Plus, I have another connection looking into it. Once we find him, we'll shut both of them down."

I twisted my fingers together as he pulled off the side of the road, my stomach roiling at the thought of food.

No, it wasn't over. Just not the way he thought. The decision I had to make wasn't whether to fall on my sword and protect Brody or to risk Val's wrath and be a united front. It was whether to fall in line and protect myself or risk Ignacio's wrath and be a ticking time bomb.

"Come on, Carrera. These *pambazos* aren't going to eat themselves."

I climbed out of the car, trying not to throw up as Brody led me toward the crowded food cart.

One thing was for sure. I should've never kissed him.

WE ARRIVED IN MEXICO CITY EARLY THAT EVENING. I PLANNED TO corner Val for some preemptive damage control, but he wasn't home. According to Leighton, he and Mateo had urgent cartel business and had been gone most of the day.

So, Brody and I spent the rest of the night pretending each other didn't exist. Not an easy task when just the mention of his name sent my pulse racing and my hormones into overdrive.

Considering where we were and the way we left things, we thought it would be best to keep this new development private for the time being. Besides, who would believe us anyway?

I spent my time alone, waiting for Val to return, lost in my own head until Ignacio invaded it. His gravelly voice echoed as I wandered the halls of the Carrera estate, the war waging inside of me tearing me apart.

"Val kneels for no one."

"He would for his son."

The walls closed in, moments away from crushing me.

"You're nothing but an afterthought. A useless inconvenience. Reclaim who you really are and stop pretending to be this pathetic shell of a queen."

I stumbled as the floor tilted, slamming me against the wall.

"I have a task for you. Don't fuck it up, or I'll kill you. But first, I'll make you watch everyone you love suffer—including Brody Harcourt."

I gripped the wall, tears streaming down my face.

"I'll put you back on top and make sure you live to see it."

It'd be so easy to fall into old habits. I could never trust Ignacio, but he needed the Carrera name, at least for now. And he offered something no one else had.

Time.

But I couldn't walk down this path and expect Brody to stand by my side. I'd never be his *princesa*. I'd be his enemy. A pariah.

There was no way out for me. If I yielded to Ignacio's

demands, I'd lose Brody and destroy Val. If I refused him, I'd still lose Brody and destroy Val. The only difference between the two was with Ignacio, the people I'd come to care about lived.

A gurgle stopped me in my tracks, and wiping my eyes, I peeked inside the cracked door. A white crib sat against a pale blue wall, and a hand-painted, navy-blue crown spanned the area above it. Right below the crown was written, *once upon a time, there was a little prince.*

Santiago's nursery.

I couldn't stop myself. I went inside and leaned over the crib. Santiago lay on his back, his tiny hands reaching for the moon and stars mobile hanging above him. As if sensing my presence, his dark eyes turned toward me, and he smiled.

Leaning down, I smiled back and rubbed his soft cheek. I traced his full lips, the sharp slant of his nose, and his angled jawline. Maybe I just refused to see them before, but they were there.

Strong Carrera features.

I saw my own face in this tiny baby. This innocent child whose blood ran in my veins. My nephew. Santiago knew nothing of my past. He was my chance to start fresh without any scars or memories. He was a child whose fate rested in my hands.

The truth hit me so hard, I gripped the edge of the crib to keep my balance. I was right. Life had come full circle. What was once ruined, now had the power to rectify. Twenty-four years ago, Ignacio was given a choice, and he changed the course of my life. Now, faced with the same one, I had the power to break the cycle or fall victim to it.

"*Familia,*" I whispered.

"My *familia*, considering he's the only blood relative I have left, thanks to you."

I flinched but didn't turn around. "I'm not the same person

I was back then, Eden."

I heard her step farther into the room, and I closed my eyes.

"Neither am I. Back then, I was just some stupid bartender who watched her brother get murdered in front of her own eyes. I had moments where I wanted to die, too. I was weak. But I made a choice when I followed Val to Mexico, and I left that woman behind. Now, I'm a cartel kingpin's wife."

I twisted around, meeting her hardened stare. "You hate me."

"Can you blame me?" she asked, silence engulfing the room as she crossed her arms over her long cherry-red hair. "You took great pleasure in telling me how you used me from the beginning to hurt Val. Or don't you remember?"

I remembered. I just wished I didn't.

⸺⤙⧓⤚⸺

Houston, Texas

One Year Ago

"HELLO, EDEN."

The moment Eden's eyes adjusted to the shock of the light, they settled right on me as if in a daze. She recognized me, but her fatigued brain couldn't put the pieces in correct order.

She would soon enough.

"How do you know me?"

"Marisol, this is Valentin Carrera's whore." Manuel motioned dramatically from me and then back to Eden, giving her a wink. "Eden Lachey, meet the beauty and brains of this operation, Marisol Muñoz, my sister."

Landing a heavy boot to her stomach, Manuel flipped her onto her back then jerked her to her feet. "Get up. We've got a party waiting for you downstairs."

"Why are you doing this?"

"Money, darling. Valentin Carrera has it; I want it. You think I spent years studying with my nose in a book at the University of Guadalajara to be stuck in an office somewhere?" My high-pitched laugh bounced off the walls. "Hell, no. What this cartel has lacked since my father's death has been intelligent direction. No offense, dear brother."

Manuel shrugged and raised a quick eyebrow in my direction before snapping Eden's arm toward a closed door.

"The Muñoz Cartel could never overtake Alejandro Carrera because it lacked strategic planning and intricate follow-through—something that required the long-term patience of a woman. You understand, right, Eden?"

"Sure," she replied, rolling her eyes in the dark.

"The men in my family want everything now, now, now. But I told them, 'bide your time and watch Carrera. He's not as inhuman as you think. Eventually, we'll find his weakness. When we do, take it. Carrera will come to us.' You're his weakness, Eden. We women are powerful creatures. In our lifetime, there will always be one man who will die for us." I stared at her and ran a painted red nail down her tangled hair. "No man is immune to our power—even the almighty El Muerte. Congratulations on being the woman who brought down the giant."

Present Day

IT ALL SEEMED LIKE A LIFETIME AGO. IN SOME WAYS, IT WAS. THE woman who took pleasure in inflicting pain didn't exist anymore. Marisol Muñoz was dead, but I wasn't sure anything I said or did would convince her.

"We've all made mistakes," I said, blotting away the memory.

"And some of us have yet to pay for them."

"You've misjudged my intentions."

"And you've clearly underestimated mine." Her words coiled around the tension in her body. "So let me be clear, I told you to stay away from my son, and I meant it. My only purpose in life is to protect my family from any and all threats."

I steeled my jaw at her insinuation. "And that's me."

She cocked an eyebrow. "Is it? You gave the order to have my brother killed in front of me. If you think I'm letting you get anywhere near my son, you're wrong. Family is the most important thing to Val, and he desperately wants to believe you. He spent his life believing you were dead, and now all he wants is a chance to have his sister by his side. I hope for his sake that you're being truthful with him." Eden crowded into me, the corner of her mouth curling up. "Because if I find out otherwise, I'll show you what kind of *puta* I really am."

Stalking toward the crib, she scooped Santiago in her arms and stormed out of the nursery.

Chapter Thirty-Three

BRODY

It was too late for *la comida,* so we all sat around the table for *la cena* which was like appetizers on steroids. It felt as comfortable as jumping into a lion's den wearing a ribeye tied around my neck. Eden stared at Adriana. Adriana stared at her plate. I stared at Adriana, then stared at Leighton because she kept staring at me staring at Adriana. Mateo stared at Val, and Val…

Well, Val fucking stared at everybody.

There was so much staring going on, no one talked. Thank God for scotch because booze was the only thing that kept me from flipping the table and walking away. I needed to either get Adriana alone and fuck this tension out of my system or get Val alone and talk it out. At this point, I didn't care which one, but something had to give.

My choice was made for me when Leighton stood, hoisting my sauce drenched niece onto her hip. "If you'll excuse me, this one needs to be hosed down."

Adriana jumped up so fast, the silverware rattled. "I'll help."

My sister cast a suspicious eye between us. "Are you sure?"

By the time she nodded, Adriana was already halfway up the stairs. "Definitely. Let's go."

Val leaned back into his chair, watching with a strained curiosity while rubbing the dark hair on his chin.

Mateo just smirked, raising an eyebrow at his jefe. "Want me to stay?"

Val waved his hand. "It's messy upstairs."

Mateo's smirk widened. "It's about to get messier down here."

Gold flecks ignited in familiar dark eyes that settled hard on the Carrera underboss. "Mateo."

Any time Valentin Carrera spoke, people obeyed, but there was a certain unmistakable tone that he reserved as a snap threat. Like that moment when you stretched a rubber band to its absolute threshold, and you knew you had seconds before it snapped. That was Val's voice. It was low and clipped, and usually just one or two words that, if not heeded, led to chaos.

Snap threat.

And Mateo heard it loud and clear.

"Right," he said, pushing away from the table. "I'll just go help two grown-ass adults give one small girl a bath."

Even I caught the sarcasm. Mateo respected Val, but he wasn't a pussy.

Val picked up his glass and stood, motioning toward the sitting room. "Let's have a talk, Harcourt."

Gripping my glass, I followed him into the same room we last met in. Val didn't sit, going straight to the bar to fill up his glass. When I didn't follow, he glanced over his shoulder, cocking a slanted eyebrow. "I'm not a fucking bartender. If you want a drink, get it yourself."

Meeting him at the marble bar, I accepted the expensive bottle of scotch he offered with a low whistle. "Macallan 1926. You don't play around."

He tipped his glass back, his gaze unwavering. "There are three things a man should never compromise quality for cost. Liquor, women..." He trailed off to take another drink so, I finished his trifecta.

"Cars?"

"Condoms," he said, lowering the glass.

I coughed, the mouthful of scotch I just took spraying everywhere. Val calmly took a napkin from the bar and brushed it down the front of his shirt before helping himself to a refill. He said nothing, but it felt like I had a flashing neon light attached to my forehead.

I fucked your sister.

Blink, blink, blink.

A lot.

Blink, blink, blink.

At least I had to come clean about my job. I owed him that much after the shit I'd pulled lately.

"I wanted to debrief you on what we uncovered," I started, but Val had other ideas.

"Likewise," he said, holding my eye. "And since this is my house, I'll go first." He let a brief pause hang in the air, no doubt for effect, or just to be an ass. "My men haven't found Cristiano Vergara yet, but we did find out something that should interest you."

I didn't say anything because I had a feeling what was coming.

"Cristiano Vergara doesn't exist."

And that wasn't it.

"I'm sorry, what?"

Sounds of glass clinking cut through the silence, and I glanced over to see Val casually filling his glass. "Doesn't exist. No birth certificate, no records, nothing. *Un fantasma en el viento*. A ghost in the wind. Innocent men don't run, but if Ignacio and Cristiano are related, I can't prove it yet."

"But you will."

His lips peeled back in a confident smirk. "I always do."

Questions flew through my mind, none of which had answers. All I knew was that I needed to talk to Carlos and compare notes.

"Also, there was nothing on the car's GPS history."

"You're kidding."

He shook his head. "Someone knew which wires to cut."

I ground my teeth. Not just any someone.

Adriana.

Val stared at me in silence for a few moments, a curious gaze in his eye. "Let's hear your debrief."

My mind still reeled from his bombshell, so I stalled with a generous drink from my glass. Every lawyer's instinct roared at me to question him, but I liked breathing and would prefer to keep doing it. "I was right when I said I thought something about Ignacio Vergara's revival of the Muñoz Cartel connected to Adriana. Ignacio was the man who kidnapped her as a baby."

Val stilled, his hand gripping the glass so hard, I expected it to shatter in his hand. "Are you telling me this is the *hijo de su puta madre* who killed my mother and my aunt?"

"Apparently, another missing birth certificate, only this one we recovered." I recounted the story Adriana told me, standing my ground when his head snapped up once I got to the part where Adriana stole the car to go meet him.

"You let her go alone? *Dios mío*, I sent you with her to make sure she didn't do something stupid, Harcourt! Meeting a killer alone in an abandoned warehouse qualifies as pretty goddamn stupid!"

"She's not stupid, Val! She's determined to protect this family! And I didn't let her go," I growled, between clenched teeth. "She snuck out of bed before I could…"

Fuuuuuck.

Val's eyes flashed pitched black. Not a speck of gold flickered in a dead sea of dark rage. "She. Snuck. Out. Of. Bed. Before. You. Could. What?" He bit out each word, his nostrils flaring.

"Stop her," I finished.

"What happened between you and Adriana?"

"What do you mean?"

"Don't play dumb with me. You left here warning me that trusting her was a mistake. You swore she had an agenda. Now, you're defending her like…" His voice trailed off, his eyes narrowing.

"Like what?"

"Like I would Eden."

I laughed. "Right."

"Did you fuck my sister?" His voice lowered to a thin rumble, and there it was.

The snap threat.

Lunging forward, he fisted my shirt. "I asked you a question."

I calmly lifted my drink and took a sip, staring him right in the eye. "Are you done?"

"I asked you to do one thing. Keep your dick away from her."

The way he spoke like we were some drunken bar fuck in a dirty bathroom stall pissed me off. "It's not like that."

"Then tell me, Harcourt." He smirked, an unbidden mocking in his eyes. "What's it like?"

It was like getting hit in the head with a brick. It was a frustrating back-and-forth with a woman I was never supposed to want. It was a dead calm stirred up in a tornado of smart mouth and brazen wit. It was fear of falling and the rush of the plunge.

"I love her, all right?" I shouted, shoving him away from me.

Val blinked. Then he blinked again. Then again. "What did you just say?"

I pressed my fingers against my forehead, rubbing against the headache brewing behind my eyes. Exhaling hard, I dropped my hand and held his gaze. "I said I'm in love with Adriana."

"It's been a week."

"About the length of time you knew Eden, I believe."

All the tendons in Val's neck pulled tight with tension, but he kept his lips pressed tightly together, tamping down his anger. It was because I was right, and he knew it.

At least I didn't have to kidnap Adriana to get her in my bed.

Gritting his teeth, he turned toward the bar again, filling his glass until it nearly overflowed. "Does she feel the same way about you?"

"I think so." I didn't elaborate. Val didn't need to know about Adriana's rules or what that kiss meant. I didn't give a damn if he stomped around threatening to cut off every protruding part of my body. This conversation was over.

But there was still one thing left I needed to say.

One thing I couldn't leave hanging over my head if I wanted to remain a permanent part of Adriana's life. She promised it would die with her, but secrets had a way of coming out one way or another, and if I wanted to open a door to the future, I had to close the one to the past.

"Look, Val, I need to tell you something."

Val's face tightened, and draining the glass, he slammed it on the table. "I'm not in the mood for any more confessions, Harcourt."

"This one you need to hear. It has to do with Adriana, and why I agreed so quickly to bring her here." Clearing my throat, I spoke slowly, making sure he heard every word. "When I took proof of Adriana's identity to Eden, it wasn't to drive her to you. It was to drive you apart."

Snap.

Val's glass shattered against the wall moments before he swung.

AFTER TUCKING HER SLEEPING DAUGHTER INTO HER CAR SEAT, LEIGHTON leaned against the door, her lips flattening into a smug smirk.

I folded my arms across my chest. "What?"

"That's a nice shiner you got there."

"Yep."

"I see you told Val."

"Told Val what?"

"That you're in love with his sister."

My eyes snapped back to find Leighton grinning like she'd just won the lottery. "Jesus, what's with everyone in this house?" I dragged my finger in a horizontal line above my eyebrows. "Do I have this shit stamped across my forehead?"

Leighton laughed, batting my hand away from my face. "A sister knows these things."

"Great."

"So, what are you going to do about it?"

"I don't know."

I didn't, and that was the thing that bothered me the most. I'd cleared the air with Val, my face taking the brunt of his wrath. Once we took Ignacio Vergara down, and whatever progeny he may or may not have, I was free to do anything I wanted to do.

The thing was, I had no idea what Adriana wanted.

I guess my silence spoke for me because Leighton wrapped an arm around my waist. "She acts tough, but she needs a hero," she said, leaning her head against my arm. "I don't know anyone who fills those shoes better than my big brother."

I snorted. "Don't let your husband hear you say that."

She laughed, knocking her bony hip against me. "You're a protector, Brody. You always have been. It's what made you such a good prosecutor. You take on everyone else's problems as your own, but when you can't defeat them, they consume you." She looked up at me, the corners of her mouth turning down as sadness filled her eyes. "It's why you have so many demons."

Out of nowhere Adriana's words came rushing back.

"You don't want me, Brody. What you want is redemption. You have a damaged hero complex, and you think saving me will absolve you of your sins."

But she was wrong. I wanted it all, and I was starting to believe that despite everything, I could have it. Saving Adriana wouldn't absolve me of my sins but repenting for them would.

I placed both hands on my sister's shoulders, her doe eyes still looking up at me. "I never asked for your forgiveness."

"You're the only one blaming you for what happened," she said, holding onto my wrists. "The only one you have to forgive is yourself."

"I'm not sure how to do that."

She gave me a bright smile and glanced up while nodding over my shoulder. "I think you already have." It was instinct that had me turning around to see Adriana pressed against the second story window. Leighton moved her hand on top of mine and squeezed my fingers until I turned back around. "Six months ago, you wouldn't have let her close enough to risk another demon. Salvation comes in many forms. Sometimes it's in the shape of your biggest regret."

My chest tightened as I processed her words. I asked for forgiveness, and she gave me clarity. A clean slate.

Wrapping my arms around my baby sister, I kissed the top of her head and rested my cheek against her blonde hair. "How'd you get to be so smart?"

She chuckled, sinking into the hug. "I had a pretty good teacher."

Chapter Thirty-Four

ADRIANA

Swallowing the lump in my throat, I turned away from the window, unable to watch any more of the sibling love fest between Brody and his sister. Not that I wasn't happy for him. I was glad to see him get the closure he needed to stop punishing himself for other peoples' sins, but I couldn't help the torrent of conflict running through me.

I grew up with a brother, at least the man I *thought* was my brother. We were close as kids. It wasn't until Esteban died and Manuel became drunk with power that the divide between us grew so wide I could no longer reach him.

But now I had a real brother. One I'd lose by my own doing no matter what I did.

Chills scattered down my arms as sweat beaded across my forehead. The fever was back. My body felt like it had been hit by a truck. I wasn't sure how much longer I could pretend like nothing was wrong.

"I'll put you back on top and make sure you live to see it."

"Shut up!" I yelled, pressing my hands over my ears.

"Interesting. Usually women wait until I speak before telling me to shut up."

I glanced up to where Val leaned against the door to my room, hands in his pockets, wearing an amused smirk. "Oh, that, I, uh, it…" Pressing the back of my hand against my forehead, I closed my eyes, forcing Ignacio's voice out of my head while silently praying for the room to stop spinning. "I'm glad you're here. I have a confession to make."

And hope to hell Brody didn't get to you first.

"So do I."

My revelation died on my tongue, and I stared at him at a complete loss for words.

Seeing he achieved his desired shock value, he pushed away from the door and sauntered into my room. I watched every step, following every shift of his eyes as they scanned everything from the walls to furniture.

"This used to be our mother's room," he said finally.

"I know."

He raised a curious eyebrow, waiting for me to explain, but I didn't. It was too late, and I was too tired to explain the memories I shouldn't have.

I shrugged. "Just a feeling, I guess."

"I put you in here on purpose," he admitted, running his finger along a thin layer of dust resting on top of the dresser. "I suppose as a test to see how you'd react."

"Seems to be a lot of tests lately," I huffed. When he didn't respond, I braced my shoulder against the tall bed post and cocked my chin. "Did Brody fail one of your tests?"

"Actually, Brody passed."

Remembering the blood dripping from his nose as he

stormed out of the sitting room earlier, I narrowed my eyes. "Your reward system is pretty sadistic."

Val let out a hearty laugh. "Brody proved his loyalty tonight by telling me something our father would have beheaded him for."

"But not you?"

"I may be Alejandro Carrera's son, but I'm not him, Adriana. When the situation calls for it, I can be just as cruel, but unlike him, I have limitations as well as standards. I expect a certain code of conduct from my men, and in turn, I exemplify it. If I'm shown loyalty, I reward it. If I'm betrayed, I show no mercy."

"What does this have to do with Brody?"

He didn't answer right away. Instead, he took slow, calculated steps designed to taunt and torture until finally, his eyes flickered right in front of me. "He confessed to using your true identity in an attempt to keep Eden away from me."

My heart fell to my feet. "He told you that? And he's still breathing?"

Pursing his lips, he gave me an unenthusiastic shrug. "I've had a long time to process it. I've just been waiting for him to grow the balls to face me."

I palmed my forehead, my vision going in and out of focus. *"Dios mío, ¿qué demonios está pasando?" My God, what the hell is happening?* "You knew? All this time, you knew?"

He had the nerve to look offended. "Why do you seem so surprised? I'm the *jefe* of the most powerful cartel in the world. I own almost all of Mexico's officials and most of the politicians in the southeastern United States. Plus, anyone with half a brain knew the minute I left Houston I had half a dozen men watching every move Eden and Brody made."

"But you did nothing," I argued, still not comprehending his logic. "You even made him a top lieutenant. Why?"

Val's calm veneer vanished. "Trust me, if he'd touched her, that would've been his last breath." Once the dark cloud passed, he uncoiled. "But Eden came back to me, and besides, how could I blame him? I can't say I wouldn't have done the same thing. Love does crazy things to a man, Adriana," he said, tapping his temple. "Makes him *loco en la cabeza.*"

Unbelievable.

I sank onto the bed, my body feeling like a sack of lead weights. If the whole thing weren't so tragic, it would've been comical. The one thing that forced Brody into this mess, Val knew about all along.

The bed dipped as Val sat beside me and clasped his hands in his lap. "Plus, how could I kill him when he confessed to being in love with my sister?"

My head snapped to the side. "He said those words?"

"Oh, he said a lot more than just those words. But judging by your reaction, they're words you haven't heard yet, so I'll keep them to myself. They're not mine to tell."

He's in love with me.

He loves me.

"Adriana, we need to talk about Cristiano Vergara."

I winced, the words like a sharp knife stabbing into my already severed heart. I had no idea what all he knew, but I had a feeling it edged dangerously close to the truth.

"I know, but not now, okay?" I couldn't sit still. I paced. I wrung my hands, and eventually I ended up right back where I started—by the window where Brody and Leighton were saying their goodbyes. Even from a distance, their embrace looked so genuine, so filled with love and trust that I blurted out, "Do you think we would've been like them? You know, if things had been different."

Val joined me by the window, watching the siblings before

answering. "I'd like to think so. When everything happened to Leighton, I saw a different side to him. He risked everything for her—his career, his reputation, his life. Over the years, I've thought a lot about the day you were taken. What I could've done. Maybe if I hadn't run like a little bitch, I could've saved you and our mother."

My heart lodged in my throat at the image of a six-year-old Val, running for his life while being chased by his mother's screams. "Or you would've died right along with her."

Val didn't answer. He just stared out the window as horrific memories played across his face. Memories I was spared, while they became a burden he carried alone.

I'd come to a crossroads. I could forge ahead and dig a trail of tears or follow the worn coward's path. It was because of that burden and the fragile bond we'd established that I chose the coward's path, once again proving I was irredeemably selfish.

"I was in Santi's nursery today."

And sadistic.

Val chuckled. "I heard."

Biting my lip, I pressed my palm against the glass. "Are you sure he's safe in there?"

He tilted his chin, his dark eyebrows bunching together. "What do you mean?"

"When I walked by, the door was ajar, and he was all alone. You have staff and *sicarios* coming in and out of this house all day. Don't you think there should be some security measures in place in case—"

"Santi is fine." The bite in his tone wasn't anger; it was conviction. His confidence wouldn't entertain the thought of anything less. "The staff is thoroughly vetted, and my men know if they step foot past the first floor, they'll be shot."

It was that unyielding confidence, and my suspicion that

he knew the truth anyway that made my decision. Rounding my lips, I blew out a nervous breath and closed my eyes. "Val, I need to tell you—"

"Hey, Danger, I've been looking for you. I…" Eden's voice trailed off as she hovered in the doorway, her bright smile fading.

Val held up a hand, his steady eyes locked with mine. "*Un momento, Cereza.* Adriana and I are talking."

The room crackled with tension, and I forced a weak smile. "It's fine, go. It's nothing that can't wait an hour."

THE POUNDING IN MY HEAD WAS RELENTLESS. A DULL ACHE SO INTENSE it blurred my vision even in complete darkness. I had no idea what time it was. Just the thought of staring at the bright light of my phone was enough to send the room spinning.

My teeth chattered as a trickle of sweat rolled down the back of my neck. I choked on the violent contrast of sensation, causing my body to spasm with a rough, rattling cough. Lifting a shaking hand to my chest, I clawed at my contracting lungs, my compressed throat, and my aching heart.

I froze, the last thought woven in so seamlessly, yet laced with so much truth.

Val said Brody confessed he was in love with me.

I didn't deserve that word, but just for tonight, as selfish as it was, I needed to pretend I did. I needed the gentle calm before the storm.

The peace before the reckoning.

I'd leave this world the same way I entered it. As a soulless pawn.

Peeling back the blanket, I padded barefoot along the cold marble, goose bumps rippling across my bare limbs. My heart lurched into my throat as I stood outside the closed door, the silence behind it making me second guess myself.

Don't turn back.

Twisting the doorknob, I stepped inside the darkened room before I could change my mind. My fingers curled by my side as an almost imperceptible exhale flitted across my ear.

"I was wondering how long it would take you."

I smiled, even though I knew he couldn't see it. "Confident, are we?" I barely got the last word out before another round of coughs almost brought me to my knees.

Sheets rustled, and the lamp ignited, flooding the room with agonizingly bright light. It felt like a thousand knives stabbing through my eyes all at once, and I muffled a cry as I pressed the heels of my palms against my eyelids.

Brody's warm hands cradled my head. "Hey, what's wrong?"

"The light," I wheezed. "Turn off the light."

His warmth disappeared along with the glaring brightness. It was a painful and welcomed loss, fighting against another one inside my head. Once again, the violent contrast sent me into a tailspin, and I stumbled into his strong arms.

"Christ, Adriana, tell me what's wrong."

But I couldn't. At least not and still claim the peace I desperately needed. "Remember when I walked in on you at Caliente?"

The tension eased with his low chuckle. "You mean when I was jerking off, pretending it was you?"

I nodded. "I want to give you that."

He let out a rough exhale, the raw need in his voice strained with hesitation. "Adriana…"

But nothing he said would deter me. Hell could rise up and drag me down piece by piece, but I was going to give him this one last memory.

My final surrender.

Sinking to my knees in the darkness, I curled my fingers around the waistband of his boxers and slid them down his strong thighs. Brody let out a low grunt as his cock sprang free. I'd never wanted to touch a man more. I'd never wanted to give without any reservations or expectations. So, I cradled him in my hands and stroked my thumbs over his swollen crown.

He sucked a sharp breath through his teeth. "Shit."

"Sit down," I instructed. "On the edge of the bed."

He didn't argue, and I moved with him as he sank onto the mattress. Without a word, he planted his feet in an open invitation. Empowered by the musky, masculine scent of his arousal, I wedged myself in between his legs and swirled my tongue around the tip.

"Fuck, Adriana, you're killing me."

"Tell me what you want," I whispered, licking underneath the head. "Every single detail. This is your fantasy. Make it come true."

His tortured groan sounded more animal than human as his hand dove into my hair. "I want you to suck me hard. I want to fuck your mouth, and then I want to come down your throat and watch you swallow it."

I let out an unsteady breath.

"Do you know why?"

I shook my head.

His fingers twisted in my hair. "Because your mouth is mine. Your kiss is mine. And God help me, I need to mark them both. Stain them. Claim them. Mine, Adriana. My body. My mouth. My kiss."

Dios mío, a la chingada.

Holy fuck.

A flood of warmth surged between my legs, and I didn't think. I acted. I took him in my mouth, giving him everything he wanted as he hit the back of my throat.

Brody hissed, leaning back on one arm as I bobbed up and down, fighting my gag reflex. "Ah, fuck. Yes, just like that. Faster."

All those things he said he wanted to do were just words. His commands flirted on the edge of dirty but didn't fall over. His hand twisted in my hair but didn't pull. His hips ground into the mattress but didn't move. He was a live wire sparking toward an explosion, but he was holding back because he didn't want to hurt me.

But that wasn't what I wanted.

This was my gift. My ending. And I wanted to give him the fantasy.

I gently pulled away and sighed. "I'm breaking another rule for you."

His pants came harsh and hard. "What?"

"I've never let a man come in my mouth. It's almost as intimate as kissing to me. I'm giving this to you. I'm giving you everything, and you're holding back. I'm not innocent, Brody. I'm not made of glass. I'm scandal and immorality and sin. Now, are you going to claim me, or not?"

It was like a switch flipped in Brody's head. Twisting his hand in my hair, he shoved my open mouth onto his cock so hard, I choked. I braced my hands on his thighs, tears streaming down my cheeks as he pulled my head back.

"You want a taste of sin, *princesa*?" he growled. Holding the base of his shaft, he flicked the head against my lips. "Lick."

I obeyed. Flattening my tongue, I dragged it across every inch, aching for more.

"Goddamn, that mouth…" It was all he said before pushing

me back down, hard steel filling my throat once more. But this time, he joined the effort, guiding me up and down his length by my hair. Just as I started to get used to the punishing rhythm, he bucked his hips, thrusting up every time he pushed me down.

His hips and his hand were in a duel, and his cock was the only weapon.

"Is this what you wanted?" He groaned out the last word, and I peeked up to see his head thrown back, his Adam's apple bobbing hard in his throat.

His movements were reckless and frantic. I didn't know how much more I could take. My jaw ached, my throat burned, and my lungs were desperate to cough, but I refused to give in. We both needed this, and I was seeing it through until the end.

"Shit!" Brody's whole body jerked right before warm spurts jetted down my throat. Letting out a primal growl, he clamped both hands against the back of my head. "Fuck, fuck, fuck!" As his body spasmed, he opened his eyes and looked down. Seeing me struggle set him off again, sending another round of his release into my mouth.

Finally, he pulled away and cupped my face in his hands. "Swallow it," he commanded. "I marked it, now show me it's mine."

So, I swallowed, and when I felt a mix of saliva and cum drip down my chin, Brody chased it with his index finger, scooping it back up to my lip. Without hesitating, I licked it off, the possessive adoration in his eyes all the reward I needed.

Hauling me up by my shoulders, he pulled me into his chest and took my lips in a devastating kiss that carved my heart out of my chest and laid it at his feet. New tears coated my wet face as I kissed him back, pouring everything I had left into that one moment.

That one perfect moment.

I hoped he kept this memory locked away, safe from the tarnished ones to come.

Pulling away, Brody brushed a hand across my cheek. He didn't mention the fresh tears coating his fingers, but he knew they were there, and the pain in his voice shattered me as he stroked my hair. "Why does this feel like goodbye?"

I forced a smile and traced his lips, memorizing every groove and crevice. "Nothing lasts forever, counselor."

"Then kiss me again."

Maybe he understood what he was asking. Maybe he didn't. I chose to believe somewhere, deep down, a part of him knew it *was* goodbye. I understood better than anyone that sometimes you were better off opting to live in ignorance than reality.

Reality was a cold and soulless place.

So, I kissed him with all the passion and hunger inside me, trying to silently reassure him that the act and the words weren't mutually exclusive.

I loved him…

And because I loved him, as he lay sleeping, I gave his lips one last kiss and left my heart next to his pillow as I walked out.

Chapter Thirty-Five

BRODY

For the second time, I woke up to an empty bed.

However, we weren't in Chapala, and this time, I had a feeling it had less to do with sneaking out to avoid an argument as much as sneaking out to avoid a confrontation.

One that had one hell of a right hook, I might add.

Despite the fact Vergara was still out there. Despite the fact the Muñoz Cartel was still intercepting our shipments. Despite the fact we now knew why he had a vendetta against the Carreras, especially Adriana, I couldn't stop smiling.

She never said the words, but then again, neither did I. It didn't matter. I felt them. She loved me. No woman had ever surrendered herself to me like Adriana did last night. If I ever wavered before, I didn't now. Adriana Carrera was mine, and God help the man who tried to take her from me.

After a quick shower, I started to shave, then remembered Adriana's nails raking through the scruff filling in my cheeks and tossed the razor in the trash. Maybe it was time to ditch the clean cut, boy next door look. After all, I was a cartel lieutenant, and an intimidating image was everything in this world.

I smirked at the reflection in the mirror.

Yeah, it was time to lay Brody Harcourt, assistant district attorney to rest and breathe life into Brody Harcourt, first lieutenant of the Carrera Cartel.

And the first thing the new Brody Harcourt needed to do was get rid of the Armani suits. Adriana was right. They made me look like an investment banker. But my choices were limited, so I pulled on the black jeans she made me buy and a white button-up shirt, rolled up at the sleeves.

Not bad. Not bad at all.

My phone chimed with a text, and I groaned, knowing if Val heard it, there would be hell to pay. However, once I saw it was from Carlos, I didn't care.

Not much on Cristiano Vergara, but Ignacio and Rosita are Colombian. Funny since I've never heard the name. Maybe an alias since I can't find any record of Ignacio existing.

I forgot I'd asked him for intel. Since he had nothing on Cristiano's whereabouts, I decided not to text him back. I had more information at this point.

Opening the door to the sitting room Val used for our meetings, I was met with silence. Val stood in his usual spot at the bar, glass in hand and eyebrow cocked. Mateo sat on the couch, one ankle crossed over his opposite knee, a shit-eating grin on his face.

"When's the rodeo, cowboy?"

I stalked past him, flipping my middle finger. "Fuck off, Cortes."

Val just poured a glass of scotch and held it out. "You're

late."

Rolling my eyes, I reached for the glass, then hesitated as Adriana's voice filled my head.

"You need to lay off the booze. I'll never understand why people willingly destroy their bodies. It's disrespectful to those who never got to make that choice."

"Hell, Harcourt. Are you drunk already?"

I dropped my hand and stepped away from the glass. "No, not drunk. In fact, I think I'm going to stop drinking for a while."

He stared at me, his face deceptively neutral. "Casual clothes? Sobriety? Who the fuck are you, and what have you done with my lieutenant?"

"Cupid shoved an arrow straight up his asshole." Both of us turned to see Mateo, not even trying to hide his arrogant smirk.

I folded my arms across my chest and glared at Val's second-in-command. "Are we going to discuss business any time soon, or is he planning to toss out shitty one-liners all morning?"

Val set down the untouched scotch and lifted his tequila to his mouth. "Shut up, Mateo. That fucker shoved his arrow so far up *your* ass, I had to bail it out of jail. You have no room to talk."

Mateo shot me a scowl, which I returned with a pleasant smirk and another middle finger.

"I have no intention of talking about this here," Val said, pacing the room. "I'm tired of being one step behind this *pinche pendejo*. My men have searched the address Adriana gave you but found nothing. He's on the move again. I've called a meeting with all my lieutenants in an hour. I want every top soldier we have on this. Ignacio Vergara will be stopped today if I have to track him down myself and send what's left of him in a box to his mother."

Mateo nodded. "So, we're invading Guadalajara."

Val's hand clenched around his glass. "We're invading

Mexico. No one is safe until I have this asshole hanging by his feet."

Blood pumped through my veins, and a rush of adrenaline awoke a dark craving inside me. "What are we waiting for?" I asked, running my hand over my gun holster. "Let's go get this fucker."

Six determined eyes, six heavy feet, and six clenched fists all moved toward the hallway when an ear-piercing scream drew three loaded guns. I rushed toward the front door, and Mateo sprinted toward the back while Val ran up the stairs, colliding halfway with a hysterical and crying Eden.

"*Cereza*! What the hell?" Val tried to take her in his arms, but she fought him like a rabid animal, fists flying at his arms, chest, and one even landing across his jaw. "*Cereza*! Calm down and tell me what's wrong." However, there were only more screams, more crying, and more fists until Val had enough. "Eden!" he yelled, pinning her arms to her side. "Talk to me!"

She glanced up at him, and the moment she looked in his eyes, the life drained out of her. Her body went limp, and she collapsed, her knees hitting the stairs with a sickening thud.

"Fuck," Val growled, sinking onto his knees with her. Twisting around, he cradled her onto his lap, and wrapped his hand around her jaw, forcing her glassy-eyed stare on him. "*Cereza*, tell me who did this to you, and I swear he will die by my hand tonight."

That was when time stopped. Eden's lifeless gaze shifted toward me, tears spilling down her cheek. "It's not a *he*. It's a *she*."

My pulse roared in my ears, and Val stiffened. "She, who?"

"Adriana." Turning her watery eyes back to her husband, Eden ripped my world apart. "Santiago is gone. His crib is empty, Val. I-I looked everywhere. He's gone, and so is Adriana. She took our son. I told you." Pain turned to rage, and she screamed, driving her fists into Val's chest. "I fucking told you not to let her come here! I told you this would happen! She murdered my brother, and now she's taken our son! I hate you for this! I hate you! I-I..." She never finished. She collapsed again in hysterical tears; her pain so raw I grabbed my own chest.

No. She was wrong. Adriana wouldn't harm Santiago. He was Val's son. He was her family. I didn't care what it looked like. Eden had it wrong.

I cleared my throat. "Val..."

Val's face blanked. It was as if he went on autopilot. Scooping Eden into his arms, he barked out orders while climbing the stairs. "Cortes, search the grounds and look for any signs of forced entry. I want every staff member questioned and don't hold back any method needed. Call the lieutenants and reroute the search from Vergara to my missing son and sister. Also, notify the doctor he's to bring over sedatives. Not later, I want it done now. And get your wife over here. Eden isn't to be left alone."

I ran my hand across my mouth. "What can I do?"

Pausing with his wife cradled in his arms at the top of the stairs, Val turned a hard stare over his shoulder. "I think you've done enough."

AN HOUR LATER, MATEO HAD DONE ALL THAT VAL ASKED, AND WE were still no closer to an answer.

All doors and windows were intact, and there were no signs of forced entry. Val insisted on interrogating every staff member himself, and they swore under the threat of bodily harm, or during bodily harm they saw no one on the grounds or near the house.

Now Mateo and I sat in the Carrera estate kitchen, my unwanted presence a thorn in his side. Sighing, he rubbed his palm across his goatee, flipping his phone in his hand. "I wouldn't if I were you."

I knew he thought defying Val's orders and sticking around was either insane or suicidal, but I didn't care.

"Good thing you're not me."

"Val just needed to lash out at someone. He'll realize it's not your fault. It's not like you had any idea what she planned to do." He stopped flipping his phone and glanced up at me out of the corner of his eye. "Did you?"

"Fuck you."

Dropping his phone, he reared back, raising his palms in the air. "I had to ask."

"She didn't do this." I still believed that. With every piece of my soul, I believed that. However, the longer both of them were gone, the harder it would be to convince anyone else. Every tick of the clock caused my stomach to plummet.

"Brody…"

"No!" I yelled. "She didn't do this. Eden is confused. Adriana hurt her before, and she doesn't trust her. I get that, but she doesn't know her like I do. She didn't hurt that baby."

"I don't want to believe it either, all right? But there isn't any other explanation. If she didn't do it, then why is she gone?"

I flinched at the question because I had no answer. That was what made me stay despite Val's warning. It was why Mateo thought I'd lost my mind. Because anyone who valued his life would've been on a plane to Houston by now.

Brody Harcourt, the assistant district attorney, would have left immediately. But Brody Harcourt, the first lieutenant, wasn't backing down.

Not even for Valentin Carrera.

"I don't know," I said, clenching my teeth.

"You don't know what?"

Mateo and I both turned to see Val standing in the entryway to the kitchen, shirt half untucked, his dark hair standing straight up, deep lines etched around the corners of his eyes, and shoulders hunched.

Never, in the years I'd known Valentin Carrera, had I seen him appear anything less than formidable. He always stood tall and proud, his shoulders pushed back to terrorize and intimidate. Even when Manuel Muñoz kidnapped Eden, he still never lost his commanding presence.

But Santiago and Adriana were Val's only family. They were his only tie to the humanity his mother instilled in him. It was at that moment I understood.

If he lost them, he lost the only thing keeping him from becoming the man he was groomed to be.

I stood. "Is Eden okay?"

Val continued into the kitchen, his movements robotic. "Her son is missing. What do you think?"

Mateo caught my eye, warning me to shut up with a slight shake of his head. But every minute I wasted worrying about my own ass was time wasted finding Adriana, so I turned my back to him.

"Val, you have to know Adriana didn't do this. She wouldn't hurt Santi." I ignored the low exhale behind me and waited for the storm.

A storm that never came.

"Do you know what she asked me last night?" Val kept his back to me as he stared at the refrigerator.

I assumed it was a rhetorical question, so I didn't answer.

"She told me she'd been to Santiago's nursery. I knew, of course. I'd already gotten an earful from Eden. She walked in and found Adriana caressing Santi's cheek. Said she heard her whisper something about *familia*. Eden lost her shit, but Adriana didn't fight back."

The image of Adriana with Santi fueled my need to do something—anything—but I said nothing and let him continue.

"But it was what Adriana said to me that keeps running through my head. She said, '*Are you sure he's safe in there?*'" He spun around, a vertical line sinking deep between his eyes. "I asked her what she meant, and she said something about having staff and *sicarios* coming in and out of the house, and shouldn't I have security measures in place. I told her Santi was fine, but there was this look in her eyes. It was, fuck, I don't know. It was sadness and fear. She said she had something to tell me, but then Eden came in, and she said she'd tell me later." He sucked in a tired breath, his eyes shifting back to the refrigerator. "But later never came."

No one said a word. All eyes just settled on the picture of the smiling baby stuck to the middle of a refrigerator that cost more than most people's cars. It was no doubt put there by Eden, but Val couldn't tear his eyes away. He traced the infant's face, his shoulders sinking even lower.

"Why did she ask all that? Was she planning? Scheming?"

Then everything hit at once. Like a song playing in reverse, then suddenly skipping to the end.

She told me, too. I just didn't listen.

"This isn't your problem, Brody. I'm not letting you take the fall for my mistakes. Past, present, or future."

Then my own sister's words rang in my ears.

"Salvation comes in many forms. Sometimes it's in the shape of your biggest regret."

Adriana hated herself for the pain she'd inflicted on Val. Her salvation would be her redemption, but how would focusing on Santiago factor in with…

"Ignacio." The word sounded as bitter as it tasted.

Val whipped back around. "What?"

"Ignacio has them. She didn't take Santi. He took them both."

Mateo's chair scraped along the floor as he stood. "Do you have proof? She could've willingly taken Santi to him. She already admitted to him initially offering her a partnership."

Val's phone rang, and he straightened, his shoulders rising. He quietly listened, his face a mask of granite. "*Si. Muy bien. Estaremos esperando por usted.*" *Yes. Very good. We will be waiting for you.* Disconnecting the call, his somber expression revived with what I knew to be the promise of blood. "No," he said, his eyes flashing. "He doesn't have proof. But I know someone who does."

Chapter Thirty-Six

ADRIANA

Tlajomulco de Zuñiga, Jalisco, Mexico

A familiar dank, musty smell hit me as soon as I opened my eyes. A metallic rust that only lingered with the stain of life. Only this time, there wasn't just a stain.

Blood.

I smelled it.

I tasted it.

I felt its warmth pool under my cheek.

"Finally, the fly finds herself caught in the spider's web." Gravelly Spanish raked over my thin nerves like fresh sandpaper.

I rolled onto my back, forcing my native language from my raw throat. "Are you the fly or the spider?"

"I'm God."

The two words hit me like a visceral blow to the chest. "Where is he? I demand you tell me what you did to him!"

"You're not in a position to demand anything."

"If you hurt him, I'll kill you."

Shaking his head, Ignacio pulled a cigar from his pocket. "Fighting until the bitter end, just like your whore mother." The last word was garbled as he bit off the tip and spat it at my feet, his gaze never leaving mine as he lit the end.

I let out a silent breath. "Where is he?"

The low laugh that followed nearly broke me. "You know they think you did it." He exhaled, a cloud of smoke pluming around his face. "I couldn't have scripted it any better. You had every privilege. Everything handed to you. You think you shined up that crown, but one apologetic text message, and you opened the door for the devil, didn't you?"

My heart free fell into my stomach as he bent down on his haunches, his lips splitting into a sadistic snarl.

"I said you were the fly, but now that I think about it, you're more of a black widow. Men have a nasty habit of dying around you, *puta*. You got the entire Muñoz family murdered, and now look at the web you've spun around the Carreras and your *gringo* boyfriend." He grabbed my hair, rancid breath heating my face. "I won't mention what you did to me." Slamming my head back down, he shrugged. "I'm all for spilling enemy blood, but you're out of control."

Fire rushed through my veins. "Fuck you!"

With a demonic roar, he drew his arm back and swung, the back of his hand driving into the side of my face, but I didn't cry out.

He wiped my blood off his hand onto his jeans, scowling with a vile hatred beyond anything I'd ever seen. Cold black eyes, soulless from both being denied and betrayed stared at me with contempt. "Shut up, Carrera whore."

I glared back at him. "Don't ever call me that again."

The hot breath on my neck disappeared as he shuffled around me. "You're not a Muñoz. You're the enemy. You proved that when you defied me, *again*. Carrera blood runs through your veins, and now it stains your hands."

"Then kill me and get it over with."

"I've already told you. I want Alejandro Carrera's son to kneel before me. I want him to beg for my mercy. Killing you doesn't benefit me yet. I need my puppet to dance for me one last time, and this time she'll perform for an audience of three."

I saw the dark truth etched in his face and tattooed in his eyes, and panic erupted through my veins. He was going to use me to lure Val here…

To Santi and to his death.

My frantic mind launched into overdrive, accusations spilling out one after the other. "You said if I defied you and didn't bring Santi back to *Tlajomulco de Zuñiga* in four days, you'd expose me to Val and Brody. Those were your words, Ignacio. You said you'd kill your own son, ruin me, and then come after all of us. You barely gave me forty-eight hours."

The more hysterical I got, the more he seemed to enjoy it, the dim light highlighting the sinister curve of his lips. "I knew the minute you walked out of this warehouse you had no intention of doing as you were told. That's what a true leader does, Adriana. He doesn't wait for shit to happen. He makes it happen."

I fought for air. "I won't help you."

"You already have."

"You're lying," I hissed. "Brody doesn't know this place exists, and unless you plan to stop hiding like a scared little bitch, no one is coming for me. This is it, Ignacio. This is the end of the line. Walk into the sun or fade into the background. I don't give a shit."

His cold eyes searched mine then hardened. "You really don't know?"

I scowled through a rattled cough. "Enlighten me."

"When I said you were nothing but a puppet, I meant it. When I said you were the rat who never failed to take the offered cheese and got her fucking neck snapped, I meant it. When I explained that you've done exactly what I thought you would do and run to exactly who I thought you'd run to for years, I fucking meant it."

"For years..." My voice trailed off, the words flitting through my head. Ignacio saw the moment they clicked together, and his smile widened along with my eyes. Slowly lifting my hand, I covered my mouth, my shoulders heaving with exertion.

Speaking the words out loud peeled back the hidden layers to reveal a truth that I didn't want to face but couldn't deny.

"What's wrong, rat? Cat got your tongue?"

"Cristiano," I whispered, the word muddled behind the safety of my palm.

Ignacio's dark gaze gleamed under the muted glow of the swinging overhead light. "How do you think I found you in the first place, *puta*?" he taunted, running his tongue across his teeth. "Did you think he really wanted to marry you?"

"It can't be." I was going to be sick. I rolled over, my stomach contracting into a coiled knot of betrayal.

As the light flickered again, Ignacio stood, a deep laugh rumbling in his chest. "I warned you not to fear the knife to your throat as much as the one in your back, *Mari*."

Chapter Thirty-Seven
BRODY

Mexico City, Mexico

Val looked up from his glass, narrowing his bloodshot eyes at the bruised man standing before him. "Your eyes are blue."

Ignoring the two soldiers holding him immobile, Cristiano centered his gaze on the force of nature across the room. "Yours are red, and blue and red make purple, which, incidentally, is the color of Harcourt's face. Care to discuss the other sixty-one colors in the crayon box?"

I shook my head.

Dumbass.

Antagonizing the man who held his life in his hands wasn't a smart move.

Val had Cristiano hauled in bleeding, bruised, and barely able to see out of two swollen eyes. To be honest, I had no idea how he could tell the guy had eyes, much less what color they were.

"I assume I'm here because of Mari."

"Adriana," I muttered. Not that anyone heard me. Those two were too busy playing a fucked up alpha chess game we didn't have time for.

However, it was Val's move, and he played to win. "You're only half Latino."

Cristiano smirked. "And yet, you're one hundred percent asshole."

"Motherfucker," Val growled, his monotone voice low and clipped. Even soaked in alcohol, it was there, stretched to its limits.

Snap threat.

Cristiano glanced my way while licking blood off his teeth. "Is he always this pleasant?"

"Shut up!" Tilting my head back, I stared at the ceiling, trying to rein in my temper.

Once he helped us get Adriana and Santi back, I was breaking that asshole's nose.

Inhaling hard, I settled my eyes on a pissed-off, half-drunk, guilt-ridden Val. "Where did you find him?" My teeth gnashed as I scanned Cristiano's beaten face. "And why didn't you let me at him first?"

Cristiano smirked. "Patience, Brenda."

I glared at Val. "Screw being first, I just want to be last."

"Stop it!" Val roared. "My sister and son are missing. I want them back. I don't give a shit if it's you…" he shouted, pointing to me, "you"—he swung his finger toward Cristiano—"you"—he tossed a nod over his shoulder at Mateo—"or the goddamn tooth fairy who makes it happen. When they're safe, you two *cabrones* can beat the hell out of each other for all I care, but until then, shut the fuck up!"

Cristiano's face paled. "Mari is missing?"

I didn't bother to correct him. "Along with Val's son, Santiago. They disappeared sometime last night."

"No, no, no, no. This wasn't supposed to happen."

The sudden shift in his demeanor set me on edge. "What wasn't supposed to happen? Do you know something, Vergara? I swear, if you had something to do with—"

"How could I have had something to do with it?" he snapped, a razor's edge away from losing control. "Your *jefe's* men ran me off the road into an embankment. I'm good, but I'm not that damn good."

What the hell?

I glanced at Val, who simply nodded.

"Ignacio," I said, speaking the one name on everyone's mind.

Cristiano laughed. "I guess I can cross running from a homicidal parent off my bucket list." A dark haze crossed his face. "That asshole kept me in a dirty warehouse for days until I managed to overtake a couple of his stupider guards. I stole a car and was trying to find Mari when I was given an unwanted escort."

Stopping his pace, Val swung around, his fists locked by his side. "So, you *are* Ignacio Vergara's son."

The room fell deathly silent as Cristiano closed his eyes, his chest rising and falling with short rapid breaths. When he opened them, the earlier arrogance was gone, replaced by dull acceptance. "Yes."

Mateo shot to his feet. "Does anyone want to tell me what the fuck is going on?"

"My father was a son of a bitch who left my mother pregnant and shamed," he ground out, cracking the surface of his façade. "Even as a boy, I knew I'd find him and make him pay. Watching my grandfather reject both of us, condemning my mother to a life of disgrace, and forcing a child to become a man to ensure our survival kind of sealed the deal."

Crossing his arms, Mateo circled around him, his stoic expression firmly in place. "I take it he didn't approve?"

Cristiano barked out a dry laugh. "Only pure blue Irish blood deserved Ronan Kelly's kindness. When contaminated by a lower-class Latino, the only thing it deserved was to be spilled."

Catching movement out of the corner of my eye, I saw Val's face morph from blank indifference to shock to blackened rage. "*¡Qué chingados*! You're Ronan Kelly's grandson?"

"The Northside Sinners," I added.

Ice shot through my veins. I heard the words and each one clawed into my head, digging through masks and lies until all that was left was a stripped away version of my own blindness.

Ronan Kelly. Cristiano Vergara. Ignacio Vergara. Esteban Muñoz. The Northside Sinners. Chicago port alliances. Missing shipments.

They all linked with one name.

Carlos Cabello.

Val's stare didn't stray from Cristiano's face. "Ronan Kelly hates cartels. It's why the Carreras have never fucked with the Midwest. It's the one policy my father and I agreed on. Kelly never had a son—only two daughters, so we decided to bide our time until the old bag of shit croaked, and then strong arm his daughters into opening up their ports."

"My mother is a good woman," Cristiano hissed, his tone dangerously close to a challenge.

I'd give it to him—Cristiano Vergara had a pair of iron balls and didn't give two shits about juggling them in front of Valentin Carrera's face. It was either the bravest thing I'd ever seen or the dumbest.

"It's true, my grandfather hates cartels," he continued. "It was why Esteban sent my father to Chicago. He didn't give a shit if he ever made it back. But he lured him into forging a trade alliance with promises to make him a lieutenant." His lips curled into a snarl. "Ignacio met my mother and assumed the way to his rank was through her."

My head snapped up. This sounded too familiar.

"He got her pregnant and never returned to Chicago. She was shunned and forbidden to give me the Kelly name. That's why I'm a Vergara." He shot me a look. "Lucky me."

Mateo cocked his head. "You must not have been too ashamed. You followed in his footsteps."

Hate seared across Cristiano's bloody face. "Fuck you. I watched her suffer because of the promises my father made and never delivered. The only truth she told me was that he was a Muñoz soldier, so the first chance I got, I came to Mexico to find him. To make him answer and pay for his sins."

A quiet click drew my eyes to my right where Mateo's fingers released his gun from its holster. It was a subtle move, but one that caught a set of pale blue eyes as well.

"I kept my mouth shut. I worked my way up the ranks from street dealer to top *sicario* while searching for any information I could find," he explained, pulling his gaze from Mateo's gun up to his face. "The path to truth was long, but then I caught Mari's eye, and I realized she was my detour. An easy and beautiful shortcut."

Her rules.

It hit me, inflaming my already burning jealousy tenfold. He was the reason for all her rules. Why she built walls. Why she wouldn't kiss a man. Why she believed she didn't deserve love.

"You son of a bitch." I flew across the room, ready to tear him apart only to be blocked by Val's outstretched arm. I glared, and he glared back, the unspoken message clear.

Let him speak.

"I said she *was* a detour! I was a kid whose only tie in this life was a heartbroken mother banished from her family. We were nothing to them. A stain on their precious empire. I'm not proud of using her to get what I wanted, but there's not a man in our world who hasn't manipulated a woman for his benefit." He swung an accusing glare at all three of us, settling on me.

I returned it with a scowl.

Val broke the silence. "Obviously, something changed."

"Esteban saw how close we were getting." My eyes bounced between them as Cristiano's shoulders lowered, his defensive stance diminishing. "He finally took the time to notice my last name instead of just seeing a face amongst men not worth his time. He sat me down and gave me every disgusting detail of my existence."

Adriana's sad, solemn voice echoed in my head.

"So why the split? Did you get cold feet?"

"No, he did."

My furrowed eyebrows faded into disbelief. "It was an arranged marriage for Chicago port access."

He didn't confirm it, but the regret in his eyes did. "Whatever benefitted Esteban, right? He thought I was his 'in'. I'm not innocent though. He dangled the same lieutenant carrot in front of my face as he did Ignacio, and I grabbed it. Sins of the father, and all that."

"But you didn't go through with it."

He shook his head. "No. Esteban died before he could promote me. Manuel took control of the cartel, and he hated me. I knew I had to stay away from Mari. Especially after knowing who her real father was and what he'd done."

I had no idea if he knew what he just said, or if there was so many hidden truths spilling out of him that it slipped out. All I knew was that I heard it.

And worse than that, Val heard it.

"You've known who she really was all this time, and you didn't say shit?" Val roared, charging forward with his arms up, hands wide, and fingers spread, ready to choke the life out of him.

But I beat him to it.

Rage and fear and the sickening images that kept filling my head consumed me. Images of Adriana and Santi. Crying. Bleeding. Begging for help. All of it spiraled out of control, and I grabbed Cristiano by the shirt, pulling him out of the guards' hands and crashed us both against the wall.

"When Adriana and I were in your office, she gave you his name. She begged you for help finding the man who was terrorizing her family, and you knew. She gave you tears, and you gave her riddles. Did you know about the safe deposit box?"

He wheezed as my forearm braced across his throat. "I told her I'd been waiting for her to come to me. That wasn't a lie. I suspected Esteban had damning information hidden inside the estate. I just didn't think she'd find it."

"So, you lied to her again!"

"I was protecting her! I sure as hell didn't want her to find out this way!"

"Bullshit! You were protecting yourself, and now your father has her!" I pushed harder, cutting off more of his air supply until a set of hands pried me off him. He dropped to his feet, coughing as I turned and shoved Mateo away from me. Still shaking with rage, I spun back around to where the piece of shit still stood. "What does he want with Adriana and Santiago?"

"He saw firsthand with Carrera's mother how quickly a parent will give their life when it comes to the safety of their child. My guess is he was using Adriana to do the same thing to

Val. When she didn't play by his rules, he made new ones."

"You never loved her," I hissed.

"Don't tell me how I felt about Mari! Maybe I was never in love with her, but I'll fight to the death for her. Adriana and my mother are the only two women who have ever given me love without wanting something in return, and Ignacio Vergara ruined both their lives. He deserves the same."

I was sick of his declarations. Any asshole could say words. It took a man to back them up. I'd crawled to the lowest level of hell for love. I wondered if Cristiano Vergara would do the same.

I flashed a cold smile. "Let's put that theory to the test, shall we?"

Chapter Thirty-Eight

ADRIANA

Tlajomulco de Zuñiga, Jalisco, Mexico

My head felt like it'd been stuffed with a bag of cotton balls. I rubbed my eyes, trying to force them open while fighting through the fuzzy cloud blocking my memory. Nothing made sense, as if my brain were a giant puzzle that had been scattered about. Nothing fit, and there was no discernible pattern.

Everything hurt. An aching, stinging, heavy hurt that made me want to give up and sink back down into the black nothingness I just came from. Frustrated, I tried to move, but my limbs felt numb and uncooperative. I blinked, the room dark except for two overhead swinging lights. The place looked industrial. Almost like a…

Warehouse.

Ignoring the pain, I pressed my palms onto the cold concrete and pushed myself up, praying the images flashing through my head were residual pieces of a nightmare and not memories. But the clearer they became, the more I remembered, and the more I remembered, the harder I shook.

The late-night text that came through on my phone from Cristiano.

Running to the back door to meet him, only to come face-to-face with Ignacio.

The sting of the needle as he plunged it into my neck.

Then pain when I awoke to the burning orange ember of a lit cigar inside a different warehouse.

And the moment I wanted to die as I heard Santiago's faint cry.

I closed my eyes, remembering how Ignacio took sadistic pleasure in telling me no matter what I did, the people I tried to protect were going to die right along with me.

All because I'd been played for a fool.

Cristiano was Ignacio Vergara's son, and even *he* was a pawn.

I tried to block out his words, but he forced me to listen. His boy. His heir. His pride. For years, he'd lied to me. He knew I was Adriana Carrera.

I brought all this to Val's door. That hurt worse than any pain Ignacio could inflict.

I'd lose my family *again*.

It was too late to save me, but I'd die a thousand deaths before I'd let anything happen to Santiago. No child should ever suffer like I did.

Or because of what I did.

Someone would come for me. Ignacio enjoyed playing with his puppet too much to leave me alone much longer. I only had one shot. One chance to find Val's son, and I refused to fail him twice.

I needed a weapon. Unfortunately, captors didn't make a habit of leaving sharp objects lying around their captive's cages.

I'd have to improvise, but there wasn't even a chair to break. No table. No window.

I scrubbed a blood caked hand across my forehead. "Great. Any more bright ideas, Adriana?"

I stilled, my hand sliding down my face.

Bright.

Rolling my eyes toward the ceiling, I watched as the two hanging lights swung back and forth.

Two lights with two bulbs.

Two glass bulbs.

I glanced down at my flimsy tank top and tiny shorts I'd pulled on after leaving Brody's bed, and for the first time since waking up in this hellhole, I smiled.

Before running to meet "Cristiano" at the back door, I put on the first shoes I could find.

High-heeled sandals.

Unbuckling the straps, I slipped them off and climbed to my feet. Aiming the heel toward the bulb, I threw hard, missing the target by about two feet and snapping the heel off as it crashed into the wall. With a deep breath, I grabbed the second one. Drawing my arm back, I threw twenty-four years of pain into the air and watched it return well over twenty-four shards of glass.

SOMEONE WAS COMING.

Warm blood trickled down my wrist as the piece of glass I tightly fisted dug into my skin.

I didn't mind. Blood reminded me I was still alive, and pain was fleeting. I'd felt less. I'd felt more. None of it mattered. All that mattered was who was on the other side of that door and how close I could get to them.

I waited. I forced everything out of my head except the turning of the doorknob. I learned the hard way that letting my guard down was a mistake, and emotions had no place in cartel life. So, I shifted on the balls of my feet, my knees protesting my crouched position against the far corner wall.

No pain, I reminded myself, squeezing harder, blood now dripping off my fingertips.

The door cracked, and I clenched my teeth.

Why didn't he just come in and get it over with?

Finally, it swung open, and a muscular figure stepped inside the now barely-lit room. I saw nothing at first but an outline of a soon-to-be dead man. However, the closer he came, the more the remaining overhead light swung, illuminating the shadow hiding his face.

The more the shadow lifted, the harder I squeezed, and the thicker the river of blood ran.

The permanent scowl he wore was dangerous, remorseless, and calculating. Tall and muscular, with skin dark enough to earn a rank but light enough to raise an eyebrow. He looked more like an underwear model than a ruthless killer.

And underestimating him had been *my* downfall.

"Cristiano," I breathed, venom lacing my voice.

His icy blue eyes turned toward the corner. "Mari, thank God!"

I let out a low laugh. "Not God. Thank your *papá*."

He froze, emotions spinning across his face like a roulette wheel. Finally, the ball settled in the resigned slot, and his smirk fell. "You know."

"Oh, your father and I had a very eye-opening chat." Standing, I moved toward him. "I learned so many things about you."

"What did he tell you?"

"Enough for me to know every word out of your mouth since the day we met has been a lie." Adrenaline pumped through me, fueling my anger. "Brody tried to tell me. He said you were dangerous. He told me I was blind, and you were giving me just enough information for me to hang myself."

"Mari…"

"I defended you! I told him he was wrong, and I knew you. I knew you wouldn't hurt me. God, I was a fucking idiot."

"Brody *was* wrong! I would never hurt you! I was trying to protect you, but you ran off to Houston, and—"

The jagged piece of glass I'd been holding clattered to the floor as my fist connected to his nose. "Don't you dare say his name. You will never be the man Brody Harcourt is!"

Cristiano swore under his breath. "Will you fucking listen to me? Brody and I—"

"Did you and Ignacio get a good laugh after you sent your text?"

He held his nose, blood pouring between his fingers. "What text?"

"Don't play dumb. I'm not in the mood. I was worried about you, and this is what I get for it."

"I didn't send you a text, Mari!"

"Adriana!" I screamed.

"Adriana, whatever he told you, he's lying. He took me from the club and held me in this warehouse. But I got away, and I've been trying to tell you Brody is the one who sent me here."

"Do I look like an *idiota* to you? Brody doesn't trust you. He'd come for me himself."

"He did! They all did. Brody sent me because I know this place."

"Right."

Sighing, he walked toward me, and I backed up. Without

taking another step, he lowered his chin, shaking his head as if reveling in a private joke. "He said you wouldn't believe me, so he told me to tell you not to make him come all the way in here just to force you to tell him everything that came after *te amo.*"

The words were both a jolt of lightning and a bullet to the heart. I love you. They were the words I said to Brody after we made love. The only ones he understood. There was no way Cristiano could've known that.

I stumbled backward. "No…"

"That man loves you, Mari, and it's written all over your face how much you love him. I know you don't trust me right now, and I'll explain everything to you, but you have to come with me. If not for me, then for him."

The room spun, and my heart thundered in my ears, the constant pounding way too fast and loud. I needed time I didn't have. My hand hurt. My head hurt. It felt like the world pressed down on my shoulders, driving me into the waiting arms of hell, and all I wanted to do was spend my last few moments in Brody's arms.

I was weak, so I nodded.

"Thank God," he breathed. "Come on, there's a back way out of here. It should be clear, but if we come across any lingering *sicarios*, I brought a friend." He nodded toward the doorway where a shotgun leaned against the wall.

Something slowed my steps as Cristiano wrapped an arm around my waist and guided me toward the door.

Santiago.

"No!" Jerking away from him, I spun around, my back toward the exit. "I can't leave without Santiago."

"Are you crazy?" he hissed. "Val is looking for him. Besides, you're Ignacio's prisoner. The two of us wandering around this place would be a flashing red sign. We'd be shot on sight."

He was right. We would be shot on sight.

We would.

We.

I had no idea if he was telling the truth, but I hoped if he was, he'd forgive me.

With my last bit of strength, I spun around, and grabbing the barrel of the shotgun, I swung. All Cristiano got out was my name before the stock slammed into the side of his skull, and he hit the floor.

Stepping over him, I crouched where I dropped the shard of glass. Holding it against the inside of my left wrist, I took a deep breath.

No one would suffer because of me again.

Chapter Thirty-Nine
BRODY

"**B**rody, behind you!"

Spinning around, I saw a flash of metal pointed at my chest and pulled the trigger. I had no idea who I just shot, but as long as it brought me one step closer to Adriana, I didn't care.

"Bet they didn't teach you that in law school." Mateo grinned, blood soaking his right arm.

"You okay?"

His face pinched as if he were offended that I asked. "Fucker had shitty aim. Too bad for him, I didn't."

We turned as a darkened hallway to our left lit up with gunshots, along with Val's very detailed instructions for the dead men to fuck their own mothers in hell.

Mateo's brow knitted. "I'm going to help him. Go find Vergara."

He didn't have to tell me twice. Staying behind to clear the field while Cristiano played the hero ate at me until my skin felt like it had turned inside out. Now I knew exactly how Val felt when we rescued Eden from Manuel Muñoz. I got why it bothered him that I was the one to find her. I understood why he left us outside and risked everything to walk into a trap.

Facing death was easier than facing a life without the woman you loved.

So, I ran. Hallway after hallway. Shot after shot. Body after body. I felt like a machine running on rocket fuel. Adriana's name rested on my lips when I collided with another *sicario*.

I raised my gun, my finger on the trigger.

"Harcourt!"

Seconds away from pulling it, I paused. "Vergara?" I lowered the gun and stepped closer. "What the hell happened to you? You look like shit."

I was being nice. Shit would've been a step up. The side of his head looked like roadkill, and somebody busted his pretty boy nose until it pointed west.

Cristiano closed his eyes, blood dripping off his chin. "I'm sorry. I tried."

My blood froze in my veins. "Where is she?"

"I said what you told me to, and it seemed to get through to her. She agreed to come with me."

"What happened?" I bit down on the words.

Frowning, he stepped backward, which was smart, because I was five seconds from putting him through the wall. "She remembered Val's kid. She refused to leave without him, and we argued. Next thing I knew, she was swinging my shotgun, and the lights went out. When I woke up, she was gone."

My breath came in short spurts, and a buzzing noise filled my head. One minute I stood there, and the next I had him pinned against the wall by his throat. "Where did they take her?"

He wrapped both hands around my wrist, but he didn't fight

back. Didn't kick. Didn't try any low blows. He just stared at me, a strange sympathy in his eyes as if he were preparing me. "I don't know, but she's a fighter, Harcourt. If anyone can make it, then—"

Fire burned me from the inside out. Releasing him, I stumbled backward, shaking my head. Then I noticed the trail of blood.

Adriana was meticulous. Most everything she did had a purpose. Cause and effect. Dominate and ruin.

Sleight of hand.

"Things at first glance are rarely what they seem. Dig deeper, and you'll find the truth lies more in what you don't see than what you do. Arrogance is the eye's worst enemy, Brody. Men always make the mistake of looking at what's in front of them instead of watching out for what's behind them."

"Things are rarely what they seem." I repeated the words, the beginnings of a smile forming.

"Agreed, but what does that have to do with Adriana?"

"Is that the room she was in?" He nodded, stepping out of the way as I bulldozed past him. The tiny room was barely lit with nothing but an overhead light.

One overhead light.

The other had been busted, the remnants of the bulb lay scattered all over the concrete floor. There was more blood in the room, and I followed the trail back out the door and down a long hallway to the right.

So, I turned left, my smile now wide and splitting across my face. "Instead of looking at what's in front of you, watch out for what's behind you."

Horizontal lines sank deep into Cristiano's forehead as he turned to face me. "Why? What the hell is wrong with you?"

"I'm too arrogant." I laughed, dropping my chin.

"I could've told you that."

I met his eyes. "And I know how to find her."

"Well, then let's go get—"

"Sorry, Vergara. No hard feelings, but I'll take it from here." Drawing my arm back, I punched him and watched him hit the ground.

Adriana only needed one hero, and he'd waited long enough to save the queen.

ADRIANA'S REVERSE TRAIL OF BREADCRUMBS LED ME INTO A LABYRINTH of twists, turns, and dead ends. I blindly followed a maze with no beginning and no end, and what pissed me off the most was that I had no doubt Ignacio was somewhere watching all of it.

Adriana and Santiago were running out of time, and I was done indulging Vergara's mind games. If Ignacio wanted to play in Valentin Carrera's league, he needed to stand at the plate and swing instead of hiding behind the batter.

So, I tightened my grip on my gun and did the one thing that went against everything I'd been taught. I stepped in front of the bullet instead of firing it.

"Adriana!" I called out, my voice echoing in the dark and deserted hallway. Pausing, I waited, listening for any sign of a response.

Nothing.

"Adriana!" This time, I didn't hold back, running full force while yelling her name over and over. "Fuck!" Turning around, I took two steps back down the same hallway I'd walked half a dozen times when the cold barrel of a gun pressed against the back of my head.

"You look lost, *pendejo*." One of Ignacio's followers ripped my gun from my hand and pressed it against my back.

"What can I say? The service around this place sucks."

"Walk," he commanded, pushing the muzzles of both guns against me.

I tried to pay attention to each twist and turn, but every wall looked the same. By the time we came to a stop in front of a large steel door, it felt like we went in another damn circle. He knocked twice, and a gravelly Spanish accent sounding like rusty nails on a bullet-ridden chalkboard answered.

"Tráemelo." Bring him to me.

My brain fired electric shocks at the familiarity I knew shouldn't be there. I knew the voice. I'd heard it in person. On the phone. Enabling me. Pushing me.

Informing me.

As soon as the guard opened the door, I took the steps on my own, my fists clenching. No one had to force me inside. I didn't care if I walked straight into a bullet. I knew exactly whose gun waited on the other side.

And after all he'd done, that Colombian motherfucker had better shoot to kill.

He stood behind a metal chair at the back of a simple folding table. I didn't know what I expected, a throne maybe? Definitely not some back-alley thrift store setup.

However, my mouth went dry the moment my eyes landed on what was in front of him.

"Brody…"

Adriana sat in the chair, with what looked to be a nine-inch blade pressed against her throat. She was pale and covered in blood, but she was here. I wanted to close my eyes and savor the sound of my name on her lips, but I couldn't show weakness. So, I held her eye, making sure she felt what I couldn't say.

I raised my eyes to meet the man holding the knife, his

top lip curled up, his gray goatee framing a smirk I'd wanted to punch off his face for weeks. "Harcourt, I'd welcome you, but it seems you've welcomed yourself, not to mention made somewhat of a mess in my warehouse."

I shot him a deadpanned look. "Carlos, or should I call you Ignacio? Which name do you prefer these days?"

He brought a lit cigar to his mouth with his free hand, ignoring me while puffing on the end. Blowing out a cloud of smoke, he swung a cold stare my way. "King."

"Fuck you."

The barrel of a gun pressed against the back of my head. "Want me to shoot him now, *jefe*?"

Ignacio waved a hand. "Leave us."

The pressure against my skull lessened. "Are you sure? I don't think…"

Ignacio rolled his eyes. "I don't pay you to think." Dropping his cigar, he stomped it out with his shoe. Before I knew what was happening, he reached for a gun, aimed it at my head, and pulled the trigger.

All I could do was blink, waiting for the inevitable white pain of the bullet or the darkness of death. Neither happened. A heavy thud hit the floor, and I turned to see the guard lying on the concrete, half his face blown off.

Ignacio let out an annoyed sigh. "Good help is hard to find."

I didn't have time to think about what just happened. Steeling my expression, I stepped out of the blood pooling under my shoe and made my way closer to the man who'd turned my life into a living hell. I had so many accusations. So many threats. So many questions. However, I couldn't stop myself from asking the main one burning on my tongue.

"Why the act?"

He shrugged. "Entertainment? Come on, Harcourt, you had

all the pieces. You were just too stupid to put them together. I toyed with you. I even told you Ignacio Vergara was Colombian after you and this whore visited my mother, remember?"

Jesus. All the information I gave him. It made me sick.

"How long have you operated on the sidelines, Carlos?"

"Long enough. I've watched all of you, but nobody bothered to see me. Nobody thought I'd have the *cojones* to come from behind and sink my teeth into both cartels' jugulars."

"Because you're a coward."

"You're nothing in my world, *gringo*. I've been under your nose the whole time, and you never saw it. Plain sight, remember? I told you it was the last place people ever looked."

Plain sight. Two words that took me back to a Chicago strip club. The defining moment that set everything in motion.

A tense breath whistled through his teeth, and another line creased his forehead before a slow smile parted his lips. "The man's name is José Rojas. I don't know how much you can find out from that, but that's all I got. We both know their reach extends far beyond border walls. They've already infiltrated Chicago. If you ask me—"

"I didn't."

The smile on his face faded, irritation flaring in his eyes. "If you ask me, whoever has the balls to rebuild is hiding in plain sight. It's the last place people ever look."

Ignacio pocketed the gun, his hearty laugh drawing my attention back to his smug face. "You fell right into my trap because you're weak. You were so fucked up in the head wanting to defy Carrera all I had to do was give you the nudge."

I narrowed my gaze. "But Leo Pinellas—"

He growled, digging the knife deeper into Adriana's neck, and the words died on my tongue at her sharp inhale. "I've been planning this for months, you stupid *pendejo*! Leo Pinellas was a

381

puppet just like the rest of you. Who do you think was in his ear telling him to give you the goods on her?" He tightened his hold on the knife, and a tear rolled down Adriana's cheek. "I knew what you'd do with it. I planned on it. I knew Carrera would be weaker without that Lachey bitch, but you couldn't even close that deal, could you?"

Blinding rage shattered my control. "Shut up!"

I was coming unhinged, and the sick son of a bitch seemed to enjoy it. An assumption proved when, with a flick of his wrist, Adriana cried out, and a trickle of blood rolled down her neck.

"You're being disrespectful, boy."

"Touch her again, and I'll fucking kill you."

He held my eye and laughed. "She led your dick around on a leash, and you're ready to die for her. How pathetic."

Letting out a roar, I didn't think. I charged. The instinct to protect her overpowered the need to keep her close. "Adriana, run!"

"Brody, no!"

My body snapped back as another arm wrapped around my neck pulling me back. "Let me go, asshole!"

Ignacio chuckled. "Run? She was with me all along, you fool. She told you as much in that piece of shit motel room, but you were too stupid to listen."

"Shipment for seventeen million, right? Disappeared near the Chicago port? Brody open your eyes. Every contact you have is being turned. You can't trust anyone. Not your friends, not your contacts, and certainly not your informants."

"Not even you?"

"Especially not me. I wouldn't if I were you."

I turned a conflicted stare toward a wide-eyed Adriana.

Panic flashed across her bruised face. "He's lying! Yes, he offered me a deal, but I was telling you the truth when I said I accepted just to get away from him. I always planned to bring him down. I didn't care who I was...Marisol Muñoz, Adriana Carrera, I told him, and I told you—I bow to no one. Whatever I did it would be on my own terms." She glared up at Ignacio. "Not yours."

"So, she went after you herself. How touching."

"You set me up," she shot back. "I had no choice."

Keeping his eyes on me, Ignacio smiled and leaned down to press a kiss against her temple. "Is this where you tell your lover that when I made my offer you were hiding out with my son?"

Chapter Forty

ADRIANA

The question on Brody's face hurt worse than any knife. "You were with Cristiano?"

"It wasn't like that! I had no idea Cris was his son!"

A laugh reverberated behind me. A sick and twisted laugh I felt in my soul. "You believe that?"

"Shut up!" I hissed. He was messing with my head, but my nerves were raw, and my body battered. I searched the tortured hazel eyes I'd come to know so well. "Brody, everything I've said to you is real. That kiss was real. I know you felt it."

Behind me, Ignacio groaned. "I know what I feel, and it's boredom. *Deshazte de él,*" he commanded, and the new guard grabbed Brody from behind. *Get rid of him.*

The guard gave a slight nod in acknowledgment and shoved a gun against the back of Brody's head. But he fought back, a dead resolve in his eyes that set everything in motion and tore one word from my throat.

"No!" Ignacio was at the end of his rope, and I knew neither of us had much time. So, fighting against the haze, I jerked against him, the blade digging deeper into my skin. "Don't hurt him! Do whatever you want to me but let him go!"

Ignacio's arms tightened around me, dragging me up from the chair to a standing position. "Are you still trying to win? I can appreciate that kind of fortitude, and if I were a patient man, I'd watch you kill yourself slowly, but you've proven to be somewhat of a pain in my ass."

Thick fingers grabbed my cheek, squeezing until I tasted blood. The harder he squeezed, the more Brody fought. Lights dimmed, and blackness swarmed in from the edges of my peripheral vision. More silent words fell from my restrained mouth until the crack of a gunshot gave them sound.

A scream of loss and heartbreak tore out of me as I closed my eyes and prayed for the knife to sink hard and fast.

"Let her go and face me like a man."

My eyes flew open to find Brody standing in front of me, gun in his hand and the slumped body of the guard on the floor behind him. I didn't know what to feel first—relief or fear. I wanted to tell him to save me. I wanted to tell him I loved him. I wanted to tell him I'd never leave him.

Instead, the words that fell out of my mouth told him goodbye. "Brody, go find Santi, please. Find him and take him back to Val and Eden."

"No! I'm not leaving you here."

"You made me love you, and now I'm lost." I choked out. "That's what *me hiciste amarte, y ahora estoy perdida* means. That's what I said after I told you I loved you. But I was wrong, Brody. I didn't lose my way when I fell for you. I found it."

I'd been strong this whole time, but time wasn't a luxury I had anymore. Desperation overtook me, and although I hated myself for it, I used Brody's own words against him.

"No one was there to save me when he tore me out of my mother's arms. I'll never forgive you if you let Santi suffer the same fate. You promised me. You told me you wouldn't make me regret kissing you, and I believed you. I told Val you'd never hurt me. Please don't make me a liar."

The pain in his face destroyed me. "Who's going to save you?"

All those nights we confessed our truths, the one I needed him to infer on his own was the one he never heard.

"I told you. No one can save me."

Stepping forward as much as the blade allowed, I kicked backward, landing a hard heel between Ignacio's legs. He let out a grunt, and the pressure against my neck lessened just enough that I managed to land an elbow into his ribcage. Grabbing onto his wrist with both hands, I spun around, both of us fighting for the knife.

"Time to die, *pinche puta*!" He shoved downward with a hard twist of his wrist.

"You first, asshole!" Chaos ensued as a second shot rang out, and pain slashed through my body, shredding every fiber into frayed threads. Ignacio's eyes widened just before he collapsed in a lifeless heap onto the concrete.

I felt like I'd slipped underwater. Everything sounded muffled and waves rippled across my vision. Arms circled around me, holding me tight as hands pressed tightly against my middle. My mouth tasted bitter, and all I wanted to do was close my eyes and sleep.

"Adriana! Oh, God, no!"

A child's cry floated somewhere above the surface, and my lips parted in a weak smile. "I broke the cycle."

Then everything went dark, and I sank to the bottom of the

Chapter Forty-One

BRODY

Guadalajara, Jalisco, Mexico

The tiny waiting room got smaller by the minute. There wasn't enough room to pace, and if someone didn't give me an update soon, I'd tear this place apart with my bare hands. Every time I passed Leighton, she pursed her lips, which I returned with a glare.

I was stalking around a hospital in blood-soaked clothes, but no matter how many disapproving looks I got, I refused to change. This was her blood. The only part of her I had with me, and I'd be damned if I'd let it go.

I glanced at the clock and ran my hand through my hair. We'd been here over three hours. Three hours since I fired the bullet that severed Ignacio Vergara's jugular. Three hours since I realized I was a second too late. Three hours since Val walked in with Santi in his arms to find Adriana in mine. Three hours since she slipped away from me.

Three hours since everyone filtered into this piece of shit

waiting room to hear if Adriana was alive or dead. I shifted a glance to the corner where a man sat by himself, his elbows on his knees and his head in his hands.

Val's hand landed on my shoulder. "It's a hard pill to swallow, isn't it?"

"What is?"

He lifted a paper cup filled with coffee toward the man in the corner. "Your pride. Cristiano was with Adriana before you met her. They have a history. You want to hate him for it, but he just risked his life to save hers, knowing her heart belongs to another man." Tipping the cup, he took a sip, giving me a side-eyed glance. "Sound familiar?"

I sighed. "Does the jealousy ever go away?"

"No. We're men. We're hardwired to protect what's ours when we think it's being threatened. But with time, you learn to trust in what you have and the person you're with. In the end, you have to remember that, yes, there was someone before you, but despite the stupid shit he pulled to get her back, and regardless of how bad you fucked up, she chose you."

I gave him a quick glance. "Are we still talking about me?

Val didn't answer. He just smiled and clapped me on the back. "Sometimes your worst enemies become your strongest allies, Harcourt. You helped me find my son. That's twice you've saved the people I love most in this world. Anything you want is yours."

I exhaled, the ache in my chest deepening. "I want a miracle."

His fingers tightened on my shoulder. "Never count a Carrera out. When we want something, we fight for it."

He walked away before I could say anything else, but it was just as well. My attention was already redirected. Letting out another breath, I walked across the room to make my worst enemy my strongest ally.

Cristiano glanced up, his gaze suspicious as I sat next to him. "I'm sorry about your father."

He didn't answer.

"Look, believe it or not, I know what it's like to find out you're the son of a psychopath." That earned me a raised eyebrow, and I shook my head. "Long story for another day."

"Yeah, well, I'm glad he's dead," he said, his jaw ticking with repressed rage. "The world's better off."

I believed him. It took balls to come here knowing whose blood flowed through his veins. I had to respect that. "I know that feeling, too. Listen, I want to thank you for what you did."

"I didn't do it for you."

"Christ, can you knock that chip off your shoulder? I'm trying to extend an olive branch here."

He started to say something, then flattened his lips, silence sitting between us like a rock. Finally, he scrubbed a hand over his face. "Is there any news?"

My pride yelled at me to drive my fist in his face and walk away, but Val's words kept echoing in my head.

"You want to hate him for it, but he just risked his life to save hers knowing her heart belongs to another man."

So instead, I did the opposite. I swallowed my pride, proving I earned Adriana's kiss. "Not yet, but you should come sit with the family. Val will be the first person they tell."

He sat up, his eyebrows bunched in confusion. "With the Carreras? I'm a Muñoz."

I chuckled and clasped him on the shoulder. "I don't think you'll burst into flames. But if you do, we're in a hospital. Besides, you could stand some scarring, pretty boy."

"¿La familia de Adriana Carrera?"

Six heads popped up followed by twelve feet hitting the floor. My heart dropped as a man dressed in scrubs stood in front of us, his dark skin weathered and wrinkled.

Val looked over at me, giving me a quick nod. *"En inglés, por favor."* In English, please.

The doctor glanced between us. "Very well. Are you Valentin Carrera?"

Val nodded. "Yes, how is my sister? Is she…?" His voice trailed off, and Eden wrapped her arms around him.

"*Señor* Carrera, the laceration your sister suffered was serious, but it could've been a lot worse. The blade missed her liver by millimeters. She lost a lot of blood, and there was some internal bleeding, but we were able to repair the damage and stop it."

My eyes bounced between them, the words twisting around in my head.

She's all right.

Val released the breath he'd been holding. "So, she's going to be okay?"

"*Señor* Carrera, the information you gave stated your sister received a kidney transplant when she was fourteen."

Val and I glanced at each other in silent acknowledgment of "Marisol's" medical history I exposed a year ago.

"Yes, she was born with type 1 diabetes."

The doctor flipped through the chart in his hands and rubbed his eyes. "Eleven years is a long time for a donor kidney to last even with proper care, however from examination and bloodwork I can tell you hers is failing at an incredibly rapid pace."

Cristiano cleared his throat, and we all turned around. "When I was in that warehouse, Ignacio told me when he took her the first time, he tortured her and gained her cooperation by withholding her anti-rejection meds."

"Do you know how long she was without them?" the doctor asked.

"Two days, maybe three?"

Everyone's eyes turned back toward the doctor. "One to two days would cause serious problems, but three days would've caused irreversible damage to an already deteriorating organ. The donor kidney is failing, and with the stab wound, Adriana's body is going into shock."

"What are you saying?" I whispered, words sounding like they came from someone else.

"We have her stabilized for now, but without an immediate transplant, there's nothing we can do."

Val exploded, shaking off Eden's arm and crowding against the doctor. "Then give her one, goddamn it!"

To his credit, the doctor didn't back down. He stared up at the man who everyone knew owned the hospital and everyone in it. "*Señor* Carrera, we can't just hand one over. There are waiting lists with thousands of people on them. I understand your unique situation, but I refuse to play God with people's lives."

"I'll donate."

Leighton whipped around, her jaw dropping. "Brody!"

Mateo laid a heavy hand on her shoulder, and she immediately pursed her lips in silence, but I didn't care. I'd give her both kidneys. I'd give her my heart. Hell, she already had it.

The doctor shook his head. "As admirable as that is, it's not that simple. There needs to be testing done. Blood matching is required to ensure the kidney won't be rejected. Ideally, she would need a parent for her best chances."

I refused to back down. "Her parents are dead."

A distant look crossed Val's face. "What about a sibling?"

You could've heard a pin drop. No one said anything until a fiery redhead attacked him like a linebacker. "Val, no! I know you want to help her, but it's major surgery. We just got Santi back, and I can't…" Tears spilled down her face. "I can't risk losing you, too."

He leaned down and kissed her forehead. "Adriana is my sister. She just risked her life to save our son. I owe her more than a kidney, *Cereza*. I owe her my life. We both do."

The doctor offered a sympathetic smile. "I think we're getting ahead of ourselves here. There are blood tests that need to be done, as well as X-rays and abdominal CT scan. Not to mention the follow-up tests that must be analyzed a minimum of three days later. This isn't an immediate procedure, *Señor* Carrera."

Val cracked a brittle smile. "Perhaps that's true for most of your patients. However, I'm sure you'd prefer the details of your trip to Monterrey remain private just as much as I'd prefer to stop discussing extraneous tests that aren't any of my concern."

The doctor's face blanched. I had no idea what happened in Monterrey, but apparently, it was enough to bypass hospital protocol.

"Of course, *Señor* Carrera, but even siblings only have a twenty five percent chance of being a perfect match, and only a fifty percent chance of being a half match."

Val kissed Eden again, prying away from the death grip she had on his arm. "Go check on Santi. I have some odds to beat."

Six hours later, I paced again, this time for an entirely different reason, but no less impatiently. I also had company as Cristiano, Leighton, and Mateo followed in line behind me. We were a train of anxiety, unsure if we'd arrive at our destination or derail and crash.

Until Eden appeared, her face chalky. "He beat the odds," she whispered.

I stepped forward, too afraid to hope. "What does that mean?"

"It means he's a perfect match."

Chapter Forty-Two
ADRIANA

*T*ethered.

That was the only way to describe the feeling. Suspended in a quiet, private space high above the world. Like a hot air balloon still anchored to the ground. I looked down as the world still went on without me, but I remained tethered by a cord.

Beeps and voices hummed below me, but where I floated, it was peaceful. I glanced down at the rope holding me down and wondered what would happen if I cut it. Where would I go? Would I come back?

Maybe I didn't want to. Up here, the air was clear. I could breathe. I didn't cough. I didn't shake. I wasn't cold. I wasn't tired. I wasn't sick.

"Pretty, isn't it?"

I spun around to see a dark-haired woman in a white flowing dress and familiar, warm, chocolate eyes dotted with gold. I'd seen her before. Not here, but in a dream.

"*Mamá*? How'd you get here?"

She laughed, the soft, lyrical sound of her voice carried by the breeze. "I've always been with you, *cariño*.

"Where am I?"

"Your safe place. This is where you keep all your memories."

I shook my head, and it suddenly felt heavy. "I can't remember any."

She lifted a hand, brushing my hair back. "Yes, you do."

Guadalajara, Jalisco, Mexico
Fifteen Years Ago

I TWISTED MY FINGERS TOGETHER WHILE STANDING *outside papá's office. I knew he was busy, and it was forbidden, but the sound drew me nearer.*

"Marisol, did you get lost again?"

Click clack click clack click clack.

I peeked into the office, keeping my eyes on the ground. "No, sir."

"Come in here."

The invitation filled me with anxiety, yet my feet moved without my permission, and I stepped into the dark office, the sweet leather scent of rain-soaked earth filling my nose. Papá sat at his desk, a lit cigar between his fingers as a row of silver balls hanging from wires clacked together.

Back and forth.

"What's that?" I heard myself whisper.

"A pendulum."

"What is it for?"

"It's a reminder that nothing is stationary. Any situation can fluctuate from one extreme to the other at any given time. One must always prepare for the unexpected and never become complacent, Marisol."

I didn't know what most of that stuff meant, but it sounded scary. I didn't think I ever wanted a pendulum. "Does it ever stop?"

He leaned forward, taking a long puff off the end of his cigar. "You should hope not, pequeña. The moment the pendulum stops clicking, the clock starts ticking."

I giggled. "That rhymes!"

A cold smile split across his mouth. One that never reached his eyes and sent a shiver down my spine. "You laugh like your mother. The voice of an angel spoken by the lips of the devil."

I frowned. "But mamá never laughs."

His gaze shifted back to the pendulum. "No, pequeña. She can't. Not anymore."

Houston, Texas
One Year Ago

"HELLO, VAL."

His dark eyebrows bunched together. "Do I know you?"

"Probably not. But I've studied you for a while now, and I think I understand you more than most anyone."

"I doubt that," he shot back with full conviction.

Stepping out of the shadows, I ran a hand through my long hair, and he immediately took a step back.

"I'm the one who ordered the hit on your new girlfriend's brother." I smiled and moved closer. "I'm the one who's been *tracking you, turning all your allies against you." I pounded my chest with my palm. "I'm the one who watched you long enough to know you had such a hard-on for your own lieutenant's bartender that it was just a matter of time before you fucked up."*

"Oh my God," Eden croaked, her voice hushed and strained from Manuel's restrictive hold. "It's you. You're the woman from the bar. You were sitting at the end the night Val came in. I remember because...because it was the night Nash was killed."

I pulled my hair to the side and tucked it behind my ear. "Marisol. Marisol Muñoz."

"Muñoz?"

"Yes, Valentin...Muñoz. As in Manuel's sister and Esteban's daughter. I've been away for many years while you've been in America. Too bad we won't be getting better acquainted."

❧

Guadalajara, Jalisco, Mexico
One Year Ago

"No!" I STUMBLED BACKWARD TOWARD THE BOOKSHELF. *"It's* NOT *true!"*

Cristiano sat on the couch, sympathy etching in the lines drawn across his face. "I'm sorry, Mari. It is."

But I didn't want his sympathy. I wanted him to take it all back. I wanted him to tell me it was all a lie.

"How do you know? He's in with the Carreras! He could be lying!"

He clasped his hands in front of him. "Brody Harcourt got the information from Leo Pinellas. I verified it myself. The birth certificate is authentic, and so are the blood records. Esteban and Carmen both have type A blood. You are AB. They can only produce children with type A or O. Adriana Carrera was born with Type 1 Juvenile Diabetes. The same thing that forced your transplant at age fourteen. Did you never wonder why your parents weren't matches? Or Manuel for that matter?"

I heard every word he said, but I didn't want to believe it. "They told me sometimes that happens."

The corners of his mouth turned down, and he sighed. "Mari…"

"Why?" I screamed, ripping a book from the shelf and throwing it at him. "Why would they do this to me?"

He averted his eyes. "I don't know."

The cry that tore from my throat didn't sound human. I didn't feel myself falling until I hit the floor. "I can't be a Carrera. I can't!"

Present Day

I BLINKED, THE VISIONS FADING AS IF THEY'D NEVER BEEN THERE. "I'm so sorry I never got to know you. I'm sorry I grew up hating you, and for turning into such a selfish, vile woman. You must be so ashamed of me."

"*Cariño*, none of what happened was your fault. We live the life we are given. A child cannot be faulted for not seeking the truth when lies are all she knows. I'm not ashamed of you. You gave your life to save my grandson, Adriana. That's the most selfless gift a person can give."

I gave my life?

I looked again at her flowing white gown and glanced down at the tether. I couldn't breathe as I spun around. "Am I dead?"

"That's up to you. However, I believe someone is waiting for you down there."

The tether grew slack. "I don't know what to do."

"You're in charge of your own destiny, *cariño*."

I glanced down once more just as the tether snapped, and a voice from below carried by me on a passing breeze.

"We're losing her…clear!"

Chapter Forty-Three

BRODY

I was staring down at my clasped hands when Eden jumped up from the chair beside me. "How are they? How is my husband? Is he…?" The words caught in her throat as tears poured down her face. Mateo slipped an arm around her, bracing for whatever news came next.

The doctor smiled. "*Señora* Carrera, your husband pulled through just fine. He's in recovery."

Eden let out a sob and covered her face.

I cleared my throat and stood. "What about Adriana?" When he didn't say anything, I repeated it louder as Leighton took my hand.

His face became solemn. "She coded on the table."

Sight and sound ceased to exist. My sister's arm tightened around me, but I jerked away from her. I didn't want to be touched.

"But we were able to stabilize her at the last minute," he

added. "The next few days will be crucial in Adriana's body accepting the new kidney. Anything can happen."

"Does that mean…?"

He smiled. "It looks real good."

Relief flooded my body, and I dropped my head back as Leighton hugged me. My heart raced with one question. "Can I see her?"

"I'm sorry, immediate family only, and *Señor* Carrera is under sedation."

No! She needed me. After all this, I couldn't let her wake up to a silent room. She'd think she'd been abandoned all over again.

I dared this motherfucker to keep me away.

But before I could do anything, Eden stepped forward and shocked everyone. "Adriana is my sister-in-law, and as Valentin Carrera's wife, I suggest you reconsider your stance on that rule. I'm a volatile woman, Dr. Torres. With the trauma my son and husband have endured, I'm sure you understand how unpleasant I can make your work environment should my emotions get the better of me."

Everyone's jaw dropped, including Dr. Torres's who cleared his throat, a bead of sweat forming on his upper lip. "I, uh, I don't see a problem in Mr. Harcourt visiting *Señorita* Carrera once she's out of recovery."

"Wise decision." Turning, Eden gave me a private wink. "Now, if you all will excuse me, I'm going to check on my men."

Two hours later, I still waited for her to wake up.

It didn't matter. I'd waited for her my whole life. I'd wait for two years. Two decades. Two lifetimes. No one was taking me out of this room until she opened her eyes.

I brushed a piece of dark hair away from her cheek, ignoring the wires, tubes, and bandages in my way. Even with ashen gray skin and the quiet drip of an IV feeding into her veins, she'd never looked more beautiful.

This woman.

This force of nature who bulldozed her way into my life with threats and a vendetta.

She challenged me. She argued with me. She made me question myself and everything around me. She was both a brazen criminal and a fierce protector.

She was selfless.

I was the selfish one. I needed her here with me. I needed to hear her voice instead of the damn beep of the machines. And once I did, I was going to kick her ass for hiding something so huge from me.

From all of us.

I pressed my forehead against her hand and closed my eyes. "Just say something. Anything. Let me know you're coming back to me."

"*Hola.*"

My neck snapped up as her eyes fluttered open. It felt like every muscle in my body gave way at one time. "You gave everyone a scare, Carrera."

She attempted a smile. "I like to keep things interesting."

I tightened my grip on her hand. "How long have you known?"

I didn't have to elaborate. By the guilty look on her face, she knew what I meant. "A few weeks."

A few weeks.

The words settled at the base of my brain, and little clues came rushing back in a blaze of truth. "When you were sick on the plane, and when I wasn't able to wake you up in Morelia, the dizziness, the coughing, all the talk about the end, and death…all of it makes sense now. I can't believe I didn't see it."

She shook her head, reaching for my arm and wincing as a jolt of pain shot through her. "You didn't see it because I didn't want you to. You were never supposed to get close enough, remember?"

I remembered. It didn't mean I was over it.

"Val gave you a kidney."

"I know."

"How?" When she just offered a secret smile, I shook my head. I probably didn't want to know. "They said you coded. I thought I lost you."

"You did."

"Huh?" Something was off about her. Her demeanor seemed too calm. Almost at peace.

"It would've been so easy to walk away from everything, Brody. This life hasn't been kind to me, so I thought the next one had to be better."

She didn't say the words, but the implication was there. I knew what she meant, and I stilled. "Do you still think that?"

"No, I'm ready to finally start living. I used to want power, but that was the old me."

"What *do* you want, Adriana?" I looked away, not wanting to see her face if her answer wasn't the one I wanted to hear. I'd laid all my cards on the table. I still had some damn pride left.

"A home," she whispered, her voice hoarse and raspy. "I want to belong."

I entwined our fingers together, turning them so her palm faced up. "You have that, *princesa*, and I'll never take it from you again."

She swallowed hard, her brows pulling together. "Does that

mean you'll be going back to Houston soon?"

"I have to. Val needs me there, and it's *my* home. He's put a lot of trust in me, and I won't let him down."

"I understand." She tried to pull her hand away, but I gripped it tight.

Maybe a little too tight.

Because what I'd mulled around while she was in surgery took a lot for me to say. It wasn't something I offered on a whim, and it made zero sense.

Maybe that was why I trusted it.

"Come with me," I blurted out.

Her mouth dropped open. "What?"

"We have hospitals in Houston. You can recover there. I'll take care of you."

"What are you saying?"

What *was* I saying?

Standing, I leaned over the bed and braced my hands on either side of her head. I got as close as I could to her without touching her, my lips hovering above hers.

Above the kiss I knew was mine and mine alone.

"I'm saying I love you, Adriana Carrera. I love the rival you were. I love the fighter you are. And I don't want to miss a moment of the leader you'll become. I don't know how to do this. I'm winging it. I've only begged a woman one other time in my life, and now I realize it wasn't out of love. It was out of fear. Fear that I wasn't good enough for anyone else, or that I was just too fucked up for anyone to look beyond the mask to see the man. Then I met you. I met a stubborn, bossy, mouthy—"

She narrowed her eyes. "Watch it."

I grinned. "Beautiful, amazing, pain in my ass who wouldn't let me kiss her. When she told me why, I stopped wanting to steal one, and started wanting to earn it."

"Brody…"

"Once this woman gave me her kiss, I knew that was it for me. I never wanted to kiss anyone else for the rest of my life." I ran the pad of my thumb over her bottom lip, and it was like coming home. Adriana closed her eyes, and I waited.

Waited for the answer of a lifetime.

When she finally opened her eyes, that smirk that I loved so much curved under my thumb.

"Does Houston have any decent food carts?"

Chapter Forty-Four

ADRIANA

Mexico City, Mexico
Six Weeks Later

I was getting cabin fever.

Well, if one could get cabin fever inside a mansion.

Still, in the six weeks since becoming the proud owner of my brother's kidney, I'd barely been allowed to lift my own fork. Val insisted on doing everything for me, and when I argued, he swore he was just protecting his investment.

Right.

However, the minute I got out from under Val's watchful eye, Eden was there to serve as his stand-in warden.

Yes, I said Eden.

I couldn't believe how much had changed in such a short amount of time. Not that we were best friends, but the animosity was gone. There was peace in the Carrera house, which only made the cartel that much stronger.

And deadlier.

Brody flew back and forth from Houston to Mexico City

as much as he could, which ended up being every week. Val just rolled his eyes, but I saw the smile when he turned his head. Those two weren't best friends either, but they'd found their peace, too.

If the four of us could get along, anything was possible.

I zipped my suitcase closed, shaking my head at the mound of clothes Leighton was making me take to Houston. I didn't have the heart to tell her half her stuff didn't fit, so I'd just donate them.

I did charitable shit like that now.

"Do you have a minute?"

I glanced toward the door where Eden stood, her bright red hair piled high on top of her head, and Santi cradled in her arms.

"Sure. Is everything okay?"

She nodded, fidgeting as she walked into the room. "I owe you an apology."

I waved my hand. "No, you don't." We'd had six weeks of peace. There was no need to open up old wounds for words that weren't needed.

Eden sighed, sinking onto my bed. "Adriana, we have more in common than I wanted to admit. We both had rough childhoods where we had to grow up too fast and rely on ourselves to survive. I didn't have a real family." She ran her hand over Santi's dark hair. "Nash was all I had and after he died, well, Val and Santi, they're my whole world. You scared me, and when I'm scared, I lash out. I can't apologize for protecting them because I'd do it again. But I will apologize for not trusting my husband's judgment."

"Eden, it's okay."

She shook her head. "No, it's not. Please let me get this out." Pressing her lips together, she took a deep breath. "You had my brother murdered, and I killed yours. I can hate you for it, but Nash wouldn't want that. In fact, I think he'd be pretty ashamed of me right now. My big brother was my hero, Adriana. He was the best man I knew, and the only one who saw the good in me when everyone else put me down. He always said, '*Edie, people do bad things, but it doesn't make them bad people. What makes them bad is when they fail to forgive.*'" Her voice broke as tears spilled down her cheeks. "Santiago Nash Carrera is named after my brother, and I want him to grow up being as proud of his mom as I hope his uncle would've been. That's why..." Her shoulders shook as she sobbed. "That's why I forgive you."

Before I knew what I was doing, I flung my arms around her. Startled at first, she soon leaned into it, pressing her cheek against my shoulder. After a few awkward moments, we pulled apart, both of us wiping our eyes, looking anywhere but at each other.

"Well," I said, glancing toward the open door, "I should probably go downstairs. Brody will be here any minute."

"Adriana, wait." She grabbed my arm, a genuine smile pulling across her mouth as she glanced down at the wiggling baby in her arms. "Santi, it's time you officially meet your Aunt Adriana." Scooping him up, she held him out to me, and I waved both hands, backing up like he was a ticking bomb.

"Oh, no, I can't..."

Her grin widened. "Come on. Consider it practice."

I didn't have time for another protest. Eden stood up and dumped him in my arms. It was either take him or drop him. Paranoid, I tugged him against my chest, looking down at the little boy I risked everything for.

"*Hola.*"

It was all I could think to say. One word that meant nothing, but then again, sometimes everything could be said without saying anything at all.

Kind of like a kiss.

VAL STOOD AT THE BOTTOM OF THE STAIRS OUTSIDE THE ESTATE, shuffling from foot to foot as Brody grinned and kissed my cheek. "I'll wait near the car and give you two a minute."

I nodded, watching him walk away as Val scratched the back of his head. "You'll be back for Santi's baptism, right?"

"Wouldn't miss it for the world."

"You sure you're okay to fly? You can rest here for a few days."

"Val, It's been six weeks. I'm fine. Stop being a big brother."

He chuckled. "Give me a break, I've got twenty-four years to catch up on." An awkward silence passed between us again, and he took a step toward me, his expression turning serious. "Thanks for saving my son."

"Thanks for the kidney."

"Yeah well, don't expect another one."

It was my turn to chuckle. If anyone had told me two months ago that I would've risked my life to save a Carrera, or anyone but myself for that matter, I would've laughed in their face. That definitely wasn't the person I was raised to be. Self-sacrifice was for the weak and the stupid. I thought the only way to survive was to ensure others didn't.

Then Brody Harcourt turned my life upside down, and it would never right itself.

I never wanted it to.

I'd learned to love. I learned to be loved.

I learned to forgive. I learned to be forgiven.

On instinct, my eyes found him, his gaze already locked on me. Those green and brown swirls that commanded such passion saw me like no other.

Val stepped beside me. "Keep that one in line."

I glanced up to see his eyes focused on Brody, the beginnings of a smile on his face. "Not a chance," I shot back with a wink.

"Hey, Adriana?"

"Yeah?"

"I…" He scratched his chin, whatever he was going to say lost as the cartel boss pushed the big brother to the back of the line. "Don't go soft on me just because you're in love and shit."

Sometimes I really liked the cartel boss a lot more. But I'd never tell my brother that.

"Not a chance. Haven't you heard? I'm a Carrera."

Epilogue

ADRIANA

Houston, Texas
One Year Later

They say life comes full circle to a place of meaning just to show you how much you've grown. I remembered thinking everything that was wrong in my life started the moment I walked into Caliente Cantina, and it would end there.

It did.

I just didn't know at the end I'd find a new beginning.

"Hey, *princesa*, this beer ain't gonna refill itself."

I rolled my eyes at the old man sitting on the barstool, twirling his empty beer mug on his finger with a shit-eating grin. Hanging the last cocktail glass, I stepped off the overturned crate and kicked it out of my way. "How many times have I told you, Frankie?" I said, snatching it off his finger before it shattered. "My name is Adriana."

"Yeah, but that blond guy calls you *princesa*," he slurred, waving a hand around the empty bar.

"That blond guy owns this place, including that stool you sit on every day. He can call me anything he wants." Tilting a clean mug under the tap, I filled it to the top and slid it into his waiting hands. "You, my friend, cannot. And that"—I pointed to the glass already at his lips—"is your last one. You're cut off."

Who knew filling bar bitch's shoes would've been so daunting? While slinging drinks wasn't exactly the best use of my particular skill set, as co-owner of Caliente, I had no choice. At least not until I could find someone with half a brain who could mix a decent drink and keep her mouth shut.

Not an easy task.

Frankie let out a groan. "Aw, c'mon, it's only two o'clock in the morning. It's early."

I glanced at the clock and raised an eyebrow. "It's four o'clock in the afternoon, and that's why I'm calling you a cab."

"Fine, man, you've sucked all the fun outta this place. Blond guy needs to bring back blonde bartender."

Bending over, I reached under the bar for my phone to call him a cab. "I'm going to pretend I didn't hear that."

"Yeah, but you've got a better ass."

My phone clattered to the floor as I felt his palm smack against my butt. Letting out a growl, I stood, ready to remind him where the hell he was, when a dangerously low, rough voice rumbled behind me.

"Franklin, you're a good customer, so I'm going to give you two seconds to get your hand off my girlfriend's ass before I shoot it off."

Frankie's eyes widened, and he flung himself back into his seat, raising both hands in surrender. "Hey, just because I admire the car doesn't mean I want to drive it, man."

I coughed into my fist, trying as best I could to cover my laugh as footsteps pounded across the floor, the scent of sage clouding around me.

Just sage. No longer scotch because Brody hadn't touched a drop of alcohol since my surgery.

I turned to see the man I'd lived with for over a year standing on the other side of the bar, his arms spread wide with his palms flat against the wood. Intense hazel eyes held mine without remorse, and I curved my lips in a private smile.

I couldn't help but stare. He still took my breath away every time I saw him. The dark sin he exuded crossed all kinds of wires in my head. He was more dominant, and the ruthless control he held in just a passing glance brought me to my knees.

I nodded. "Counselor."

Heat flared in his eyes. "*Princesa.*"

Crossing to the other side to meet him, I placed my palms in the same position, our fingers touching. "Be nice."

A patch of unruly blond hair dipped over his eyebrow as he slid a hand around the back of my neck, drawing me to him. "Why?"

"Because I said so." My stomach flipped at the command in his voice, and even though a handful of patrons were scattered around the bar, it felt as if we were the only two in the place.

"You know, this benevolent leaf you've turned over seems to only be geared toward men." He nodded at Frankie, who now swayed so hard in his seat, I wasn't entirely sure both he and the stool weren't about to hit the floor. "I thought women were all about equality?"

"Are you saying I'm gender biased?"

"I'm saying maybe I preferred the vindictive bitch over the insatiable flirt."

"Don't pout, counselor," I laughed, ignoring his penetrating stare. "I'll show you later how I can be both." Leaning farther across the bar, I pressed my lips to his for a tempting kiss. One meant to serve as a promise for things to come.

But Brody had other ideas.

Cradling my face, he turned tempting into torrid. There was no prelude. No gentle nip or taste. He demanded entrance, and I surrendered. Our tongues clashed with an urgency distance had denied us. It was warm, desperate, and hungry. With a final bite to my bottom lip, he pulled back with a satisfied smirk.

I let out an unsteady breath. "You're wound up today."

"You're damn right," he groaned, dropping his bag on the floor. "Between me being in New York, and you going back and forth to Chicago, we've hardly seen each other."

I barely held in my own groan. He wasn't kidding. The last three months had been hell. We'd been two proverbial ships passing in the night. Brody established an alliance with the Italians for New York port access and had been busy solidifying distribution channels while I spent my time building a rapport with Cristiano's grandfather in Chicago.

I still held out hope I'd be able to mend that bridge between them. Cris said it was a lost cause, but I didn't give up so easily.

"Are you feeling neglected?" I grinned, running the pad of my thumb over the scruff on his chin.

Brody grabbed my wrist and dragged it toward his mouth, his tongue tracing my pulse. "Don't test me, *princesa*. I haven't touched you in over a week. Don't think I won't throw you on that bar and give Frankie something to really stare at."

"I ain't lookin' at nothin'," Frankie slurred behind me.

I chuckled. Brody's possessiveness was one of the things I loved most about him. I accused him once of smothering women, but it was just the opposite. He made me feel secure in a domineering yet endearing way.

He threw me over his shoulder but always made sure I landed on my feet.

I cupped his cheek. "This bar could be filled with men, and

I wouldn't see anyone but you. You're all I need for the rest of my life."

"I'm glad to hear you say that."

I let out a squeal as Brody grabbed me under the arms and lifted me up and over the bar. My feet barely hit the floor before he spun me around and guided me to a barstool near the end of the bar.

"What the hell are you—?" Before I could get the rest of my question out, two strong hands landed on my shoulders and pushed down until I gave up and sank onto the barstool.

"Do you remember the last time you sat here?"

"Tuesday?" I smirked.

He sighed heavily, visible tension in his neck. "No, *princesa*, this chair." He tapped his finger against the wood under my ass then slid onto the stool next to me.

Something about this didn't sit well with me. I didn't know what it was until I scanned my eyes down the length of him. It was only then that I noticed what he was wearing, and my smile faltered.

Black tailored Armani pants. A white button-up starched shirt rolled-up at the sleeves, and a blue tie hanging around his neck. I hadn't noticed it when he first came in because it had been a long time since he traded luxury and design for leather and denim.

"Why do you have on a suit? You haven't worn one in over a year."

"I know. Still not ringing a bell, huh? Maybe this will jog your memory." I was still confused when he stood on the bottom rung of the stool and leaned over the bar. I watched dumfounded as he poured a beer and a shot of tequila. After placing the beer in front of himself and the shot glass in front of me, he tugged his tie off his neck and tossed it onto the bar.

None of this made sense. He knew I didn't drink, and as far as I knew, he'd quit.

"Brody, I have no idea—"

"Wrong," he said, shaking his head. "Your line is, '*bad day*,' and then you're supposed to push your tequila to the side and point out my tie."

He'd lost his mind. However, he had that look on his face. The one he got right before he blew someone's head off. So, regardless of how much I questioned his sanity, I complied.

"Bad day?" I asked. Pushing the tequila to the side, I held a perfect smile while nodding toward the discarded tie.

Brody didn't bother to look up, while still gripping the hell out of his mug. "Something like that."

We sat there for moments of uncomfortable silence as he waited for me to say something else. Something obviously, I was supposed to know by the clench of his jaw and grit of his teeth.

After what seemed like forever, Brody pierced me with a fiery stare and placed his hand across my forearm. "Want to…?"

My eyes snapped toward the connection. It was such a simple move. An insignificant touch that said everything. It grabbed me by the throat and spun me back in time. Back to when I had nothing to lose.

Before I'd ever been kissed.

As if it were yesterday, I knew my next line perfectly. "Want to talk about it?"

The fire that lit his eyes before blazed even brighter. Turning away, he stared blankly across the bar before lifting the mug to his mouth. "Not particularly."

"Well, then can I buy you a drink?"

"I own the bar, sweetheart."

"I get it," I recited as I shifted toward him and leaned my elbow onto the bar. "I'm just a stranger. What do I know, right?

But you've got a chip on your shoulder the size of Texas. You obviously need to unload. If not me, there's got to be someone you can talk to."

And just like a year ago, Brody said nothing.

"Girlfriend?"

Still nothing.

I opened my mouth to say the memorable line I hit him with next. The one I remembered set him off on a chain reaction of events that led us here, but he beat me to it.

"I don't have a girlfriend."

"What?" I reared back, confused. That wasn't what he was supposed to say.

Before I could move from my chair, Brody took my hand, his throat bobbing on a hard swallow. "I'm hoping I have a wife."

I couldn't breathe. My chest felt like a team of horses trampled over it, and my heart raced with disbelief. Those words. I couldn't process those words.

"Brody…"

I was caught off guard when one corner of his mouth twitched in a cocky smirk, and he reached forward and pinched my lips shut. "Baby, I know you love to argue, but shut up and let me get this out."

I nodded as best I could with his fingers holding my lips in a vice grip.

He smiled, tilting his chin toward my lap. "This is where it started. When you walked into my bar and sat down on that stool, I hit rock bottom. I didn't think my life could get any worse."

I narrowed my eyes. "*Hmmfwhhhaa.*"

Which loosely translated meant, *watch it.*

Brody let out a low laugh and ran a hand up my cheek. "You came here to destroy me, Adriana, but you ended up saving me. We're not perfect, and we'll never be normal, but I don't think

I'd want it any other way. I know I don't want you any other way. I love your stubborn attitude. I love that you always have to have the last word. I love that you can't cook, and damn near set the bar on fire." He grinned. "But mostly, I love you, *princesa*. I love the sentimental woman, the passionate lover, and the ruthless queen, and I want all three by my side forever."

It didn't matter that he held my lips closed. I wouldn't have been able to string two words together anyway. All I could do was stare at him as he reached into his shirt pocket and pulled out a diamond ring.

"So, what do you say, Adriana Carrera? Will you marry me? Will you be my wife?"

I nodded.

Partly because he still had my lips clamped shut, but mainly because words failed me. Even the simple three letter one that answered his question. That was the thing about Brody and me— we didn't need something as trivial as a word to solidify what we felt. We didn't need ceremonies or vows or huge diamond rings.

We'd proven our commitment to each other over and over.

But I sure as hell wouldn't turn any of those things down.

Frankie, along with the few patrons in the bar, cheered as Brody whooped and scooped me off the chair, kissing me and spinning me around until we were both delirious and dizzy.

"Did she say yes? We're dying over here!"

As the familiar voice filled the bar, my head shot up, and I glanced over Brody's shoulder, my legs wrapped around his waist and my arms twisted around his neck. "Is that Eden?"

Brody just shrugged with an unapologetically guilty grin plastered across his face. I knew that look all too well, so I hoisted myself higher over his shoulder, my gaze landing on the brightly lit cell phone sitting next to his tie.

I narrowed a gaze at my new fiancé. "Speaker phone, huh?

You play a dangerous game, counselor. What if I'd said no?"

He leaned in close, his mouth brushing against my ear. "Why do you think I pinched your lips shut?"

I threw my head back and laughed, then turned my attention toward my intrusive family. "How long have you guys been listening?"

"Long enough to hear things about my sister's sex life I can't unhear," Val grumbled on the other end of the line.

"Val, stop it!" Eden hissed, then as if flipping a switch, her voice rose about twelve octaves, and she let out a squeal I was fairly certain only dogs could hear. "Congratulations, you two! You have to have the wedding at the estate! Oh, a Christmas wedding would be beautiful! Leighton and I could plan it. You wouldn't have to do a thing but show up, and—"

The rest of her exuberant tirade ended in a series of muffled grunts.

"*Cereza*," Val chastised as the muffled sounds got louder. "While I'm sure they appreciate your adorable, yet disturbing enthusiasm, they just got engaged. Besides, you're five months pregnant. You don't need to be planning anything."

There was static and shuffling before another big squeal almost shattered my eardrums. "Congrats, big brother!" Leighton shouted.

Brody grinned. "Thanks, Lil' Bit." With a peck on my cheek, he set me on top of the bar and retrieved his phone. "Okay, I think that's enough family togetherness for today. We'll call everyone later once we've celebrated privately."

I couldn't help but laugh at Val's growl of disapproval. We'd come a long way from trying to kill each other to being insanely protective of each other. I suppose blood really was thicker than water.

Once we stopped trying to spill it, of course.

Everyone said their goodbyes, and Brody ended the call with promises of video and a visit to the estate. I mixed a few more drinks, and after pacing the floor for fifteen minutes, he gave up and closed the bar early.

As soon as Frankie left, Brody locked the door behind him and swept me into his arms. "I get to kiss the bride now."

I laughed and ran my hands through his thick hair. "That's only when we get married."

"When have we ever followed tradition?" His lips twitched in a half smile seconds before his mouth claimed mine in a slow and seductive kiss. Brody's fingers tightened in my hair, and he pulled me closer. He tasted and took, and I happily gave.

I told him once that my kisses were all his, and I meant it.

His mouth left mine and marked a heated trail across my jaw and down my neck. I closed my eyes, reveling in the feel of his lips on my skin, and the feel of his ring on my finger.

"You know, I never thanked you."

Brody pulled back and eyed me closely as he brushed a piece of hair away from my face. "For what?"

"For exposing who I really was. I hated you for it at the time, but if you hadn't, I would've died. I was convinced you wanted to take my life, and you ended up saving it."

He backed me against the bar, and the space between us disappeared. "I think we saved each other."

We did. In every sense of the word. We risked our lives for each other, but it was so much more than a sacrifice of pain or a gift of life. Both of us were headed down our own dark path when they unexpectedly crossed. It would've been so easy to keep running deeper into the shadows until those paths consumed us, but circumstance, fate, or whatever you wanted to call it, stepped in.

We still walked in the dark, but we didn't walk alone. This

life we led wasn't bathed in sunlight. Neither of us was all evil, and neither of us was all good. Extremes were what brought down empires.

And what we'd built was indestructible.

As if reading my mind, Brody brought my left hand to his lips and kissed the diamond now residing on my third finger. "So, what do you think, *princesa*? Ready to be a queen again?"

It was funny. Reclaiming my crown was why I came to Houston, but it turned out that the one thing I wanted ended up being the last thing I needed.

"Only yours, counselor. Only yours."

THE END

Acknowledgments

I've run out of people to thank, so, thank you to Pinot Grigio for keeping my glass filled and my laptop from flying through the window.

Catherine Wiltcher, I'm not even sure what to say at this point except that "person" who sprouted horns and a tail two days before deadline? That was my twin sister, Dora. We keep her in a kennel downstairs. Not sure how she got loose, but I apologize for the sixty-four messages she sent you at four a.m.

A huge apology to my family for being MIA the last four years. In case you wondered, I was upstairs the whole time. Thanks to whoever brought me water, Cheetos, and Febreze.

Crystal, what can I say that I haven't already said in nineteen acknowledgments? Thank you for not complaining when I asked you to Google things in the name of research that probably have both of us on some kind of FBI watch list. Thanks for always being by my side, for championing this series, and for not being afraid to tell me when I've done your man wrong. Thanks to you, Val got his groove back. You are now and forever, Mrs. Valentin Carrera.

Thank you Ginger Snaps and Alina Kirshner for making me seem like I'm fluent in Spanish and Russian. Spoiler: I'm not. Because of you both, Val and Ava's dialects are authentic. You are my translation goddesses.

Thank you so much to KC Fernandez for your mad proofreading skills and your insane attention to detail. Simply put, you saved my ass. I'm not sure how I managed to rope you into my inner circle, but good luck getting out of it now.

To my incredible beta team, Carrera's Guerreras, thank you. You never complain when I roll in at the last minute with either a paragraph or seventeen chapters, or when I post them at two a.m. and type in all caps, *WHERE ARE YOU* because I forget that normal people sleep. Thank you for your love and support, and for telling me when something really sucks. Love you, Crystal, Sarah, Sienna, Ronda, Sheri, Tami, KC, Tiffany, Amy, and Melissa.

To my editor, Mitzi Carroll, thank you for your dedication to this series and for always making room for me when the manuscript is a week later than I promised.

Many thanks to Danielle Sanchez and the staff of Wildfire Marketing Solutions for your help with this release and for being my sounding board. I'm so blessed to be a part of your team.

To my reader group, Cora's Twisted Alpha Addicts, and my street team, Cora's Twisted Capos, thank you for being there every day to make me smile and give me the push I need to keep the words flowing. I couldn't imagine the book world without you.

Mom, thank you for seeing the stars, grabbing one, and holding it for me until I believed in myself enough to know I belonged among them.

Lastly, to the bloggers, readers, booktokers, and bookstagrammers who have read and shared this series over the years, a very heartfelt thank you. As always, without you, I'm just a chick with a laptop.

About the Author

Cora Kenborn is a *USA Today* Bestselling author of over twenty-five multi-genre novels, including the Carrera Cartel Trilogy.

While best known for her dark and gritty romances, Cora infuses sharp banter and a shocking blindside in every story she writes. She loves a brooding antihero who falls hard for a feisty heroine who stands beside him, not behind him.

Although she's a native North Carolinian, Cora claims the domestic Southern Belle gene skipped a generation, so she spends any free time convincing her family that microwaved mac and cheese counts as fine dining.

Oh, and autocorrect thinks she's obsessed with ducks.

*Join her newsletter for updates and get a **FREE** ebook.*
www.corakenborn.com

Author Library

CARRERA CARTEL
(Dark Mafia Romance)

Carrera Cartel: The Collection
(w/bonus novel)
Blurred Red Lines
Faded Gray Lines
Drawn Blue Lines

CORRUPT GODS
Spinoff of Carrera Cartel
(Dark Mafia Romance)

Corrupt Gods Collection
(w/bonus chapters)
Born Sinner
Bad Blood
Tainted Blood
City of Thieves
Bullets and Thorns

MARCHESI EMPIRE
Spinoff of Carrera Cartel
(Dark Mafia Romance)

Torched Spades
Tortured Hearts

LES CAVALIERS DE L'OMBRE
(Dark Mafia Romance)

Darkest Deeds

BRATVA'S MARK
Spinoff of Les Cavaliers de l'ombre
(Dark Bratva Romance)

Illicit Acts
Wicked Ways

Made in United States
North Haven, CT
09 February 2022

15897702R00259